Kingdom Series Collection
By Marie Hall

Smashwords Edition
Copyright © 2012 by Marie Hall
All Rights Reserved

Contents

<u>Her Mad Hatter</u>
<u>Gerard's Beauty</u>
<u>Red and Her Wolf</u>

Her Mad Hatter

"Bad boys need love too."

Alice is all grown up. Running the Mad Hatter's Cupcakery and Tea Shoppe is a delicious job, until fate--and a fairy godmother with a weakness for bad boys--throws her a curveball. Now, Alice is the newest resident of Wonderland, where the Mad Hatter fuels her fantasies and thrills her body with his dark touch.

The Mad Hatter may have a voice and a body made for sex, but he takes no lovers. Ever. But a determined fairy godmother has forced Alice into Wonderland--and his arms. Now, as desire and madness converge, the Hatter must decide if he will fight the fairy godmother's mating--or fight for Alice.

Her Mad Hatter

by

Marie Hall

Her mad Hatter

Copyright 2012 Marie Hall

Cover Art by Claudia McKinney of www.phatpuppyart.com Copyright October 2012

Photographer, Teresa Yeh
Model, Danny
Edited by Jennifer Blackstream, Brent Taylor, and Anne Marsh

Formatted by L.K. Campbell

www.MarieHallWrites.blogspot.com

Smashwords Edition

    This is a work fiction. All characters, places and events are from the author's imagination and should not be confused with fact. Any resemblance to persons, living or dead, events or places is purely coincidental.
    All rights reserved. No part of this publication may be reproduced in any material form, whether by printing, photocopying, scanning or otherwise without the written permission of the publisher, Marie Hall, except in the case of brief quotations embodied in the context of reviews.
    This book is licensed for your personal enjoyment only. This ebook may not be resold or given away to other people. If you would like to share this ebook with another person, please purchase an additional copy for each person you share it with. Thank you for respecting the hard work of all people involved with the creation of this ebook.
    Applications should be addressed in the first instance, in writing, to Marie Hall. Unauthorized or restricted use in relation to this publication may result in civil proceedings and/or criminal prosecution.
    The author and illustrator have asserted their respective rights under the Copyright Designs and Patent Acts 1988 (as amended) to be identified as the author of this book and illustrator of the artwork.
    Published in 2012 by Marie Hall, Honolulu, Hawaii, United States of America

Dedication

To those who never stopped believing in me. Especially Joyce and Mom... ya'll are crazy, but awesome!

Table Of Contents

Chapter 1
Chapter 2
Chapter 3
Chapter 4
Chapter 5
Chapter 6
Chapter 7
Chapter 8
Chapter 9
Chapter 10
Chapter 11
Chapter 12
Chapter 13
Chapter 14
Bonus

Chapter 1

Danika, fairy godmother extraordinaire, ran her glowing hand over a shadowy bump in the mushroom cap wall of her home. It was the hiding place for her most treasured and valuable item-- her wand. She grabbed hold of the smooth wood, the hum of its power echoing down her fingertips like the swelling vibrations of water dripping on thin metal. And though the wand was worn down from years of granting wishes, there could be no doubt she was the best at what she did.

Of course that stupid fat cow- oh what was her face, the one who worked with Cinderella- thought she was the best. But honestly, what was her claim to fame? Turning a pumpkin into a coach? Or, how about making mice footmen?

Preposterous.

She was a disgrace to all the fairy godmothers out there with her ridiculous bippity-boppity-booing.

Not to mention her clientele. That simpering little doll-- a classic Mary Sue if ever there was one. *Oh save me, Prince Charming, for I am pretty and cannot do a thing for myself.* *Bat lashes, wiggle bottom, ad nauseum.*

Blah!

Pathetic little creature. Danika would rather gouge her eye out with a spoon. A rusty one! And... and... roughened at the edges. She humphed. That's how much she hated the simpering princes and princesses of her world.

Thankfully, she'd never have that problem. The moment Danika had graduated from Fairy Godmother Inc.- three hundred years ago- she'd applied to work as godmother to the lowly. Since none of the other godmothers wished to work for them, they'd given her the position posthaste and left her to do her thing. Quite happily too, she might add.

Danika worked for the bad boys of Kingdom.

The degenerates; low lifes, and naughty villains. She snorted, shaking her head at how little anyone knew about her boys. Why any self-respecting fairy godmother would pass them over for an inane twit who relied on animals to do her housecleaning was beyond her. Grabbing her star-dusted cloak from off the coat rack, she tossed it over her shoulders. Glittering bits of stardust drifted to the floor.

A golden bolt of power flowed down her arm, through her fingers, and out the tip of the wand. It swirled like a flame, dousing out the candles. She shut the door behind her.

Tiny iridescent wings broke free of her vest, lifting her high into the bejeweled night. Her path cut through trees with branches thick as the fattest snakes.

Stargazers shivered at her passing.

"Thank you, Fairy Godmother!" they crooned as the stardust settled on their beautiful pink petals. They swiveled on thin green stems, lapping up the powder like a fine wine.

Danika winked, gave them a jaunty wave, and continued on. Most days she'd stop to chat, maybe sing a song or two, but tonight she traveled in haste.

Once a year, the Bad Five (the truly worst of the worst of her boys) gathered, to drink, to discuss who'd they'd plot against next, and generally muck it up together. It was perfect timing for her-- because she had five birds to kill and one stone to do it with.

Miriam the Shunned-- fairy godmother of wishes and visions-- had given Danika some sobering news last month. Either get the Bad Five hitched, or great misfortunate would befall them.

Not like Danika hadn't made many love matches already. Her resume was quite hefty. Why just last week Mr. Fee Fi Fo Fum himself had fallen madly for the wicked witch of the West. Next month was to be their nuptials. Danika had received her invitation to the gala only today. And last month she'd introduced Tweedle-Dee to La-Di-Dah, sparks ignited, and Danika was fairly certain there'd be a second wedding in the future.

Danika was good at love matches when given sufficient time, but love matches weren't as simple as poof there she is, kissy kissy, and sailing off into the sunset. Finding a perfect mate took patience and due diligence. To suddenly be told the Bad Five had a year to find their mates... the thought twisted Danika's stomach in knots.

Not like Danika hadn't tried already, many times. But love was much more than chemistry; it was a melding of hearts and minds. Of seeing someone and knowing unequivocally she or he was *it*.

Thankfully, Miriam had gifted Danika with a boon. There'd been an incident several years ago, one nearly forgotten by all but Danika and Wolf. A sad affair really... Danika shook her head, shoving the haunting memories aside before they grew too strong and claimed her thoughts, now was not the time to think on that, eventually she'd have to address the wrong and pray to the gods she could make it right. But today was for her boys and thanks to Miriam's *sight* Danika now knew the names of the women, the very ones her boys were destined to be with.

But she'd been shocked. Not at the names, rather at the reality of just how close she'd been to finding Hatter's match once before. All within Kingdom knew *Alice* was destined for Hatter. Their story had been entwined since the very beginning; problem was of the millions of Alices in the world, 'twas hard to know exactly which one she was.

When Danika was around a viable option her entire body would tingle. Her body had tingled many times and each time she'd been wrong. But a few years ago she'd come across an Alice who did more than make her tingle; her body had surged with power so intense that Danika had momentarily blacked out.

Her name had been Alice Hu.

Miriam had told Danika that Hatter's true match was also named Alice Hu, great-granddaughter of the original. And Hatter had *hated* the original.

Flapping her wings harder, Danika tried to ignore the sick pit in her stomach. She'd agonized about this all night and finally came to the only conclusion there was: she would not tell him who the girl was beforehand.

A squawking noise broke her from her musings. Startled, she looked up and just in time too. A large white stork carrying a blue bundle in its long beak headed straight toward her.

"Stork!" she cried, and beat her gossamer wings in a furious fashion, hoping to sail clear of the sharp dagger that was his beak tip. She clutched her chest, breathing deep to calm frazzled nerves.

"Mmm, so shorry, Danika. Muss make me drop time, hiss Excellenshe will tar and feather me if I'm late." His words were slurred, unable to open his beak too wide lest the babe drop out.

"Honestly." Danika straightened the ends of her dress in an attempt to settle herself.

The stork didn't pause, but he dipped his head in apology. Ruffled, but not vexed, she nodded back. He was, she supposed, in a hurry much as herself.

A tiny green fist poked out the top of the bundle.

Danika curled her nose.

She hated ogres, no matter what form they came in. Nasty little boogers they were, always smashing through trees, destroying her precious forest home with their big gigantic ham fists and warty feet.

With a shake of her head she hurried on. She couldn't wait to see the Bad Five. Of all her charges they were her favorites and for the life of her she could never understand why more fairies didn't feel as she did. Bad boys needed love too. Her boys weren't dangerous— just naughty. But naughty could be very, very fun. Unfortunately, Kingdom was mostly made up of goodie two shoes with a very dim view of good and evil. They were completely unable to look beyond her boys' slightly colorful pasts. So the Wolf had killed a time or two. Big deal. He was a wolf! What did they expect? That he'd lick his balls all day and howl at the moon?

She chuckled at the thought.

In no time she spied the lights that Leonard-- the Hatter's pet mouse-- had hung branch to branch. She hovered in the air directly over their table. The Bad Five were already thick in their cups, laughing and eating. Danika took a moment to study her motley crew before they noticed her presence.

The Hatter, as always, slouched in his seat at the head of the table with a fist tucked under his chin. His dark eyes stared blankly into the night, distant, thinking... who knew what thoughts.

Hair disheveled, clothes ripped, but all of it with that flair of style that made it seem possible he'd contrived his appearance to look just so.

Danika had known him several years now, and each year he seemed to sink deeper and deeper into the quagmire of his mind. He needed a mate, someone to help offset the residual madness that built up like toxins in the bones without an outlet. A mate would force him to get out of his head

Wonderland was wonderful, but without a counterbalance, it could turn its inhabitants completely insane.

The man was dangerously close to irreparable damage. He'd been here too long, with no one to pull him from the cliff's edge. And now, with Miriam's warnings ringing in her ears, she knew he'd only a year left before the madness completely consumed him. Maybe even less. Her heart clenched— what would Wonderland be without him? Not near as fun, that was for sure.

Hatter took a sip of his tea. She sighed. He truly was a lovely man, with a face that seemed a kiss from the gods, a strong jaw, molten brown eyes, and a mouth made for sin. Her pulse raced. Old as she was, she was not impervious to his charms. Charms he never seemed aware of. Hatter simply was what he was.

"Has the witch arrived yet?" The deep timbre of Gerard's voice shivered through the cool night. He tipped his head back and chugged from the tankard he held fisted tight in his hand.

"I'm sure I don't know," Hook said, eyeing the French drunk with a sharp black brow.

"She's not a witch," Jinni sipped at his tea, "she's a fairy. *Kahar*." The last dripped from his tongue like venom.

She covered her mouth, containing the mirth that threatened to spill when Gerard's face mottled a dark shade of red.

"I detest when you speak Chinese."

"To vilify a man is the readiest way in which a little man can himself attain greatness," Hatter said, never taking his eyes from some unknown spot in the distance.

Gerard's face screwed up, as if contemplating Hatter's words and whether to take umbrage or not. Finally the effort seemed too much for him. "Argh," he growled, dismissing him with a flick of his wrist.

Hook rolled his eyes. "He's Persian, you idiot."

Gerard clenched his fist. "I can take you, *une main*."

"Beauty with no brains, Calypso save us," Hook said in a whiskey-thick drawl. "He called you an idiot, you dolt." Never a patient sort, his silver hook tapped the table.

Tap.

The wolf's nostrils flared. Yellow eyes narrowed to thin slits.

Tap.

A low guttural growl.

Hook's lips twisted as he looked toward the wolf whose hackles were raised, eyes glowing with threat of violence.

Tap.

"Bloody hell!" Gerard smashed his fist into the table, knocking a silver platter full of crumpets to the floor. "Shut up," he snarled and snatched up a roasted leg of turkey. Straight white teeth ripped into it with animal aggression.

"Oy," a tiny squeak rang from a ceramic teapot.

Hatter sighed and flipped the lid up. Leonard popped his furry brown head out. Whiskers twitching as he said, "I'll give ye a nibble to yer hind, I will."

"Oh hush, rat. And why do you bother with such a stupid creature anyway?" Gerard asked, looking at Hatter and pointing his ravaged turkey leg at the mouse whose eyes bulged with indignation.

"I never," Leonard huffed, looking back at Hatter.

Hatter patted his furry head, handed him a sugar cube, and tucked him back into his favorite cubbyhole.

The Wolf gave a gentle whuff, whether of agreement or not-- it was hard to say-- and continued lapping at the cream within the silver dog bowl.

"Uncivilized." Jinni sniffed. His form shimmered like heat rolling off the desert sands. Cursed years ago to a semi-corporal existence, Jinni might never again know the touch of another soul. A curse Danika still worked diligently to try and reverse. Of all her boys, he was the most confusing. A naturally magical creature, he was Djinn- genie to most. With powers that rivaled her own, by all rights he shouldn't have a godmother. But... he'd screwed up big, gotten himself cursed, lost his ability to use magic, and was now her problem to fix.

However-- stubborn, difficult man that he was-- he was offended by the very notion of a godmother. Which made her job all the more difficult.

Danika knew beneath Jinni's icy exterior flowed lava. A spark so hot it consumed. If a woman could ever get into that cold heart, his passion would burn as bright as the desert land he'd hailed from. However there was still the minor problem of his near invisibility.

But she was not here for Wolf, Hook, Jinni, or even the lovely, thick-headed, Gerard.

Hatter slouched even further in his seat, his stare a mile long. Antipathy clung to him like second skin.

She tsked.

Wolf stilled, sniffed, then looked up. The others followed suit.

"Fairy godmother, here to grace us with your presence. Oh goodie." To the untrained ear Hook's greeting smacked of sarcasm, but she knew the raven-haired brute well.

She dropped to the center of the table, dwarfed by heaping trays of food and enveloped by the scented aroma of tea and spices.

Danika walked toward him, gossamer skirts swishing in her wake. "Were you hoping maybe for Tinker? Heard tell you had a thing for waifish blondes." She patted the back of her bun, pointing the wand at her chest. "I could always turn myself..."

"Bollox," he growled, but couldn't quite hide the smile twitching the corner of his full lower lip. "I've a Pan to conquer, madam, so do let us hurry."

"Ravishing as always. And is that stardust? Why, Danika, you shouldn't have dressed so formally for us." Gerard smoldered, his words layered with sex and decadence. Promises of dark seduction and wicked nights danced in the air.

Her stomach quivered and heat bloomed in her cheeks.

He smiled and scratched his own. The rascal. She'd find a woman to bring him to his knees. Too bad Belle had fallen for the Beast-- she'd seemed so perfect. But alas...

She turned on the Hatter. He looked even more bedraggled up close. His tie was undone and skewed. She flitted to him, attempted to tuck the dark strands of hair in his eyes back, but it was useless. Finally, she sighed.

"What has happened to you, Hatter?"

There were no emotions on his face and no smile to betray a hint of what he felt. "Life happened, fairy. Surely you know. Or haven't you heard? Cursed I am. The sky is gray, the sky is light, and still the Hatter bemoans his plight."

That voice made her think of hot nights, cool sheets, and heady moans.

A choir of mingling voices began to sing. *The Mad Hatter bemoans his plight. Oh nay, oh my, the Hatter bemoans his plight...*"

"I hate those flowers. *Enfer*, why did you plant your abode here, Hatter?" Gerard's French lilt grew rough with annoyance and he chucked a bone toward the garden of singing dandelions.

Shrieks resonated and then flowery roars reached a cacophonous pitch as they cursed him full of boils, warts, and pustules.

"I do wish you'd hurry this on, starflower," Jinni said with an exotic inflection that rolled over her skin like heated honey.

Dizzy, and slightly breathless, she returned to the center of the table. Too much testosterone, too many fine pairs of eyes studying her. Heaven help the women these men paired with, they'd be the devil in the sheets for sure.

"As you know, I'm your godmother, and as such I've duties to fulfill."

"*Mon dieu*," Gerard groaned. "Must we abide this horror every year? Be done with it, *fée*. It's not worked yet."

"Again?" Jinni crooked a brow.

Hook fiddled with the end of his mustache. A glint of something in his dark blue eyes led her to suspect he was not as opposed as the rest.

The Wolf gave a moaning growl-- human in its whining undertones.

Hatter jerked. It was the first reaction she'd seen from him so far. She might have been pleased, were it not for the threat of violence that quivered through the air like the strike of a finely honed blade.

"No more. I told you last time: no more, fairy."

She held her chin high. "And I've given you leeway and your space. But it is more than time to get back in the game. We will keep searching until we find your Alice. We must." The lie settled heavy on her tongue, Alice had been already been found, and she knew without a doubt he'd be irate. Danika raised her chin. She would not give into fear though, not now.

Gerard threw himself back on the chair, causing the legs to rock precariously, and laughed. A great big booming sound that rent the night. Pigwidgeons scattered like falling rose petals in a thousand different directions.

Gerard picked his teeth. "Mates. I'm in. I'll take three, no make that four. All blonde. Big..." he framed his chest, "and no readers. *Dieux*, I hate readers." His nose curled as he grabbed his magically full tankard again.

"One will do. And that goes for all of you." She eyed Jinni hard.

His tipped his head. "In my Kingdom we are expected to maintain a full harem, oh magnificent one."

"Aye, well…" She stomped her foot, wagging her finger at him. "Women from Earth will not abide that arrangement. Besides," she grinned, recalling one in particular that would be perfect for him, "she'll be more than enough for what you need doing."

"Earth?" Hook roared. "Never!"

The Wolf licked his lips.

"Enough, enough." She raised her hands. "You'll not have a say. It is my duty to see to your needs. Happy endings are not the sole domain of Prince Charming." She bristled, remembering the heated battles between herself and her kind.

Love might never tame the beast fully, but it would certainly temper the wildness in each of them.

The Hatter's face could have been carved from ice. He was as still as a snake ready to strike. She took a step back; he was certainly crazy enough to do it. Heart thundering, feigning a boldness she did not feel, Danika shook her head. "No, Hatter, not even your madness will affect my decision. It is as I say. When the clock strikes midnight-" She waved her wand and a golden antique clock stood before him, its metrical ticks making Hook shudder. "She will be here."

"Science has not yet taught us if madness is or is not the sublimity of the intelligence." Hatter's voice was whisper soft, but full of some hidden torment.

Filled with an ache to hold him, she clenched her teeth. She could not. She had a task, and she'd see it through.

"Be... be that as it may, she will come and you will mate her."

He didn't seem to notice she'd spoken. "But I have promises to keep, and miles to go before I sleep, and miles to go before I sleep."

She frowned, looking to the others for help in deciphering some meaning behind his cryptic words. The Wolf blew air through his muzzle. Gerard only shrugged.

Hatter was worse, no doubt. There used to be a time she could at least piece together his meaning. Now-- oh dear-- he truly needed his mate. She knew he was tired of searching. So was she... Especially after the last Alice. The great-grandmother Alice Hu.

Danika clenched her wand tighter. What if the girl looked like the original? She swallowed hard. The last Alice had been cruel, a charlatan. She'd fooled them all. Especially Danika herself. She'd fallen prey to the girl's outwardly loving exterior. But she'd soon learned they'd had a viper in their midst. The girl had wanted nothing more than the power of Wonderland. She'd never wanted the Hatter.

A reality made all the more sad because she'd never seen Hatter so taken. He'd made a fool of himself-- in his mind anyway. He'd shown Alice the wonder and strange beauty of Wonderland, expecting her to love the talking flowers and vaporous cat-shifting loons as he did. But she'd despised it all, wanted to change everything; she'd rejected his uniqueness as madness and mocked him behind his back to others.

Once he'd discovered her deception, something in him had fractured; where once he'd been irreverent, often laughing, he'd turned moody and withdrawn.

Now Danika was set to bring him another Alice, knowing this one to be the right one, but what would he feel knowing this Alice came from that Alice? Would he even give the girl a chance? Would he hate her because of who she was? The thought made Danika sick.

If the magic hadn't demanded Danika find him an Alice, she'd have brought him a blasted Jane and to hell with all the Alices everywhere.

"Yes, just so." She sighed in answer to his nonsensical ramblings.

Gerard snorted. "Only bride who'll have him is one freshly buried. Honestly, *fee, cruel* torture."

She planted hands on her hips in her best authoritative pose. Not easy for one barely 10 inches tall. "Your turn will come soon enough, Gerard."

He shuddered, and she nodded, pleased her words hadn't faltered. "Now off with the lot of you. Freshen up, get sober, and for the gods' sakes, wash." She eyed Gerard in particular.

They all sat staring at her. She glowered. "Go, I say!" And gesturing at them with her wand, she lifted them from their seats. Wolf yelped the loudest as Danika tossed them from the garden.

"Blast you, *sorciere demon*," Gerard's thick growl rose above the grumbles of the rest.

She grinned and twirled towards Hatter. He was staring at her, eyes full of pain, of hunger, of something he felt would be forever out of his reach.

"Cursed," he whispered.

She patted his cold fingers. "Hatter, you are not cursed. We just haven't found the one yet. But we will. I swear it."

Danika's words sounded sure, but in her heart she trembled. *What will he do*: was now the chanting mantra tattooed in her skull. She didn't have a choice, he was unwell, and he didn't have much time. She bit her lip.

"Let me be, Danika." He stood. "I do not want a mate out of necessity, or one chosen for me by this crazy up-is-down and down-is-up world. I will not do this again."

"I love you, Hatter, but hear me well. I'll never stop."

He clenched his fist, brimstone burning in the depths of his cold black eyes. Then he blinked and smiled, a slow curling grin. "Do you know, fairy?"

She frowned. "What, my dear?"

His eyes were glazed, his body swaying. "The answer to the riddle?"

Danika's lips thinned, heart bleeding. He couldn't even hang on to his anger before the madness claimed him.

She swallowed hard. "I do."

"And?" He lifted up on his toes.

"Poe, dear." She touched his bristly jaw. "Poe."

He snapped his fingers and with a sharp nod, walked off muttering, "I knew it."

If Miriam hadn't told truth, if this wasn't the right Alice, Hatter wouldn't survive another year. Alice Hu had to be the one, because without the Hatter, Wonderland could never be the same.

Chapter 2

The bell above The Mad Hatter's Cupcakery and Tea Shoppe rang as the last customer of the day walked out.

Alice heaved a huge sigh of relief, ran around the counter to the door, and turned the sign. She giggled-- the place was a mess, with napkins scattered everywhere. Tons of plates to wash and clean in the back and yet she felt like she'd just completed the Honolulu marathon. Her giggling held a frantic pitch to it. They'd done it. They'd started a business and made money. Lots of it. She hadn't counted, but she was pretty sure they were well on their way to being in the black.

In another two years.

Her frilled mini dress was covered in powdered sugar, her hair smelled of a million different varieties of tea spices, and she didn't care. A sense of accomplishment filled her: *they'd done it*.

Of course, it didn't hurt that she'd landed the sweetest location in downtown Honolulu-- right across from world famous Waikiki beach, aka Tourist Mecca. That meant one thing: a constant stream of customers.

Tabby-- her baker's assistant-- squealed, grabbed both of Alice's hands and jumped up and down.

"Girl power," Tabby sang. "We so rock!"

"I know!"

It took at least five minutes before exhaustion finally worked its way through Alice's brain. Grabbing her forehead, but still wearing a goofy smile, she dropped down in the seat nearest her.

"Oh my gosh, we did it." Her words were quiet, more thoughtful, as the full impact of what they'd done finally started to settle in.

"Yeah," Tabby agreed. "Wow."

Tabitha planted hands on her slim hips and grinned. "I think this calls for a celebration, don't you?"

"Can you believe it, Tabby? We're true blue business owners."

"Look out world." Tabby nodded, a smile as radiant as a burst of sunlight, tightened her face. "Feels good, yeah? After all these years, all the tears, all the sacrifices? And our moms thought we'd be good for nothings." She snorted, reached into the cupcake display case, and grabbed two desserts.

Alice groaned as another dull throb shot up her left calf muscle. She kicked off the four-inch heels Tabby had sworn were appropriate cupcakery attire, and massaged the stiff kink from her thigh-high clad leg.

She'd felt slightly ridiculous in the frilly blue dress that barely covered her butt cheeks, but as Tabby had said time and again: sex sells, even in cupcakeries. Apparently, it was true. Easily half the customers today had been men.

She'd not eaten anything all day, too anxious to get food down. But now it was seven, the day was done, and her stomach suddenly reminded her how neglected it'd been.

Tabby sat across from her. "Mad Hatter's Surprise, or Hooka's Delight? Hmm? Hmm?" Tabby wiggled the plates under Alice's nose. The creations were mini works of art.

The Mad Hatter was a vanilla bean-based cupcake. At its center was a caramel covered slice of jalapeno-- the Hatter's surprise-- but it was the tequila cream cheese frosting that made Alice have a mouthgasm every time. She gestured for the Mad Hatter.

Tabby handed it to her, and then picking hers up said, "to a wildly successful day, and to many, many more."

"Hear. Hear." Alice nodded agreement; they tapped cupcakes together and then bit into them with simultaneous groans.

"O.M.G. Alice." Tabby's eyes were twin saucers of joy. "I'm beyond happy that you decided to waste your life and become a professional baker."

Alice snorted. Her mother's words. Mom had had different thoughts in mind for her fourth and youngest daughter. Each Hu child had become something wildly successful. Her oldest sister, Verona, was Honolulu's most renowned cardiologist. Alma-- second oldest-- the vet. Tanya-- White House correspondent.

Then there was Alice. Head in the clouds Alice. Nose always in the books Alice. Well, one book in particular. Alice in Wonderland.

As a little girl she'd thought it was cool to have a book named after her. Of course, she hadn't known it wasn't really, but by the time she'd figured it out, she'd already fallen in love with the dark and quirky prose of the book.

Always imagining it was she-- Japanese goddess Alice Hu-- who'd fallen into Wonderland, met the white rabbit, become both big and small, met and... since the Tim Burton adaptation had come out... kissed the Mad Hatter. Yes, he was certifiable, but after seeing Johnny Depp play the part, crazy had never looked so yummy.

She licked the frosting swirl and moaned as her taste buds erupted with sharp hints of tequila and notes of lime.

"I love this." Tabby chuckled and blew out a puff ring of smoke. A nifty trick Alice had learned at culinary school. Pop rocks flash frozen in dry ice. "We're gonna be rich. Oh hey, did you hear?"

After ten years of being best friends, Alice had grown used to Tabby speaking in stream of consciousness. She peeled the paper off her cake. "What?"

She nibbled, content to be lazy and eat slowly. The kitchen could be on fire and she doubted she'd get her tired butt off the chair. Her feet ached and her toes tingled. She wasn't sure that was totally normal, but at the moment, she couldn't even muster up a grain of 'care.' She was blissed out.

"K 1 News Now called this morning, wants to do an interview with you tomorrow."

When the words finally registered through the fog in Alice's throbbing head, her pulse fluttered and she sat up straighter in her chair. "No way! And I'm only hearing this now?"

Tabby shrugged as she popped the last bite of her cupcake in her mouth. "What? We were busy. Not like I had pet mice to do my bidding. Some of us," she pointed at her chest and raised a brow, "were actually working."

"Cinderella had mice, not Wonderland."

"Pssh, who cares? I get them all confused anyway."

"Sacrilege. Off with her head!" Alice shrilled in her best Red Queen impersonation.

Tabby rolled her eyes. "And that's why you never get laid anymore. You. Are. Weird." She patted Alice's hand. "Honey, you do know they don't actually exist, right?"

Alice chuckled. Tabby always gave her grief about her love of-- okay... obsession with-- all things Wonderland. "What? You mean to tell me the face painted man who crawls in my window and makes wild monkey love to me every night isn't actually real?" She tapped her finger to her chin. "That could be a problem."

Tabby chuckled. "I've got dishes to clean. I'd like to get home before ten anyway."

"Ooh la la," Alice winked and sat back, "another hot date with Mr. H.P.D.?"

Tabitha bit her bottom lip, a shy look in her eyes. "I don't know, maybe."

Alice giggled and rubbed the back of her neck. "Then I suggest you get those dishes done." She winked.

Tabby ran back, a spryness to her steps Alice couldn't hope to match. She was exhausted.

Not, "I was out working in the garden exhausted" either. More like, "I've run ten miles, hiked Mount Kilimanjaro, all while lifting twenty pound dumbbells" tired. She rubbed her nose, feeling the beginnings of a headache spreading behind her eyes and shooting down the back of her neck. She winced.

Too many long nights, too much stress of opening day, too much. She needed a break already. Tired as she was though, it was a good tired. She brushed some crumbs off the table, filled with a sense of accomplishment.

Alice sighed; content to stay put a moment longer. Tabby teased her about her lack of a love life, and even though she played along, the truth was Alice was beyond sick of being alone. She wasn't that crazy. Really.

Her bedroom might be decorated a bit like an enchanted garden, full of potted plants and candles and gauzy silky drapings. And so maybe there were the wall clocks, faces painted to appear like the Cheshire cat, the Queen, and of course... handsome Mad Hatter, Johnny Depp. But that wasn't that weird, right? She had a thing. Didn't everyone?

Alice shook her head, slipped her shoes back on and with a heave, was headed toward the register when the front door jingled. She smacked her forehead. In her laziness, she'd forgotten to lock the door.

"Sorry, we're closed." She turned, spying an older woman-- maybe in her late fifties-- wearing a sad look.

"Oh my. I smelled something so heavenly and knew I must, *must* get a taste of whatever special surprises were in here." She threaded her fingers together. "Truly, could you not find it in your heart to allow a tired old woman, frail too I might add..."

Alice couldn't stop the smile. The woman had balls. She kind of liked her.

"Oh come on, Auntie," the local island patois slipped from her tongue as she jerked her hand. "But lock that door behind you. I don't have much left."

Blue eyes, still as sharp and bright as they must have been in her youth, lit up. She rubbed her hands in anticipation. "I've heard so much about you, Alice Hu."

Alice frowned. How did the woman know her name? Paper maybe? Had she given her full name? She rubbed her forehead.

The woman's face went soft, eyes deep in contemplation. "Extraordinary likeness," she spoke quietly and reached out a hand to frame Alice's jaw. "Oh, Alice. I've found you."

Alice's heart clenched, she wanted to jerk out of the woman's grasp, but something made her pause as an answering awareness fluttered desperate wings in her chest. Then the lady gave a tiny shake of the head and laughed, as if suddenly recalling where she was. She dropped her hand and took a step back.

Alice released a breath, suddenly confused by what'd just passed between them.

The woman flashed straight teeth at her. "Wild, reckless child you were. Head in the clouds, nose in the book. Hatter in the heart." There was a lyrical, chiming quality to her laugh that made Alice think of bells. "But now you are a woman grown and my, what a woman you are. You look so much like her."

This was all too weird. "I'm... I'm sorry," her brows dipped, "do I know you?"

The old woman was now at the counter. Her clothes were stylish, fashionable even. But the fabric was unlike any Alice had ever seen. As if someone had gathered the finest spider silk, still sparkling with morning dew, and woven a pale white top from it. She wasn't a large woman, but her personality swept in like a tidal wave, filling the room with its bubbling presence and making her seem much larger than she was.

"Oh, dear me, no." She laughed, her blondish-gray curls bobbed attractively around her pixie face. "How could you? Why this is the first time we've ever met."

Ookay. The woman was clearly one bat short in her belfry. "Right, well... let's see," Alice turned to the display case, trying to hurry things up, "seems all we've got left are the Red Queen's Revenge."

"Oh," the woman shook her head, "that old hag? Surely you could have come up with something better. Off with your head."

Had she not made that same joke to Tabby a few minutes ago? A shiver of strange zipped down Alice's spine.

"What's in it?"

"Umm." It took a second for her to gather her wits. This woman was seriously weirding her out. Memo to her, check the web for any reports on missing mental patients. "Uhh, it's red velvet. Frosting is Italian butter cream with flecks of pink peppercorn."

Cupcake lady groaned. "As much as I despise that fat bag of poo, that sounds lovely. I'll take one, if you please."

"Sure." She handed her the second to last cupcake. "Here you go."

The woman took the cake, unwrapped it and took the largest bite Alice had ever seen a woman take. It didn't even seem like she chewed, before she crammed the rest in her mouth. "Mmm. Ohhh." She made breathy cooing noises the whole time, a look of pure delight creasing her brows.

Crazy or not, Alice bloomed with pride at the obvious enjoyment that had the other woman licking her fingers and pointing to the last one. "Yes, please. Thankfully I've no man to worry if my hips grow to the size of a hippopotamus."

"Yeah, well that makes two of us." Alice smiled her first true grin. "Here, on the house."

The woman did another one of her man bites, sighed, and then patted Alice's hand. "Oh, but, you do, dear."

"Mmm? Do what?"

"You do have a man to worry about, although," she leaned back on her heels and eyed Alice with a calculating glint, "he'll go mad for each and every curve. Oh yes," she nodded, now seeming to speak more to herself, "you'll do very well."

Was this woman trying to set her up with one of her grandchildren or something? Bet he was just as creepy and bizarre as the old crone.

"No thanks." She frowned. Had it only been five minutes ago that she'd been having the best day of her life? "Auntie, I'm sorry, but it really is closing time. I have to clean up."

The woman smiled a secretive sort of thing. "Of course you do, my dear. Don't be late. He'll be waiting." With a jaunty wave, she turned on her heels and left. The door jingled behind her.

"Oh my gosh, Tabby." Alice ran to the door and locked it. She leaned against it, heart beating frantically in her chest. "What the freaking hell was that?"

Tabby popped her head out of the kitchen, a frown on her full lips. "What?"

Alice pushed the teacup themed curtains aside and glanced out the window. Though the sun had set, the streets were still crowded with hundreds of tourists. Thankfully, crazy cupcake lady wasn't one of them.

"That woman." She turned, with a swift shake of her head. "She was nuts. Kept trying to set me up with someone. Total creep job."

"Alice, are you okay?"

She stopped. Why was her friend looking at her like she was a bug under a microscope? "The woman?" She hooked her thumb over her shoulder. "Ate my last two cupcakes."

"No." Tabby shook her head, her face a mask of confusion. "Honey, it's been quiet as death out here. In fact I'd wondered if you'd fallen asleep."

She laughed. "Tabby, shut up. You're just trying to freak me out."

Tabby planted her hands on her hips. She wasn't laughing and now her look went from confusion to true concern. "Hun, are you feeling okay? Sleeping good?"

Her voice was soft and patient, but wrinkles marred the corners of her eyes. She knew that look, had seen it before. A long time ago. It'd haunted her then, it haunted her still.

Alice clenched her fists, her anger intensifying the dull ache in her skull, which in turn only wound her nerves tighter.

A million thoughts buzzed in her head. Was Tabby lying? Trying to make her think she was crazy? She didn't seem to be. How could she not have heard the woman? Quickly her eyes zoomed toward the case. Empty. Not crazy. She licked her lips and gave a self-effacing chuckle. "Yeah, you got me. I fell asleep."

Tabby shook her head. "You know what, sweetie. Let me call Beany. He can come help me finish up. Why don't you call it a night, go take a bath, drink some wine and hit the sack? I think that's what you need. Okay?"

Alice knew she wasn't crazy. The woman had been there. As equally sure of that as she was, she also knew trying to convince Tabby of it would only make her seem crazier. Not less.

She pinched her nose. "Yeah, think it's these heels. Air's too thin up here."

Tabby smiled and walked back to the kitchen. "Leave the keys on the counter. I'll lock up."

Alice undid her apron and tossed it onto the counter, knocking a white business card to the ground. That hadn't been there before. Frowning, she walked over and picked it up, flipping it back and forth. The only thing on either side was a large picture of a white rabbit with the words: *rub me*.

With a shrug, she tucked the card in her bra, set the keys on the counter, and headed to her apartment three blocks away.

***

Steam curled around Alice's face as she wiggled her pruny toes. She'd have to get out soon, but not yet. Instead, she took a long, slow sip of the tart red wine, studying the card.

No matter how many times she turned it, nothing changed. The smiling rabbit mocked her.

"That crazy lady probably left this just to torment me." Finishing the last of her wine, she set the glass down and got out. It took a second for the room to stop spinning. A silly grin split her face. She felt *niiice*.

The tiny blare of her bedroom TV filtered under the crack of the bathroom door. She hated silence, especially because she lived alone. She quickly dried off, grabbed her boy shorts and cami top off the towel rack, and slipped them on.

She'd not been able to resist the items when she'd spied them at a local boutique shop. The cami was a picture of Alice, bent over a table looking at the plate of cake with the sign that read: Eat me.

She tied her hair back into a messy bun, quickly brushed her teeth, and groaned when red drops plopped into her white sink. Alice reached for toilet paper, dabbing at the nosebleed until it stopped. Stress always worked weird things in her body and this was not her first nosebleed. It probably wouldn't be her last, either.

Satisfied she was done bleeding, she tossed the papers in the waste bin, grabbed the card off her washstand and headed to her room. Thankfully, because she was sure the room was spinning. Needing to lie down, she plopped into the tangle of sheets and sighed.

Every bone in her body throbbed and her muscles burned. But at least they were no longer stiff-- the hot water jets had done wonders. Lifting industrial size mixing bowls all morning was no joke.

She flipped the card, obsessed beyond reason with why it'd been left there. Stupid that she should care. It was a dumb card. And yet...

Rub me.

Really? As simple as that?

It's not that she hadn't considered doing it from the moment she'd seen the card. But honestly, this wasn't Wonderland. In the real world when someone left a card like this, that person was usually hiding in wait until you rubbed it so he could then howl in laughter at how stupid you were.

Of course, she was alone now. Her thumb twitched, the obsession intensified tenfold.

She laughed. "I can't believe I'm falling for this." But her head was a little swimmy, the room slightly out of focus, and she was feeling just crazy enough to give in to insanity.

She rubbed her thumb across the words and waited. A quickening, like the flutter of moth's wings pulsed across her skin. Alice sucked in a deep breath.

The clocks ticked.

The fake laughter of news anchors blared through her TV's tiny speakers.

She snorted.

Nothing.

"You're such an idiot, Alice. Tabby was right--"

"You're late," a nasally voice said.

It *did not* come from the TV.

Alice screamed and shot straight up. Every nerve in her body tensed for flight or fight. Her eyes grew wide and her jaw dropped. At the foot of her bed stood an enormous white rabbit in red livery, blinking huge bunny eyes back at her.

"No way." She glanced at the card. It was blank.

"Come. Come." He hopped toward the window, gesturing frantically.

"Whoa." How much had she had to drink? Two glasses, three maybe? She rubbed her eyes. "You're not real."

He rolled his eyes. "As real as you, I'd reckon. Now come, come." His hand...paws? … were on the window sill. He pushed it up, letting in a cool hibiscus-tinted breeze.

"As if." Oh my gosh, she'd cracked. Her mother was right. Too much Wonderland and sugar had finally rotted her brain.

"Oy, why must all the Alices be so vexing?" the small voice growled. He hopped back to her. "Come." He held out his paw.

She scooted back on her heels, bumping hard into her headboard. "Get away from me. You're not real. You're not real."

"Bloody hell, Alice, you called and I came. But I must get back to me Duchess. So please hurry."

She shook her head, denying his words. Not real. White bunnies didn't swear. Or talk. Yeah, they definitely didn't do that.

He hopped up on the bed and her stomach dove to her knees when the mattress caved in. "Oh my gosh, oh my gosh. This is so not happening."

Soft fur touched her bare flesh. She shivered as he grabbed her wrist in a surprising hold, taking them both toward the window. She dug in her heels, but he was really strong. All she managed to do was drag her sheets along with her.

"We're late..."

"For a very important date," she added, giggling with a note of hysteria.

His eyes crossed. "Yes, well... upsy daisy now."

Then his paws were on her butt and she slammed her hands against the window frame. The crazy thing was trying to shove her through the window. She lived on the eighteenth floor.

"Hell. To the N. O." She wiggled, struggling. Her muscles flooded with adrenaline. Fear was a raw, consuming thing. She screamed, crying for help.

But it was no use.

With one final grunt, she fell.

Chapter 3

Air surged past Alice in a dizzying rush. She threw her hands over her face, stomach tickling as she waited for impact.

But as the seconds ticked by, she cracked open one eye. She should have hit pavement and been a memory by now. "Oh, ah..." Words failed her. She'd expected to see blacktop, looming like a nightmare, instead... there was dirt. Everywhere. She was in a tunnel of it. Tree roots, gnarled and twisted, reached out toward her like writhing fingers in a haunted house.

And then the dirt was gone, and suddenly there was nothing but clocks. Masses of them. Thousands. Zooming past in a Dali-esque blur.

After a few minutes the tickling in her belly stopped, but still she fell. She huffed, wondering if this hell would ever end. Almost the moment she thought it, she was there. Wherever there was. She slammed her head and shoulders into something hard and cold, groaning at the webbing of pain that exploded in her body upon impact. It knocked her dizzy for a second and, when she opened her eyes, her vision blurred. The scent of crushed grass and sweet smelling flowers enveloped her in its heady embrace.

"The Alice girl is here."

"Alice? Yet again?"

"Little girl. Little girl."

"No, she is a woman, gnatty old fool. Look at those boobs."

The voices were constant, random and sing-song. She shook her head and groaned. "My head."

"She's busted her head. What, what."

"Ohhhh," crooned a teeny voice, *"the Hatter won't like that."*

She froze at the sound of that name. Where the hell was she? She rubbed her eyes. It took a moment, but when she could finally make out what was before her, she couldn't believe it. She grabbed her head. Flowers, too many different varieties to count, were looking at her.

Looking at her!

She yelped.

They blinked.

"She's as loud as the rest. Truly, dearie, do ye not see 'tis night?" a fluted yellow flower honked at her.

She had to get home. Maybe she was home? Maybe this was all a dream. A bad, weird dream.

"Deep into that darkness peering, long I stood there, wondering, fearing, doubting, dreaming dreams no mortal ever dared to dream before."

The voice was hot and gravelly, rolling over her body like a lover's touch. She followed the voice and her thighs tingled.

It was him. Alice swallowed. She'd know the face anywhere. She'd seen it before. A long, long time ago.

She smiled, so many words on her tongue, none of them able to make it past numb lips.

It was hard to gauge his height. He was sitting on a chair, a cup of tea in his hand, staring at her with a hard black glare. There was violence and madness burning in that gaze. And something else. Something that made her burn, made her nipples tighten into hard, almost painful buds.

Last time she'd seen him he hadn't looked so foreboding, or so sexy. She licked her lips.

Silvery moonlight made his hair glint with shades of the darkest chocolate. The pressure of his gaze felt like a hot brand.

Her pulse stuttered. Dreams shouldn't make her so hot. Needy.

It hadn't before. Then again, she'd only been 13.

"You."

She bristled, not because of what he said, but how he'd said it. A depth of meaning had been conveyed in that one word. Anger, disdain, even hate. Alice held her chin up, but her nails left crescent marks on her palm.

His nose curled. "Bloody, damn fairy," he spat.

Alice was so startled she couldn't even speak. Why the hell was he so angry? What had she done? And who was this fairy? She rubbed the back of her head. Was she dead? Maybe this was hell?

With his dark hair and sharp brows, Hatter looked more like the devil than the white knight of her youth. The man she'd idolized, the very one she'd credited with saving her life. She could still see it in her mind's eyes, her body lying weak and pale in the hospital bed, calling out for an imaginary savior. She'd never been more surprised than when he'd answered her...

But clearly that memory belonged only to her. He didn't seem to remember her at all.

His lips thinned and a spark of something hot flashed through his eyes when he set his cup down. On freaking air! It literally hung, suspended as if by strings.

She'd dreamed of Wonderland many times, but never like this. Never with so much detail. She could smell the wind, and colors she'd never seen in her life dotted the landscape. Vivid didn't even begin to describe this.

"Follow me."

Was he serious? "I'm not going anywhere with you." Alice bit the inside her cheek. An owl hooted and she shivered.

"Fine." He narrowed his eyes. "Then stay."

He got up and she gulped. Though he stood a distance from her still, she knew he towered her by a good foot. At five foot two there wasn't much that didn't. He turned to go and she clenched her teeth.

A thwamping sound rang through the sudden stillness of the field and her pulse thumped. She jerked, glancing over her shoulder. A chilling echo of laughter flitted through the dark silhouette of trees.

Just a dream. She squeezed her eyes shut.

Thwamp.

"You're not really going to just leave me here, are you?" she yelled at his retreating figure.

He stopped and, even though it was dark, there was enough moonlight to the see the heated glare on his face. "Follow or stay."

"Follow or stay. Follow or stay," she muttered under her breath, but rushed to catch up when she heard the next slithering thwamp.

He wouldn't look at her and he wouldn't stop. Alice wanted to kick him. If this was a dream, he'd be nicer. Which meant it wasn't a dream. But then there was that whole white rabbit thing.

Each step they took the more and more she seethed. One step blurred into the next and the next until she wasn't even sure how much time had passed. Only that it'd felt like forever and the silent treatment was quickly starting to wear thin.

"You know, it wouldn't hurt to be a little more polite." The moment the words left her mouth she wanted to kick herself. Why the hell did she care?

He didn't stop and the field was now no longer a field, but rolling hills full of ruts.

She panted, calves screaming as she gripped her side. Shoes would have been great right about now. Barefoot was so not fun, especially when dirt got between her toes and stones dug into her heels. But she would not stop and she would not beg him to either.

Since he wouldn't talk and she couldn't at this point, it gave her plenty of time to think. Whatever had happened tonight, she was pretty sure she wasn't dreaming.

The sights, the smells, the burning pit of anger gnawing at her gut. No, she wasn't dreaming. And she wasn't dead. Because she was pretty sure dead people didn't want to murder something.

She eyed the back of his brightly painted pin-striped suit. What was with the stupid get up anyway? Just how many pocket watches did one man need? She counted at least thirty, and that was on his back! Who did that? All her life she'd been infatuated by the man. Now...

She rolled her eyes when her heart fluttered at the sight of his broad shoulders. Stupid traitorous emotions.

A bead of sweat plopped off the tip of her nose. Annoyed, she wiped her brow. When would this torture end? Where was he taking her?

"Dammit!" she hissed when she stepped on a twig, its rough edge easily slicing through her heel.

Alice grabbed hold of a thick tree branch and hopped on one leg as she tried to peer at the bottom of her foot.

Blood. She growled, swiping at the wet warmth of it. "I could kill him. I will kill him. That bastard. Why am I following him? This is stupid, stupid, Alice. Why did you rub that card?"

"Alice!"

Startled to hear him call out her name, she glanced up. He was looking at her, his face stone cold, but his eyes held a frantic edge to them.

"Listen to me."

She swallowed hard. His tone held a note of "Stay calm, and don't panic." Never a good sign when someone started a sentence that way.

A long sibilant hiss sounded in her ear.

She froze. Swallowing hard, she turned her face and came eye to eye with the black, beady eyes of a ginormous snake. A snake unlike any she'd seen before. Its forked tongue came to within inches of her nose. And now that she was aware of it, she wondered why the hell she hadn't noticed the tree sported purple polka dots.

"Hatter," she squeaked and slowly dropped her hand.

Her *branch* moved.

"Hatter," she hissed, she couldn't take her eyes from the beast, as if looking at it would somehow prevent it from wrapping its thick body around her own. "Help. Me."

Strong hands latched onto her shoulders. Her eyes were still wide and her knees felt locked in place. Hatter pinched her and she jumped, glaring at him.

"Get behind me," he said.

She didn't need to be told twice. Alice stepped into the shelter of his back. Her fingers clenched the edge of his jacket, watching in horror as he lifted out a hand toward the creature's broad head.

"And truly I was afraid," his deep voice hypnotized her and she buried her nose in his jacket, "I was most afraid. But even so, honored still more that he should seek my hospitality from out of the dark door of the secret earth..."

There was nothing after that save the stillness of the breeze, the Hatter's even breaths, and the wild rush of blood in her ears. It seemed an eternity before he turned.

"He's gone, are you okay?" He touched her face and she hated that his soft touch felt so good.

"Does it matter? Do you care?" she snapped, jerking her face out of his hand. Even though that was the last thing she wanted to do. She wanted to touch him, to remember again the man who'd saved the dying little girl years ago, but she couldn't forget how he'd been earlier.

His hand hung in midair for a moment until, with a slow nod, he dropped it. Hatter turned on his heels and started forward again. "Almost there," he rumbled.

"Fine," she said, equal parts wanting to cry and wanting to pick up a rock and throw it at the back of his head. But she did neither; instead she limped along behind him, her gashed heel stinging every step of the way.

Moments later, Alice was surrounded by a swarm of dancing fireflies. They zipped in and out through trees, lighting the canopy of leaves with their golden liquid radiance.

Hatter stopped. "Stay here."

Their rest stop didn't look like much. There were trees and glowing mushrooms, the spotted glowing kinds you'd see in cartoons and in an assortment of colors. A large swarm of fireflies congregated in and around them. She wiggled her toes, wanting to moan at the lush smoothness of soft grass beneath her feet. She needed to sit. Now.

"Whatever," she groaned and plopped down. Her feet were a mess, covered in dirt and oozing blood. If there was a time to cry, now would have been the perfect time for it.

Instead she watched Hatter reach out and swipe at one of the bugs. It bounced around in his palm frantically.

He was saying something. Growling it actually, but she couldn't hear and really, she didn't care.

Mad as a hatter.

Why had she ever thought that was sexy?

Chapter 4

"What kind of black magic is this?" Hatter hissed.

Danika's wings fluttered against his palm as she shoved and pushed at him. "Hatter!" she squealed, "for the gods sakes, open your palm! Damn you, man. You're bending my wings."

He shook his fist and eyed the little ball of light hard. "I told you not to bring her. Not only do you bring her, you bring *her*! What have you done? She should be old and withered, and yet she looks the same. How is that possible?"

The muscle in his jaw ticked when she didn't answer quickly enough. He shook his hand harder.

"Open," she roared, "or you'll get no answers from me."

He flung her from his hand. She rolled in a ball through the air before finally righting herself and glaring at him. Danika pointed her wand at his chest. "How dare you!"

"I dare much," he growled. "What have you done, Danika?"

How could Danika have done this? How could she have returned that venomous, viperous woman back to him? How was it even possible?

How could he have these feelings for Alice, these soft feelings that made him face a snake's constricting coils to help her? He should hate her, he did hate her. After all she'd done to him, he wanted to shake her, kiss her, whisper his undying hate in her ears. Hatter grabbed his skull, willing himself to ignore the huddled bundle on the grass behind him. Up is down, down is up. Emotions made no sense. No sense.

"Look at me, I say." Danika snapped her fingers.

"What?"

Danika's face crumpled. "Are you not pleased, Hatter?"

"Pleased." He wanted to roar, wanted to stomp on Danika's mushroom home and smash his fist through her tree. "Pleased?" he asked again. "Why have you returned her? How have you returned her? Wonderland said no. No. No." He grabbed his head again. Dizzy, gods he could smell her. Like caramel and the salty brine of sea.

When she'd clutched his jacket and pressed her nose into his back, he'd been aware, so very aware. Every inch of his body screamed for her. Wanted her. She was his Alice, the one he'd surrendered his heart to years before. Wicked, wicked Alice. She'd whispered of love, touched his body, made him yearn and need.

Betrayer. His nostrils flared. Evil little Alice with the forked tongue, just like the snake. He should have let the snake have her. Damn her.

"It's not her, Hatter." Danika grabbed his fingers, peeling it away from his eye.

He shook her off. "Of course it's her."

"No." Her curls bobbed around her tiny head. "That Alice is nothing more than a withered husk."

For a moment, a yawning chasm of ice filled his empty, shattered soul.

Danika pointed over his shoulder. "That is her great granddaughter."

Not the same Alice? "But her eyes, and the face. Pretty, pretty hair. Long and black with a widow's peak. The itsy-bitsy spider crawls up the water spout..."

A sharp slap stung his cheek. "Snap out of it. Now is not the time to lose your wits."

Hatter blinked. "Why her? I hate her."

"Hatter, no." Danika petted the cheek she'd slapped, her cold little hand soothing. "You do not hate her. You do not know her. She is not the same. I swear it."

He grabbed his head, trying to recall why he'd been so angry. Trying to hang on and remember, lest he lose the thought like he'd lost so many others. "You reached into the same bloodline. Why didn't you tell me?"

She gave him a soft smile. "Because I know you. If you'd known, you'd never have come to get her."

He took a breath, and Alice was there, her sweet, caramel warmth permeating the breeze. Hatter looked over his shoulder. She sat huddled on the ground, staring at her foot, a tiny frown marring her brows. He'd been cruel, forcing her to march without shoes. Forcing her to follow without speaking a word.

"I can't, Danika." He shook his head. "Take her back. Take her home."

"You know that's not how it works. She's here. For three days. Try, Hatter." Her blue eyes filled with tears. "You must try."

He sighed. Couldn't Danika see it was hopeless? And now she brought him the granddaughter of the woman who'd betrayed him and expected him to what-- trust the same blood didn't run through her veins?

"Heal her feet. They... bleed."

"Oh, Hatter," Danika sighed. "Open your eyes, boy, see what I can, before it's too late."

He ran his hand through his wavy hair. "Wonderland's not accepted her."

She frowned. "She's only just gotten here. Give her time."

He curled his lips, always so positive Danika was. Every time it was the same thing. Next time. The next one. He was sick of it.

"No promises. Heal her feet," he demanded again.

With a sigh, Danika flew toward Alice, becoming a golden streak of light that bobbed and weaved around her feet.

Alice yelped, snatching her feet back and then sighed happily when the bleeding stopped. Their eyes met and Hatter had no words, all he could do was stare and hope and hate. He clenched his jaw as Danika flew back to him.

"Take her to the waters, have her wash her feet. They'll be healed after that."

Hatter nodded his thanks, then walking up to Alice he cleared his throat. "Come with me," he said, much gruffer than he'd intended.

She frowned, pulling her bottom lip between straight teeth. "Where?" Wariness shone in her gaze.

"Just... come." He grabbed her elbow, wishing he had more kindness in him. She wasn't the same Alice, or so Danika said, and yet... the truth was hard to reconcile.

Huffing, she stood and jerked her elbow from his lax grip. "I can walk just fine, thank you."

Hatter led them to the fairy waters a short distance behind the glen. Fairies, looking like lightening bugs the way they danced above the surface of the placid stream, added a magical, almost surreal setting to their surroundings.

He pointed to a depressed section of verdant grass. "Sit."

She lifted a brow, an annoyed look creasing her forehead.

"If you please." The words were thick on his tongue.

Reminding him of a Queen the way she lifted her chin proudly, she sat cross-legged. "Well?"

Knowing he should apologize, not knowing how to even begin, he did the only thing he could think of. Hatter knelt by her side, a shiver rippling through him as her scent of caramel and sunshine tickled his senses, filled his head. He dipped his hand into the water. "Give me your feet."

"Why? My feet feel fine, really?"

She grabbed hold of them, tucking them tightly against her shapely thighs. He put her through this, he'd make it right. Gently, he traced the instep of her left foot.

"Give me your foot?" he asked again, gently.

Her big brown eyes softened and she didn't resist when he tugged it free. Dipping his hand into the chill waters, he scooped up a palm full and let it drizzle against her soft flesh. She moaned, when he rubbed it in.

"Oh wow, that's so... wow," she sighed, leaning back on her hands, silently opening herself up to him further.

He smiled, knowing the magical properties of the water did more than heal a scrap or seal a wound, the waters here were the purest essence of life. Making new what was old. He rubbed it in, kneading the hurt and rawness away.

Leaning in so close, feeling the breath of her body flit against top of his head, he licked his lips. Alice Hu, whatever incarnation she came in, had a way of affecting him in the deepest marrow of his soul.

Her body heat so close, it wrapped around him like hug, making him forget that he couldn't lean in and kiss her, that she wasn't his. That he didn't want her. All he knew was this moment, this touch, the rhythmic movement of her breasts as she exhaled slowly.

His fingers trembled as he moved to her other foot, forcing himself to repeat the same torturous massage, trying in vain to forget how soft she felt, how good she smelled. How her lips parted ever so slightly, fuller on the bottom than the top.

Hatter swallowed hard, she wasn't his. Not now. Not ever.

Jerking back, he waved his hand over her feet. His own magic ran hot through his veins as he called forth a pair of sparkling silver flats to cover her feet in.

Standing, he nodded, molars grinding so hard his jaw ached. He could never forget who she was. What stock she hailed from.

A snake could shed its skin many times in its life, but it never stopped being a snake. New Alice couldn't be so different from Evil Alice.

What do you want from me, Alice? What do you want?

Chapter 5

They walked again. Thankfully Alice's feet were fine. Which was amazing. One second she wanted to cry from the stinging pain, and then, the next second, the ball of firelight ran across her feet and she'd felt better. And then he'd washed her feet and she'd felt amazing. Not an ache or pain anywhere the water had touched. Like she was a new person. Well, from the feet down anyway. And though there'd been nothing erotic or even sensual about his ministrations, her stomach and heart had fluttered like a girl with her first crush. He'd washed her feet, stood, and stared at her.

Maybe it'd been her imagination, but for just a moment, an infinite second in time it'd seemed like he'd shared a piece of his soul, letting her peer deep into the burning depths of his heated gaze, but then he'd blinked and the spell (or whatever it'd been) had passed, leaving her shaken and tongue tied.

He seemed different now. Not completely kind. Hell no, nothing that drastic. But there was much less hostility, which, she supposed, was better than nothing.

"I'm..." he cleared his throat and glanced at her from the corner of his eye. "The Hatter."

Alice lifted her brow. "I pretty much figured that out."

"Right," he sighed and glanced to the side.

She rolled her eyes and huffed. "I'm Alice. Alice Hu."

His jaw went rigid, but even so, her heart skipped a beat at the pure beauty and masculinity of his face. He was so much more than she remembered. Didn't mean she'd forgiven him for what he'd done earlier. Not by a long shot.

But she hated silence. "So is this a dream, or what?" At this point, she was 99.9999 percent certain this wasn't a dream, but she wanted to talk. Even if that meant talking with the most sexily infuriating man she'd ever met in her life.

"All that we see or seem is but a dream within a dream," he said, words laced with a bitter sadness that made her heart tremble.

"Sure." She was confused. Was he agreeing with her or not? Why did she suddenly want to wrap him in her arms? The haunting sorrow in his gaze touched something in her heart.

She set her jaw and tapped her hand against her thigh. The man was ridiculous, spoke in riddles, and yet-- her stomach did a somersault-- she couldn't stop the mental pictures of him nude with her sprawled on top of him.

She groaned. He was mean. She didn't like him. He'd freakin' made her walk through a forest without shoes on. Her tender feet had gotten bruised and bloody and it was so easy to give into the hate, but then he'd saved her from that damn snake, washed her smelly feet, and nothing made sense anymore. Since the moment they'd left the mushroom glade, he'd been acting different. Not so angry and cold.

Stems of grass brushed against her ankles like the softest satin. Stars gleamed brighter than any diamond in the navy blue sky. Wind, pregnant with the fragrance of flowers, sifted gentle fingers through her hair.

"I'd swear I was drunk as a skunk right now, except for the fact that I don't feel in the least bit tipsy. I just cannot accept I'm in Wonderland, though. This is ridiculous."

A loud snore, like the braying of a donkey, startled her. She yelped and Hatter pointed to a shadowy lump beside them. A huge skunk lay sprawled on its back, a glass bottle by its head. Its bushy black and white tail twitched back and forth, tiny feet jerking like a dog's when asleep.

"Is that a-"

"Words have power." His eyes narrowed and he was looking at her different now, not shocked or amazed exactly, but different. He turned. Alice hadn't been aware he'd been standing so close until suddenly it seemed as if he took up all her space. She licked her lips, skin tingling with a rush of blood. He looked like he wanted to say more.

"Alice-" His Adam's apple bobbed, as if he were working up the courage to say more.

The hot shiver of the Hatter's sherry-tinted breath fanned her face. She squirmed. She wanted to touch him, touch herself. Anything, just to end the madness of lust spreading through her veins like a sickness.

Then his gaze grew hooded and he turned back around. She sucked in a shaky breath, knees suddenly weak. What was going on? Hadn't she just been pissed at him?

"What the hell happened back there? Did I make that thing come?" she asked his back.

He stopped and she caught back up to him. He looked down at her. "You tell me."

Pulse trapped in her throat because suddenly nothing made sense, she grabbed his hand. "Why am I here?"

There'd been one other time in her life when words had shifted her reality, and it'd not been magic at all but a tumor the size of a golf ball in her brain. Was she sick again? Stomach revolting with worry she squeezed his fingers.

His jaw clenched. He looked at their clasped hands and she expected him to let go. Hatter sighed and pulled her in for a hug.

Stunned, she didn't move. It didn't seem like a kind hug, or even an I-want-to-strip-you-and-make-love-hug. He trembled and she sensed, that much like the snake, power rippled behind the touch and if he wanted to he could hurt her. Maybe he did want to.

A part of Alice wanted to shove him back, make him let her go. His hard fingers bunched into the back of her shirt. But she just couldn't because this was the man she'd loved her entire life. The man she'd craved since age thirteen.

"You smell like cinnamon and tea," she shyly admitted. "My favorites."

He cleared his throat. "It is time." Was his voice shaking? Time for what? She wanted to ask, but doubted he'd elaborate as he hadn't done so yet and, if she'd learned anything in her short life, it was not to ask stupid questions she knew would never get answered. For now, she'd wait and watch.

Alice looked and then blinked, trying to rattle the image loose. Much like the fictional Alice, she was presented with a table, empty, save for the small slices of strawberry-festooned cakes. Each one had a sign in it. One read: Eat Me. The other: Poison. And she couldn't stop the delighted thrill that zipped down her spine as she recognized one of her favorite scenes from the book.

Nibbling on her lip, she glanced at him. What was she supposed to choose? Alice hadn't had a choice, so this was kind of different and whole lot confusing. Hatter didn't move for one or the other and his blank face gave nothing away. There'd be no taking a lead off his cue.

Was he testing her?

She looked around for any sign or clue, but it was pointless. Nothing could or would help her. Taking a deep breath, she reached for the Eat Me slice. Just as she ripped the tip off, the sharp slap of his hand made her drop it. Shocked, she glanced at her stinging hand. "Did you just slap me?"

At least he had the good sense not to deny it. Most people would have said, I didn't do that, or, that's not what I meant. "Bad is good. Good is bad."

Then he tore off two chunks from the Poisoned one and handed it to her.

The white frosting looked delicious, but the cake was green. And not St. Patty's Day dyed green either. No, this was sitting out on the counter, rotting from humidity, green. She wrinkled her nose as the smell finally smacked her nostrils. Spoiled eggs and ten day old banana peels.

Her stomach soured. "You know, I'm not actually all that hungry."

He rolled his eyes, popped his into his mouth and before she had a moment to protest, he'd slid hers between her teeth. Reflex forced her to chew, her tongue bursting with the unexpected notes of strawberry cordial.

But the delicious buzz lasted only a second before Alice was slammed with vertigo. The bit of rotten cake revolted in her stomach. She reached out blindly, almost falling as the world slid sideways and her with it. Like looking at fun house mirrors while the walls around her rolled and rolled. She screamed. A firm set of hands clamped onto her waist and then she could breathe, because he felt so real and immovable. Blessedly still. She gulped in air and clung like a baby monkey to its mother's back.

"Breathe, Alice." His hands petted her hair, calming the panic laying siege. After a second, trusting herself not to throw up, she opened her eyes.

Either the world had grown, or she'd shrunk. Grass towered around them.

"Come." He gripped her hand, and she allowed herself to be led, still feeling drunk and wobbly.

He wound a tight path through the emerald forest. Any other time she might have enjoyed it, looked around and absorbed it all. She was finally in Wonderland. But right now she was too tired to care and simply wanted to get to where they were going.

In the distance she spied a teapot with a twilight meadow scene painted on it. As they neared, she noticed a white cottage covered in thorny roses at its center.

He walked up to the teapot. What exactly did he plan to do with that thing? Gah, she hoped that wasn't his house. While fitting, she had zero desire to curl up on a cold ceramic floor.

Then he did a strange thing. Which was kind of stupid, because was the Hatter capable of doing "strange?" His name sort of implied the fact that he was as bizarre as seeing a man-sized white rabbit swearing at her.

He reached for the red door of the cottage and his hand phased through the teapot like it was little more than a mirage. The door swung open.

She frowned and tapped the teapot, shocked at its solidness. He looked at her and somehow she understood his intention.

"This is your home?" she asked.

"Yes."

The way he acted, the apprehension in his gaze, she sensed this cost him a great deal. But she wasn't sure why. Though she really shouldn't care. He was a brute. Totally rude. And yet his hug and touch made her want to melt into a puddle of goo at his feet. Much easier to hate him when he was a jerk, and so much harder to do it when he wasn't.

Damn her soft heart.

The cottage was quaint, the roof slightly sunken in, and the paint chipped off in spots or two. The thing was in desperate need of work and it was a wonder it still stood.

"Hmm. It's... nice." She didn't want to lie, but really, it was pretty bad.

His lips twitched and, oh man, she forgot everything. His rudeness? Gone. His indifference? Gone, too. All she could see was that smile. She was pathetic. Seriously crazy. If he'd been sullenly handsome before, now he was HOT to the nth degree. Her stomach flopped.

The painting stretched, bulged, and when he stepped through it almost seemed to absorb him. He hadn't released her hand. She didn't have a moment to panic or think, disoriented the moment her foot slid through the door.

She was upside down. Or was that right side up? Hard to know for sure because the furniture and bookcases sat inches from her. But she clearly stood on the roof, or, rather, a roof beam. The door they'd stepped through was definitely below her.

Maybe?

Then the world around them rolled like the display of a slot machine and she plopped down on the floor, landing on her backside with a thud. She wasn't moving, but felt like she was in the dizzying rush. When it finally stopped she rubbed her butt.

He snorted.

"Don't you laugh," she wagged her finger.

Hatter pressed his lips together and mumbled something.

She narrowed her eyes. "What did you say?"

"I said..." and that was as far as he got before he started laughing.

She crossed her arms, but the longer he laughed the harder she fought not to join him. Finally, he held a hand out to her.

Grumbling, she took it and noticed the door was where it should be and the beams above her head. "That gonna happen again?"

His lips twitched. "No."

"You know what, Hatter, I don't think you're as crazy as everyone else thinks you are. I think you're a big fraud." She tried to be stern, but she couldn't stop herself from smiling.

Light danced in his expressive, suddenly warm brown eyes.

"Ah, I knew it." She couldn't resist teasing further.

He snorted. "I became insane, with long intervals of horrible sanity."

"And now it's gone." She rolled her eyes. "And just for the record, you might want to read something other than Poe. Incredibly depressing."

He jerked, shocked. "You know Poe?"

She grinned, crossing her arms under her breasts and experienced a momentary thrill of feminine delight when his eyes zoomed to her chest. "I know a great many things, Hatter. Like the fact you find my *shirt* fascinating."

He shrugged. She smirked-- he hadn't denied it. "Come on." He turned and continued on down the winding maze of corridors. The cottage outside had been tiny, but this place was an M.C. Esher nightmare.

Hatter would walk through one door and suddenly it was day, the sun beating so hard, she'd been ready to chant: "I'm melting" in her best Wicked Witch impersonation. Only to then enter through another door and plop face first in a mound of silver dusted snow.

Shivering, rubbing her arms to generate any heat, she stuttered, "cold," through clenched teeth.

Then they were walking through yet another door, and before she had a chance to breathe a loud sigh of relief at the blast of warmth, she was free falling. Again.

She threw her arms out, attempting to grab anything to stop the mind numbing terror of total darkness.

"Relax," his deep voice rumbled next to her ear. She turned, blindly reaching out toward his voice. He grabbed her hand and the fear vanished, replaced by a thrill of excitement that bordered on lunacy.

Wind surged past in a sickening rush. All she could focus on was the heat emanating from long fingers wrapped around hers. Her stomach dipped when his thumb caressed her knuckle.

Then they landed on what felt like a hundred soft pillows and she lost him.

"Hatter," she cried, scrabbling to stand. Everything was dark and she was disoriented, turning in circles, trying to find some source of light.

"Hold my hand."

His hand slid into hers and for a second, a whisper in time, she felt the world shift. Small. Minutely. Like a butterfly's wings taking off from a rose petal. She jerked, eyes widening, feeling his heat spread through her palm, up her arm. Her heart twisted almost painfully in her chest at the rightness of the very strange moment.

He didn't slow his pace or turn as they advanced on door after door, each room more strange than the last. A green sky with blue grass. A room filled with thirty moons. Another smelling of the heavenly scent of vanilla and spice. One after another, shifting in a blurry daze she couldn't track.

They stepped through a door and all she had time to do was groan, "Dammit." Just how many times would she have to free fall?

She closed her eyes when she got too dizzy to keep them open from the constant rotation. Her hair hung above her head. Lovely. She was falling headfirst. At this point, she wasn't even scared. Sort of like riding a rollercoaster twenty times in a row, after a certain point, it failed to terrify.

She wrapped her arms around his waist, snuggling in the best she could. With his big frame shielding her, she felt safe, protected in the madness of his home.

And then they were there. Landing gracefully on their feet. She looked, breathing in the wonder of a land that defied description.

The world sparkled with the deep hued shades of jewels. They stood on an open meadow. Flowers, petals looking like they'd been dipped in gold, swayed from a gentle breeze. A flock of birds gracefully sailed overhead, their birdsong a trilling, haunting melody that pierced her heart. And in the distance, she heard the faint roar of rushing water.

"My home is this way." Somewhere between her falling at his feet, and her falling in his arms, he'd gentled. Reminding her forcibly of the man etched in her memory from years ago.

She nodded, feeling as if the world hushed around her, held its breath with an expectant hum.

Hatter led her to a white cottage with a red door. It looked exactly the same as the one painted on the teapot. She halted, narrowing her eyes.

His lips quirked and heat nestled deep in her belly.

"Don't worry," he shook his head, "no more tricks. This is home. You're probably exhausted."

He'd read her mind. For a second she'd been afraid she'd have to endure more tricks and turns.

A thick wave of dark brown hair fell into his eye and she felt the oddest desire to reach up and tuck it back into place. Run her fingers through it and see if it felt as soft as it looked. She bit her lip and nodded.

The moment they stepped inside, she waited for the dizzy inertia of a spinning room, but he'd told the truth. It was a simple living room. A blue stuffed love seat and rocking chair sat before a fire burning in the hearth. Beside it a wooden bookshelf lined with books. Colorful rugs were strewn haphazard around the low lit room.

She sniffed and her stomach rumbled when she identified the scent of buttery scones. Everything had a homey, comfy feel to it. Not at all what she'd expected from the Hatter's home.

The crazy rooms, and falling into nothing, sure... but not this. This was nothing short of a dream home for her.

She'd always wanted to live in a place just like this. A simple, cozy, warm haven. She could picture herself here, reading in front of the fire.

Alice glanced at Hatter from the corner of her eye.

Or maybe making love, while outside a storm raged and the world seemed bathed in madness and chaos. Safe in her lover's arms.

Heat crept up her neck and she rocked on her heels as she become aware of his large presence and the fact that they were very alone.

She swallowed, wishing she knew what he was thinking.

His eyes were shaded, and it was hard for her to make him out. But he kept casting her shifty glances. Maybe... he was nervous? Her heart skipped a beat-- did he like her being here?

"This place is so awesome. So un-mad-like. In fact," she gushed, not filtering her words, "in fact, I wish I could stay here forever."

He dropped her hand. "But I am mad, Alice," he muttered and the ease they'd shared just seconds ago vanished.

The air thickened with tension and even though he stood right next to her, it was like a wall had suddenly slammed up between them. If he'd had fangs, he'd be growling.

What had she done now? His moods were as random as trade winds, up and then down. Hot and then cold. For a second she'd thought he'd wanted her here, maybe she'd been wrong.

Her stomach rumbled, a loud sonorous boom in the stillness. He turned and walked into another room, leaving her to wonder whether to stay or follow.

A second later he came marching back in holding a golden brown bun in his hand. "Here," he tossed it at her. "Eat something, you're too skinny. Like all the rest of them."

She caught the yeasty projectile. It was sticky and warm. It smelled so good and she was so hungry. Rest of them, who? She was curious and even recognized a hot tendril of jealousy spark through her veins despite her resolve not to care that other women had obviously tramped through his home. But she wouldn't ask. It was the Hu pride.

He was hot one second, cold the next. It aggravated her, because she wanted to like him, wanted to see him as she'd seen him before. And just when she thought maybe she'd been wrong about him in the beginning, he did something to bring it back. The man was just like Wonderland, always throwing her off balance.

She tore into the bread with her teeth: not like she asked to come here. Tabby was right, she was sick in the head to be so turned on by him.

"Come on." He turned and walked off.

"Come on. Come on." She mocked. "It's always come on with you. I've got a name, you know." She swallowed the bite of bread, unhappy to find she'd liked it. It tasted like butter and honey. Any other time she'd lick her fingers to claim all the sticky goodness, but she refused to show him how much she'd enjoyed it.

"Alice." Again, he sounded aggravated.

There'd not been a thought in her mind to do it, but, as if having an out of body experience, she watched her arm draw back. Saw the half-eaten bun sail out of her hand towards the back of his head.

The moment it hit him, she gasped, then covered her mouth, horrified. He jerked, came to a complete stop and grabbed the back of his skull, crumbs still clinging to bits of his hair. When he looked at her... all she had to say was, if looks could kill. But then his stare turned incredulous, as if to say: *'did you really just throw that piece of bread at me!'*

Her fear turned to laughter and she couldn't stop it. She grabbed her stomach and pointed. "I'm so sorry. I have no idea what I was thinking. I've never..." Tears gathered at the corners of her eyes as she lost all words and laughed until her sides ached.

His anger quickly subsided and he cocked his head as if confused by her. Which only made it funnier. He was the Hatter, yet she was the one acting like a complete idiot.

She held up her hand. "I'm sorry," she huffed, gulping in air. "Sorry. Won't do it again."

"Yes, well, I... deserved it." His lips tipped up and she knew he fought back a smile. And seeing that was like pouring salt on snow; it killed her laughter cold. She grabbed her chest as her blood heated and her head swim with naughty thoughts.

Like shoving the stupid jacket off his broad shoulders, stripping him of the colorfully striped pants, and then proceeding to lick her way down his body until she came to the bit of male beauty that would be hard and proud. Just for her.

She shivered. His nostrils flared, as if he sensed her thoughts. Something wicked, and not altogether displeasing glinted back at her in the depths of his chocolate brown eyes.

The room charged with a snap of sexual hunger so intense, so arousing, she knew if she touched herself, she'd be soaked.

His hot gaze danced across her form, lingering in all the right places. Heat coiled like a sling between her thighs. Focusing, trying to remember to breathe around the lump in her throat, she held her ground, pretending he wasn't making her tremble.

Her reaction was more intense than any she'd had in years, maybe ever. She wanted him with a need that came a hair's breadth to being insane.

His mouth thinned. "Come on. Please."

She nodded regally, and tried to pretend his words hadn't just turned her insides to mush, and followed him down another hall. This one was full of closed doors. At least twenty. The dimensions of the place made her lightheaded; it was small, yet large. Compact, yet unending. Madness. Like the man himself. Was he taking her to his room?

The thought made her want to purr.

Stopping at the seventh door, he turned the knob and opened it to her. "Is this okay?"

Her eyes widened as she stepped in behind him. "My room?"

Had it really been a dream? She could have sworn... She sighed. Seeing the clocks and scattered plants, all Alice could think was how drab it all looked. She'd gotten Wonderland all wrong. What must he think, seeing her room, knowing how silly her notions of his world were?

She felt his eyes on her, hot and searching. Drawn to him, she looked back. And for a moment it seemed like his eyes swirled with light, round and round and round. Mesmerizing her, locking her in place, black rolling into brown and then into amber. *Around and around, over and over, pulling her in with its sad, haunting symmetry. A staircase that fell into forever, unending, unceasing torment.*

Then he blinked, and it was gone. His hand hovered above her head, so close she felt the heat radiating from his palm.

His hand shook as it lowered inch by agonizingly slow inch. She moaned when he touched her— she couldn't help it. His touch did something to her, made her feel alive, tingly and on fire. The sound spurred him on and, with a sharp groan, he wrapped a strand of hair around his shaking finger, lifting it to his nose.

He closed his eyes and inhaled. Tremors wracked his body as he moved closer. Something thick and large pressed against her thigh. She purred, responding to the primal lust. Alice wanted to touch him, hold him. She slid her arms around his back, wishing she could touch naked flesh, hating that he was so covered up. She settled for laying her head against his chest.

Bump bump, the beat of his heart was a song in her ears. Again her world tilted, flipped on its side, and made her question where up was, where she started and he began. She clung to him; he was the hope in a swirling torrent of senselessness.

"I know everything there is to know about you, Alice." His voice, whiskey rough, was an erotic caress against the nape of her neck. "I always have."

Alice's heart thrilled, raced and she could taste the adrenaline surge on her tongue. But then he stepped away, and she felt bereft. She dropped empty arms as he walked away.

Chapter 6

Hatter paced the length of his bedroom. His arms were crossed behind his back, fingers flexing as he contemplated what to do about Alice.

Danika said she wasn't the same Alice. But she looked the same. From her almond shaped brown eyes to the beguiling widow's peak at her forehead.

He rubbed his jaw, pulse thudding. She even talked the same-- soft, with an exotic lilt to it. And her hair, all black and silky and when he'd inhaled he'd known she'd smell of salt and hints of buttery caramel. Just like the other.

He paused against his bed frame. But she did not act the same. Watching his world, her eyes sparkled with wonder rather than greed. She'd called a creature. Other Alice hadn't been able to do that. She'd only been able to summon small things. A teacup, butterflies... his pulse pounded so hard he thought he'd choke on it.

Was this Alice really the one? Was she his? Blood rushed to his groin and he groaned. Danika wouldn't lie; she was many things, but not a liar. She'd said this wasn't the same girl and, as much as he wanted to hate New Alice for reminding him so forcibly of the evil one, it would be cruel and wrong.

Damn that meddlesome godmother. This was all her doing anyway. His nostrils flared, the essence of Alice's scent lingering on his coat, his skin. She was beautiful and spirited. His lips curved in a slow grin. She'd thrown bread at him.

The minx.

Hatter couldn't stop thinking about the skunk. She'd called it. With her silly nonsense words, she'd called it into being. Other Alice had manifested magic and he'd thought then she may have been the one, but it hadn't been enough. Wonderland had said no.

But a skunk, a large, fat and drunken skunk, was vastly stronger magic than a mere cup of tea. His heart raced. And her look when he'd touched her, she'd not shied away from the contact but had leaned in. She'd wanted his touch and he'd wanted to keep touching and petting and caressing. Pretty, silly little Alice. Maybe. Maybe...

He jerked as if slapped; he'd not go down this road again. He punched the wall, heart hammering a wild rhythm in his chest. Sick beyond endurance, he slammed a mental door on that thought. He could not afford to grow soft.

To want.

She had to go.

"I am not yours, not lost in you. Not lost..."

Chapter 7

Alice lay in her bed. The constant tick tock tick tock of her Cheshire Cat wall clock kept her from sleep. She stared unfocused eyes at the ceiling fan, her breathing taking up the singsong rhythm of the clock. She shoved the silk sheets down, hot and confused, too awake to sleep and yet too tired to move.

It was strange, the dichotomy of feeling like she was at home, when in fact, this wasn't her house and she wasn't in her room. She'd thought crossing that threshold would somehow usher her back to her own time and reality. But no, she was still here-- in Wonderland-- stuck, maybe forever.

It was enough to make a person question her sanity. Too many times to count, she'd opened her door, thinking any moment she'd see her living room and hear the thud of Auntie Hamaka's ten house cats running amok in the apartment next to hers. But each time she'd swing the door open, she'd simply seen door after door after door. Brightly colored throw rugs, frames with no pictures on the wall. Not her house.

Her stomach rose with each breath. The fan turned. She didn't blink.

"Hello, dear."

Alice yelped. "Bloody freaking hell!" She grabbed her chest and then did a double take when she noticed who was in her room. Crazy cupcake lady, but smaller. Like ten times smaller. Fairy size and flitting through the air.

"You're that woman!" She stabbed her finger at her. "Who the hell are you? Where the hell am I? What's going on?" The last almost came out a wail, her words warbling and she clamped her lips shut on the hysteria threatening to choke her.

The fairy stared at her with sympathetic blue eyes, a soft smile on her round little face.

"I know how you must feel, dear..."

Alice snorted. "Oh, I seriously doubt that. What did you do to me? Who are you?"

Crazy cupcake lady held up pudgy little fingers, shaking loose a blond curl of hair. "I'll answer all your questions, but first," she pointed to the bed, "let's do sit."

Startled, Alice realized she'd stood to a defensive crouching position. How frightening she must look in her boy shirts and cami. She rolled her eyes at the absurd picture and plopped back down with a huff.

She eyed the little woman evilly.

"My name is Danika, fairy godmother extraordinaire, and this is very real."

Alice lifted a brow. "I've pretty much accepted I'm here. How that is even remotely possible, I can't fathom. But *why* am I here? Why can't I go home?"

Crazy lady didn't bat a lash. "I told you."

"Umm. No, you didn't. You laid a card on my table and walked off. You told me nothing."

The lady rolled her eyes. "You really must listen. I told you, you had a man-"

"I thought you were freaking kidding. Like yanno, loco." She rolled her finger against her temple. "Am I here forever? What's happened? I can't stay here, you know that. I've got a family. They're probably worried..."

Danika held up her hands. "Three days, Alice. That's all. If in three days you two do not fall madly in love, you're free to go home." She said it as if it wasn't a huge commitment she asked for.

Alice wanted to laugh. Was she nuts? "Oh, is that all? Well, thank you for this honor."

Danika frowned. "You're... welcome?"

Alice scoffed. "Sarcasm, fairy. Ever heard of it? No, I will not stay here three days. He's a tyrant. Do you know what he made me do? Walk barefoot for miles." Alice curled her toes. "My heels were bloody-"

Danika nodded. "Yes. Yes, he came and saw me. Total misunderstanding— he'll be much nicer now."

Alice pinched the bridge of her nose. "What? When? I was with him, we never saw you."

"Yes, dear. In the woods."

Alice's eyes grew large. "You were the lightning bugs!" She chuckled, feeling stupid that she hadn't put that together immediately. Lightning bugs couldn't heal feet. Then again, it wasn't everyday she discovered fairies really existed, either.

Danika bristled. "Lightning bug, indeed!" Her full face flushed a rosy red as she inhaled long and slow several times through her nose. "I am a fairy."

Alice grinned. "Of course you are." And suddenly she wasn't mad, just tired. She wanted to go home, pretend none of this had happened. Pretend she hadn't met the man of her dreams, the man she'd obsessed about as a child only to discover he wasn't at all what she'd thought he'd be. "Why don't we just cut the three days down to one? Chalk it up to a failed experiment and move on?" She laughed, a short humorless sound.

Very small hands gripped the sides of Alice's nose, forcing her to look back at worried blue eyes. "This is no joke. You must know, he needs you."

"Stop it." Alice swatted the fairy off her.

Undeterred, Danika grabbed Alice's cheek. Her fingers were cold and it was ridiculous how Alice suddenly felt like she was ten again when her mother caught her reading instead of doing chores.

"Send me home. Now."

"I cannot. You rubbed the card. You agreed..."

Alice crossed her arms. "I didn't agree to a damn thing. I rubbed the card, yes..." she frowned, man she'd been stupid to do it, trying to remember if there'd been any fine print. But the card had only showed a bunny with *rub me* on it. "I didn't," she asserted again.

Danika huffed. "Humans and your nonsense of science and disbelief..." she grumbled. "This is a world of magic and mayhem and rules do not apply here. You cannot control this chaos, my dear-- you must let it be. You agreed by rubbing. Period. You must accept it for what it is."

Alice jerked out of Danika's hold. "And just what is that?"

"Truth."

Truth? The fairy spoke of truth and Alice wanted to hit something. She'd spoken truth once before-- and that truth had nearly ruined her life.

Alice had seen Hatter when she was 13. She'd known the encounter had been real and she'd told anyone who would listen.

Her parents had taken her to psychologists; her friends had given up on her. Called her crazy, psycho, a nut job. Eventually her mother had threatened to commit her if she didn't quit talking like that.

So she'd stopped talking. She'd stopped telling others about it, and as the years wore on, she'd come to the realization it was easier to say they were right. It hadn't been real. She'd never seen him. It'd been a dream, a result of a disease-ravaged mind. Nothing more, nothing less.

Her parents slept easier, she'd made new friends who knew nothing about her temporary "episode," and the love that'd burned brighter than the hottest flame had cooled to an ember. She'd moved on. She'd still loved the Hatter and all his maddening ways, but as a favorite story. Nothing more, nothing less.

"He doesn't want me." The words spilled from Alice's lips before she could censure her thoughts.

Danika bit her lip. "And that is partly my doing, love." She looked suddenly anxious, flitting around Alice's head in a dizzying circle.

"I wish you'd be still," Alice grumped, "you're making my eyes cross. What exactly did you do?"

The crazy fairy toyed with her fingernail. "You are not his first Alice. In fact, you're not even his tenth."

The words brought Alice up short. "What do you mean?"

"I've tried for decades, maybe centuries now-" Danika pinched her nose, exhaustion heavily lacing her words, "to find his perfect match. The Alice to offset the madness leaking into him." She threw her hands wide. "With no success. Some feared him, others tolerated him, and still others coveted the power of the land itself. But none ever loved him."

Alice heard Danika like a buzz of white noise in the background. Other Alices? She wasn't his first.

"Did he sleep with them?" she snapped and then clamped her teeth shut, wishing she hadn't blurted that out, but desperate to know. Who was Hatter? Did he have a sick kinky fetish to get it on with as many Alices as he could? Well he was S.O.L.. Alice wouldn't be another notch in his belt. Hot or not.

Danika's jaw dropped as if shocked. "No!" Her voice rose in pitch like a howl. "Dear me." She grabbed her chest. "The man is not a pervert, dear."

The furious pounding in Alice's chest eased somewhat. "Then why bring so many Alices?"

"Because that's the way of it here. Hatter and Alice, Big Bad Wolf and Red... the stories are written with a grain of truth to them. It must be an Alice." She shrugged and Alice licked her canine, refusing to analyze why she suddenly felt like a huge burden had lifted.

She didn't want to share Hatter with anybody else.

Shaking her head, Danika said, "But that is not all."

Alice narrowed her eyes wishing the fairy would stop dragging this out. "Yes?"

Danika blew out a breath. "You see, I may have dipped into a certain bloodline. Brought back a ghost, if you will."

"What?" Alice was totally confused.

Danika sighed and dropped her hands to her sides. "Many years ago I brought an Alice to the Hatter. She was a lovely thing. Doe-eyed and of gentle disposition." She snorted. "At first anyway. I think he fell for her beauty more than anything." She shook her head. "She was an awful woman. Wanted the power she could glean from the land. She did not want him at all."

"I don't understand what that has to do with me?"

Danika's tiny hand traced Alice's jaw, giving her goose bumps. "You two could be twins. He sees her when he looks at you."

Alice sucked in a breath, finally understanding the bloodline reference and the cruelty of the woman. "My great-grandmother," she whispered.

Danika nodded gravely.

And though she had no right to jealously, a flinty spark of passionate hatred flared to life in Alice's heart. No wonder Hatter hated her. Alice loved her great-grandmother, now... because she was blood and it was the honorable thing to do.

But loving her didn't mean Alice could forget being locked out of the house during the heat of the day because her comings and goings let in too many flies. Or being told not to eat the second piece of birthday cake because she'd get fat and ugly and no one would want her then.

The bitterness her grandmother had always thrown at her great-grandfather, calling him stupid and a hairy Okinawan who was no good for her and she'd almost had better. Should have had better...

In hindsight, the crazy mutterings made more sense. But anger solved nothing. Jealousy was useless. Obviously it hadn't worked out between them, but that past was coming back to bite Alice in the ass now because she wasn't her grandmother. She was nothing like the old shrew and yet Hatter judged her based off that.

She looked at the little fairy. "My mother always told me it was uncanny. I've seen the pictures. We look exactly the same." Deflated, she leaned her head against the wall. No wonder Hatter had been so cruel. She understood it, didn't mean she forgave him, but she understood it now. "Why in the hell would you bring me here? He'll never be able to look beyond..." Alice traced a hand down her body.

Danika grabbed Alice's numb fingers and gave them a gentle rub. "You must make him see you, Alice. You." She shook her finger for emphasis. "The moment I saw your grandmother my body shot with sparks of right. But I know now it wasn't for her— it was the bloodline, the eventuality of *you*. He's never responded to any of the Alices the way he did her. But how he responded to her is but a drop in the bucket to the way he feels for you. I know my Hatter and I know you've completely disrupted his narrowed worldview. I believe the only reason why he got swept up in that Alice was because he sensed as I did the tremblings of your coming."

Alice snorted. "Oh yeah, cutting up my heels was his way of showing his undying devotion."

"Does he not show any warmth toward you? Any sort of spark?"

Alice remembered his touch, his eyes... how they'd gazed at her, as if seeking to slip into her soul and she shivered.

Danika smiled. "Aye, you call to him. You are his, Alice. I know it. Now we must convince him."

Alice crossed her heels and shook her head. "What if I'm not ready? Huh? What if I don't want to?" A part of her totally did, but another part, the rational side of her was afraid. She had a life back home. She couldn't be expected to stay here forever. Could he come back with her? Did she want him to?

Danika alighted on the end of her bed. "He's dying, dear." The fairy's words echoed with anguish so thick Alice's throat tightened.

"Dying?" she whispered.

The fairy looked around the room with a sad smile and as she did the walls literally seemed to vanish into mist, revealing the outside beauty of nature surrounding his home. "He is Wonderland. This beautiful madness? It's all a product of his deliriously wicked mind. It's lovely chaos, and it's consuming him. Surely you've noticed his preoccupation with riddles and gibberish?"

Alice bit her bottom lip, rocking backwards. Dying? The Hatter? The beautiful, sexy man who made her want to scream and throw herself on him? "You're lying," she hissed, her lungs heaving for oxygen as the images conjured made her want to weep.

Alice might be upset with him, might even want to hurl sticky buns at his head every once in a while, but she couldn't imagine a world in which he didn't exist.

"I wish that I were." Danika's lip quivered.

Alice swallowed hard. "But, how can I save him?"

"Love." Danika smiled. "True love. He must find his mate, his perfect match and equal. She is the only one who can pull him from the ever increasing insanity of his mind."

The enormity of that burden was daunting. How could she do that? He didn't even like her. "What if I'm not the one? What if you're wrong again?"

Even saying it hurt. Did she want to be? She'd never been so angry, or so aroused by anyone else. For years Hatter had been her constant thought. What if he could never get past her looks? She couldn't help who she was and she'd never be content in a relationship if he wasn't as wildly in love with her as she was with him. Especially if he only considered her a replacement for the one he'd really wanted.

"You are. I know it," Danika said, cutting into her thoughts.

"Oh yeah, how? He thought he was in love before— you said that yourself." She lifted a challenging brow. "He might still be in love with my grandmother."

Danika pressed her lips together. "Wonderland did not accept her and Wonderland is not just a place in a book, Alice. Wonderland is an extension of the man himself. Wonderland will open like a flower to the sun, the land will roll and the wind will hum when the true Alice is found."

Her heart sank like a rock. "Well there you go," she muttered, "it hasn't done that. Obviously, it's not me."

Danika shook her finger. "Your time is not yet up. You've only just met; it takes longer than a mere night for true love to bloom."

Alice rolled her eyes. "Well if that's what you're basing it off of, it sure as hell takes longer than three days."

"Not so, dear. True soul mates know. They always do."

Alice couldn't stop the nagging thought that she had known. Even at 13, she'd fallen in love. As much in love as a child could be. But he didn't remember her. That much was clear, because he'd made no mention of that earlier meeting.

In all her years, she'd never once heard her great-grandmother speak of the Hatter. Alice would have guessed the woman hadn't even known of his existence. And yet she did and when Alice had spoken of Hatter in her hospital room, her grandmother had been there. It'd been her great-grandmother who'd insisted her mother take Alice to an asylum. That spiteful wench! Alice ground her molars as fire burned in her gut.

How could he ever see beyond that?

It hurt thinking he didn't remember her. Didn't see her. She saw him— all of him. It'd taken years to excise Hatter from her heart.

At twenty-four, she was okay with that and was ready to move on. To find a real love and a real man. To get married and have kids.

To live in the real world and not in the book.

And now this evil little fairy came and told her, *he needs you. He doesn't know it yet, but he needs you, Alice,* and she wanted to cry. Because a part of her had always needed him. Hatter was her white knight, he was the hero of her every fantasy. When she'd dated at home, she'd always sought some aspect of him with guys and had found every last one of them wanting, because in the end, they weren't him.

Only Hatter had those soulful eyes that made her melt, the full bottom lip that made her desperate for a taste. The shoulders, so strong, firm, offering reassurance when she'd fallen into total blackness. The Hatter she'd always pictured within the pages of her beloved book. Not the slapstick caricature of the cartoons, but a hero. A savior to a frightened little girl lying in a hospital bed.

How she'd tenderly rubbed her fingers over pages with any mention of him on it, her small heart swelling with an impossible feeling of love, tenderness, and a yearning for something she hadn't been able to comprehend then.

In her way, she'd always loved Hatter. With a madness that had consumed her. A madness she wanted more than anything to embrace now.

But she knew if she took this plunge, if she chose to believe it was true again, that this was real, she'd never be able to forget. Never be able to pretend again. She'd be ruined for anyone else. She licked dry lips, pulse beating so hard she felt the echo of it in her head. But wasn't she ruined already? She'd never been able to date a man for longer than two months before she was finding excuses to dump him.

The flood of emotions she'd bottled away for years, burst forth. She loved him and she could no longer pretend it wasn't so.

She sighed, body warm and alive and filled with a desperate need to go to him-- the arrogant brutish jerk who couldn't remember her. But she'd make him remember. No matter what and in the process she'd make him forget her great-grandmother. Alice was not her, and she'd make him see that.

She flattened a hand on her nervous belly. Somewhere in this crazy house he existed. "Three days to make him love me?" She glanced up and Danika nodded. "I want to break the curse."

Danika's smile was radiant.

"But I can't stay, fairy. You have to understand. I can't just bail out on my family. I have to go back. At least for a little while."

Danika inhaled. "If it is meant to be, it will all work out in the end, Alice. You just wait and see. Trust in this, in him, make him love you, make him see you, and it will work itself out."

A cold chill nipped at Alice's nose. She shivered, startled to notice Danika beginning to turn amorphous. She hovered like a ghost surrounded by light.

"Love him, Alice. Only love him." The ephemeral ball of light whispered before disappearing in a sun fire burst.

Alice hugged her knees to her chest and started rocking, staring at the door as if she'd divine an answer from it.

Three days.

She stood up and, before she could second-guess her decision, she went to the door, turned the knob and stepped out into the hall. Empty portraits stared back at her. Vines, not there before, crawled like green fingers through cracks, covering the wall in a living canvas. She walked; as she slid her hand along the wall, a trail of tiny purple flowers blossomed under her touch.

It'd only been a short walk from the living room earlier, but now she found herself walking through a maze of twists and turns.

"Hatter," she called quietly. Afraid to speak too loudly, afraid she'd lose her nerve.

"Alice." That deep voice, like a fiery caress, made her gasp and turn.

He leaned against a wall. The jacket he'd worn earlier was gone now. A white shirt, top three buttons undone, tapered to his body, outlined taut curves and gave her a tantalizing peek of tanned male flesh.

She licked her lips. *I am woman, hear me roar*, became a thunderous backdrop to the wild beating of her frantic heart.

"I... I wanted to..." She cleared her throat, realizing she was still staring at his sliver of nude flesh. Her fingers clenched.

He smiled with a wicked gleam in his eyes. He knew. She lifted her chin. So she found him attractive. She didn't care if he knew. Three days, three days to stop being mousy, shy Alice. Three days.

"I wanted to see you. I missed you."

He shoved off the wall and gave her a smile with no heat. "I'm assuming you've finished your cozy tête-à-tête with a certain fairy?" Disgust laced his words.

"How did you..." Then the light bulb came on, literally, a ball of silver light flashing above her head. Talk about weird. For a second she wondered where clichés had originated and if, perhaps, they'd come from a place like this. A place where words had power.

Of course he'd know. She wasn't his first. Alice buried her nails in her palms.

A moon, heavy and round, materialized, flooding the hall-- which now looked more like a garden than a hallway-- with light. A gentle breeze, redolent with the sweet smell of fresh grass and rich earth surrounded her.

She looked around in awe. "What is this, Hatter?"

He was silent so long, she didn't think he'd answer. "It's me, Alice. It's my magic, my moods. I create all this," he tapped his head, "with just a thought."

She wanted to tell him she knew that, that she'd wanted to know what the place was and if it held any significant meaning to him, but words failed her. Suddenly she wasn't standing before him in boy shorts and a cami, but a frilly blue dress with thigh-high striped stockings and large, chunky heels.

She planted hands on her hips, fighting the grin, and tapped her foot instead.

He grinned. "Though I find I prefer you like this."

For a second, she thought she'd be naked. But she was once again wearing her boy shorts and cami. His look, his voice, it did something to her. Curls of heat spread between her legs, tightened her belly, made her nipples tight. He was so beautiful. Like a gothic devil with his shaggy dark hair and sensual lips that promised wicked delights..

"Are you searching for me, Alice?" The teasing glint fled and his voice went empty and hollow again. Almost like he didn't want to have fun with her, didn't want to be easy going.

She sighed. "I don't know. Maybe."

His hard gaze was steady. Such a short distance between them— it would take nothing to close the gap.

She'd had boyfriends in her life. Losers. Winners. None of them made her feel what she felt in that moment. Heat. Fire. Longing so profound she wondered if it were possible to die from it.

She wondered how her great-grandmother had acted. Alice could only picture her as she was now-- hunched over, an old, old woman well past her prime. How had her grandmother seduced him?

Because she wanted to be just the opposite. Alice never wanted him to see her grandmother again.

Be yourself, the echo of her mother's gentle words flooded her mind.

He stared at her, waiting for something. For some sign. A truth to pass between them, a kindred sharing. Some awareness of who he was.

Alice remembered an elective she'd taken in high school. Who knew the meaningless English lit class would someday come to good use? Since he seemed to love Edgar Allen Poe so much she'd start there.

"The true genius shudders at incompleteness-"

He closed his eyes and his breathing hiked. She took a timid step forward.

"-and usually prefers silence to saying something..."

He recited the last part with her. "Which is not everything it should be."

He stepped forward. The air shivered between them, a tremble, a kiss of wind at her temple. Her hand was on his cheek, the whisker-roughened skin tickling her fingers.

Haunted eyes stared back at her.

She pulled his face down until their lips nearly touched. "I've known you all my life."

He gripped her fingers, squeezing hard.

"I discovered you when I was 10." She looked deep into his eyes, peering into the mad soul, and poured out her truths. "I saw more than pages or a name in a book. I saw a brave man. A kind man. Even then I knew, even then I craved that which I could not name. And when I was 13..." she swallowed, wanting to share, wanting to see a flare of recognition in his eyes, a remembered memory.

He looked at her, brows drawn, waiting for her to finish. She couldn't, not yet. If he didn't remember, if he hadn't cherished it as she had, it would be a wound.

She shook her head and smiled. "And when I was 13, I knew. I always knew, Hatter."

"Alice, don't. Don't say these things. They aren't true." Wine-tinted breath stroked her lips and she sighed. And though his words begged her to stop, his hands wrapped around her waist like a vise, defying her to step out of the circle of his arms.

"I wish I was lying. I wish I didn't feel this. Do you have any idea how hard it was to be in love with a man in a book?" She closed her eyes, aching as the memories flooded her. "It's always been you, Hatter."

For a weird second, she was sure the grass beneath her feet trembled. She looked at him, his gaze riveted to her face, searching her, like he was trying to peer into her soul.

He shook. "Three days, Alice. Three days and you'll be gone just like your wicked grandmother. She also gave an oath of love."

"I. Am. Not. Her." She shook her head. "Three days to prove to you that I," she grabbed one of his hands and forced him to cup her cheek, "am real. Three days to make you see me. Not her. But me, little Alice Hu. Lover of all things Hatter."

He didn't yank his hand away. "No, Alice."

He smelled of sweet smoke and wine. Such a delicious combination, it made her want to purr and curl her toes into the dewy grass.

Alice stopped thinking, stopped wondering right from wrong. She wanted this. Always had. She laid her head against his chest. The muscle flexed beneath her cheek.

How would she ever be able to leave?

Chapter 8

Alice slept. Her silky black hair trailed along the white pillow like cracks in the earth and he ached to touch her. To kiss her gently awake. To watch her eyes grow soft and liquid with lust, with love.

Hatter gripped the door frame. Once he'd been certain she'd fallen asleep, he'd tiptoed back to her room and stood outside, watching. Hoping. Dreaming. Hating.

Hating his existence. Hating her for coming. For looking so much like the other one. Hating her because he needed her so much, knowing she'd leave him like all the rest.

Each Alice had been an adventure. Each wild, unpredictable incarnation had imprinted an indelible mark upon his soul. He remembered one who'd loved to fish out treasures from the sea and another who'd spun dresses from the cotton candy orchards. Some had sat three days locked away in their rooms, never venturing out, never trying to know him. He'd enjoyed some more than others and at the time had mourned their not staying.

In the end they'd all left, ripping out a piece of his soul. For a time, he'd grown excited knowing another Alice would come, dreaming the next one would be different. But after several years the constant parade had lost its zeal and he'd yearned for the moment they'd leave him to his solitude.

She sighed, and rolled over. Her outstretched arm pointed toward him. A wild sleeper, she'd moved from one corner of the bed to the other, as if seeking something, even in sleep. Her fingers curled and her mouth tipped down.

So damn beautiful.

Skin the color of wild spring honey with hair like shadow, hanging long and low, with the tiniest widow's peak on her forehead. A short thing, this Alice barely reached the top of his chest. Petite, but full figured in a ripe, luscious way. Her hips flared out, and his heart pumped harder. She was the perfect size to hang onto while she rode him, passion gleaming from the depths of her big doe eyes.

Heat pooled in his groin. It grew stiff, frustratingly so. But he did not touch himself. He'd stopped doing that a long time ago, when the other Alice Hu had left. After her, he'd sworn never again. Never again would he allow himself to care because to do so would weaken him.

It'd been years since she'd left and, with time, he'd realized he'd not loved that Alice at all. He knew because he'd survived, but it was that knowledge that made him fear to love. Because though he'd not loved her, the weeks that had followed had been some of the worst in his life. Only Danika's stubborn willfulness had brought him back from the fog of his mind.

The episode had so frightened Danika that she'd stopped bringing him Alices for a while and he'd reveled in the peace and quiet thinking surely Danika finally understood there was no match for the Hatter.

Hatter leaned against the door, his eyes drinking her in. His body trembled remembering the rush of heat and fire that'd blanketed him when she'd touched him and forced him to touch her. This Alice was more dangerous than any of the others because not only did he not mind her presence, he sought it out like a man parched for drink. She needed to leave. To forget him in the hopes that he could forget her. In the hopes that, someday, he'd not be plagued with night terrors, with the dreams of having a life he was never supposed to have.

He was the Hatter, a lunatic, a madman. His life was nonsense and mayhem. Everyone within the Kingdom said so. So had the other Alice Hu— she'd hurled the words at him like a blade, cutting him to the quick. He ground his jaw.

This Alice whimpered. He wanted to rush to her, soothe her. Touch her fine skin and inhale the sweet scent of her body.

His mouth tipped, remembering her startled look in the hall. The shorts that had exposed a long expanse of thigh. He'd nearly come undone. It had been all he could take to stand there and watch, his throat working with a need to yank her to him, to beg her to end his madness.

And he couldn't stop the queer feeling that they'd met before. But she hadn't looked like this. He frowned and grabbed his head. Why couldn't he remember?

All he knew was that when he looked at her he heard the haunting strains of a repetitive beeping noise. But then the sound vanished and he was left with questions.

She mumbled.

She'd quoted Poe. So different than all the others, even her grandmother had never done that. Evil Alice had never tried to know him. But this Alice made him want to know *her*.

Other Alices had lied before. Some had claimed love, others kindness. None of it had been true.

His jaw flexed.

Why did he want to believe her?

"My Hatter," she murmured, pink lips curling into a slow smile and his heart turned over. Lovely. Deadly. Peril. He closed his eyes and backed slowly out.

***

Ignore her. Make her want to leave.

The room trembled as a thousand clocks rang loud with the new hour. He stared at one in particular— a simple clock. No adornments, nothing about the small round pocket watch seemed particularly valuable.

He traced the grain seam, fingers gentle, the wood smooth from years (or was it decades? centuries? he could never remember anymore) of touching. Time. Always too much of it, and never enough.

It ticked on, endless, unceasing, unmerciful.

Tick.

Tock.

Tick.

Tock.

Unable to roll the hands back, unable to make it stop. Moving, always, always moving on and on and on. Marching forward in an endless cycle of time, time, time...

He drew his hand back, squeezing his eyes closed. Beautiful brown eyes filled his head. The scent of vanilla was so strong, he swore he could still smell it.

Satin skin, buttery brown, smooth and delicate. Hair as black as midnight. His body strained and he hardened. It made him sweat. Made him need.

He would not surrender. It was madness. Wonderland would say no and she would leave. As it'd always been.

But he'd never wanted another the way he did her. The moment he'd seen her, something inside him had quickened. Finally, he'd thought. Finally here. And that had confused him. He squeezed his eyes shut.

Her with the vanilla sunshine-y smile.

The widow's peak, alluring, sexy, devilish. Beautiful, dangerous creatures, black widow spiders were. Luring you in with their beauty. Killing you without remorse.

"Dangerous creatures. Dangerous." He closed his eyes, resting his head against the mantle. "Dangerous, dangerous beauty. Beauty. Beautiful. Alice," his voice cracked.

She'd leave him. Like all the rest. He must make her go.

His spine stiffened, fingers clenched against his thigh. Did she think of him at all? Even a little? Beautiful, sane, wicked little Alice?

Tick.

Tock.

Time moved on.

Chapter 9

Alice jerked to a sitting position, tired, and just this side of pissy. Sunlight poured in through the window. She glanced around: her room was the same as it'd ever been.

Just a dream. Maybe, she'd call in sick. A horrible thing to do to Tabby, and it was only the second day of her grand Cupcakery opening.

With a loud sigh, she got up and headed to the shower. But when she reached the bathroom door, there was no bathroom. It was the most enormous and empty walk in closet she'd ever seen. It stretched for miles.

Not a dream. Or a dream within a dream, she thought of Hatter and her pulse sped. Where was he? Was he thinking about her?

She glanced down, she didn't want him to see her in the same clothes, but there was nothing here. She wished she had some clothes, something sexy, something that would forever erase any memory of her grandmother from his mind.

And this time when she glanced up, a crushed velvet gown hung from a hanger in a shade of burgundy so deep it almost resembled blood. Velvet dresses had always made her think of fake wigs and hideous dollar store Halloween costumes. Plus, it looked several inches too long, but... she shrugged and slipped it off its rack. Beggars couldn't afford to be picky. It was either this, or wear the same thing for three days.

She wrinkled her nose at the thought, took her clothes off, and was pulling the sleeves on when she grumbled, "give anything for a toothbrush and shower right about now."

No sooner had the words left her mouth her tongue tingled with the sharp nip of mint. Her body shone with a wet sheen, and the scent of flowers filled the room.

She hadn't bathed, and yet, she was clean. Man, if she could patent this back home, she'd make a killing.

The dress was a perfect fit. But she didn't question it, it was Wonderland, nothing seemed to follow any conventional rules of reason. Most especially when it came to the Hatter.

The dress fell to mid-thigh. Thankfully, she had great legs. Her stomach fluttered and she wished she had a mirror.

A displaced shiver of air brushed against her back.

She turned and there was a mirror. Suddenly she wondered, was Wonderland responding? Was the wind right now humming and the land rolling? She strained to listen, but there was nothing but empty silence.

Her heart sank and she shook her head. Silly Alice... hoping for what couldn't be. Of all the Alices in the world there was no way she'd be his perfect match. The odds were more astronomical then winning the lottery ten times straight. In all of history, she was his Alice. The thought gave her a pang and she had to take several deep breaths before she could shrug it off.

Alice studied her reflection. The dress was tight, but comfortable. Though, she didn't like the sleeves. Instantly they vanished, exposing the long lean muscle of her bare arms.

"It would look a lot better with a choker collar." The fabric moved, sliding up her neck until it resembled the choker she'd requested.

She pointed her toes. He'd put her in heels last night. "Thigh-high boots." The softest black suede she'd ever felt in her life suddenly hugged her legs. A stupid, wide grin covered her face from ear to ear.

This was crazy. She was crazy. *Paris Hilton, eat your heart out*. Free clothes— it was enough to make her head spin with dizzy possibilities.

Alice had gone through a Goth phase in a high school, much to her mother's everlasting shame. She'd even managed to sneak an Alice dress replica to prom. She'd poofed her black hair and touched up her face with a light tint of lip gloss and a few strokes of mascara. A large black and white striped bow was the only accessory she'd worn. Rather than make her look like a Lolita, the effect had been stunning.

That'd been the night boys had finally started noticing her. Overnight, she'd turned from the nerd carrying around the worn Alice in Wonderland book, to the hot nerd carrying around a worn copy of Wonderland. It'd also been the night of her first real kiss.

Clinton Issac. Tall soccer player. Gorgeous, and with the cutest dimple in his right cheek. She'd closed her eyes, puckered her lips, and the rest was a gross blur of slobber and sweaty hands trying to unclasp her bra.

Gross kiss notwithstanding, she wondered if lightning would strike twice. She bit the corner of her lip and wished.

A large stylish bow materialized in the palm of her hand, a small blood ruby winking from its center. She slipped it on, her stomach a nervous mass of butterflies. What would the Hatter think of her now?

Two days left.

Feeling like she might puke, she walked out, not knowing what she'd see today. Now that she was here, she was ready and willing to embrace the impossible.

The hallway was just a regular hallway. She frowned, disappointed for a quick second that it all seemed so mundane. There were no empty frames on the wall, no vines appearing like slow moving snakes. Instead, the walls were painted with fresco designs. A carnival at night, its neon lights aglow.

She narrowed her eyes and walked to the wall. It all looked so real and when she closed her eyes she couldn't help imagining the happy roar of a crowd. The sway of rides. For a moment, she could almost smell the greasy whiff of corndogs and funnel cake. Her stomach rumbled, snapping her instantly back to reality.

Food. Time for food. Lots of it. With a little sigh she turned on her heels-- and smacked head on into an unmovable wall.

"Oww." She rubbed her forehead.

Hatter chuckled and the vibrations that laugh sent through her body weakened her knees. His hands slid down her arms and his touch was like fire. Her skin prickled as every cell became hyper-aware of his proximity.

"You look..."

Her stomach flopped. Did he like it? She held her breath.

Then the heat in his glance died, leaving his eyes cold and distant. "Hungry."

The switch was almost too abrupt to follow. Hungry? She screwed her face up. "What?" After all the time she'd taken with her appearance— that was all he had to say to her? What about that initial heat, the look that said he wanted to turn out all the lights and do naughty things to her? She stifled a sigh of frustration. She wanted that heat back.

"I've not fed you well." His deep voice rumbled.

She should be more than annoyed. She'd dressed up for him, tried her best to turn his head, and all he could talk about was food. In high school, that sort of passive aggressive rejection would have sent her scurrying back to her Wonderland book, too embarrassed to try again.

She pressed her lips together. That was the old Alice. The Alice that had been convinced by friends and family that her dreams were all just that-- dreams. This Alice knew better. She knew her dream was real-- he was standing right in front of her. And she wasn't giving up without a fight.

He waited, a strange wariness in his dark eyes.

"I think food is a great idea. I'm starving."

She didn't think he was aware of the way his body heaved a gentle sigh as the tension flowed out of his bones. She wasn't sure how he'd expected her to react, but she was glad she hadn't given a voice to her annoyance over his less than desirable reaction to her attire. There would be plenty of time to be alluring later.

Besides, when he smiled like that, her heart did a crazy tilt that left her feeling almost breathless. He really was gorgeous. She let him take her hand.

He led her back down the hall and then they were there. Wherever there was? They were still in the cottage, she supposed, as they'd never actually walked out... and yet, she was now in a garden.

She glanced behind her, staring back into the hallway, and shook her head with a tiny shrug.

A sturdy white tea table sat in the middle of a large swath of sunlight, bathing the garden in a heated buttery glow. Roses, dripping with scent and a multitude of colors, covered the garden from the ground up. Tiny yellow butterflies flapped lazy wings from petal to petal. It felt like stepping through a Monet.

She smiled and clasped her clammy hands together. "High tea?"

He shoved blunt fingers through his thick wavy hair, his posture unsure as he nodded. "If that's okay?"

Alice was proud of herself for not hopping and skipping around like Tweedledee and Tweedledum. She sat, trying to look elegant, but she was afraid the way she was dressed, she looked more like the best friend in Pretty Woman. Low brow hoochie, though the heat returning to his eyes made her think... maybe he didn't mind?

Dainty trays of food manifested, filling the table's top to capacity. Teacakes, finger sandwiches, salad, fruit, and cheese cubes as far as her eye could see.

She groaned, mouth salivating at the sight.

Two teapots appeared. Hatter grabbed the one with steam rising from its spout and poured a generous amount of the amber liquid into her cup. The heady aroma of anise and five-spice curled under her nose like a fog bank. She inhaled, taking the scent deep. Like a fine wine, it flooded her senses.

"Thank you." She grinned, adding "I feel like I should be wearing gloves and a bonnet or something."

Cream lace gloves, with a string of small pearls laced at the side, appeared next to her hand. She snorted. "I have got to watch what I say here."

He glanced at the gloves, staring at them so hard she was sure he'd say something.

But he didn't. Instead he dropped a sugar cube into his tea and nodded toward the bowl.

"Yes, one, please," her voice quivered a little. The cube dropped into her cup with a soft plop, disappearing in moments. Alice slipped the fingerless gloves on, just to have something to do and nodded. "Am I decent?"

His brows lowered. "For what?"

"For tea, of course." She rolled her eyes, laughing.

The cup in his hand paused at chest level. "I wouldn't know. Tea is just tea." He shrugged and then sipped.

Embarrassed, she pressed her lips together. "Of course." Suddenly, she felt ridiculous in the gloves, in the dress, in the top hat that'd appeared from thin air atop her head. It was silly of her to get so excited. Just because this was straight out of her favorite scene from Alice in Wonderland. Just because it was the scene where she'd always felt the Hatter's presence the strongest. She swallowed the tea, but hardly tasted it. This was so stupid, so impossible.

"But..."

Alice hated that her heart fluttered. She didn't want to care. Damn him, how many times would he make her feel like a fool?

"You look very good to me."

Her gaze shot up, locking onto his. His compliment echoed in her ears and she suddenly realized she was smiling. Pathetic— she was so pathetic. She hadn't been a virgin for some time, and yet right now her stomach tickled and her knees knocked. He made her feel like she was back in high school, gazing adoringly at Clinton Issac, waiting for the day he'd finally notice her. All over one little compliment.

Her smile wilted at the edges. Clinton had been an awful disappointment. She swept her eyes over Hatter's face. Would he be, too?

"What's your real name?" She hadn't meant to ask him that, but it just sort of plopped out of her mouth. He looked at her, head cocked. Her eyes widened and heat rose in her cheeks. "I'm sorry, I don't know where that-"

He held a long fingered hand up. Her stomach dove, remembering the feel of those hands on her body last night. How those hands had dipped lower on her waist until, for a moment, she'd thought he'd grab her. Pinch, knead, do something. Fire licked her veins and she guzzled more of the tea, eyes burning as the hot liquid scalded her throat.

He gave her a weak grin. "The longer I stay, the less I know? Hatter? Mad Hatter? T. T." He shook his head and stared at his hands as if he could divine the truth of the universe from them. He growled and rubbed his eyes. "I... can't, remember. Too long ago."

She was sorry she'd asked him. A frown tugged at the corners of his full lips. She wanted to smooth the anxious lines between his eyes. Instead, she plucked at the hem of her dress.

"The longer you stay? What do you mean?"

He looked up, butter knife held loosely in his hand. The smile she'd glimpsed only last night, the real one, the one that peeked out when he wasn't afraid to relax, came out for a fleeting moment.

"I was a man once."

She lifted a brow and gave him a knowing grin. "Oh, I think you're still a man."

His lips twitched. "This," he gestured, taking in their surroundings, "this is all an illusion. Frightening fragments of time and space, magic, moment, memory. Thoughts tumbling, tumbling down." His eyes grew distant and she knew she was losing him to the thoughts in his head. She tapped his arm, bringing his eyes back to her with a jerk.

"Illusion? Madness? This place doesn't seem so mad."

Hair slipped into his eyes. Emboldened, she reached up and patted it back.

He stilled. She curled her fingers into a fist she brought quickly back to her lap. "What I mean is," her words faltered only a little, "I love this place."

"Why?" The question tore from someplace deep inside him. She sensed his desperate desire to understand her, understand why she felt as she did.

"There's magic here and rooms that lead to nothing. Clocks that tick in perpetual motion, flowers that come alive at my touch, and..." *there's you...* She looked down, distracting herself by taking a bite of the lemon curd laden scone. The sweet tang tingled her tongue and she moaned, a little jealous at his cook's ability to make such delicious curd. Her stuff was good, but this was like biting into a lemon plucked fresh from a tree with a drizzle of sugar on top.

"So good," she cooed.

She felt his gaze like a brand. "What was the last part you did not speak?"

He'd caught that. She wiggled, took a deep breath and gathered her courage.

"I want to know you, Hatter. Is that so strange?"

"Yes."

She licked her lips, the tip of her tongue swiping up a crumb from the corner of her mouth. His eyes homed in like a beacon and it was unnerving, exhilarating. She touched her chest, feeling suddenly very hot.

"What am I to you? You do not know me." His voice dripped scorn, anger, and something else. Hope? Maybe.

She drummed her nails on the table. She knew he liked his poems. Pride shaded the corners of his lips when he threw out a particularly obscure one.

His hands were long, fingers strong and firm. There was strength in those hands; she'd felt them tighten at her waist. He wasn't an idle man with hands like that. Many might be tempted to think he drank tea all day and guzzled wine all night. Mad as a Hatter, they all said, but though, at times, he seemed to lose touch with reality, there was a hawk's gaze behind those eyes. A quickness that saw more in a blade of grass than many could read within the pages of a book.

And the hell of it was she didn't know how she knew that. She just did. Alice had dreamed of him for years, talked to him, told him her most cherished and heartfelt dreams, knowing in her child's heart that he heard her, understood her, and knew her just as well.

"I know we have two days, Hatter." She did not wish to give him hope. She had a life she needed to get back to. Responsibilities. She had a Shoppe to run and Tabby was probably crazy with worry. Not to mention her mother and father were probably, even now, calling every cop on the island to do a thorough search for their missing daughter. They'd all think something horrible had happened to her.

Somehow, someway she'd figure out how to save Hatter, how to get Wonderland to accept her. But she couldn't stay permanently. If there was some way to hop between realms, then that could be a definite possibility. But she had to go back eventually.

The light in his eyes dimmed and he sat back, staring out at the garden with unseeing eyes.

Her fingers shook as she reached for a small bowl of grapes. "The food is wonderful," she said, desperate to get him to look back at her. She hated to see the sadness touch his eyes.

"Leonard will be pleased."

Her lips quirked and she glanced around. A tiger-striped butterfly touched down on the table. Its gossamer wings moved gracefully. The animals and flowers were so normal today. She'd kind of hoped for more, maybe a butterfly with pads of butter for wings or rocking horse flies. Of course, that had been a cartoon and she shouldn't have gotten her hopes up. "I'd like to tell him thanks. I know I love it when a customer tells me that."

He nodded, tapping the other teapot on the table. "Leonard, awake. Alice wishes to thank you."

Shock made her drop the succulent red grape an inch from her mouth as the furry head of a tiny mouse popped its head out.

"Oh my gosh!" she squeaked. "A mouse. A...a-"

The food that'd settled in her stomach with the sweetness of sun warmed honey, suddenly felt like a brick. She breathed hard around the gag.

He rubbed black little eyes, large ears twitching as he looked around with a furtive sneer. "Mice!" His high-pitched squeak matched her own. "Where? A pox on them." The teapot rocked precariously as he shook a tiny fist. His nose wrinkled at a furious pace. "Nasty flea ridden vermin they are! And in me garden no less."

Huh? She looked at Hatter. What was... didn't the mouse know... he was the mouse?

Hatter patted Leonard's head with the indulgent grin of a proud parent. "Leonard's my chef, and friend. Are you not, wee one?"

His voice had gone soft, gentle. The cadence left her spell bound, watching as a shaft of light suddenly filtered through a hole in a fluffy white cloud, illuminating his features. He looked like an angel.

But only the fallen would make her fell the sudden violent lust rushing hot through her veins. She swallowed hard.

"Right o', guv'nor," Leonard chirped. "Indeed." Black beady eyes glanced up at her.

Alice tried to see him as Hatter did. Soft brown fur, long whiskers twitching with each breath. The little eyes turned soft, filled with light as he reached his hand out to her. "Oh aye, yer majestic Hatter, she is a lovely one. Ain't she?"

His hand was still open, plump pink fingers curled toward her, and she realized he wanted to shake hands. She smiled. He really was kind of cute. Alice gave him her finger and he shook it.

"I loved your food, Leonard."

He beamed, winked at Hatter as if to say I-told-you-so, and turned back to her.

"I'm a bit of a foodie myself," she said.

"Are ye now?" Leonard twitched in delight. "And do ye prefer the sweet to the savory, as I do?"

"She owns a Cupcakery." She glanced up at Hatter who'd answered for her. "The creations would make you green with envy."

How did he know that about her? Had all the other Alices baked too? She bit her tongue at the irritating thought.

Leonard gave her a sage nod of respect. "As it should. As it should." He raised his arms high above his head, exposing sharp teeth and a pink tongue as he gave a mighty yawn. He smacked his lips and patted his head. "Perhaps, Alice girl, we'll swap recipes."

"Did you make the curd too?"

For a second the sleep left his eyes and he nodded. "Me mum's recipe, God rest 'er soul."

"Best I've ever had."

"True enough." The little mouse accepted the compliment with the air of one who knew they weren't idle words, tapped the side of his nose and then yawned again. "Had meself a frightfully long night, Miss. Apologies," he slurred the last and then sank gracefully back down into the pot.

She giggled. "What in the world could keep a mouse up all night?" She looked at Hatter and the laughter died in her throat. He was giving her that look again.

The look that stripped away all pretense, that said he was looking at her soul. A woman could melt into that look, lose herself and never find her way back home. She gripped the edge of the table.

"Have you eaten enough, Alice?"

She shivered, warm, but not because of the sun. His voice, rough, scratchy, set her body on edge. Alice nodded, not able to speak.

"Come." He pushed away from the table and held his hand out to her.

Holding his hand felt as natural now as breathing. Trying to be as inconspicuous as possible, she moved into step with him, getting inside his bubble just so that she could feel the heat from his body.

His jaw tightened, but he didn't move away.

"Where are we going?"

He was leading them deeper into the garden; a black wrought iron fence in the distance drew closer. The garden slowly morphed from swaying flowers to towering tree trunks whose overhanging branches obscured the sky.

The moment they stepped through the gate, it was like someone had grabbed an enormous window shade and drawn it across the sky. The sunlight melted into moon glow. Stars studded the sky like thousands of glinting diamonds. The royal blue veil of the heavens was broken only by an occasional fluffy white cloud floating past. The night smelled of heat and exotic spices. Somewhere, frogs croaked a gentle song. She shivered.

"Where are you taking me?"

He glanced at her from the corner of his eyes. Her heart thudded. "A secret," was all he said.

It was becoming hard to remember why she needed to go home. Why staying here was a bad idea. When he looked at her like that, like she was a precious jewel and he was the dragon sworn to protect it, she forgot lots of things.

Something in her recognized that for the first time, she was truly beginning to feel alive. That the world before was the dream, and this one was the truth. That she'd finally come home. Scary how good the thought was.

A small clearing opened up, revealing a placid lake that stretched a good distance in every direction. Bugs darted and zipped over calm water while small bubbles popped at the surface. Cattails swayed gently.

"It's beautiful."

He shook his head. "Not this."

It was on the tip of her tongue to ask him what, but he was already leading them straight toward the water, splashing in, and giving her no choice but to follow. She braced for the cold, but it never came. It was warm, soothing. They sank in, water covering their heads. She held her breath.

Everything was black. How long would she have to hold her breath? Did he know where they were going? She looked around, searching for a cave, an opening with a pocket of air. Trying to stave off the panic, she hoped it wouldn't be too much longer. He wouldn't hurt her. He might want to, but he wouldn't. She know that, trusted that, felt it in the depths of her soul.

They sank deeper and deeper and she was growing more and more dizzy

She tried to yank her wrist out of his hand; she needed to get back to the surface. Air was a desperate need now, her body shaking and her throat on fire. A blue glow radiated in a flash around them. He looked at her and frowned.

"Alice?" The glow added shadow to hollows, giving him a sinister appearance. "You can breathe here." He demonstrated by inhaling deeply.

Her lungs burned, they were empty, deprived of sweet oxygen. She'd never gone more than thirty seconds at the beach without gulping for air. Black dots swam in her vision.

She wanted to trust him so badly.

He shook her shoulders, wearing a frantic look. "Do it, damn you, breathe!"

And then the matter was out of her hands, instinct took over and she sucked, waiting for the fluid to fill her lungs. Drown her.

It was thicker than air, but clean, fresh with a hint of salty brine. She could breathe. She sucked in harder, greedy for more. And then she laughed a desperate choking sound of disbelief. "I'm breathing water."

He closed his eyes for a brief moment. Then that hot gaze of his, the one that made her want to strip her clothes and his off, demanded she look at him.

"You must know, Alice, I would never hurt you. Never." His knuckles grazed her cheek and she felt that touch move like lightening through her limbs. Her nipples hardened into painfully sharp peaks.

His eyes danced with light again, a swirling pattern of movement, a chaotic rhythm that matched the frenetic beat of her heart. She held her breath again as he leaned closer, his body heat pressing against her. Lips touched hers, a feather soft whisper at first, hesitant. Exploratory.

She curled her fingers into his jacket, and he groaned. The rumble vibrated her chest and then he was not so soft, not so gentle. He was demanding, kissing, touching, tasting, sucking on her lip, and swiping his tongue across the seam.

She parted her mouth on a loud moan and he darted in, massaging her tongue with his own. He tasted so good, like spring rain and wildflowers and then his hands cupped her ass, making her burn and shiver as she moaned loud and long.

Alice pulled him closer, wishing she could crawl inside him, lose herself completely to the untamed sensations he yanked from her soul. Her fingers slid through the thick waves of his hair. Soft silk.

He was kissing her face, her cheeks, her jaw, her forehead, the tip of her upturned nose. Her body was alive and dizzy with joy.

She slipped her hands under his jacket and taut muscles flexed under her touch. If she were a cat, she'd be purring. She pouted when he pulled back. His breathing was hard, but his grip on her was tender. The caress of this thumb trailed fire, raised goose bumps.

Had anyone ever looked at her like that before? She touched the corner of his mouth, a mouth that had consumed her. Passion lay buried in the man, deep and bottomless. She wanted more. She wanted all of it.

A loud croak shattered the mood. Without her even noticing, they'd stopped sinking. She was standing on the bottom of a lake and a 50 foot frog stared at them.

"Hatter?" She gripped the collar of his jacket.

"This is what I wanted to show you." His nose was in her hair. Alice felt hot and cold at the same time, her body tense and loose. How could having a man sniff her hair turn her on so much?

She dropped her head onto his chest, loving the sound of his heart beneath her ear.

"Would you like to see?" He sounded anxious and nervous. *Sweet*, she smiled.

Did he realize how hard it was for her to focus when he touched her? She looked back at the big, ugly frog and wrinkled her nose. "A warty frog?" His eyes glinted. "Oh, Hatter," she couldn't help teasing him, "just what every girl wants to see when she's out on a date with the hottest man alive." She fanned her face, not noticing how he'd stilled.

He dropped his hands, almost making her stumble back from his abrupt release. She frowned as he walked toward the green-skinned beast.

Just like before, when it seemed she was finally starting to make headway, he'd gone cold and walked off. She clenched her fists, nails biting into the palms of her hands.

Damaged goods, he was totally damaged. So why did it not make her want to run away?

It went deeper than her lifelong obsession with all things Wonderland. This wasn't a book, and he wasn't a faceless ideal. The Hatter was in pain. For reasons she could barely understand, she didn't just want to help him; she wanted to make him better. Wanted to see him whole again, the perfectly wonderful madcap Hatter.

She rubbed her arms and followed. He stopped by a webbed foot. The frog didn't budge. It just sat, staring at them with the empty eyed stare of a predator.

She tiptoed to Hatter's side and slipped her hand into his lax one, trusting him, though her knees knocked having to stand so close to the thing.

His fingers were spread, loose, and for a second she worried he might reject her. Then he sighed and gave her a squeeze.

"Ancient frog beneath the waves," his deep voice rolled through the eerie blackness, "hiding treasures of olden days."

The frog's giant mouth opened a red yawning maw of death. Its pink tongue whipped out and wrapped around their bodies, the sticky wetness making her yelp. And then, it swallowed them.

Alice held tight to Hatter's hands. She'd show him she didn't always panic, even though in her mind she was frantically screaming.

Thankfully, the ride didn't last long. She landed with legs sprawled, flat on her butt.

Hatter, of course, looked as devilishly delicious as before. Not a thing out of place. His clothes were perfect, his brows were raised, and every hair on his head was exactly as before.

He was laughing, and while the sound made her legs weak and stomach flutter, she was not happy that it was at her expense. Alice held her hand out to him with what little pride she had left.

"You know you could be a gentleman and help me up instead of staring at me like I've grown a third eye." Her cheeks burned when he jerked her up.

His hands rested casually on her hips. It seemed like he found any reason to touch her now. Not that she minded; she only wished it wouldn't always be so hot and cold with him.

She crossed her arms and huffed.

He grinned and her heart jerked. He was breathtaking when he did that.

She turned her face to the side and then her eyes widened when she finally noticed where they were. And the moment she noticed, the cave came alive with a roar of tick tocks.

Thousands, hundreds of thousands of clocks hung and sat in every conceivable corner of the place. They were mounted inside the rock face, beneath the thick sheet of glass she walked on. Funny ones, nautical ones, bedroom clocks, grand domed clocks with large golden chimes dangling beneath; she never knew there were so many different types.

Each clock was set at different times, so that some rang the top of the hour, while others were just starting a day's rotation, and some even spun in reverse.

"What is this place?"

He dropped her hand and walked to the center of the room, spreading his arms wide. "My tick tock life. Six o'clock, teatime. Don't be late. Time. My time." He was mumbling again, his eyes glazed, lost in a different time and place, looking lovingly at each clock.

It was easy to believe he was crazy when he looked like this. His smile became a frown. He looked at her and the madness evaporated. "I've lost my way, Alice. I'm no good. I'm lost in time. Pieces of myself. Do you understand?"

She'd started walking toward him, before she was even aware of doing it. Like he was the spark to her fire, she needed to touch him, needed it as much as she needed her next breath. She reached, smoothing her fingers over his pinched brows and he shuddered.

"What happened to you, Hatter?"

He took her hand, fingers tight on her wrist.

"Is it Wonderland? Has the magic made you crazy?"

He shook his head, eyes wounded, distant. She gripped the side of his face, forcing his eyes back to her and away from the madness that always pulled at him.

"I am time here. Don't you see?"

What did that mean? "Are you saying you are time?"

He nodded.

"You?"

"Sometimes..." he whispered, "Sometimes I wish I could leave." His voice was so low she barely heard him. As if he was afraid to speak too loud. "To be free, unhindered. To work with hands," he blinked, and she knew he struggled to remember something in the way his shoulders tensed up, "but I can never leave. And you never stay."

She dropped her hands. "But I've never been here before, Hatter."

He gripped his hair with his hands and yanked, hair stuck out in different directions. "Always you. Haunting me, driving me crazy. Making me want what I cannot have."

She denied it, shaking her head so hard the top hat slipped off. "Hatter, that wasn't me. That was my grandmother. I'm not her!"

He growled and walked up to a cherry wood mantle that appeared like a specter behind him. He rubbed his fingers against a clock face with the obsessive compulsion of a man who'd done it many times before.

"All the same," he muttered, "you all come, so beautiful. Smells," he shuddered, "gods you all smell so good and I want you, but you're all selfish, spoiled, and the land says no. And so you go and you never look back; you never remember the man lost in time. Time moves and it gets easier. I can breathe; I can forget. But then it's time again and I'm weary, weary...weary of you all."

She covered her mouth, a lump in her throat, and hot tears behind her eyes. He didn't want her at all. Danika was wrong-- he couldn't forget her grandmother, or apparently any of the others. She wasn't special to him. How could she be? They barely knew each other. She was just a face passing through.

He turned, brown eyes sparking with frosty hints of frightening anger. "And then you. You're the worst of them. Quoting poems, telling me..." he swallowed, "things that I cannot believe. Trying to understand me. Always touching me, the heat of your body reaches to me. None of the others did that, none of the others cared. They only wanted the power or they wanted to go. You want to go too, don't you, Alice?" He didn't give her a chance to respond. "Why aren't you afraid of me?"

She lifted her chin. "Because I'm not."

"Why!" His face contorted into a mask of rage and it was more than anger, pain glittered in the depths of his eyes.

Alice squeezed her eyes shut, her truth burning the tip of her tongue. Did he really want to know, did she have the strength to tell him?

She gazed at him. Others might see him and see anger, fury, blinding rage. But she couldn't. "Because..." she swallowed, opening herself up to someone in a way she'd never dreamed to do again, "when I was 13, I-" *had brain cancer*. She couldn't say it. She desperately wanted to. Wanted to explain, but she didn't have the strength to dip into memories that brought back nothing but pain and paralyzing fear.

"What?" he demanded. "I share my soul with you and you give me nothing? What!" His demanded, and her heart bled.

"Oh, Hatter." She covered her face. "I... I want to, but..."

"But," he sneered, "but, but, but! Prove to me you're different and choose to stay, Alice. Be mine. Choose me."

She jerked, wanting to so bad. More than he could ever know. "What if I jump back and forth, visit family. Then..."

"No," he growled it and her eyes widened.

"It can't be all or nothing, Hatter. I've got responsibilities." She didn't want to go. But why did he demand all or nothing? Why couldn't he share her? Fact was she'd be more here than there, but she didn't want her family to worry. She wasn't like him— this wasn't home. Why couldn't he understand that?

"I want you more than I've ever wanted another. Damn you, Alice, damn you all!"

He threw his fist out. It crashed into a clock, forever silencing it beneath crushed glass. Like a frightened, wild beast, his eyes were wide-- the whites large and the irises menacing. Heaving air like a bellow, lungs and chest expanding like the devil come to claim her soul.

But instead of frightening her, it only made her sad. Yes, she wanted him to see her, Alice Hu, the slightly geeky girl who loved to read, bake cupcakes, and paint her toenails. The girl who'd dreamed of someday becoming a success like the rest of her sisters.

But she couldn't blame him. How long had Alice after Alice been thrust at him? No wonder he didn't remember her. She couldn't imagine having to endure this torment year after year.

"I've only got two days left, Hatter." She held up two fingers. "Just two. Why fight?"

He cast his eyes down, jaw clenched, muscle ticking.

She thumped her fist against her thigh, the clocks' ticking sounded like thunder in her ears. "Can't we try to be friends?"

Why did she want that so bad? If it was all or nothing with him, then she couldn't stay. She'd be leaving. So why couldn't she just let this thing fade into nothing?

"Go away, Alice." He whispered and the words hurt her more than she'd thought they would. She winced. "Go back to your room. To the garden. I don't care." He turned his back on her. "Just go away."

He didn't want her. She closed her eyes, feeling disturbingly close to tears. He was a mess, a red hot mess. Too much baggage, too much trouble. He was not the man she remembered, maybe he never was, maybe she'd seen him through rose colored glasses, turning him into something he could never live up to. "I don't know how to get back." Her calm voice betrayed nothing of her quiet despair.

An outline of a door shimmered before her.

He leaned against the mantel, fingers running over the same spot as before. "It will take you anywhere you wish to go."

He wanted nothing. He didn't turn, didn't move, not when he she walked toward the door, not even when she turned the knob. She peeked around the corner, hoping he'd turn around; tell her he didn't mean it. Hoping that the Hatter who'd kissed her senseless, would return.

He didn't move.

She wanted to laugh, not because it was funny, but because she was bleeding and if she didn't laugh, she'd cry. Alice opened the door and walked away.

Chapter 10

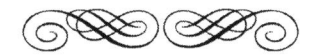

"Why are you here?" The high-pitched voice pierced Alice's skull.

Alice glared at Danika, hating the fairy in that moment. Hating her because she'd been happy, she'd had her dreams and hopes and coming here had dashed them all and made them seem much less exciting and wonderful. "Because he doesn't want me." She shifted on the bed, pulling her knees further against her chest. "I wanted to go back home. The stupid door was supposed to take me anywhere I wanted." She looked at her feet. "I wanted to go home," she said again in a reed thin whisper.

Four hours later, alternating between anger, woe-is-me, and a horrible need to cry, she'd finally come to the realization... the Hatter she'd known (or thought she'd known) had been a figment of a child's overactive imagination. He'd never existed. Her crazy, kooky, Prince Charming did not exist.

He was just a shell, too damaged to love anything.

"The door cannot return you until the three days are up— 'tis the way of it in Fairy. Your time is not yet done, Alice. You must go back to him."

"Why?" she snapped, angry again. "Why did you freaking bring me here? He doesn't want me," she laughed, a thread of hysteria lacing her words. "He's damaged goods, Danika. There's nothing cracking that shell."

"No, no," Danika shook her head. "Not so. I've seen how he looks at you."

Alice jerked to her knees, crawling forward on the bed, backing the little fairy into the wall.

"The same way he looked at all the others I'm sure. I'm just another Alice, another loser. Just like my great-grandmother."

Danika dropped to the bed, her tiny wings buzzing like a hummingbird's. "You don't believe that. And neither do I. You surprise him, dearie. You understand him. None of the others did, or could."

Alice stopped and sat back on her butt, wrapping a strand of hair around her finger, tugging on it like she used to when she was younger. "I want to free him, Danika. I do." And she did. Even though he made her angry and want to cuss and do things her mother would blush to know about, she still wanted to help him. Save him. "But it's impossible. He's too wounded, too fragile. Every little thing I say or do seems to piss him off. I can't do this. He doesn't want me. He sees her when he sees me, I can't win." The last came out a petulant whine.

Danika hovered in front of her, splaying her tiny hand on Alice's chest. Heat poured through Alice like molten lava and her heart felt like it swelled, growing to twice its size.

"But don't you see? The land has already begun responding to you."

She shook her head. "What does that even mean? How can I make this place fall in love with me?"

"By making him fall in love with you."

"But he loved my grandmother."

"No," Danika was adamant, blondish gray curls bounced attractively around her head. "What he felt was pretense. Lies. Lust masked as love. Had any of the other Alices encouraged him, his love would have turned to hate and that is why in part, he despises them now. It wasn't real. In fact, I believe deep down he knew that. That's why he never laid with them. Not one. In fact, I doubt he touched many of them."

"Then neither is this." But then Alice remembered his caresses, his kiss. Her heart thumped. He'd touched her.

"No, dear, you're wrong. I know you're his equal. The mate I've searched for all these years. I've seen how he looks at you."

"Why do you think it's me?" And why was her freaking heart pounding so hard? It didn't matter. None of this mattered. She couldn't stay. She couldn't. Right? She shook her head, trying to stop the weird thought that said it was totally possible. Totally do-able.

"Because you've loved him all your life. He's been real for you all along, Alice. You have to make him see that. He must know the truth. Make him see you. Do whatever it takes-- but make him see you. If you can make him see you, the land will accept you as part of itself. The curse will be broken, Alice." Her blue eyes sparkled, black lashes quivering with gathering moisture.

Alice closed her eyes. "I can't stay, Danika." Though it was a ripping wound to say it. But she couldn't abandon her life, her family. Not for a man she barely knew who didn't want her anyway.

The smile turned into a frown. "We'll cross that bridge when we get there, wee Alice." Danika patted her hand. "Go find him, girl. Do not listen to the mad ramblings of a broken man. He means none of what he says and only half of what he doesn't. You've got but two days, not even." She glanced out the darkened window.

"That literally made no sense."

Danika grinned, the twinkle back. "Aye, well, I guess he's rubbed off on me."

Stupid hope stirred like a lazy cat waking up, but Alice didn't need hope. She needed to go home, back to the real world, and away from the pervasive temptation of a man who was no good for anybody.

"Do not abandon him now, there's more to you than this." Danika's words echoed as she began to fade. When she was gone, the same door Alice had stepped through earlier reappeared.

It was her choice. She couldn't look away from the door. The knowledge that he was on the other side of it was an incessant hammering thought. She bit her tongue. It was her choice.

No! She wouldn't go to him.

She just couldn't.

Her foot twitched.

***

Rain poured around Hatter. The thunderous boom of the darkened sky made him feel not so alone. He sat in his favorite recliner, in the center of a wildflower studded field. Wind howled, long saw grass swayed violently back and forth, cutting grooves into his bare hands, but he barely felt the pain.

Rain, like needle pricks, slapped at his face, drove hair into his eyes. He didn't care, didn't bother to move or turn. He welcomed the rain, welcomed the deluge, hoping it would somehow erase the torment gnawing at his guts. Because she was here, in his world, and he wanted nothing more than to be where she was. Bathe in the beauty of a simple smile, touch her soft flesh and inhale the sensual scent of her body.

He'd kept his place normal. For her. Seeing how she'd panicked when she'd walked through the twists and turns of his home. She was a mortal. Human. A being incapable of comprehending and accepting the dichotomous nature of Wonderland where up wasn't always up, and down could sometimes lead nowhere.

So he'd muted it, kept it pretty. Banal. A white bird tumbled over and over, unable to catch its bearings in the tempest. It hurtled toward him, stick legs poking up in odd angles.

He snatched it just as it blew overhead.

What was this bird? He frowned. He should never have muted the magic. It was unnatural. And she wouldn't stay. She should see it for what it really was and who cared if he scared her off? She'd leave and never come back. Just like the rest. All of them so fickle, foolish.

He'd sworn no more. Not after *she'd* left. The one he'd felt certain would be *his* Alice. But she'd been wicked, wanting nothing of him or what he'd offered.

The bird struggled in his grip, warmth flooded his palm, and suddenly the creature began to morph. Become what it really was. Its beak elongated, broadened at the tip.

So similar were the two Alices.

Its body thickened, turned a dusty shade of rose. Lightning struck right in front of him, but he didn't jump. The bird flapped broad wings, the silver handle of its spoonbill tinkling with music as rain plopped harder and faster upon it.

Ozone swirled around him. He closed his eyes. But not all the same. This Alice was soft and sweet. She told him things. Wonderful, crazy things. Hunger for her, for his woman, clawed at his gut. He wanted to take her, claim her and make her forget any petty desires she'd ever had for returning to her world.

His fingers clenched and the bird grunted, clawed feet scrabbling to jump from his lap. But he held tight, squeezing harder.

Because the moment she returned to Earth she'd never come back, if she left, she'd stay gone. Alice would forget Wonderland. She would forget him.

The bird thrashed now, talons shredding his pant leg until he felt the heat of it grazing flesh.

"No Alice," he muttered. Rain fell down his face like tears. Maybe they were tears. He swallowed hard, looking down at the bird. It labored for breath.

Ribs expanding, black eyes stared at him.

"Why do you look at me like that, bird?"

The spoonbill stopped struggling, but reproach burned in the depths of pain-filled eyes. He petted the wet feathers.

"Rose feathers. Tea roses. She rose in the moonlight. Moonlight shadows her face." He closed his eyes again, his grip relaxing infinitesimally. "Face of a goddess. My Alice, my Alice."

"Hatter?"

That voice. The singsong rhythm made him tremble, made his blood stir and his cock twitch.

Tiny hands caressed the lines of his jaw. His breath stuttered.

"Let the bird go, Hatter."

Soft words, gentle, gentle. Like cashmere's caress. *Anything, anything for you, Alice.*

He released the bird. And Hatter drowned in eyes that sparkled with shades of bitter beer. Her midnight hair was plastered to her face, the tiniest blue body-hugging dress he'd ever seen fitted to her like a second skin. Beautiful, so beautiful his Alice was.

"Why didn't you leave me?" His voice cracked. "You always leave me. Always."

She shook her head. "Hatter, I'm not them." That luscious mouth turned down in a frown and he touched the corner, lifting it. Never wanting to see her sad, not her. Not his Alice.

She kissed the tip of his finger and it was fire. Flames. Scorching him, making him shake. Want, need. More than ever. More than before.

"It's raining, Hatter." She glanced around, worry in her eyes. "Lightning. It's not good to be out here. Let's go someplace else."

The rain relented, gray clouds broke apart and sunlight peeked through. A fine mist swept in, bringing with it the fresh scent of springtime and flowers.

She was trembling, but not from desire like he was. Alice was rubbing her arms. "I don't know. I don't know why I'm here. Why am I here, Hatter? Why do I keep coming back to you, when you don't care?"

He did care. He cared too much. Why? He didn't know. Because she was so beautiful? But the others had been beautiful too. Because she liked poetry? But she wasn't the first.

Because she looked like the other one?

He didn't know. She was different, but he wasn't sure why. He didn't know how to put that into words.

"You shouldn't be so wet," he growled. Not a good host. A good host would never let his lady get sick. Sickness killed.

His heart clenched. Black eyes. Lifeless eyes, staring at him from a pale, heart shaped face. His breathing intensified as the image, always fragmented and fleeting, rammed his skull.

For just a moment, he remembered. Mother, pretty mother. Sick. Coughing. Wet, she'd been wet and he'd been young. So young. He'd wanted to play. The sky had grown dark. She'd told him. Warned him. Come home when it gets that way.

He hadn't listened. He'd just wanted to play.

She'd come to look for him.

Two weeks later, she was dead and he was alone. Crying, with no family and no home. Then he'd fallen. Fallen.

Sickness brought death.

"Hatter?"

That voice was a dulcet lovely thing and it brought him back, snapped him from the violence of his mind. He jerked and she watched him, wondering if he were truly insane.

He frowned. *I'm not crazy, not, not crazy.* He wanted to scream it and yell it, to convince her not to give up on him and his wild ramblings as the others had.

Instead, he wrapped his fingers around her slender wrists. So very gentle, he could snap them. So frail were they. Gentle. Gentle. She did not resist.

He pulled her onto his lap. She sat, stiff as a board smelling like caramel and salt, honey and warm cinnamon. He wanted to trace her with his hands and his tongue, to see if she tasted as sweet as she smelled.

He moved his hands, running them along the length of her spine, slow and sure. She shivered and let out a tiny whimper. But this time, he didn't think it was from the cold.

Hatter pushed heat into his palms, drying her off, steam rose from her clothing. She sighed and dropped her head onto his shoulder.

His cock grew heavy, hard against his thigh. He trembled, feeling twitchy, almost on the verge of losing control, but he didn't stop touching her or running his fingers down the sides of her thighs, up again, and around the generous swells of her breasts. Hard nipples rubbed against his palms and he growled.

"Lovely. My Alice."

She nodded, voice liquid as she said, "Your Alice. Oh yes, Hatter. Yes."

He no longer skimmed her body, he began to apply pressure, to knead and touch. He licked his lips, noticing a pearly drop of water slide down her neck, coming to rest at the base of her throat.

Such a perfect little drop, clinging to her neck, suspended, frozen in time. Refracting light, catching every color of the rainbow inside its liquid cocoon. Alluring, tempting him to kiss it off, but he couldn't, couldn't. Because to kiss it would ruin its symmetry. He blinked. The drop quivered, then continued on its journey and he shuddered, aching from the absence of it.

"Oh gods, Alice." He rested his forehead against her neck. "Why you?"

She turned, straddling his thighs. The warmth of her center enveloped him like a hug and he groaned. Nothing stood between them but a mere scrap of fabric and his pants. He wanted to shift, rub himself against the heat of her body.

Her fingers toyed with the wet hair on the back of his head.

"You make me crazy," she said, then her eyes widened as if she hadn't meant to say that and his heart sank. Did she think him as mad as all the others had?

She smiled, all teeth and full lips curving up so prettily. He wanted that mouth on him, all of him. He gripped the armchair, refusing to touch her anymore.

The sky started to darken again.

She shook her head. "I have to tell you something. Something that's painful for me, but you have to know."

His body tensed, waiting to hear her say she hated him too, that she'd lied, that she would leave, that…

"You remember in the cave when I stopped talking?"

He narrowed his eyes and nodded. She shook and he couldn't stop from rubbing her arms, trying to calm her, aching to hold her, yet sensing this cost her a great deal and if she didn't tell him now she might never muster the courage to tell him later.

"When I was 13," she began, wiggling closer, eliciting a thick groan from him. "I used to have headaches, every day."

She stopped wiggling, looking beyond him. "Sometimes they were so bad, I couldn't stop crying." Her mouth thinned. "I didn't think anything of it. My mom would give me some medicine and I'd feel better the next day. But then I started to forget things. Like my homework, and feeding our cats. Dumb stuff." She shrugged and gave him a small smile.

He frowned, sensing this was more than just silly stuff.

"Then one morning I woke up, and I couldn't remember my mother's name. My sister's. My dad. Nothing."

He stilled her fidgeting fingers, rubbing his thumbs along her soft wrists.

"My dad was a doctor and knew something was wrong. So they took me to the hospital." Her eyes were haunted, far away, glittering with unshed tears. "Do you know what brain cancer is, Hatter?"

His upside down crazy world paused. He couldn't seem to catch a breath. He grabbed her head and tucked it against the crook of his neck, running his hand over the back of her thick hair.

"Are you sick, Alice?" His voice was gruff, feeling like he might choke on the question.

She didn't say anything for a moment. "No," she said it so calmly that it was eerie. Was she sick? She shook her head emphatically and smiled. "No," she said stronger, "not anymore."

The greasy ball of fear in his gut eased up and he took a shaky breath.

Alice pulled away from him, looking at him, as if she were imprinting his face to memory. Her eyes traced the curves of his face before she spoke again.

"It was the size of a golf ball. They gave me a twenty percent chance of surviving the surgery." She grinned, but it wasn't a happy one. It was sad, laced with memories both bitter and hard to relive. "Only time I ever saw my mother cry. But I remember after the surgery, I was lying in bed and you came to me."

He bit his lip.

"You grabbed my hand and whispered that I would be okay."

A wiggle, a worm of a memory tried to work its way through the muddle of his thoughts. Ephemeral dreams, never to be remembered, such fleeting silly things.

White everywhere. The memory that had nagged at him from the moment he'd seen her began to form. Like riding through a dark tunnel and finally reaching the light... blurry images took shape and in an instant he recalled the dream with perfect clarity.

He'd been asleep, when he'd heard a voice. A sweet little voice, crying and pleading with him to please come. *Please come, my Hatter.*

The call had become desperate, incessant.

Please, Hatter, I need you...

And he'd had no choice but to follow. He couldn't sleep, not with the tears, and the pleas, the way that voice had driven a spear through his heart. She'd needed him. Rarely did he visit the dreaming, rarely could he enter the consciousness of others, but he'd gone to her.

Such a little thing. Frail, skin so gray and chapped. A delicate china doll lying within a white cloud. She'd been so beautiful, silent. She'd opened her eyes and told him...

"Do you remember this at all? I'm such a freak sometimes. Of course, you don't remember. It was only a dream." Her laugh was self-deprecating, as if she were embarrassed to admit it. Like she expected him to mock her, so she mocked herself first.

"You asked me: was I real?"

Her face turned sharply toward his.

A black strand of hair slipped over her eye. He couldn't help himself— he had to touch her. He wrapped the silken strand around his finger. She shivered.

His voice was raw, scratchy, but he forced himself to speak, knowing how desperately she needed to hear this. "When I said, I was, you said-"

"That you were so beautiful." Her tender words were a benediction to his ears. "And you said?" she waited for him to continue, a challenge-- he knew-- to see if it'd impacted him the way it had her. If after all these years, he could remember.

He smiled; the words as clear to him now as they'd been that day in the strange cloud full of beeping sounds. "Everything has beauty, but not everyone sees it."

"My favorite Confucius quote." She turned her cheek into his palm. "You saved me that day, Hatter. I always felt like it was your magic that saved me. I fell in love with you that day."

The ice around his heart thawed. She'd called him and he'd answered. His chest ached as the sky broke open with radiance, netting them in its golden wash.

"Oh, Hatter," she half sobbed and then started kissing his face, his cheeks, his nose. Planting hot kisses and the fire that had simmered while she'd told her story, roared back.

Gods he wanted her, more than he'd ever that other Alice. He growled, grabbed the back of her head and slammed their lips together. No gentleness in this touch, he couldn't. It'd been too long, and he'd been so empty. He needed this, her. Now.

"Yes, oh yes." Her tiny moans drove him to distraction.

Her tongue flirted with the seam of his lips and she tasted of sunshine. And magic. Magic? His heart's blood sang in his ears. She was the one. She had to be. He could barely think. All he knew was he had to have this woman. This human mortal who'd cried out for him.

The Mad Hatter.

She'd not been afraid.

She'd wanted his touch.

He traced the curve of her neck; his fingers framed the hollow of her throat, thumb resting against it, feeling the frenetic beat of her pulse. He groaned, twining his tongue with hers.

His body throbbed, ached. He pushed back on her shoulders, laying her down and she squealed. Alice glanced around. "Where are we?"

He'd not been aware he'd transported them until she'd asked it. Barely pausing, he whispered, "My room." Then he was kissing her again, tasting the sweet saltiness of her neck, licking the dip behind her ear.

She moaned, wiggled on him and blood pooled heady and thick in his cock. "I want you," he groaned.

Alice fumbled with dress. She yanked, tugged, and then finally threw her hands out to the sides. "Just rip it."

Grinning, he tore it and immediately was entranced by the sight of the red lace bra covering perfectly rounded breasts. His hand shook. "You are beautiful."

Her lashes fluttered. "Touch me."

He didn't just want to touch her. He wanted to taste her. Lowering his head, he kissed the swell of each breast; his hands massaged their prizes before tugging the bra down. She had dark brown nipples, so pointed, so lovely.

He took one in his mouth, rolled it between his teeth, his tongue swirling over the tip. Her moan bounced around the room, her fingers desperate, yanking at the back of his head, tugging his hair. Sharp nails dug into his scalp, drawing welts and he growled. Pain, and so much pleasure.

"I want to touch you, Hatter," she pleaded. All he could do was mumble. She pulled at his still wet shirt. It stuck, refusing to slide up.

In her frustration, she ground her center on his blood-engorged cock. "Dammit it all to hell," he growled, ripping the shirt off, unbuttoning his pants. He needed her hands on him now, needed her to end his agony.

She pushed his hands away and started shoving his pants down, using her feet to push down further when her hands could no longer reach. He lifted up on the tips of his shoes.

Never had he been this reckless, this wild to slake his lust. His kisses left a moist trail from her breasts to her navel. She bucked and lifted up with a soft ah.

"Too many bloody clothes," he snarled and then chuckled when their clothes disappeared. In his rush to have her, he'd forgotten a few simple words could have made the process much easier.

Her brown eyes sparkled with mischief. "Well, that was easy."

He kissed her, turning her laugh into a throaty growl. She wrapped her legs around his waist; the movement brought him against the heady wetness between her thighs. He clenched his teeth, trying to hang on, trying to make it special for her. Not wanting to rush this, but knowing he was already so close.

Hatter crawled down her fevered body. For a moment, they stared at each other, the moment transcending more than carnality, more than a meeting of lust.

Two lost and broken souls meeting, discovering that in each other they'd found the missing half. Fall and spring, ying and yang. He breathed, she breathed. Both afraid to speak, to ruin the perfection of a moment suspended in time.

But time was fleeting and they both knew it.

He broke eye contact first. He didn't want to get lost that way, couldn't afford to. He licked his lips and froze when his gaze landed on the springy black mass of curls at the juncture of her thighs.

"Alice." Her name, a whisper, a prayer-- fell from his lips in a trembling voice.

Unabashed, she spread her legs, exposing her swollen pink pearl. His limbs felt too heavy, the air too thick. It was hard to breath, to move. All he wanted to do was lie down and pet her, taste her.

"Hatter, please."

It was his undoing. He lowered his head, inhaled, taking the heady aroma deep into his lungs.

"Please," she whispered again.

The moment his mouth touched her clit, she hissed, rocked back on her heels and squeezed her thighs around his face with a punishing grip.

He drew his tongue long and slow down her slit. She tasted of tart raspberries. Delicious. Hatter teased, running his tongue back and forth until she gleamed wet with her dew and his tongue. When he heard her murmuring incoherently, he took her clit into his mouth and sucked hard.

"Oh my gosh," she cried, "yes. Oh my gosh, oh my Hatter, my crazy Hatter."

Her words enflamed him, drove him insane. He sucked harder, swirling the bit of flesh around his tongue. Her fingers scratched him everywhere, raising the fine hairs on his body. Using his bristly jaw, he rubbed against her while he continued his onslaught.

Then she was clenching again, her entire body rocking on his face for several intense seconds before she went limp.

"Oh," she laughed, and bit her finger. "That was, oh wow..." Her laid his chin on her belly, still tasting her on his tongue and watched as her dusky cheeks burned crimson.

Skin glowing, eyes sparkling, black hair fanned out behind her like blades of shadow... she was the prettiest thing he'd ever seen. He would always remember her, just like this.

She held her arms out to him. "Come here."

He slipped into her arms, warmth flooded his entire body. He still burned for her, but beneath that drive, was a confusing ebb and flow he'd never felt before. Ice and fire.

Wanting to cry, not knowing why. Maybe he was mad, maybe the rumors were true.

She kissed him, wrapped her legs around him again and slid that hot heat along the thick, painful length of his cock.

"It's your turn, my love," she whispered, kissing the crook of his neck, setting his blood on fire.

He adjusted his hips and moaned as he finally slid home. Her sheath was like a tight warm fist as he pumped. Sweat dripped from his brow.

He started whispering, lost in his head, in the feel of her body pressed to his. He didn't know what he was saying, but he couldn't stop the words.

So good. So damn good.

Gnashing his teeth, his body tightened and tingled as the pressure built.

"Love it," she kept whispering over and over.

With one last surge, he fell over the cliff. Fractured into a thousand pieces of nothing and sank into the peaceful oblivion of the little death.

It took a moment to come back and when he did he knew he'd never be the same. She'd slipped under the cracks, found the chink in his armor and wiggled her way in. He'd never be able to excise her and he never wanted to.

He hugged her to him, knowing he'd found his Alice. After all these years, he'd found her.

"Hatter." She looked at him, a small frown marring her brows. "You're crying?"

How could he tell her? How could he explain that it wasn't him who'd saved her? *She'd* saved *him*? His heart was so full it hurt. He buried his nose in her hair, she smelled like caramel. Gods, he loved that smell.

This wasn't supposed to happen.

"Hatter." She touched his cheek. "I'm... I'm sorry."

He shook his head. "Don't be sorry. Ever. It was perfect."

"It was perfect, wasn't it?" He heard her smile.

Swallowing hard, he looked at her.

"Hatter." She patted the bed. "Can I sleep here tonight? In your arms?"

He should say no. Gods, he was a masochist. He should guard what fragile bits of it were left, she would leave him. They always did. He closed his eyes, but opened his arms. "Yes."

They lay, neither one speaking, hanging on, as if clinging could stop the hands of time.

Chapter 11

Alice stretched in the morning light. Her arms high above her head, she woke from the best night's sleep she'd had, ever.

"Good morning," he said in the whiskey-roughened voice that made her shiver and her stomach tingle.

"Back 'atcha."

He touched her cheek. She'd slept, but a part of her had been aware of his light caresses throughout the night. Her lover. Her Mad Hatter. Her stomach fluttered... just thinking it was unreal. Who got this lucky? Never her, never geeky little Alice Hu.

And yet here she was. In his bed. With his big, naked body exposed for her to look her fill. He sat next to her, one knee bent, his cock at half-mast and wearing an expression of wonderment. She licked her lips.

"I'm hungry." She bit her lip.

He frowned. So cute when he did that, he was so clueless. He was looking around; she could almost see the wheels in his head turning, wondering what she would like.

She laughed and sat up, then wrapped her arms around his neck and nuzzled it. He still smelled of rain, but also with a rich earthy musk that made her body burn.

"I'm very hungry," she murmured licking the vein at his neck.

"Oh." A flash of light manifested above his head and she knew he finally understood. He wrapped big arms around her and she trembled. "Oh," he said again, that sexy voice of his dipping to a lower octave, "well, I'm starving."

Last night he'd given her the best orgasm of her life. It was only fair she returned the favor. Alice straddled him, pushed him down and watched as the cat-ate-the-canary grin stole across his face. He crossed his arms behind his back.

"I'm at your disposal."

She bit her lip. "Mmm... what a tempting offer." She touched the tip of her finger to the center of his chest, feeling him twitch against her thigh.

So large and lovely and perfect. She wanted him in her again. But first...

"Maybe I should kiss you here." She touched one nipple and it puckered into a hard bud. The muscles of his stomach strained.

"That would be nice," he agreed.

"Or maybe," she batted her lashes and continued her fingertip exploration, circling his navel, "I should kiss you here."

His Adam's apple bobbed.

"Or," she grabbed him, giving him a gentle squeeze, "maybe here."

His eyes squeezed shut as his head jerked. "Oh gods, Alice. Yes, please, yes."

Her mouth watered and she scooted back on her heels, unable to wait another second. She brought him to her mouth, and brushed her tongue against the opening. He jerked so hard, he nearly pulled out of her grasp. Then his hand was framing the back of her head, guiding her to take his full length.

She took him in with a greedy gulp. His hips twitched and she knew he wanted to shove in, but he was being patient. Gentle.

She loved him. She knew that now. She always had, there'd never been a question of that. Alice wanted to show him just how much.

Humming, she took him in to the hilt, loving the feel of his silken skin against her tongue. He started murmuring again and her heart almost exploded from her chest.

"I love you, Alice. Oh gods, Alice, only you. It's only been you. Never again. No more. Just you. You're mine. Always, always."

He was senseless in his ramblings, and she wondered if he even knew what he was saying. She toyed with him, pretending he meant each and every word. Pretending she was that precious to him, that loved and cherished by him.

His legs stiffened. "I'm coming, my love. You might want to pull out." His words were thick, slurred with lust.

She shook her head, wanting everything he had to give. He shot in her mouth with a loud roar and it was sweet and creamy. She swallowed it with a happy little grin and wiped the back of her mouth with her hand.

He sat up, a look of utter astonishment on his face. "Alice," he grabbed her, pulled her tight to him, "I...I..." She never heard what he meant to say, he kissed her.

They stayed in bed for hours, eating, playing, making love. Discovering each other and themselves.

Hours later, sated (for now), they finally ventured from the bed. Hatter was dressed in his outlandish clothes again and her heart beamed with pride.

"You know," she said, "you're all sorts of perfect."

He smiled, but she saw pleasure in his eyes. "I want to show you something. Will you come?"

She nodded. "I'll go anywhere with you." Her hand slipped into his and they were once again walking through the weird door that lead nowhere and everywhere. Suddenly it dawned on her the door took them anywhere. When she'd first gotten here, had she really needed to travel through so many crazy twists and turns? Probably not. She smiled, her crazy silly Hatter. He'd probably been trying to make her run off, scare her. Alice squeezed his fingers. But she wasn't the giving up type, never had been.

When he pulled her through, she looked around, expecting something grandiose, quirky... what she got was a dusty old workshop full of wood working tools and machines.

His smile was radiant. "This is my refuge."

He was looking around and she was looking at him. So different from the moody Hatter she'd first met, now he was bouncing on his feet, gripping her hand like a lifeline while he waited for her to say something.

There were several unfinished pieces around. Something that looked like shelves sat on a far bench and closest to her, a large chunk of driftwood with a scene etched into its side. She squinted.

The scene was a depiction of trees and nature, but within the copse of trees were rounded shapes. She smiled, when she finally recognized it.

"That's a carnival." She looked at him. "Like the one on your wall the other night."

His knuckled her cheeks, brushed against the corner of her lips. She kissed him and his laugh was relaxed, easy.

Gone was the madness, the mayhem of irony, and the gloom of depression. "As a little boy, my mother used to take me to the fair." His eyes shone. "I loved the rides, but most especially the giant wheel with lights. Round and round it went." He shook his head. "I could have ridden it all night."

She grabbed his hand, turning it over, finally noticing the thick calluses on his palm. She brushed her fingers over it, and then brought it to her mouth and kissed each one. Such strong hands, loving hands. A true artist, he'd touched every inch of her with these hands.

She didn't want to leave. Ignoring the heat starting to gather behind her eyes, she asked, "Why don't we?"

He took her chin, lifting her eyes to his. "Alice?"

She shook her head and sniffed. "Why don't we ride all night, Hatter? Eat cotton candy until we're sick and can't think anymore?"

He said nothing for a moment, and she knew he sensed her sadness, it was in the way his mouth thinned, his fingers clenched, but he nodded instead. "Yes. Let's ride, Alice."

They stepped outside the workshop and, as Alice knew there would be, a Ferris wheel sat tall and stately, just waiting for them.

He led her to a basket and when they sat, the ride started of its own accord. Lively carnival music filled the woods and it was so perfect. So wonderful she wanted to cry.

Her heart was breaking.

This wasn't fair.

He hugged her, pulling her to his side. The air was sweet with the scents of night.

"Alice," his voice shook, "I want you to stay."

She bit her lip and turned her face into his side. Wonderland had not accepted her. Of that she was positive, there'd been no music, no land shaking-- her stomach churned-- it'd rejected her too.

Then a thought came and she grabbed the lapel of his multi-colored jacket. "Come with me, Hatter. Come back." He blinked, his eyes went hooded and she didn't want him to say no. "Not forever," she rushed on, "just long enough for me to get my life in order. Then we can go anywhere. Anywhere you want. We can be together. I'll stay here permanently if that's what you want."

Already she imagined introducing her crazy boyfriend to her parents, to Tabby, and fought a snicker at the thought. Her conservative parents would flip. Tabby on the other hand would probably love him.

"No."

She jerked. "What?" Alice drew a blank on her thoughts. "No?"

"No." His jaw clenched and her stomach dropped like the ride she was on. He couldn't say no. Hadn't he just said that he wished she could stay?

"But it's perfect." She should stop talking, stop embarrassing herself further, but she had to make him see.

His nostrils flared and he looked away. "I wish..." He squeezed his eyes shut. "Gods," he moaned, "so many things. So many things, Alice. Please," and she heard the same desperation in his plea as had been hers, "please stay with me. Don't go back."

A lump wedged in her throat. "Hatter, you know I can't. Not if Wonderland rejects me. Danika told me the ground would rock and the air would sing." She had no way of knowing if she'd broken it or not, but it didn't feel like anything monumental had changed. There'd been no songs, no quakes. Which meant another Alice would come.

It was a bleeding wound type of thought.

He shook his head. "It's over. I don't care. Let them come, let a million more come. I won't have them, any of them." He touched her chin, forcing her to look up at him.

"I just want you, Alice Hu. You. You perfect china doll in the white clouds with that beautiful widow's peak," he touched her hair, "and your dainty feet, and bow-shaped lips that utter poetry and make me feel... alive."

Tears started dripping then.

"I," she sobbed hard, the tears obscuring his face, "Hatter, what are you doing? You know I can't. I haven't been-"

"Dammit!" he snarled. "Always no. Always, always no."

She shook her head. Couldn't he see she had nothing to do with this? She couldn't control this, why couldn't he understand that? Why was he making it so difficult on her? "Hatter, come. With me. Please." Her words came between stuttered sobs.

"I can't." Two simple words, but they rang with the finality of a death knell.

He pulled his arm out from behind her and Alice couldn't believe it. Not after last night, this morning, all the heated whispers of love and adoration. He felt something. She knew it. "We still have time. Please don't do this yet. Please don't turn away from me. I have responsibilities, but I love you, Hatter. It's always been you. Please."

He closed his eyes, the ride stopped and he lifted the gate. "Don't say things you don't mean, Alice. I will not go and you cannot stay."

"Stop telling me what I mean," she snarled, "I'm so sick of you thinking you know me. Thinking you know at all how I feel."

He didn't react, but simply said, "love opens the gates, Alice." His eyes were distant and she knew the truth. It was over.

He stood up and started to walk away, then stopped and came back. She thought maybe he'd changed his mind, her heart leapt and she wiped at the tears running freely down her cheeks. She didn't know why Wonderland still rejected her, but it wasn't for lack of love. She burned with it.

He took her hair, slipped it through his fingers and shuddered. "I..." he swallowed and dropped his hand.

Desperate for his touch, unwilling to accept this, she leaned in. It couldn't be over.

"Goodbye, Alice girl." Then he turned, head held high, and walked off.

She stood numb, watching the scene unfold with cold detachment; her brain unable to accept the reality of the moment.

What had just happened?

He'd left her.

Why?

She hugged her arms to her body. Her hero. The man who'd saved her life, he'd walked off, never looking back. No kiss. No nothing.

Why couldn't he have come home with her? She sucked in a breath, body shaking. She'd said she would say good-bye and go anywhere. She'd be happy, so long as they were together, it didn't matter where. Here. Earth. Anywhere.

The tears came harder, fatter, and hotter. She could hardly breathe out of her nose. Blue light shimmered in front of her and then she stood face to face with the door.

Alice looked around. The Ferris wheel was gone; the woodshop was gone. She stood in the middle of an empty field.

Heart miserable, she reached out and took hold of the knob. Her foot stood poised above the threshold as the memory of his words to her in the hospital room crowded her mind.

"Everything has beauty," she said, "but not everyone sees it." Her stomach hurt, her eyes burned. "I saw you, Hatter." Her words whispered through the night. "I saw you."

She walked away.

***

Hatter stood behind the shadow of a tree and watched her walk away; taking the last shreds of his heart with her. She'd lied. Just like the others. Told him she loved him, but she hadn't. Because Wonderland would have said yes. She'd been perfect. So perfect, his tiny Alice with her piercing eyes and wicked mouth. He trembled, remembering her touch, her tongue.

"I saw you too, Alice." His words carried like a whisper on the breeze. Wonderland shuddered, the wind sang with a choir of a thousand bells and the ground swayed.

Hatter gripped the tree and horror blanketed his mind. Wonderland said yes, not because of her words, but because of his.

Chapter 12

Alice was gone and his heart bled crimson. Hatter grabbed his temples. She'd not lied when she'd said she loved him. Wonderland accepted her, wanted her. And she'd left them both.

Because of him. He'd not told her the truth, why he couldn't go with her. Why he could never leave. She'd thought he'd rejected her. He should have told her the truth.

"Damn me," he pounded his fist on his chair. The sky outside the window rolled with thunder, black clouds bloated with rain drenched the lands. She'd left and it was all his fault.

Frogs dropped from the sky by the thousands, their dying croaks lingering in his ear like a macabre lullaby.

All his fault.

Dueling rams knocked horns, their strikes raged with the sound of thunder. His house shook, but Hatter wouldn't move. He'd stay and watch as Wonderland ripped herself apart.

He swallowed the bile in his throat.

He should never have kissed her. Touched those soft pink lips, tasted the dew between her thighs. Heat spiraled down his legs, made him weak in the knees and stirred his blood. Gods she'd smelled so good.

Like salt and caramel. His mouth watered, wishing he could taste it again, sink into the mindless oblivion of her beauty.

He was the Mad Hatter; he should have known he could never have a happy ending. He'd never allow it.

"Insane. Stupid. Insane." He muttered. "And the raven, never flitting, still is sitting on the pallid bust of Pallas just above my chamber door; And his eyes have all the seeming of a demon that is dreaming, and the lamp-light o'er him streaming throws his shadow on the floor; And my soul from out that shadow that lies floating on the floor Shall be lifted nevermore..."

"Hatter." A golden ball of light materialized before him, the humming flit of wings became an irritating buzz. He swatted at her.

"Damn you," he snarled, eyeing Danika. "Why did you bring her?"

Her blue eyes grew wide and sparkled with tears. "Oh, Hatter." She grabbed her chest. "What can I do? I cannot bring another Alice, she's been found and Wonderland..."

Hatter pounded his fist. Black birds dropped like cannon against his roof, landing in front of his window with unblinking eyes. "I don't want another! I want her. I want my Alice. My AlicemyAlicemyAlice."

He grabbed his head, it hurt. It hurt to think of her, he closed his eyes and she was there, but when he opened them she was gone. Gone, gone, gone, and he was lost.

Come to me my, Hatter. The words tore through his skull. He dropped to his knees, heart thundering. "Alice!" he screamed. *Come to me my, love. Come to me,tometometome…*

"Alice!" Hatter cried. He heard her— she called to him. Wanted him. Needed him, just like before. But there was only blackness, no white clouds, blackness and beeping and his heart tore into a thousand fragments of fear because he tasted her sickness, the bitter nip of cancer spread inside and through his head. "Alice?" he screamed again, but the faint voice did not return.

"I cannot go to her. I cannot find her. Lost to me. Should have told her. Should have said why... She'll never know..." He rocked, grabbing his chest and moaning loud. Why had he sent her away? Stupid Hatter. Stupid. A dark void swirled in his vision; thoughts crowded his brain sucking him down into a bog of nonsense. He couldn't go to her. Couldn't find her.

Danika shook him. "Look at me, Hatter. Tell her what?"

He shook his head. Thoughts scattering, rolling, mucking him up. Sweat beaded on his forehead as he squeezed the last lucid memory from his mind. "Love her. Alice is dying. My Alice. My Alice. Get her, Danika. Please…"

Then the voices crowded him, a million talk talking sounds and he stopped fighting. Too hard to remember, too easy to forget.

"Prophet! said I, 'thing of evil!' – prophet still, if bird or devil! – Whether tempter sent, or whether tempest tossed thee here ashore..." Hatter never tore his eyes from the storm, his nails bled from scratching at the wood of his armrest as the madness of his mind consumed him.

Chapter 13

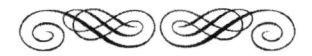

All Alice wanted was her room and her bed. She wanted to lay down and never move, never have to remember or think about the man who'd stolen her heart. Again. She almost crawled up the last flight of stairs, shaking the knob with weary hands. It was locked.

She frowned and patted her body. She was wearing the cami and shorts she'd worn the first night. No purse, which meant no keys and no cell phone. And it was late.

She didn't want anyone to see her like this, her face all puffy from crying. Tabby had told her once she was an ugly crier. It was true. Her nose always got cherry red at the tip and her eyes would turn puffy and purple.

Exhausted, annoyed, she kicked the door and then headed back down. She'd walk to the shop. Maybe Tabby was still there.

She grabbed her head. It was throbbing again. Somehow, and she couldn't even remember doing it, she walked the three blocks to her storefront. Waikiki was dark, with few stragglers around. It had to be well past midnight, but things didn't slow down until at least two or three in the morning.

"Dammit!" She sobbed, the tears started back up again. Last thing she wanted was to be locked out all night. She wanted to sleep, to forget him, to forget that. To forget it all.

In frustration, she yanked on the door and yelped when it gave way, nearly causing her to fall down as she stumbled through.

"Alice!" Tabby's cry was unmistakable and filled with panic.

"Tabby?" she looked around the dark room, and finally saw a small movement slip away from shadow.

Then arms were crushing her and she was crying loud. "I knew it, I knew you'd come back here. Alice, where the hell have you been?"

Tabby clung to her so hard she could barely breathe. Wanting to kick herself all sorts of stupid, only just realizing she'd been gone three days. They'd all probably been sick with worry.

"I..." she pulled a blank, not knowing what to say, who would believe this story? She wouldn't believe this story if she hadn't lived it. "I'm fine," she laughed, trying to play it off and disentangled Tabby's arms from around her neck.

Tabby growled. She walked to the wall, flipped on the light switch and pointed at her. "How dare you leave like that? How dare you." Her brown eyes were thin slits and Alice had never seen Tabby so angry. Vibrating with it. She looked like hell too.

Her eyes were puffy and dark, like she hadn't slept in months.

"Do you know how hard it's been running this place without you? Wondering if you were dead or alive? Your mom has been crazy with grief."

She laughed. "Jeez, Tabs, I've only been gone three days. I'm sorry but..."

Her eyes widened. "Three days! Try three months, you asshole! Three months!"

"Shut up. Don't be stupid." She laughed, but Tabby didn't crack a smile. In fact, she didn't even blink. She walked up to Alice, grabbed her shoulders and shook. Panic so thick on her, Alice felt it choking the breath from her lungs like smoke from a fire. "Tabs?"

Her lips wobbled and Alice could see she had a hard time swallowing. "Three months, Alice."

Knees suddenly gave out on her, thankfully Tabby anticipated that reaction, and pulled a chair out just in time. She plopped onto it. Grabbing her head. It was splitting and each time she swallowed she tasted metal on her tongue.

Alice shook.

Tabby dropped to her knees, wrapped her arms around her waist and held her tight. Hot tears soaked the front of her shirt. But Alice was cold. Calm. She knew.

The pain in her head, the visions. She closed her eyes. The loss of time.

"It's back, isn't it, Tabby?"

"Oh Alice, Alice," she repeated her name like a litany. "Best doctors. Best care. We'll catch it in time."

Empty words. Three months. That was a long time. The longest blackout ever. They both knew. The tumor was back.

She should be crying. But there was nothing there now. She was empty. Devoid. And a part of her had suspected, when she'd told him her story. It was back. She closed her eyes, remembering dark brown eyes that made her want to melt at his feet. Made her want to forget this world.

Something wet slid from her nose and when she brushed the back of her hand against it a red streak smeared her hand and the strong scent of blood filled her head.

Had it only been a dream?

***

The doctors had done all they could. But the tumor was too large, too deep, and two weeks later she battled for life. Wonderland was a fairy tale that no longer existed for her in the new reality of doctors and cancer. In a matter of days she'd become an emaciated skeleton. Doctors had been shocked at her rapid decline. Even she'd been amazed, as if the three months she'd been missing and healthy suddenly spun time forward the moment she'd stepped foot back on Earth. She was skin and bones, with nothing but a few stray hairs on her head. She looked dead already.

She'd had a dream last night, one where she'd called his name and he'd screamed hers in return. It'd been wonderful, but too soon she'd woken up and now the pleasure was pain.

Tabby grabbed her hand. "This room's so much nicer than the last one," she said with a weak grin. "Yellow too," she pointed to the walls, "your favorite color. Yup," she nodded, "I like this one."

"It's okay, Tabs." Her voice was weak. She was so tired, so very tired. It was time and she was ready. But first she had to let them know it was okay. "I'm dying. And it's okay."

Tabby's beautiful face twisted up into an ugly mask and she pressed a white tissue to her face as the silent cry wracked her body. "I love you, Alice. You know that, right? Sisters?"

Alice smiled. "The best."

Beany-- a.k.a. Mr. H.P.D.-- grabbed Tabby's shoulders and gave them a gentle squeeze. Alice closed her eyes. Tabby would be okay-- she'd found her man. They were going to marry next year. For a second it hurt, hurt so bad Alice's jaw trembled. They'd have beautiful kids, a beautiful life.

Tabby wiped her nose with a tissue. She glanced at Beany then back down at Alice. "You should know we've renamed the Shoppe. It's now going to be called Alice and Hatter's Cupcakery and Tea Shoppe."

Tears lodged in her throat. She wouldn't cry. It would kill Tabby to think she didn't love it. She did, it was a comfort to know in a small way she'd always be a part of the place that'd brought her so much joy.

Alice opened her mouth to say thanks when a stab of pain shot down her spine and broke her out in a clammy sweat. She hissed.

"Does it hurt, sweetie?" Her mother's voice was soft as she gently pushed Tabby aside to grab Alice's hand. She nodded, fighting the nausea, the need to puke food she'd not eaten in days. Her mother's hands were warm. Loving.

The machine beeped as her mother increased her dose of pain medicine. It wasn't enough, never enough to fully blunt it. She trembled when the worst of it passed, opening weary eyes.

Her mother's face, lined with wrinkles, so like her own smiled down at her. She closed her eyes. Doctors said it would be any day now. They kept saying that. Kept whispering, thinking she couldn't hear, but she heard.

A part of her wanted to go now. But something kept her hanging on. More than the dreams of him, more than the memory still as clear as a picture in her mind, she had to wait, and so she did, astonishing her doctors, family, and friends. But soon she wouldn't be able to hang on.

Alice took a rattling breath. The cancer metastasized on a daily basis. It was in her lungs, blood, spleen, kidneys, you name it... it was there. At first doctors had suggested surgery, but she knew it was like trying to put a Band-Aid on an arterial bleed. Useless. Eventually, the doctors had decided to "control the pain." She'd known what that meant: it was over. No more hope.

"Alice," her mother rubbed her fingers over Alice's bald brows. "*Tutu* is here. She wants to speak with you."

Since returning Alice had refused to meet with her great-grandmother. Not because she was still angry, but because seeing her would make her remember him.

"Please talk with her," her mother pleaded, "She's old and travels down here every day only for you to say no."

Alice didn't say anything, but gave a gentle nod. Her mother gave a swift smile, glanced over her shoulder and nodded.

"Love you, Alice," Tabby whispered, leaned in and gave her a kiss on the cheek as Alice's father wheeled her great grandmother into the room.

Her frail grandmother-- covered in wrinkles and liver spots-- looked the epitome of health compared to her. Filmy brown eyes studied her. *Tutu* let out a heavy sigh.

Alice looked up at the ceiling, unable to meet *Tutu's* scrutiny.

"The fairy-" *Tutu* began.

Alice sucked in a breath.

"She came to you." It wasn't a question, but a statement.

Alice's heart bled anew, she bit her bottom lip as the tears she'd refused to cry in front of Tabby finally came. She nodded.

Tutu was near blind, but even so, Alice felt that heavy gaze to the depths of her soul. "Go back. Call her to you and go back, *Kuuipo*. Wonderland will heal you. Will save you."

Alice let the tears fall, uncaring who saw them. "I... I can't. Wonderland said no." She sucked in a hard breath, trying in vain to fill lungs that refused to fully inflate.

Tutu patted her hand, her skin was so soft. "They did this to you. They owe you."

"No." She shook her head. "Hatter didn't do this. Neither did Danika. My. Time." She huffed, no energy left in her body to feel anger, spite, or jealousy toward the woman who'd ruined Hatter for so long.

Tutu's lips pressed into a thin slash and for a moment Alice saw the stubborn jaw, the legendary angry glint in her eyes.

"I... I loved him. Won't go back." She sucked air, needing to get this out, working harder than she'd worked in days, but knowing she had to tell someone the truth. "Not for healing. Never want him to think it wasn't for... love."

It was out, and maybe that's what she'd been holding out for, because now Alice was tired- dead tired, ready to let go.

"Love him... so much." The last words ended on a ragged whisper.

***

Danika had to find her. Alice had to know the truth. Why Hatter hadn't followed. How it'd been the Hatter and not her that'd needed to confess his love.

Her wings fluttered. Maybe there was still hope. Danika waved her wand with a jerk, transporting herself back to Earth. She *would* fix this.

The briny smell of ocean water greeted Danika as she stepped through dimensions. Palm trees swayed in the gentle breeze. People shuffled about and kids squealed running through Waikiki's waves. Earth wasn't all bad.

But when she walked past the bakery, she frowned. The lights were off and the store empty. It was only midday.

Danika knocked on the door. No one came. She wiggled the lock. It didn't budge.

A friendly face poked out of the neighboring building. A petite Asian woman with kind brown eyes smiled at her. "Girl not here," she said in a gentle lilt.

Shocked, she pointed. "But they just opened."

The old woman nodded. "Yes. Very sad. Girl sick. Very bad sick. She go hospital. No long time left." She shook her head; a tiny frown tipped her mouth.

Her heart clenched. "Which one?"

She scratched her head. "Queens. She no long left." She tsked. "Good girl, good cake. Too bad." With one final shake of her head, she walked back into her shop.

Finding Queen's Center was easy-- finding Alice's room was not. She walked down hallway after hallway, asking if anyone knew of Alice Hu. Finally a kindly nurse pointed her to the front desk. But Danika wasn't family and wasn't allowed access.

She frowned, knowing there had to be a way. The very rude young man turned his back, and she smiled. Danika turned invisible, glanced at the computer screen and finally located Alice's room. Room 5A, I.C.U.

The moment she walked through the halls and heard the quiet hush of death, she knew it was very, very bad.

Each room held a sad scene. People around a bed, machines beeping and whirring, sustaining a life that would end in days or weeks.

The sterile hallways made her want to run away. Her skin prickled with cold, the sounds of wheezing and sometimes... no sounds at all, it was almost too much. She stopped walking, clung to the wall and took a deep breath.

"Hatter needs her." Steeling her resolve, she moved again. Three more rooms and then she saw her. She was alone.

Alice seemed dwarfed by the bed she lay on. The once vibrant honey hue of her skin was now ashen and gray. She looked like a skeleton; there wasn't even any hair on her head, just thin wisps.

Her hands shook.

Clear, plastic tubes ran up her nose.

"Oh, Alice girl, I'm so, so sorry."

Alice's lashes fluttered. She opened her eyes, her breath coming short and choppy. "Danika? You're here?"

She walked up to her, grabbed her hand, afraid to hurt her, afraid to let go. The vibrant beauty of before was gone, all that remained was a shell. Her eyes were bloodshot, wide and shining.

"I... Oh, dearie, I never knew." Words spilled from Danika's lips, mingled with the tears from her eyes.

Alice smiled, her lashes fluttered, as if the effort to hold her eyes open cost her everything. "It was nice. I was," she breathed, a shallow sucking in of oxygen, "happy."

"Who is she talking to?"

Danika turned at the sound of another voice. A woman-- bearing an uncanny resemblance to Alice, but older-- asked a man in a white coat. He put an arm around her shoulder.

"It's part of the process. The drugs have dulled the pain." His voice broke and he looked at Alice with love shining in his eyes.

Alice's laugh was weak. Danika looked back at her. "They don't see you. Think. I'm. Crazy." Her lips trembled. "As a Hatter."

The woman behind them sobbed. Heels clicked loudly on linoleum as she ran from the room.

"He misses you desperately," Danika whispered.

She coughed, and then gasped. A sheen of sweat glistened on her forehead. "Wonderland. No."

Danika shook her head. "No, Alice. Wonderland said yes. It wasn't you, see." She rubbed her knuckle. "It was him. He had to declare himself, had to truly fall in love. He loves you, Alice."

For a moment, Alice's face crumpled, then she grew calm, unnaturally still. "All that we see... or seem is but a dream... within a dream."

It was hard to listen to Alice speak, each word forced out between labored pants for breaths.

"Alice, look at me." Danika patted her hand, forcing the girl to work through the lethargy and open her eyes. They glimmered with tears. She licked her lips. "You can still come back."

Alice snorted. "Dying."

"I can take you. Wonderland will heal you. You'll never die. Never. You'll be perfect and healthy, with your Hatter. Always."

The tears started to fall, each one like a blade to Danika's heart. Alice had to come back. Not just for Hatter's sanity, but also because the thought of such a young life being extinguished was a tragedy Danika couldn't endure.

"Didn't want me. He wouldn't come..." Alice coughed, the booming sound painful to Danika's ears. She winced in sympathy, waiting for it to pass. After a minute Alice laid back down, her lips tinted blue.

The girl had minutes. A shadow of death hovered above her, reaching out its cold skeletal fingers, ready to claim her any moment now.

"Here? He wouldn't come here, is that what you're trying to tell me, Alice?"

Alice nodded weakly.

"Oh, Alice. He wants you beyond endurance. He's locked himself up in his house, the land rages beyond his door. Wonderland is in chaos. Creatures die and kill each other. The violence of his mind has exploded upon the land." She shuddered. "Alice, he couldn't come. Do you hear me?"

The girl was unnaturally quiet. Danika patted her cheek and Alice stirred and mumbled.

"Listen to me." Danika pried Alice's eyes open, forcing Alice to see her. "He couldn't come because, outside of Wonderland, he's not immortal. He was like you. A human who stumbled in." She rushed through the explanation, hoping the girl would hang on long enough to listen. "Time would catch up with him. Why do you think he's surrounded by clocks? Each Wonderland day is a month here."

Alice's eyes widened, trying to focus. "A month?"

Danika nodded. "A month. He's so old now time would catch up with him in seconds. He cannot exist beyond Wonderland."

Alice's nostrils flared, she was trying so hard to think it through. Danika could see her struggle; see her fight to hang on to reality. "Want me?"

"Yes." Hope leaped into Danika's throat. "The land accepts you. Wants you. So does he. Return to him, save him, save yourself. Oh Alice, come home with me."

Alice frowned, her eyes looking out at the door. "How will... you. Take. Me?"

Danika touched the tip of her wand to Alice's stomach. "With magic."

Alice shook her head. "Body? Or..." she inhaled, "just soul?"

Danika's eyes widened. "This is not heaven, child. I cannot divide your soul from your body. All of you. I would take all of you."

Alice closed her eyes.

Danika's heart stuttered as she waited for the girl to take a breath. She shook her hand. Not yet, please not yet.

Alice's family would surely worry when they came back to find an empty bed, to always wonder. But it was the only way. Alice was dead to them anyway. It was over for them. But not for Alice.

Alice's lashes fluttered.

Good enough. Danika tapped her with the wand, shrinking them both. With a final flick of her wand, she pointed to the bed. A white letter appeared on the empty pillows, the words: *I'm happy*, written on it.

That was the best she could do.

She gripped Alice's hand and wouldn't let go as they barreled through dimensions.

Chapter 14

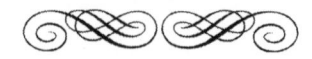

Wrapped in shadow, Hatter stared out the blackened window. Words from poems fell in repetitive motion from his lips.

Alice's heart swelled, aching in her chest. To go from being so close to death, to inhaling a breath free of pain. To seeing her lover. It was almost too much.

Would he think she returned only to be saved? She bit her lip.

"Hatter," she whispered, afraid he might not hear her.

His shoulders stiffened, but he didn't turn.

"I...I..." She was stuttering again; he always made her feel like a girl with her first school crush. She rubbed sweaty palms down the front of her cami and shorts, the same ones she'd worn the first time they'd met. The same ones he'd said she liked her in best. Her heart flipped. "Do you love me?"

Hatter shot to his feet, his eyes wild and his hair longer than she remembered.

"Alice?" he croaked, eyes glistening with a powerful emotion that tugged at her heart, gave her feet wings.

She flew into his outstretched arms, resting her ear against the firm beat of his heart.

His body trembled. "Love you," he whispered, nuzzling her hair, his hands were frantic on her back, pushing her shirt up, touching her bare flesh. "Loveyouloveyouloveyou, always, always, my Alice, my love."

She purred, needing to touch him, to feel the hard press of his body again.

"Clothes off," he said, and they were naked. He picked her up, pressing her against the wall. He lifted her, forcing her to wrap her legs around his waist. The thickness of him rested against her aching opening.

So good. If this was a dream, death, she didn't care. She never wanted to wake up.

"Hatter, I was sick."

"Gods," he sobbed and kissed her cheeks, her throat. "Gods, Alice."

She gripped his face, forced him to pause and look at her. He needed to know. "I didn't come back because of that. I almost died, but I came back for you. None of this matters if you don't believe that."

His eyes closed and he gently planted a kiss on her mouth, his tongue tracing the seam of her lips, and she knew he believed her. Alice's heart thrilled.

There were no playful teases, no petting or sweet nothings whispered. This was primal need. He pushed into her liquid heat and her body was so primed, so ready the moment he slipped in fully she felt the quickening thrum of an orgasm. Her blood resonated, it moved through her like crystal song.

He was kissing her neck, his hands grasping her breasts.

"Love you, so much," he muttered, taking her tongue, dueling with it. "Don't ever leave me. Sorry I'm such an ass. Sorry I didn't tell you why. Sorry for so much."

She shook her head, feeling dizzy and lightheaded from the overwhelming sensation of him. He slid in and out, her legs tightened. She was close, her thighs started to shake.

"Never leave," she mumbled. "Love you, so much too."

Then they were there, he tipped his head back and roared. His hot seed came in torrents, flooding her body. His touch, his soul, it was hers. All hers.

He was her Mad Hatter and Alice was finally home.

Alice Hu's Red Queen's Revenge Cupcakes:

Ingredients

- 2 1/2 cups flour
- 1 1/2 cups sugar
- 3 tablespoons unsweetened cocoa powder
- 1 teaspoon baking soda
- 1 teaspoon salt
- 2 eggs
- 1 1/3 cups vegetable oil
- 3/4 cup buttermilk, room temperature
- 2 tablespoons red food coloring
- 1 tablespoon white distilled vinegar
- 1/2 tablespoon vanilla extract
- Cream Cheese Frosting, recipe follows
- A small palmful of pink peppercorns, roughly chopped

Directions

Preheat the oven to 350 degrees F. Line mini cupcake or muffin pans with 48 mini cupcake liners or line regular-size cupcake or muffin pans with 24 regular cupcake liners.

In mixing bowl, sift together the flour, sugar, baking soda, cocoa powder, and salt. In another mixing bowl, stir together the eggs and oil. In a mixing cup, mix together the buttermilk, food coloring, vinegar, and vanilla extract and lightly whisk. Gradually add the dry ingredients and buttermilk mixture to the egg mixture, starting and ending with the dry ingredients. We are trying to achieve a dark brown, red cupcake color, so add more cocoa powder, if the red is not deep enough. Then add the batter to the mini cupcake liners until they are 3/4-full and bake for 13 to 14 minutes, or until done. Alternately, fill the regular-size cupcake liners and bake 22 minutes, or until done. Let the cupcakes cool completely.

Cream Cheese Frosting:

- 4 cups confectioners' sugar
- 8 ounces cream cheese
- 1 cup or 2 sticks unsalted butter
- 1/2 teaspoon salt
- 4 teaspoons pure vanilla extract

Combine the sugar, cream cheese, butter, salt, and vanilla extract in a large mixing bowl and blend for 2 minutes.

And finally, the Queen's Revenge, take a small dusting of pink peppercorn and carefully sprinkle the tops of each cupcake. Both sweet and spicy!

Leonard's Awesome Lemon Curd: Words in parenthesis courtesy of Momma Leonard…

Ingredients

- 5 egg yolks
- 1 cup sugar
- 4 lemons, zested and juiced
- 1 stick butter, cut into pats and chilled

Directions

Add enough water to a medium saucepan to come about 1-inch up the side. Bring to a simmer over medium-high heat. Meanwhile, combine egg yolks and sugar in a medium size metal bowl **(mind the fur now… 'tis quite disgusting should any get into the concoction)** and whisk until smooth, about 1 minute. Measure citrus juice and if needed, add enough cold water to reach 1/3 cup. Add juice and zest to egg mixture and whisk smooth. Once water reaches a simmer, reduce heat to low and place bowl on top of saucepan. (Bowl should be large enough to fit on top of saucepan without touching the water.) Whisk until thickened, approximately 8 minutes **(or 20 twitches of me whiskers)**, or until mixture is light yellow and coats the back of a spoon. Remove promptly from heat and stir in butter a piece at a time, allowing each addition to melt before adding the next. Remove to a clean container and cover by laying a layer of plastic wrap directly on the surface of the curd. Refrigerate for up to 2 weeks.

And Leonard being Leonard, he wanted me to let you know that some good old fashioned English scones are a must to truly savor the tangy sweetness of his momma's curd.

Leonard's Awesome Scones:

Ingredients

- 3 cups flour
- 1/3 cup sugar
- 1 teaspoon salt
- 2 1/2 teaspoons baking powder
- 1/2 teaspoon baking soda
- 3/4 cup (1 1/2 sticks) <u>unsalted butter</u>
- 1 cup <u>buttermilk</u>
- 1 tablespoon <u>heavy cream</u>, for brushing

Directions

Preheat oven to 400 degrees F. Combine the flour, sugar, salt, baking powder and baking soda in a large bowl. Add butter and mix with your fingertips to a coarse meal. Add buttermilk and mix just until combined. Add currants, if desired.

Transfer dough to a floured board and divide into 2 parts. Roll each to 3/4 inch thick rounds. Cut each round into 8 wedges and place slightly separated on a greased baking sheet. Brush the tops with the cream, and bake for 15 minutes, or until lightly browned. Serve warm, split in half and slather with lemon curd.

Hatter says it tastes best with a good Earl Grey.

Acknowledgements

Thank you to Sonya, Jennifer, Anne, and C.C. You gals are awesome and I could never have done it without you.

Gerard's Beauty

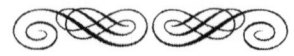

"Bad boys need love too…"

Betty Hart has had it with men. Jilted in love, her life now consists of shelving books by day, watching too much Anime by night, and occasionally larping on the weekends with her fellow 'Bleeding Heart Rebel' nerds. Men are not welcome and very much unwanted. Especially the sexy Frenchman who saunters into her library reeking of alcohol and looking like he went one too many rounds in the ring.

Gerard Caron is in trouble. Again. Caught with his pants down (literally) he's forced to seek asylum on Earth while his fairy godmother tries to keep Prince Charming from going all 'Off with his head'. Maybe, messing around with the King's daughter hadn't been such a great idea after all, not that Gerard knew the silly redhead was a princess. But his fairy godmother knows the only way to save his life is to finally pair Gerard with his perfect mate, whether he's willing or not.

From the moment Gerard lays eyes on the nerdy librarian he knows he must have her, but Betty is unlike any woman he's ever known. He thought Betty would come as willingly to his bed as every other woman before her, but she is a woman who demands respect and even… horror of all horrors… love. Is it possible for a self-proclaimed Casanova to change his ways?

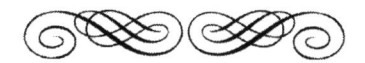

Gerard's Beauty

by

Marie Hall

Gerard's Beauty

Copyright Marie Hall 2012

Cover Art by Claudia McKinney of www.phatpuppyart.com Copyright October 2012

Photographer, Teresa Yeh
Model, Danny
Edited by Brent Taylor

Formatted by L.K. Campbell

Smashwords Edition

    This is a work fiction. All characters, places and events are from the author's imagination and should not be confused with fact. Any resemblance to persons, living or dead, events or places is purely coincidental.
    All rights reserved. No part of this publication may be reproduced in any material form, whether by printing, photocopying, scanning or otherwise without the written permission of the publisher, Marie Hall, except in the case of brief quotations embodied in the context of reviews.
    This book is licensed for your personal enjoyment only. This ebook may not be resold or given away to other people. If you would like to share this ebook with another person, please purchase an additional copy for each person you share it with. Thank you for respecting the hard work of all people involved with the creation of this ebook.
    Applications should be addressed in the first instance, in writing, to Marie Hall. Unauthorized or restricted use in relation to this publication may result in civil proceedings and/or criminal prosecution.
    The author and illustrator have asserted their respective rights under the Copyright Designs and Patent Acts 1988 (as amended) to be identified as the author of this book and illustrator of the artwork.

MarieHallWrites@gmail.com

MarieHallWrites.blogspot.com

Published in 2012 by Marie Hall, Honolulu, Hawaii, United States of America

Dedication

To Iliana. Because you are perfect just the way you are…

Acknowledgements

To Joyce and Mom, because you girls just get me

Table Of Contents

Chapter 1
Chapter 2
Chapter 3
Chapter 4
Chapter 5
Chapter 6
Chapter 7
Chapter 8
Chapter 9
Chapter 10
Chapter 11
Chapter 12
Chapter 13
Chapter 14
Chapter 15
Chapter 16
Bonus

Chapter 1

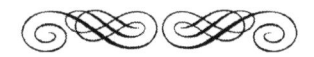

Danika-- fairy godmother extraordinaire-- blazed through the night like a tiny falling star.

Damn that pompous bastard Gerard.

She shivered, holding her wand tight to her heaving bosom. Trying to think up a few more bad words for the odious man, but words failed her. He'd turned her into a laughing stock in front of her peers.

Galeta the blue-- Head Mistress of Fairy Godmother Inc.-- threatened to rip Danika's title from her. From her! How dare they even insinuate that she'd lost control of her charges?

Of course Gerard's pending trial only strengthened their allegations. *The oaf.* If he'd only kept his nose clean like she'd implicitly instructed. But the man was incapable of thinking with something other than the snake in his pants. She'd hoped after his last trial he'd be a little more thoughtful of whom he seduced. Last time they'd been lucky that the father had been willing to settle the debt for a few gold coins. She doubted gold would appease this situation.

Cinderella's daughter... of all the lass' Gerard could have beguiled, why her? Now Prince Charming was all 'off-with-his-head' and Danika had a serious problem on her hands.

She ground her molars so hard her jaw ached. "Relax, Danika. Must not allow yourself to get angry." Even though she suffered a violent urge to turn Gerard into a toad, it would only prove to her peers she had lost control and unfortunately it was not a viable option. Using magic for revenge was the very thing that'd cursed Jinni to non-genie status. Danika had no desire to be striped of her powers as well.

She beat her wings faster, streaking through the trees with a furious buzz.

She had to get to Gerard first, before the angry mob could get their hands on him. Thankfully she'd sic'd the best tracker in the Kingdom on him, and just received the missive she'd been waiting weeks to get. Gerard had been found. And not a moment too soon.

For tonight the jury and tribunal convened-- comprised of jilted lovers, fathers with revenge on their minds, and the three most powerful godmothers in the land-- if she could get Gerard out of Kingdom, perhaps she could convince the court he'd not return unless reformed.

Perhaps... just perhaps, that would be enough to mollify the crowd and prevent a retaliatory execution.

And after her smashing success with the Hatter and his Alice. None had thought that romance possible. She'd proven them wrong, had made a true love match. In fact, the two were so in love it bordered on disgusting.

But now none of that mattered, thanks to the French baboon. If Danika had been smarter she'd have known Gerard planned to flee. He, more than the others, hated the very notion of love. After Alice and Hatter's successful match Gerard had become withdrawn and quiet. That was so unlike the gregarious Frenchman that at first Danika had thought him jealous. What a fool she'd been to let him have his space. She'd thought nothing of his leaving, but as time progressed and he'd not returned, an awful suspicion rose in her gut.

He'd gotten himself into trouble.

By that point so much time had passed his trail had gone cold. She'd searched his favorite haunts, to no avail. Out of sheer desperation she'd questioned the flowers, as they always knew what was what, but the flowers had been less than helpful. One saw this, another that, but none could pinpoint him accurately. It seemed the moment his location was discovered, he'd hie himself off to the next pair of plump arms and ample bosom.

The man was a nitwit. Did he not see she had his best interest at heart? But maybe it was her fault for the whole Belle debacle.

To Danika's credit making a love match was no easy feat. Still she did feel partly responsible. The night Belle had married the Beast she thought Gerard had gone as mad as the Hatter.

Gerard had gotten thick in his cups-- face splotchy and red-- sniveling that Belle was a tramp all along and he'd known and wouldn't have her anyway. However the insult of her marriage was nothing compared to the greater insult he believed he'd suffered afterwards.

Forced anonymity.

Through the ages mortals had learned of the lives and roles of the Kingdom's inhabitants through song and tale. All knew of Hook's obsession with Pan, Wolf's run in with Red's grandmother-- but of Gerard, well... he wasn't even a cliff note in a text book. He simply did not exist outside of Kingdom. Ironic, since his story was easily one of the better known, but... as he'd so often done, he'd screwed the pooch (to use an oft used Earth phrase). He'd angered the wrong people and they'd exacted their revenge. Danika might have felt sorry for him if he were anyone else, but Gerard was Gerard. He angered everyone.

Spying Leonard's lighted gardens in the distance she sighed, feeling a little more in control of herself now that she could act. Danika alighted on the empty tea table. "Wolf," she hissed.

A shaggy black shadow pulled away from the tree. His long pink tongue lolled out the corner of his fanged jaws. Huffing, he appeared to be laughing in his dog like way.

"Did you find him then?"

The Big Bad Wolf dipped his head, and turning, trotted back to the tree he'd hidden behind earlier. A flash of white light lit the rose garden and then a tall, muscularly built man stepped out from behind the tree.

The books had it all wrong. Shifters never turned human with clothes on. They returned to human form as nude as the day they were born. His muscles, like thick ropes, flexed as he strode back out. She fanned her flushed face, entranced by his predatory loping grace, even on two feet, he walked like a beast.

My, but her boys were pretty. She cleared her throat, attempting to remember why she was here.

Eyes, the golden shade of a lion's hue, glinted back at her. "I've brought him." His throaty growl made her shiver. "He seduced a mermaid, was hiding out in her lair." He spat, disgust evident in his tone.

"Yes, well, you know how he is. No woman can resist him. Beautiful, abhorrent man." She pursed her lips.

He lifted a shaggy black brow. "Do you think it's fair then, what you've planned? Not that I care about the bastard, but the woman."

Ah, her wolf always did have a soft spot for the female form. Much maligned he'd been for eating Red's grandmother, though the stories were mostly exaggerated.

"I must." She shook her fists, her wand spurted with firework bursts of energy. "'Tis more than a mere matter of finding his mate. He's in danger of losing his very life."

He frowned and rubbed his stubbled jaw. "I see. Well, then. He's behind that tree. Bound and gagged, as ordered." He pointed to a gnarled oak.

She smirked and started toward it.

"Our bargain?" he asked quietly, a low growl undercut his words.

She bit her lip, heart speeding just a tad. Danika had kind of promised him something. The godmothers were not going to like it. She wrinkled her nose, rubbing her forehead, bit of a pickle that situation.

"Danika," his voice grew sharper, more wolf like, less human.

"Yes, yes, bloody hell, Wolf. As I've promised."

His nostrils flared, as if he were trying to scent her out. Sweating below her collar, she gripped her wand tighter. She did not lie, though perhaps she'd embellished the truth a wee tiny bit. But no need to let him know that.

Just yet.

Her grin wobbled.

His lips thinned as he finally nodded. "Aye, then. You know where to find me."

"I do indeed." She watched him go. "Oh my." He was really not going to like what she'd done. But then again, neither would anyone else.

"I do what I must," she sighed, as she rounded the oak. Being a godmother was often a thankless job. It'd only taken her two hundred and fifty years and twenty ones days (but who was counting) to stop being offended by it. Though every once in a while, it still rankled.

Like now, when her boys should be deliriously happy by the prospect of finding their match. Not like she'd asked them to chew their own leg off. Her mouth curled. Given the choice between self mutilation or marriage, she wasn't sure which they'd choose. But she was almost 99 percent positive it wouldn't be the girls.

Stupid men.

Case in point, Gerard,-- hog-tied at the base of the tree-- eyes closed, hair disheveled and filled with bits of bramble. He'd looked better. And had obviously fought like a rabid dog to escape Danika's clutches.

Danika walked to him, the closer she got, the more overpowering the odor of alcohol became. She pinched her nose, getting woozy.

Gerard was covered in gashes and scrapes. A long cut ran under his right eye, a slight bluish tinted bruise shaded his cheek, and she was sure he'd not be able to do much more than sip liquid nourishment for the next day or two. Swollen and bloody, his lips were painful even to gaze upon.

Wolf, perhaps, had been a bit too thorough in bringing him back.

She rolled her eyes. "Fine mess this is, Gerard." Though angry with him, her heart ached to see him like this.

He'd been jovial once. Oh, he'd always had a touch of the devil in him-- no doubt-- but good where it'd mattered most. Not since Belle though, and especially not since the night his legacy had been forever tainted by lies and half truths.

Danika tsked. "I should let you face their wrath, Gerard. Truly I should. No less than you deserve." Her words were tough, but her touch was soft as she gently caressed his smooth brow. Even after all he put her through, she still loved him. Loved them all, they were her boys, and she'd fight to the death to protect them.

He snorted and then sneezed, showering her in a cloud of dust. She shuddered and stepped away from his mouth.

"Sad, pathetic man you are now." She shook her head. He gave a soft moan, whether he understood her or not, she wasn't sure. "Yes, I said it. Pathetic."

"*Non*," he grimaced and twitched, as if becoming aware of the bonds that held him.

She coughed and waved her hand in front of her nose. "This is horrible. Horrible!" She stomped her foot. "Gerard, she'll be terrified of you. You look like a beggar. No. Worse. You look like a beggar who's been waylaid in a distillery vat. If this were any other time I'd wait."

"Bloody Wolf." He spit a crimson streak. "Told him I'd come."

"Yes, I'm sure you were quite the angel. Wolf completely in the wrong." She crossed her arms and tapped her foot.

He cracked open a blood shot eye and shifted, trying to move to a sitting position. His body jerked and he groaned, laying his face back down in the dirt. "Perhaps I did attempt to cold cock him first. Bit fuzzy on that."

"Of course you did." She pointed her wand at his bonds, a bright pink glow wrapped around the leather hide on his wrists and ankles.

Gingerly, he sat up and rubbed his chapped wrists. Taking a deep breath, he winced. "I think the bastard broke a rib." He felt around his waist. When she didn't respond to his obvious ploy to baby him, he sighed. "Fine. Fine," his deep French lilt grew heavy with exasperation. "I concede. You made your point, but you cannot bring her here with me looking like this."

She leaned back on her heels. His shirt was shredded in several spots. One-- a particularly long rip along his chest-- exposed the tiny bud of a brown nipple. Blood stained his collar. But it was his pants, with the laces loosened, that told the true tale. Wolf had obviously found Gerard rutting like a mad fool. She lifted a brow, looking back at him.

He grinned and then winced when his cracked lip oozed. "I am a man, *fee*," he said it unabashed, almost prideful.

Danika thinned her lips. She'd studied the girl-- Betty Hart. The mortal had good insight into a person's true psyche. A rare gift in a human (apart from a disastrous and much too recent relationship with a boyo named James) her instincts were normally spot on. Unfortunately now that she'd been burned, Betty questioned her intuition. This pairing could work, but only if both Gerard and Betty let it. Problem was convincing them of it.

"I never said I'd bring her here," she licked her teeth, studied her nails and waited.

One second.

His face scrunched up.

She tapped her foot.

Two seconds.

His jaw dropped.

She smiled.

Three seconds. And...

"*Non*! No. I refuse. I will not be sent to that vile," he ground his jaw, "Earth!"

She planted her hands on her hips. "Oh, but you will."

Anger glittered like hellfire in the depths of his inky blue eyes. "You didn't send Hatter."

"He could not go. You, however..." She eyed him hard, trying to pretend her knees weren't currently knocking. He could be quite imposing when he wanted to be. "Are another matter. You were not born of Earth therefore you can safely walk its roads."

His nostrils flared. "You cannot make me, I will not go."

She almost laughed at his petulant manner. "You are very wrong there, me boy. I most certainly can and will. Just this evening a tribunal's been called."

He stiffened and she smiled. "*Oui, mon ami*. You know exactly what I mean. Princess Arabella! Gerard, what were you thinking?" she screeched, finally free to vent her frustration.

Gerard scrubbed his face. "It is not what it seems. I swear, *Marraine*, I did not touch her. The *coquine* threw herself at me. I'd never force myself on a woman, much less a princess."

"I find it hard to believe you could not tell it was her, she's a wild mane of orange hair. 'Tis impossible to mistake her for a commoner!" Danika threw her hands up.

Gerard shook his head. "She was in disguise, I swear it. Once I discovered who she was, I put her aside, but by that point I was found and well..." He tunneled blunt fingers through his messy hair. "I ran. I knew they'd lock me in the dungeon."

She believed him, which made the situation all the harder. "Oh, Gerard," she touched his chin, "your past returns to haunt you."

"But you do believe me?" His dark blue eyes were large and earnest.

She rolled her wrist, the wand burst with pink bolts of energy. "I do."

He sighed, his shoulders visibly relaxing.

"But, you know they will not. You've bedded too many of the town's women..."

He frowned. "All willing. I don't care what they claim now."

"Be that as it may," she shook her head, "you've angered most, if not all men folk, and now the King. You must leave. I'll go in your stead and speak on your behalf."

"Good. Good."

She pursed her lips. "I hope you don't expect this to go as smoothly as before. You only slept with the milliner's daughter then, this is a Princess."

"Ah," he grabbed her by the waist and holding her like a doll, planted a quick kiss on her cheek, "you'll do fine. You'll show them all's well and I'll be free to return. Besides, I did not bed the wench. She's as untarnished as before. Mostly."

She growled, even while her heart pounded. He thought it would be as simple as the last time, she knew by his light hearted teasing that he did not understand the magnitude of his earnest mistake. This time Gerard had angered a King, a King bent on retribution. Galeta would respond as she'd been dying to do for decades now, he'd finally given the head godmother a legitimate reason to exact her revenge.

Danika had no clue why Galeta hated Gerard so much. He'd never shared, but knowing her mistress as she did, Danika feared the worst.

Danika would fight like the devil to see the punishment fit the crime, unfortunately she was pretty sure she'd be the only one coming to his defense.

His smile slipped. "*Fee*? You're keeping something from me. What?"

"I..." Danika sucked in a breath, hating how transparent she always was. She gave him a weak grin and wiggled free of his grasp, not wanting to be accidentally crushed. Perhaps she should tell him. Just in case, prepare him for the worst possible scenario.

But in that moment he looked like the boy she remembered from his youth, eyes clear and free of guile. Beautiful face made more handsome because he wasn't oozing sex, but being himself. If Gerard could ever learn not to depend on his looks, but to let a woman see the kindness buried so deep she wasn't sure he even knew it still existed, he'd bend even more hearts his way.

That peek of his humanity made Danika bite her tongue. Perhaps by some miracle she could convince the court of his innocence in this. "It is nothing, Gerard."

"*Non*," he snarled, fists clenching, "I know you well, fairy, there is fear in your eyes. You tell me the truth."

Danika held his gaze, wanting desperately to turn away and not meet the blinking fury he directed at her like a lethal blade. He said nothing, only vibrated with the strength of his mounting anger.

She knew he was not angry at her, but at his circumstances, which was the only reason why she didn't quiver like a sapling. "Be on your best behavior, Gerard. Her name is Betty Hart. Find her, mate her. You'll thank me."

She swished her wand and Gerard shot to his feet. "You cannot mean to do this," he barked, "Danika, what aren't you telling me?" His body already began to fade into the glowing tunnel that would take him through dimensions. He looked over his shoulder.

Her heart squeezed.

"I'll be better," he said, "no more whoring. Drinking," his French accent thickened. "I'll... stop."

The road to hell was paved with good intentions. He might mean it, but Gerard would never be able to stop. It was his way and who he was. The only thing that could possibly change him would be falling in love.

"Gerard, do not forget why this is now a necessity. You've placed yourself in this situation. I'm doing my very best to fix what has now become a matter of life and death." She flew to him, briefly able to touch the corner of his jaw before he became insubstantial. "I'll return to you once I've received verdict."

"A pox on that," were his last words before he vanished.

Chapter 2

"*Merde!*" Gerard snarled when he landed... no dumped was a better word... when he got dumped on hard stone. His body, already bloody and beaten, exploded with sharp stabs of pain on impact.

Stars danced in front of his eyes. Taking two deep breaths between his teeth, he glanced up. Blurred vision made it difficult to figure out where he was.

It took a second for the ringing in his ears to stop, when it finally did, he was slowly able to get to his feet. Grunting heavily with the effort to stay standing, he looked up.

First thing he noticed were the trees. Massive things, tall and towering to the sky, with leaves a dark shade of yellow and red. Second thing he noticed was a thick slab of gray stone leading like a trail to a building. And the third thing he noticed made him growl.

"*Fils de salope*," he swore and spat by his boot. Damn that meddlesome witch. A library! He'd specifically told Danika he wanted nothing to do with readers, or smart women, stupid and pretty, that's all he'd wanted. But of course Danika did not listen, she never did.

The muscle in his jaw ticked. He squared his hips, studying the building like he would an enemy. No way in hell he'd go there. *Non!*

She'd not make him. Nostrils flaring, he sat on the edge of the path and stared at a world both similar and yet alien to his own.

A cool breeze stirred branches. Squirrels scampered up long limbed trunks, cheeks bulging with their hidden treasures. Birds flew overhead and every once in a while a car would idle slowly by.

He only knew what the metallic contraptions were because while he'd never been to Earth before, he'd seen pictures of this place. A long time ago, in a pub-- Skull and Crossbones, or maybe the Silver Dagger (who cared)-- point was, a man had walked in with a large box full of things he'd called pictures.

The man had claimed a fairy had dumped him on Earth. Of course they'd all laughed at his wild claim. Fairies wouldn't do that, especially not godmothers, t'was truly a heinous thought to imagine one of them dumping a charge within Earth's mad realm.

But the man had insisted, pulling out his box and pointing to it as proof. Gerard had dug through the box, intrigued despite himself at the frozen moment in time encapsulated within the glossy paper. He'd still not fully believed, but he'd grown a fondness for the paper, for the strangeness of the place called Earth. He'd tossed the pictures of kids and men aside, but had swiped one or two-- okay, ten-- of the one's with women on it. He'd studied the entire contents of the box, almost to the point of obsession, entranced by the foreign beauty of the Earthly realm. In no way did that mean he'd ever wanted to see it for himself.

He sighed. None would believe this.

Gerard rubbed his temples, brows drawn at the pain throbbing behind his skull and ribcage. "Bloody, damn *fee*." He groaned. What hadn't she told him? That more than anything else worried him and gnawed at his gut.

And why was she so insistent he find this Betty Hart? Didn't she see he would never mate, could never be happy with one woman? Who could? Once the beauty faded what more was there?

He'd tried once, tried to open himself to the possibility of a life with just one woman. Belle. The name alone made him want to spit. Legend made her out to be a virtuous woman, in love with a beast whose heart beat golden. He snorted. More like in love with the endless supply of coin to be had in the shaggy dog's pocket.

Though none ever believed the tale, why... because that damn book! Nothing but lies. Lies told by one very conniving godmother. The very godmother heading the tribunal for his trial. He swallowed hard. Gods his only hope was Danika's ability to convince a crowd full of angry citizens he was harmless.

He rubbed his temple. Damn, damn, damn, that orange headed tramp might cost him dearly.

Gerard glowered as the chatter of people interrupted his thoughts. A women scowled when she spotted him, a pair of brats exited the car. She hugged them to her, her frown deepened.

Gerard shuddered. He hated kids. Squawking screaming things. Too needy by half. Then a terrifying thought struck. What did Betty look like? Good gods he hoped this was not her. His pulse hammered wildly.

The woman wore bright blue glasses. What in the devil possessed her to wear that hideous color when she also sported a frizzy mane of red hair boggled his mind. But that was not the worst of it, her shirt was stained and she wore trews one size too large. A more hideous creature he'd never seen.

Her eyes widened, studying him with the wariness of prey spotting a predator. The strange creature grabbed her brats and bustled them into the library.

He rolled his eyes. Gerard would stay out here all damn day, the night even, Danika could not make him go to her. And if that'd been her, forget it. Surely the jury would return verdict soon, they'd been quickish last time. Pay some coin, apologize profusely... blah, blah, blah, and he'd been freed. This time should be no different, he'd done nothing wrong. But dread curled like a big greasy ball in the pit of his stomach. Would Galeta believe the lying tramp had tried to seduce him, would the King?

Gerard shook his head, ignoring the sick feeling. Danika would prove it and he'd be fine.

He breathed, ignored the burning pain in his shoulder and waited. Danika might even now be coming for him.

Any time now.

Chapter 3

"I hate men, a curse on all of them!" Betty growled, slamming some trashy romance into its spot on the shelf and rolled her cart to the next stop.

Trisha lifted a shapely brow. "Careful. Don't take it out on Nora." She petted the spine of the book with a small pout. "Besides, I told you James was no good. After hmm..." she tapped her chin, "oh, I don't know, the second date. Loser." Her upper lip pulled back with disgust.

"Pig," Betty joined in, "he's a...a..." Her face scrunched up when a customer glanced up with a sharp frown.

Trisha rubbed her arm and stuck her tongue out at the man. He huffed, and waddled off to a different section of the library. "That's right, sweetling. Total jerk off. But let's not scare the people with our tirade's. K?"

Betty clenched her jaw, blinking back the hot pulsing anger flowing through her gut whenever she thought about James. Even now, ten months later, she couldn't believe what an idiot she'd been. Her friends, family, they'd all told her he was scum. Always hitting on this and that person, probably even sleeping with a few-- she thought of her cousin Linda in particular, and sighed-- though none would ever admit to it.

If it was just a matter of getting over him, she wasn't sure it would be so hard. But his new girlfriend was making Betty's life a living hell. Somehow the queen B was convinced she was trying to worm her way back into James' life and was now harassing her any chance she got.

"That woman is driving me nuts, Trisha. Three freaking messages she left me. All detailing in graphic description what they do in bed and how I never did for him what she can and ugh..." Her nails dug into the palms of her hands. Not like they'd just broken up, which made the phone calls all the weirder.

"Ssh." Trisha pushed the cart away and took Pride and Prejudice out of her hands, then pulled her in for a tight hug. "That woman is an idiot and in desperate need of therapy. You ask me, I bet James is up to his old tricks and inciting her jealousy because he hasn't tossed pictures of you away or something equally idiotic. That man always did want what he couldn't have."

Betty's lips twitched and she shook her head. "Well he's not getting me back. I can't stand him. I hate him. I hate her." She trembled. "I can barely sleep, some nights I got calls back to back. And when I tell the cops all they say is she's not a danger to me and there's not a darn thing they can do about it. Men suck."

Trisha's green eyes were soft. "Oh, honey, he's so not worth it and I wish you wouldn't judge every man based off one bad seed." She gave Betty's upper arm a gentle squeeze. "But the cops are right. Gretchen's not a killer, just jealous. She knows she can't hold a candle to you and it's burning her up inside."

Betty chuckled. "You're right. I'm not fearing for my life or anything, it's just... I want to move on."

"There you go," Trisha's voice brightened. "Who knows, maybe Mr. Right is just around the corner. True love, le sigh." Trisha clapped her hands together dramatically.

"Oh yeah, true love my butt." Betty rolled her eyes. "Says the girl who can't hold down a relationship for longer than the next release of the newest Coach purse."

"Hey, do not mock the Coach." Trisha wagged a finger. "Those bags are to die for. Besides," she shrugged, "it's not like I don't want a permanent man, but I'm picky. Until I find him, I'm very happy to flirt." She winked. "Makes life worth living."

Betty grabbed another book and took a deep breath. "Yeah well, I'm so over guys."

Trisha's green eyes sparkled as she grabbed a book from the cart. "Mmm. You'll change your mind."

"I doubt it." Betty's lips thinned. Men were dogs. She'd seen enough in her twenty six years to know it was total fact. They had sex on the brain and little else.

"Excuse me," a woman's voice interrupted her thoughts. Betty turned to see a redhead standing with two boys pressed to her legs.

"Yes?" Betty asked.

"I just thought I should tell you, there's some guy sitting outside. He looks like he's gotten into a fight and he totally gives me the willies. You should probably call the cops or something."

Betty glanced at Trisha, heart sinking as their eyes met. It wasn't often they got complaints like this, but she never liked dealing with them.

"Trisha, can you?"

Trisha sighed. "Fine, I'll deal with the perv. Finish racking and stacking." She glanced at her watch. "Wanna get out of here by five. Got places to be."

Betty snorted. "You mean losers to see."

"Hey," Trisha tapped her chest, her red nails standing out bold against the crisp white of her top, "you know how it goes, one woman's trash..."

"Yeah, whatever." Betty turned around and got back to work.

Betty was halfway done when Trisha finally returned, but she was acting weird, glancing over her shoulder every five seconds with a big, goofy grin on her face. Trisha's low pitch giggle was so unlike her that Betty's brows dipped. "What in the world is wrong with you?"

Trisha fanned her flushed face as she pointed to the library sitting area. "Him. That. Boy is he a tall glass of water. And his voice," she sighed, "made me have a mini-orgasm."

"Ewww, Trish." Betty slapped her arm, but couldn't resist taking a peek. Trisha rarely lost her composure over a man that way.

And though she was hating men at the moment, that didn't mean Betty was blind. Hot was hot and she liked to look. She was surprised when all she saw was a man, scowling face all covered in scratches, staring at the kids bookshelf in front of him with the look of a man intending to do it bodily harm.

"Him?" She pointed.

Trisha licked her lips and nodded. "The voice, Betty." She grabbed her arms and shook. "He *iz*, how do you say," Trisha said in her best Lauren Bacall growl, "*zee* French." She smirked and Betty was pretty sure her friend had lost it. She'd finally cracked under the strain of late returns and the stress of cataloguing.

Betty looked back at him. Sure he was big. He shifted, his thick muscular thighs obvious behind the thin scrap of brown fabric. What in the world was he wearing anyway?

The cream shirt with the laces in front and black Santa Claus looking boots, jeez, he looked like some stupid pirate right off the pages of a Halloween Emporium magazine.

Looking beyond the stupid clothes, and the multitude of scratches and bloody lip, he was kind of okay looking.

Square jawed with a light dusting of hair. Her pulse thumped. She always did have a thing for the five o'clock shadow.

"Look at his hair," Trisha sighed.

Sighed?

Really?

Wow, Trisha had it bad.

Betty's gaze went back to him, Trisha was right though, his hair was… for lack of a better word, beautiful. All thick and wavy and brown, like a dark roasted chestnut and her fingers twitched.

As if sensing her stare he looked up.

His eyes narrowed and she stopped moving, stopped breathing. From her vantage point his eyes looked deep black. But instead of them being lifeless and flat like a shark's, they gleamed like oil in moonlight.

Her heart beat hard and her mouth went dry. Then he lifted a brow and reclined, reminding her of a loping panther the way his massive body relaxed on the chair. One large leg sprawled out, skin peeking out from behind his ripped shirt. The words power and grace popped into her head. His lips curved into a slow liquid grin and it was like getting smacked in the face.

She bristled. James had done the same thing. Thinking he was God's gift to all womankind. The bastard. She rolled her eyes and purposefully turned her back on him.

Trisha clapped her hands. "Hot, right?"

"Whatever," Betty huffed, "he's got womanizer written all over him. You can have him." She went back to work, shoving the books in with force.

Trisha sighed. "Can't. Date tonight. Too bad."

"Besides," Betty continued, irritated at herself because all she wanted to do was turn back around and look, "he's clearly violent. He's been in a fight and why haven't you called the cops, anyway?" She rounded on Trisha with a snarl.

Trisha's eyes widened and she held up her hands. "Whoa there, little lady. Slow your role. I didn't call the cops, because he's not a threat. He said he's waiting for his ride to come get him."

Betty rubbed her nose. It wasn't Trisha's fault, she knew that. It was just aggravating that even after the nightmare that was James she found herself turned on by a red hot mess. She sighed. "I'm sorry. Not your fault."

Trisha's lips thinned as she nodded.

"It's just, he's all beat up and," she sniffed, "I smell alcohol, even here. He's been in a bar fight, Trisha."

"Yeah, so? Small town, it happens." Trisha's eyes were wide.

Betty tapped the spine of a book. "The closest bar is twenty miles down the road, thataway," she pointed over her shoulder, "and secondly, drunks don't make it a habit of raiding the library afterwards."

Trisha rolled her eyes. "You worry too much. Look, I'm sure his friend is coming." She punched Betty's arm playfully. "Besides, it's not like he's here to rob us. Right? No cash." Shaking her head, she walked back to the front desk, laughing as she went.

Betty frowned and eyed the stranger hard. Trisha was right. Lebanon, Missouri was many things... big, it was not. Not like she'd know everyone in town, but she'd have noticed him.

His eyes blinked, his hard gaze never turned from her face.

"I've got my eye on you," she muttered low enough that there was no way he should have heard it five bookshelves down.

He chuckled and Betty's spine went rigid as her legs grew soft.

Stupid men.

Chapter 4

Gerard moaned as sunlight pierced his closed eyelids. He couldn't stop the groan of pain spilling from cracked lips as he rolled off the hard bench. It'd been his bed for the night. He'd expected Danika to return before the night was through. Earth hours were much shorter though than Kingdom ones and he probably shouldn't be worried, but knowing that didn't stop the uneasy knot from forming in his gut.

The sounds of chirping birds set his teeth on edge. He grabbed a rock by his foot and chucked it into the large oak full of nesting birds, they scattered with a loud squawk. Black tail feathers drifted lazily on the breeze behind them.

"Bloody, damn *fee*," he muttered and grabbed his lower back. Gods what he wouldn't give for a toothbrush and some rum.

"Oh, heck no."

He scrubbed his whiskered jaw, the sound of a woman's sharp tongue grated on his nerve sensitive skull. Gerard turned, only to stare into a pair of fine brown eyes. Very angry, fine brown eyes.

The *fille* had her arms crossed, her black hair was pulled high into a severe pony tail. She was a tall one, and nicely curved. He couldn't stop his grin when he gaze landed on a perfectly rounded pair of breasts. Too bad it was covered up by such an ugly red top.

"Hey," she snapped her fingers, "my eyes are up here, jerk."

Feisty. He looked that too. "*Exscuze-moi, Madame*. But you've a lovely pair of breasts, can you blame a man for looking?"

"I...you--" A faint red blush stole up her swan like neck and settled in her cheeks.

"Mmm," he trailed his finger up her neck, "such a lovely thing."

She slapped his hand away. "You're a pig." She stomped her slippered foot and marched around him, heading to the door with the key in her hand. "If you don't get the heck out of here, I'm calling the cops. In fact," she turned swiftly on her heels-- Medusa couldn't have been more frightening in that moment. Her black hair snapped behind her head like charmed snakes. "In fact... I've already called them." Her fingers shook as she yanked on her purse strap and pulled out a small black object, waving it at him.

Gerard leaned back on the bench, crossed his booted heels, and enjoyed the sight of a woman bluffing.

"Yeah, I called when I pulled up. I saw you." Her lips pressed into a tight line and then she shooed him. "Now, go. Go before they get here."

"Liar," he drawled.

Her entire body went stiff as a board, and then her eyes narrowed into dangerous slits. She flipped the device open. A glowing screen hooked his attention. What the devil was that thing? Did she think to scare him off with it?

Gerard bit his tongue to keep from laughing. He pushed off the bench and lazily walked up to her.

She pushed her hand further out, shaking the thing as if it were a weapon. "Get back.

I told Trisha you were dangerous. Where's your car ride? Huh? You were supposed to be gone."

He licked his lips, stopping only when he felt the heat of her body invade his own. Gerard had spent a chilly night out in the open, he'd had no food for two days, and he was royally pissed at the fairy for dropping him off in this godforsaken place. But he couldn't deny he enjoyed bantering with a beautiful woman, no matter where she hailed from.

"I noticed you yesterday."

She trembled, he knew his words affected her. Could see it in the tightening of her lips and her heavy breathing, but even so she pushed her tiny palm against his muscled chest and urged him back. She'd not make this easy.

A good tumble-- that would help ease the past night's humiliation. She was not the first damsel to pretend she did not want him.

He licked his lips and she went still. The morning was cool, crisp with the rich scent of pine and autumn leaves and now her. She smelled of flowers. Gerard touched the shell of her ear. Such a tiny exquisitely shaped thing. A diamond glinted from her lobe.

"Such a lovely creature," he moaned, his body reacting instinctively to the soft touch of feminine flesh. Already he could picture sliding her panties off with his teeth, exposing the treasure within.

Her lashes fluttered. "What... is my name?" she whispered and he laughed.

Women... always wanting to be cosseted and praised first. He grinned, nuzzling the edge of her ear, inhaling the sweat scent of soap and flowery perfume.

"*Mon petite chou*," his voice was thick with want. Gods, were his thighs trembling? He'd not ached for a woman like this in years.

He'd had beautiful women aplenty, one, two... sometimes three at a time. Gerard was not picky. But rarely did they make him weak in the knees like a lad seeing naked female flesh for the first time. He wrapped his big hands around her elegantly shaped waist and yanked her into him.

She fitted-- her every contour molding to his as if she'd been expressly made for him. He growled when she let out a tiny whimper. His cock so hard he thought he might explode from the pressure.

The woman mumbled something, but it was all nonsense in his muddled brain. The touch of her skin against the heated press of his lips was so soft, so yielding. He shivered, the intensity of his desire making him clumsy as he tugged at her shirt.

"Mmm, I'll make you weep, my beauty," he murmured, her flowery scent making him dizzy.

Her fingers slipped through his curls and he grinned as she lightly scratched his scalp. She liked it rough. So did he. Gerard fingered the bottom button of her shirt. Too much clothes, why did women always insist on covering so much?

But what had at first been gentle sex play, was now more than rough. It was pain. She wasn't simply scratching, she was clawing, gouging groves into his skin.

"Ow, damn!" He released her and grabbed the back of his head.

Those pretty lips were fixed in a permanent scowl. "Are you freaking kidding me?"

He rubbed his tender head. "What? Do you not find me attractive? I felt your body tremble."

Her eyes bugged. "First off, my name's not cabbage."

Gerard lifted a brow.

She laughed. "Oh yeah, jerk off, spent a year in Paris, I know what that mon petit chou," she mimicked his voice in singsong, "means. It's a lame, standard pet name. Everyone uses it. Especially when," she stabbed her finger in his chest, "they don't know the person's name, you bastard. Just who do you think I am? A slut?"

"Well..."

She glowered and he swallowed the yes on his tongue. Admitting that wasn't the best way to get laid. Gerard racked his brain. When was the last time a woman had rebuffed him? None, except for Belle.

His jaw clenched.

"Secondly, your breath stinks. Get a breath mint. Seriously." She rolled her eyes. "Seducing me at eight o'clock in the morning. Gah, you're so lame. Get the heck out of here, before I really do call the cops!" And with that she turned on her heels, marched to the door, and disappeared inside the library. The word made him want to gag.

Gerard balled his fists and bellowed at the top of his lungs. "Bloody hell, *fee*. Get me out of here!"

But she did not answer and she did not come.

Chapter 5

"It's raining." Trisha pouted blood red lips and glanced back out the library window.

"So?" Betty set her jaw and stamped an overdue notice on yet another envelope.

Trisha sighed. "Sweets, he's harmless."

"How the heck do you know that? He accosted me today--"

"Okay, first of all," Trisha flipped a book into her library cart and held up her hand, "he's been sitting out there all day."

Betty deliberately turned her back on the window. She wouldn't deny he looked pathetically miserable out there, sitting on the stoop, his large body shivering in the cold Missouri rain. And that maybe, just maybe, she was starting to feel kind of sorry for him. Or that his kiss had made her toes curl and that only by sheer force of will had she been able to push him off her. That she'd lied when she said his breath had stunk, the truth was he'd tasted of a fine aged brandy-- how that was possible, she had no clue. A French thing? And that even though his clothes were in tatters she'd never seen a hotter guy in her life. The shadow of his beard playing against her sensitive skin-- her stomach flopped just thinking about it.

Even bloody and bruised he'd moved that huge body with a skill unrivaled by any lover she'd ever known. Not like she'd had many, James had only been her second. But still. With just one touch he'd made her skin tingle and with a glance her blood hot, hot, hot. And the bulge in his pants... mmm, oh yes, she'd felt that too. She bit her lip, fighting the urge to look back. Knowing if she did she'd forget why she shouldn't care.

The man was dangerous. If James had been dynamite, that man was a nuclear bomb. He was a player with a capital P. Something Betty could not afford to forget.

"Secondly," Trisha continued, ticking off another finger, "who the hell speaks like that? Accosted? Seriously," her green eyes twinkled, "and you say I read too many bodice rippers."

"Whatever, Trisha. I'm going home." Betty kept glancing at the clock, seemed like the more she looked, the slower it went. She'd eyed the clock with an obsessive nature today, desperate to get away. Not from the library, but from him.

Betty had fixated over sorting, organizing the next week's activities. In short, she was all caught up with work and still had another ten minutes to go. "At seven, I'm clocking out."

There hadn't even been more than three customers today.

"Methinks the woman doth protest too much," Trisha laughed.

"What?" Betty planted her hands on her hips, feeling the tingling start of a headache burn behind her eyes.

Trisha stepped out from behind the counter, flipped the closed sign on the door and smiled. Her brown and green Sunday dress made her look young and innocent. Gorgeous, exposing her perfectly shaped calves and Betty couldn't stop wondering what he'd think if he saw her.

Had he seen her? Had he tried to hit on Trisha too? She frowned, not liking that thought one bit. Worst part of it was she didn't even know his name. Hottie McHoster? "Ugh," she moaned.

Trisha grabbed her shoulders. "Look, he's been here two days."

"So why haven't you called the cops yet?" Betty asked.

Trisha's lips quirked. "Why haven't you?"

Betty rubbed her nose. Not like she hadn't threatened it, many times. So why hadn't she?

Trisha looked over her shoulder and sighed. "He's not on private property."

Betty shook her head and stepped away from Trish to go grab her purse and rain coat. "He's loitering. Probably homeless."

She was shrugging on her jacket when Trisha flipped the lights off. "Nope," she said, "not. Have you seen his teeth? Too clean."

When had Trisha seen his teeth? Betty huffed, she so didn't care and if she kept telling herself that, maybe she'd eventually believe it.

"But he's obviously not from here. French accent, crazy clothes... I've got it!" Trisha snapped her fingers, her grin huge. "He's been shanghaied."

Betty laughed, grabbed her tube of pearl pink lip gloss and refused to analyze why she was primping when she was getting ready to run through rain. "And dropped in the middle of a landlocked state. Makes perfect sense, Trish."

Trisha snorted. "S'all I got. But whatever he is, or wherever he's from, he needs help."

A man dressed in jeans and a gray sweater knocked on the glass. He smiled and waved, exposing a big dimple in his left cheek. Betty jerked her thumb at him. "One of yours?"

Trisha sighed and buttoned up her lime green pea coat. "Young and dumb, just how I like 'em." She winked and blew an air kiss at him. "Look," she turned back toward Betty, "I know men, trust me, he's a cad. But he's not dangerous. At least take him to a hospital before he croaks on us."

Betty shook her head. "I'm not driving that man anywhere. Not alone."

The guy knocked harder.

"Really?" Betty turned and scowled at him. He jerked as if slapped and pointed to his watch.

"Yes. Yes." Trisha waved him off and fluffed her hair, applying a quick coat of mascara. "Waterproof, gotta love it." She winked. "Anyway, he needs a doctor. Call Kelly, he'll come."

"Can't," Betty shook her head, "he just finished a forty-eight hour rotation at the clinic. He's sleeps harder than the dead."

"Trishelle," the guy's voice blared through the doors, "movies. Gonna be late."

Trisha smirked and rolled her eyes, ignoring him. "Call a million times, that's what big brothers are for, to come to their baby sister's aid," she grabbed Betty's hand, "just please... don't call the cops. At least give him his dignity."

Betty bit her bottom lip. Her heart raced at the thought of letting that guy in her car-- that big powerful body cramped into her small sedan. Breathing the same air.

She gulped.

"He's just a harmless bastard sitting in the rain." Trisha tapped Betty's chin. "Have mercy on him. You know where the shelter's at right?"

Betty lifted a brow. "You know I do. Do you?"

Trisha giggled. "Nope. That's why you're the perfect person to go drop him off!" With a wink and a wave, Trisha joined her impatient date. Betty licked her lips.

All day she'd pretended he wasn't out there, and it was easy to do with work to be done. But now she was going to walk past him and there would be no ignoring him then.

Then don't look, can't miss what ya don't see-- her grandma Nani's sage words suddenly sprang to mind. Advice she'd given Betty the night she'd wept on her fragile shoulder's about James dumping her and spotting him shopping for groceries at her grocery store. The last bit of advice her grandmother had given her, she'd died in her sleep two nights later. Betty sighed.

"Yeah. Won't look. Totally." She gripped the strap of her purse like a shield and exited the library, locking the door behind her.

The blast of chilly air up her jacket broke her out in a wash of goose bumps. This morning it'd been sunny without a cloud in the sky. Now, the weather was downright nasty. The unofficial slogan of Missouri: Wait around long enough, it'll change. And boy had it, it now felt like ten degrees shy of freezing.

Her skin tingled, but not from the cold. He was looking at her. She felt the heated press of his eyes like a hot brand.

"Don't look." She kept her eyes down and her head low as she ran down the sidewalk, rain smacked her in the face like tiny needles and she winced. This was a miserable night to be out. Where would he sleep this time?

Betty bit her lip and all her plans went to pot when she glanced over her shoulder. He wasn't looking at her as she'd expected, instead, he was looking at the old tree and wearing the fiercest scowl she'd ever seen.

He had his arms wrapped around his body and jeez... she just couldn't do it. She'd never treat a homeless person this way, she wouldn't do it with him either.

Betty marched back to him, stopping only when she got to the bench. This was so dumb. What if he was a deranged lunatic? People didn't just sit outside for two days, sleep on a park bench overnight even-- without some serious issues.

"What?" he growled, turning his frosty glare on her. "Come to crow some more?"

Her lips tipped and she held her purse over her head, trying to ward off the rain-- but it was useless, rain ran down the back of her neck and under her jacket. She shivered. "Look, you shouldn't be out here tonight. Don't you have some place to go? Somebody to stay with?"

And though his bottom lip was still healing, and looked angry and swollen where it'd been busted, he still had the most sensual lips she'd ever seen. Her stomach fluttered remembering the feel of them this morning.

Betty glanced at the dark green sky. This was tornado country, it wasn't unheard of to have twisters come down unexpectedly and wreak havoc out of the seeming blue.

That's when she heard it-- the soft ping of hail hitting asphalt. She winced. They had seconds before they started getting pelted too.

"Dammit," she grabbed his hand and tugged, "come on!"

She knew he could shake her off if he wanted to, but he didn't. It was a two hundred yard sprint to her car and by the time they'd made it to her beat up Toyota, she'd already been waylaid by four golf ball sized chunks of ice.

"*Enfer*," he growled, "what type of sorcery is this? Ice from the sky?"

Betty heard his mutters, wondered at the strangeness of it, and just as quickly dismissed it. The man was nuts and she needed to get him away from here and away from her. The sooner the better. She shoved her key in the lock, wishing yet again for the funds to buy a car with an automatic unlock button and swung her door open just as another cold stone bit into her cheek.

She muttered as she reached over to unlock his side.

His big frame took up all the passenger space and then some. His knees pressed tight to the dash and his arms were bent at the shoulders, large hands in his lap. He looked like a sardine in a tin can, but a sardine had never looked so sexy.

She laughed. She couldn't help it. It bubbled up from her belly and spilled from her mouth. At first he scowled harder, which of course, only made her laugh harder.

Then his lips twitched. "This is ah... comfortable?"

She snorted and grabbed a napkin out of her purse to mop up some of the wetness dripping from the tips of her bangs. "You look--" She shook her head. "It's all your fault."

The stern lines framed his eyes again.

"Who told you to get so big anyway?" she teased.

Once he seemed to realize she wasn't mocking him, he visibly relaxed and the sexy as sin grin tipped the corners of his mouth, killing her laughter instantly.

Gorgeous. So gorgeous. Heat settled in her cheeks, and she shifted on her wet car seat, trying to ignore the sudden heat slithering down her belly through her thighs.

Betty distracted herself by glancing in the rearview mirror, pretending to dry off, to try and forget her reckless attraction to the man.

But it was useless, and so was drying off. She needed to get home and change. She tossed the crumpled napkin onto the dash and cranked the car. Blasting the air to heat, she sighed as the warmth penetrated through her chilly skin.

They drove in silence. She glanced at him from the corner of her eye, but he was looking out the window with a grim set to his stubbled jaw.

Betty licked her lips. Wanting to hear some sort of sound, she clicked on her stereo and groaned when the childish blare of "*I love you. You love me...*" crackled through her speakers.

He curled his nose, his eyes wide with horror, and she giggled. "Umm... oops, Briley's tape. Forgot he left that here." She popped the cassette tape out and switched it to FM. Some song about '*I want to rock your body all night long*' came on and she sighed. Not much better. She turned the volume down until it was nothing but background noise.

Betty drummed her fingers on the steering wheel, easing through the empty Leba*non* streets, headed toward her brother's house. He might not wake up for a phone call, but he'd wake up if she pounded on the door.

"Who's Briley?" McHotster asked, his voice low and growly.

A crime how sexy that was, and how much she wished she could hear it in the morning. She shook the silly thought aside, shifting gears to slow down for the red light.

She looked at him, he was looking back out the window. "He's my nephew." She smiled. "He's going to be eleven next week."

He didn't say anything. Betty bit her lip, tasting the strawberry sweetness of her lip gloss.

"I wouldn't have been caught dead listening to such infantile music at that age," he mumbled and she bristled. He didn't know, and that was the only thing that stayed her tongue.

She counted to ten before she trusted herself to speak. "I don't even know your name."

He looked back at her, his eyes wary. "And that's a problem because?"

Her eyes widened and she gripped the wheel until her knuckles whitened, but she was proud her voice did not betray her shock at his blunt way. She turned left, heading down the tiny two lane country road toward her brother's one bedroom farm house. Trees, appearing like black specters in the moonlight, framed either side of the road. The rain had trickled down to a fine mist and it felt like driving through a fairy tale. The teal and navy blue sky twinkled with starlight, the full moon filled the sky like a giant golden orb.

Her heart sped with the driving thought that this was a great place to be abducted and raped. Fear turned her words sharp.

"Look, I'm trying to be a good Samaritan here. I could have just called the cops, but I didn't. You've been loitering on our grounds, scaring away the customers and I just want to know the name of the man who--" Betty gasped, and then paused, realizing her near mistake. What she'd almost said, almost admitted.

The tilt of his head and narrowing of his eyes spoke volumes. She scrunched down on the seat, stepping harder on the gas.

"Who what?" His accent went supersonic gravelly and her nipples hardened. Betty felt like one of Pavlov's dogs-- ring a bell and it's time for food-- except in this case it was hear that deep French burr and her body tingled with a hot rush of sexual arousal. *Gah*, she'd never been so turned on by the sound of a man's voice before.

He shifted his muscular frame and she hated how aware of him she was. His clothes were still the same horrible things from the day before, ripped, tattered, and sexy as hell. She bit her tongue and his eyes danced with light.

"Turned you on," he said, his finger trailed feather light along the back of her hand and she jerked the wheel hard to the left, the tires squealed as she pulled to the side of the road. Her pulse thundered in her ears.

Perfectly shaped teeth bit his perfectly shaped lips and...

"I could smack you!" Betty parked her car and flicked his hand off. "Do you always have to get so... so, grabby? Ugh!" She wrapped her arms around herself.

Cocky arrogance touched his face and she gnashed her teeth. Had she learned nothing from James?

"Don't tell me you don't like my touch, *femme vipere*. I tasted the sweetness of your surrender, you lie to say you do not."

Angry, ashamed, she panted for breath as her nails dug into her palms. "One, don't call me a viper. So not the way to get on my good side. Two--"

He raised his brow, seeming more amused by her than offended. She trembled, but she wasn't exactly sure it was just from rage because he was leaning in again. Absorbing all the oxygen in her bubble, the heat of his body snapped across her skin with the shock of static.

"T... two," she stuttered and he pushed his finger against her lips.

"Has anyone ever told you, you've the voice of a harpy--" Betty sucked in a sharp breath, "but the lips of a succulent sweet fruit?" He said the last with his lips feathering across hers and she was going to slap him.

Any second now.

"I... I." Was all she got out when his lips pressed hard and firm and with a desperate moan she opened her mouth, hating him, herself, and all of mankind.

His large hands framed her face, so gentle and warm while his mouth plundered hers. His tongue swept in and she tasted him and how he tasted of brandy and cherry pipe smoke, she'd never know and at the moment, could give a rat's patootie. All she knew was she wanted more.

Betty nipped at his lip and though he hissed, he didn't pull back and neither did she. What was he doing to her? She wrapped her hands around the back of his head, twining his thick wet hair around her fingers. Now he was running his big hand down her arm and somehow, he'd unbuttoned her jacket and was now stroking the front of shirt. Touching her, molding his fingers around her heavy breasts and she flexed her body, opening up to him.

A sound like a whimper rang in her ears. She struggled to pinpoint where it came from only to start with a jerk when his fingers slipped under the hem of her shirt. His touch burned a path straight to her aching core.

There went that whimper again and this time she was startled to realize it was coming from her. She pushed against his chest, his muscle slid beneath her palm and it was a little bit of torture to push him away.

She squeezed her eyes shut, leaning her forehead against his as she struggled for breath. "You can't keep doing that."

"Gerard." He said simply and sat back.

"Do what?" Betty looked at him. His hair poked up where she'd twirled it. He scrubbed a fist down his face.

"My name. It's Gerard." He didn't breath heavy, his face was calm, and without the slightest hint that he suffered the same internal turmoil she did. He'd rocked her world, she might as well have been a weed in his garden for all that he noticed her.

She licked her lips, still tasting him. "No last name?"

He growled, shoving his fingers like forks through his messy hair. And though he still bore bruises and looked frightening as hell when he scowled, Betty knew James had nothing on Gerard. This man was a woman's wet dream made manifest.

"I'm not asking for your hand, *Madam*. Why do you insist on knowing me?"

Aaand now she could think again. "Wow, you really are a jerk. Oh no wait," she tapped her jaw, "you're a misogynistic jerk. Twice now you've shoved your tongue down my throat..."

Gerard snorted. "You're not the one who bares the love marks." He patted the back of his head. "I'd say you were shoving that delicious tongue of yours down my throat as much or more." He sat back, and though cramped, he still managed to look like a king relaxing on his throne.

Anytime Betty got mad as a kid, her dad would always tease and say, *'watch that one percent, Betty, its explosive'*. One percent meaning the negligible drop of Panamanian blood flowing through her veins, that hot Latin temper that could spark a flame with just one word. Normally, she could breathe through it, but not tonight, not with him.

"Fine, you wanna play that game, fine. Yes, I think you're hot. Beyond hot. You're every girl's wet fantasy come true."

His smile grew wider and she could just see that already enormous ego inflating.

"You're also a pig..."

He frowned.

"A stranger, and if it wasn't for the fact that my mom raised me to help those less fortunate than myself, I'd have left your sorry ass back there."

"Ah." He flicked his wrist in a gesture of dismissal. "Leave me, take me, I don't give a damn. I'll be gone soon and then I won't have to worry about you, this world, or any other damn stupid, meddlesome, conniving..."

She froze, latching onto one thing. "What do you mean this world?" Betty had seen first-hand the effects of suicide on a family. Was that why he'd been sitting out there for two nights? Contemplating his end? He didn't seem the type, but then again, neither had Trisha's sister. Sometimes you could never tell.

He shrugged. "You wouldn't believe me if I told you."

Betty eyed the beefy Frenchman. Not able to understand one bit her burgeoning obsession with the man. "Try me," she dared him with lifted brow.

"*Non.*" Gerard went back to staring out the window and though she didn't know him from Adam, she was pretty sure if he said '*non*' than it was no. "Leave me, or let us go. I care not," he muttered. That more than anything proved his non-dangerous status.

Weird, yes. Hot, without a doubt. A knife wielding psycho-- probably not.

Suddenly it seemed pointless to drive out to her brother's. He'd be dead to the world, exhausted from his long shift, and not a little ticked off with her for bringing a big burly man to his doorstep just to dump him off so she could appease her conscious. Not to mention the fact that she suddenly felt an inexplicable urge to keep Gerard by her side.

He was probably spouting off nonsense, with no intention of killing himself, but she'd always promised herself that if she should ever be able to help someone contemplating suicide, she'd do it.

With a long sigh, suddenly exhausted and more than ready for a long, hot soak, she started her engine and turned the car back toward town.

She expected him to ask where she was headed. But he didn't speak another word for the five miles it took them to get to her townhouse.

She punched in her code to open the gate and pulled into her assigned parking spot.

"C'mon," she huffed, grabbing her purse.

He looked around with pursed his lips, and with a powerful heave, managed to extract himself from the car.

Betty walked to her bright red door, potted plants lined her stoop. "Home sweet home," she said, swinging the door open and stepping back to let him in.

"This is your home, then?"

She bit her lip. Maybe it hadn't been the right thing to bring him here. But apart from Trisha, she didn't really have that many friends. What if he thought she was asking for a booty call?

Her cheeks flamed at the thought and she muttered a quick explanation. "It's late, and I thought maybe you'd like some dinner."

His face lit up like a little boy's on Christmas morning. "Gods yes," he groaned, "I could eat a horse."

Chapter 6

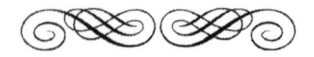

The *fille* looked around like a cornered rabbit, darting quick glances over his shoulder, over hers, as if uncertain of her decision to bring him into her home.

"I'll not kill you if that's your worry," he said with a grin.

She stopped moving, her brown eyes widened and she held up her hands as if to ward him off. "Why did you say that? I didn't think that. Did I make you--"

Her voice had shot to a high pitched squeak and he pressed his finger to her lips, stilling her. Gerard found himself intrigued by the quirky proud woman who reeked of fear and yet stood her ground. Not that he wouldn't mind a quicker capitulation than this-- but he'd learned the prize was often made sweeter by the chase.

"*Mon petite*," he traced the line of her heart shaped chin with his thumb, his body responding to the barely discernible trembles running through her, "women are like a fine wine, meant to be savored slowly and often."

Her ears blushed a deep shade of pink, Gerard chuckled and touched the hot tips; he'd never known a woman's ears could flush scarlet.

She grabbed his hand, stopping his caress and her voice was a low throaty chuckle. He knew women, knew when they were sexually aroused and though her lips said no, her body told the true story.

"Frenchmen and their wine, next thing you'll be telling me is I taste of escargot."

He wrapped his hand around the finger she pointed into his chest. "And butter. Don't forget the butter," he teased, "escargot, wine, and butter."

"The French trinity." She snorted and the curve of her luscious lips told him she fought the laugh. "I brought you here to eat, to have a warm bed for one night. That's all. No seductions." She stepped out of his arms. "One night, Gerard. Period. So don't get too cozy here."

Gerard smiled. But it wasn't just any smile, it was the slow spread of lips, the narrowing of eyes, and the tilt of his chin that he used like a weapon against her. He'd won many hearts by simply being patient.

"As you say, *Madam*," he purred; his raspy growl grew even deeper and caused her pupils to dilate.

Let the woman believe herself in charge. That was the trick. Make her feel secure in her power and she'd never know the seduction had ever happened until she was in bed with him. By that point she no longer cared about nonsense like roses and words of affirmation. She'd take whatever he gave, but what he gave was plenty good. None had ever been less than satisfied. At least in that, Gerard succeeded.

She bit her bottom lip. The lass was truly delicious, a tempting mix of minx and innocence. His heart beat hard at the thought of finally making her his.

"What is your name?" Why was he asking that? He didn't care. Truly. It didn't matter and yet his entire body tingled with the need to know. This had to be Betty Hart, of all the women he'd seen, only she intrigued him on a visceral level.

Her lips quirked. "If you're nice, maybe I'll tell you."

Gerard grinned, did she sass him now? How very interesting.

"After dinner." And with that, she turned on her heels. "I'm dripping water all over the floor and so are you. Let me get us some clothes and then we can start thinking about what to do for dinner."

***

"Wow," she pushed her plate away and rubbed her belly, "where did you learn to cook like that?"

"A woman," he said, stabbing another red potato on his fork before popping it in his mouth.

She twirled her glass of red wine between slim fingers. "Ah, of course."

He swallowed and nodded. "Food is not the way to a man's heart, it's the other way around. Men don't care if beef is boiled, grilled, or sautéed. No," he shook his head, "so long as it's warm and fills our belly, we're content. But a woman..." he licked his lips eyeing her chest. The tight fit of her gray top outlined her rounded breasts to perfection, making him hungry for something other than the smoked cod on his plate. "Cook for her and she's all yours." He held out the palm of his hand.

She leaned back, lifted her foot on the chair and rested her hand on her knee. "You're a dangerous man to know, Gerard. Somehow I don't think many women get to walk away from you with their heart intact."

Wine had loosened her tongue, gave her a becoming pink flush to her cheeks, and Gerard wanted her with a mounting desire that bordered on the insane. She wore a pair of checkered boxers, so masculine, but not on her. Not with the long expanse of creamy legs peeking out beneath and the tight fitting top-- there could be no mistaking she was pure woman.

His cock stirred. It'd been days since his last tup. Desperately wanting to adjust himself, he resisted the urge, not wanting her to realize just how badly he wanted her.

She licked her lips, her lids were slightly heavy, lazily opening and closing. He ground his jaw, no longer even tasting his food. With a growl, Gerard swiped the bottle of red off the table and filled his glass for the third time and chugged.

Either he got himself thoroughly smashed, or he'd make a move on her, and he knew she wasn't ready. Not yet. He did it now and he'd never get another chance.

"Rented a movie last night," she slurred a little.

"You're a featherweight, *mon cherie*. Perhaps you shouldn't drink more."

She hiccupped and then giggled, covering her mouth. "Don't drink usually. Love it," she drawled, "but drinking alone makes one a drunk." She nodded as if to punctuate her statement.

Gerard took the glass from her hand, she pouted, and bloody hell he was close to shooting off in his pants. Pants he'd still not changed out of.

She'd brought him clothes earlier, something she'd mentioned a prior beau owning. The idea had settled like a brick in his gut, he'd not wear the clothes of another lover. Gerard didn't follow, he led.

Thank the gods they were sitting, otherwise she'd notice the tent in his pants for sure.

"Indeed, beauty." He gently grabbed the stem of the crystal glass and took it from her.

She made a grab for it and he shook his head.

"I do believe you'd be very unhappy with yourself in the morning if you went to bed drunk with a big, straping," he grinned, "virile..."

She snorted.

"Handsome man in your house," he finished.

She laughed. "Only two glasses."

He shook his head. "*Non, belle*, this was the third and," he glanced at the half empty crystal, "it's almost empty."

She wagged her finger. "You. You. You." She touched the tip of his nose and it was a bloody torture to remain seated and not grab her, pull her to his lap and fondle every inch of her luscious body. Her eyes went blank for a moment, then she blinked and finished her thought. "Make me nervous with all your '*non*' and *mon petite chou*'ing and," she sighed, "I hate players. Hate them and you're just so you and I'm me," she ran her hand down her body and now her chuckle started to wobble with the first hint of tears and he groaned.

Gods why had he urged her to bring out the wine? Beautiful or not, he could not deal with a woman's tears, made him jittery and anxious to get away.

She sighed and shook her head, the smile back in place. "Rented a movie."

His eyes widened. "Yes," he pounced on her words.

She frowned. "Did I ask a question? I don't remember asking a question."

"Bloody hell, woman," Gerard mumbled, louder he said, "*Non*. You did not ask, but yes, I'd like to see this movie." He tasted the word, the crazy man in the bar that long ago night had talked on and on about talking pictures, Gerard was fairly certain a movie was that thing. He was curious despite his misgivings of spending too much time alone with a drunk woman who had uppity morals when sober.

She flipped hair out of her eyes. "Beauty and the Beast," she snickered and he went still as a corpse. "Best non Anime movie ever. I mean I know it's a cartoon, but it's my favorite. Usually Briley comes to spend the nights and it's his favorite too." She stood. "Want to watch it with me?"

Gerard licked his teeth, fire burned in his gut and he shoved his plate away. "What is your name?"

She pursed her lips. "Ohh," she mock shuddered, "so growly. I don't know..." she tapped her chin.

"Argh," he flicked his wrist and standing, grabbed their dishes, depositing them in the sink. "Forget it."

She wiggled her brows. "You're hooked on me. Admit it."

"You're a woman," he said.

The woman was crazy, drunk, and hell if she sighed once more and lifted those breasts any higher he'd forget his fledgling morals and rip the shirt off her. Gerard gripped the sink. "Name?"

She stuck her tongue out and stood to wobbly feet. Her eyes bugged as she laughed. "Grounds a little rolly, no?"

"*L'enfer sanglant*, woman. Why do you keep wine in the house if you can't handle it?" Gerard walked to her side, grabbing her elbow as he led her to the living room. She was going to smash her face in.

She wrinkled her nose and glanced down. "Bloody hell to you too and you have sexy hands. You know that. I bet you do. I bet women throw themselves at you, right? Jeez, I'm drunk. I'm never drunk... did you do that?"

He rolled his eyes. "*Non*. You're a closeted lush that can't handle her spirits."

She snorted. "Betty Hart."

Gerard pushed her down onto the couch, she did a little mewling sound in the back of her throat and snuggled her face into the cushions. Gods the woman had the sexiest legs he'd ever seen. Endlessly long and curvy, toned, and a pale luscious cream. He growled, and shoved his fingers through his hair. Blood pooled in his aching cock, and he took two steps back. But he still smelled her flowery perfume everywhere, and now she was yawning, stretching her arms high above her head, and baring her smooth belly-- and it wasn't enough. He needed distance, space.

She was drunk.

Gerard had few moral hang-ups, sexing up a drunkard was one of them. His nails dug into the palms of his hands.

She eyed him. "Did you hear me?"

"Yes, damn you. I heard your name. Where's your shower?"

Betty's eyes crinkled at the corners, and she pointed behind him. "Down the hall, and you're really rude. Why did I bring you home? I'm a single woman, this is so stupid. And why am I drunk? Again, so stupid."

She grabbed her forehead and muttered under her breath and she was right... so stupid. Because right now Gerard wanted to strip her, himself, and make her come until she screamed.

With a groan he turned on his heels and headed toward the shower. The colder the better.

"*Fee*," he muttered, "come get me now."

This time the air around him shuddered with a pop of pressure and he knew Danika had finally heard. Thank the gods, one more night around Betty and he'd lose any vestige of chivalry. It was time to go home, to the waiting arms of a lover who expected nothing more from him than a no-strings attached romp and away from the maddening temptation of Betty's viperous tongue.

Chapter 7

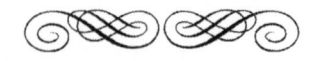

Betty knew on some level that she was in trouble. A. She should never have brought him home. B. She most definitely should not have had that third glass. She'd known after two glasses she was just shy of buzzy. But Gerard had made her more nervous than she'd thought possible.

The dull sound of running water echoed down her hall, and she grabbed her furry pink throw blanket off the back of the couch, cuddling down into it. The man was huge, gorgeous, and he was staying in her house.

What the hell had she been thinking? In what universe would she EVER do something like this? Betty had always been the designated driver, even in college-- she'd known she couldn't handle any type of liquor. Hell, everyone knew that. If she went to a bar, it was virgin's all the time.

She closed her eyes.

Gerard would be naked. She licked her lips. Soaping that hot, hard body of his. His long fingers stroking the length of his thick, bulging...

Panting, she snapped her eyes open. Oh man, she totally could not think that. It was too easy to picture the water sluicing down his rock hard abs. Not that she'd seen him without a shirt on, but no one that yummy would ever sport anything other than a six pack. The man screamed gym rat.

Heart racing, pulse pounding, and her thighs tingling with a powerful need to stroke herself she grabbed the D.V.D. off the coffee table and slowly made her way to the TV. She popped the movie in and settled back. A cartoon, that would kill the wicked voice in her head demanding she go join him.

But she couldn't focus on it. She'd seen the movie at least five hundred times by this point. She basically knew it line by line. But it failed to keep her attention. Thirty minutes into it, she kept glancing at the empty doorway with a profound longing for him to return.

How long did it take him to shower? What exactly was the man doing? She strained, lifting up on her knees to peek around the corner. This was her house, she could totally walk down the hall without making him think she did it because of him. But yeah, her butt wasn't moving. With her luck she'd trip and fall in front of the bathroom door just as he opened it and she'd catch a glimpse of... She shook her head. *No, stop that Betty.* She bit the corner of her lip and then crossing her arms, turned her back on the hallway and scowled at the blurry screen. She'd taken her contacts out earlier and she needed to put on her glasses.

Normally she had no problem grabbing them, but the black horn-rimmed glasses-- while comfortable-- were far from sexy. Not that she should give that a second thought.

"Ugh," she swiped her case out of the basket next to the couch and plopped them on, who cared what he thought so long as she didn't get a headache.

Betty focused on the screen, soon lost in the story and giggling when Beast acted like his beastly self--snarling at poor Belle for exploring the wrong side of the castle. She could totally picture Gerard acting the same way, all snarly and proprietary and her heart pounded wondering why she was so damn intrigued.

Maybe because he was big and French and she'd had a major thing for French men in college. Betty had jumped at the chance to study abroad for a year, especially when she'd discovered she'd be staying in gay Paris. She'd been wildly disappointed though.

Not because of the land, it was beyond beautiful. Or the food even, the food had been nothing short of heaven. But she'd not experienced a passionate French affair, her only regret.

She tapped her foot, bouncing it in rhythm to the song as she glanced over her shoulder again. "Where is he?"

Sure she'd told him no seduction, but he didn't need to be so literal about it and stay away completely.

"Trying to forget you, my dear."

Betty's eyes bugged and she twirled around, making the room spin for a split second and giving herself a wicked case of vertigo. She grabbed her stomach and couldn't even squeak out a sound at the sight of a doll sized woman hovering in front of her.

Her hair was blonde, piled in large curls atop her head and threaded through with a string of... well, it looked like dew. Like perfect miniature dew drops shimmering in mother of pearl. Her wings were a see through, blue-tinted gossamer color. Reminding Betty more of dragonflies wings than a butterfly's. She had an open face, not breathtakingly gorgeous, but friendly.

Betty rubbed her eyes. "I know I'm not that drunk."

The fairy-- who'd been tapping her blue star tipped wand in into the palm of her hand-- lifted a brow. "Oh is that it? Well, I can fix that right up."

Before Betty had a moment to gather her thoughts in protest, pink lightning arced from the wand and encircled her head. Her heart raced as she breathed in ozone tinted air, the breath burned her nose with mini volts of shivering current. And like a balloon popping, the wine laced stupor she'd been in vanished in an instant.

She yelped and scooted to her feet. "Gerard!" She screamed. There'd been no thought to call Gerard, pure instinct drove her to yell for him, wanting him suddenly near her. "Come here. Come quick."

The fairy grinned. "First name basis, already? How splendid!" She rubbed her hands. "I knew you were the one."

"What?" Gerard's thick burr snared Betty's gaze, she pointed at the fairy, ready to demand if he saw her too or if she'd totally lost her mind, but the words died.

"You're...you're--"

Water puddled at his feet. His very bare feet. She licked her lips, mentally chanting at herself not to look up. Black springy hair covered extremely muscular calves, and his thighs... she gulped, like a cedar trees.

Even the girlie pink towel he'd wrapped around his waist could not detract from the sheer male beauty of him. Something thick and halfcocked bulged from behind it and her stomach flopped.

"*Cherie?*" he questioned again and she jerked, realizing she'd been gawking like an awkward teen. His eyes glimmered with a knowing light and when he bit his bottom lip, she knew he knew what she'd been peeking at. "Say the word, love, and the towel comes off."

Her cheeks flamed.

"Oh gods," the bell like voice dripped disgust, "you are a fine piece of work, Gerard. Does that ever work?"

His body tensed and he shoved off the wall. "*Fee*, you damn..."

The fairy circled in front of Betty and wagged her finger. "Uh, uh. Mind your words, *mon ami*."

His mouth snapped shut, but his eyes narrowed into twin slits. That's when Betty knew she wasn't nuts. Either they were having a shared hallucination or this fairy was real.

Betty's smile faltered when the fairy turned toward her.

"Well, what do you think?" she pointed at Betty while talking to Gerard, "beautiful like you like them. She can string a sentence together, and best of all she knows nothing of your colorful past."

"*Fee*," Gerard snarled, cutting her off. He sauntered into the middle of Betty's living room, one hand gripping the edges of the towel together, the other flexing like he wanted to strike something.

The dichotomous image of a hulking man wrapped in fluffy pink made Betty want to laugh, even while she also wanted to drag him to her bedroom and scratch the itch he'd started the moment she'd spotted his cocky self lounging in her library.

"Wait," Betty pinched the bridge of her nose, "what's going on here? Who's that?" She pointed to the flying fairy and jeez... that sounded weird just thinking it.

"That's Danika--" Gerard said.

"Fairy Godmother Extraordinaire," the fairy said with a snap of her head.

"I'll be honest," Betty chuckled, "this is so not what I expected when I brought you home with me. I'd swear you laced my brownies with weed, except we didn't have any and could somebody please explain what the heck's going on here!" Betty did always tend to talk too much when she got nervous, and right now she was about as nervous as she'd ever been.

Danika took a deep breath, her friendly smile growing even wider, which was just creepy as hell. In theory coming face to face with a doll sized fairy seemed cool, in reality... not so much. Betty had no desire to go through pink electroshock 2.0, thank you very much, once had been more than enough. The thing might be small, but she packed a punch.

"My dear," the fairy's voice filtered through the room like a choir of bells, "I promise to answer all your questions, but first I must needs speak with Gerard. If you could give us some privacy please?"

Betty's eyes bugged. Was she freaking kidding? A stranger-- fairy or no-- coming into her house and asking her to leave? Yeah-freaking-right. She crossed her arms.

Gerard shook his head. "Her house, she can stay." His voice was calm, but there was an undercurrent of nerves Betty had never heard from him before. For reasons unknown, her stomach sank with a horrible sense that all was not well.

"So?" he asked, his knuckles blanched white.

Danika looked down at the carpet, and Betty rocked on her heels as anxiety riddled her gut. It was obvious she was intruding on something personal. But the compulsion to know over rode any desire to give them privacy. She tip-toed closer.

"Stay," Gerard commanded, obviously thinking she meant to leave. He didn't turn to look at her, his unswerving gaze stayed put on the fairy.

"I've been given a brief reprieve to meet with you first. Galeta the Blue herself comes to hand down verdict, Gerard."

He scrubbed his face, and his silence was deafening. Betty's heart beat so hard she was sure they heard it.

"They did not believe me then?" he asked in a flat tone of voice.

Danika didn't answer, but apparently she didn't need to, because Gerard nodded. The little fairy glanced over at Betty. "My dear, I'm truly sorry for what is about to transpire. I do what I must, but always know it is for the good. Trust that. Please."

Betty didn't even have a moment to ask what, or contemplate the cryptic statement before a loud whooshing sound poured through the stillness. A dazzling blue light seared Betty's retinas, and she blinked against the sudden onslaught of tears.

Another fairy hovered beside Danika when the light finally faded. Her shoulders were rigid, and though her skin still held the firmness of youth, there was an ancientness to her presence that Betty felt in every nerve of her body.

The fairy could only be Galeta the Blue, and it was obvious from one glance why she'd been named that. Her eyes were the blue of an arctic ice tunnel, clear and mesmerizing. The dress she wore sparkled like ice refracted in sunlight, and on her head was a large golden crown dripping with sapphires. But it was the blue ringlets of hair framing her head in a wild halo that really drew Betty's eye.

"Gerard," Galeta intoned, his name rolled from her tongue with the steely reverberations of a bottomless echo. "I've come to pass judgment."

Beside her Danika trembled, and Betty would bet anything it wasn't with fear. The tiny woman literally had steam rolling from her ears.

For a fact, Betty had never seen anything more bizarre in her life. A whole new world of weird was opening up before her eyes and all she could do was stare like a mindless drone, hypnotized like one watching a car wreck unfold.

"The tribunal convened," that deeply feminine voice thundered, "and you've been found guilty."

Gerard, who'd been silent, now growled. "You know it's not true. Glean my memory if you must, fairy," he pleaded, but the tiny blue woman gave him a wicked smile, made all the more sinister coming from the china doll beauty.

Betty swallowed when Gerard grabbed her hand, squeezing hard and making her wince.

Her heart stuttered, what was going on here? Who was this demon fairy and what did they want with him?

Then those glacial blue eyes turned to her, and the smirk became a full-fledged grin dripping with malice and spite. "Is this the mate you spoke of, Danika?"

Mate?

"Yes," Danika squeaked.

Betty jerked as if slapped. "What? Whoa." She took a step back, holding up her free hand. "What's going on here?"

Galeta flew toward Betty, stopping inches from her face, forcing Betty to take another step back just so that she could see her without being forced to cross her eyes.

"Ugly creature you are," Galeta spat by her foot.

"Hey!" Betty cried.

Gerard squeezed her hand again, and stepped part ways in front of her. As if to shield her.

"Galeta, the verdict, if you please," Danika spoke up, her voice projecting a calm Betty most definitely did not feel.

Right now Betty kept imagining plucking Galeta the freak's massive electric blue butterfly wings off her back and permanently grounding her. Ugly! She'd give that fairy ugly.

"*Veritas*, Gerard Caron, that is your sentence."

He stiffened, his entire body went so still Betty feared he'd had a heart attack. Danika closed her eyes.

"Bound you will be for one month. Slave to her whims..." While Galeta spoke, she twirled her wand, a blue spray of light coalesced into a tight ball. Rolling like a wave on top of itself, faster and faster.

Betty planted herself square in front of Gerard. A split second impulse she immediately regretted when Galeta's hard glacial stare turned on her. Galeta's smile revealed baby fangs, and Betty's knees knocked so hard she thought she might pass out.

"Indeed she must be your mate to throw herself in front of you like that," Galeta sneered.

"Not... no," Betty gulped, unable to even finish the thought.

The light faded, and a floating silver necklace with a black heart shaped pendant dangled before her eyes. Galeta snatched it, the pendant was twice the size of her head-- but the fairy hefted it as it weighed no more than a feather. She buzzed around Betty.

Betty twisted as the fairy slammed the pendant against Gerard's naked chest. He hadn't moved. But his jaw flexed, and the muscle in his cheek ticked as his dark blue eyes burned holy fury.

"Bound," Galeta continued.

As she spoke, the black pendant swirled with bands of thick crimson and swirls of liquid gold. A blue light pulsed from around Gerard's chest where the pendant rested. His teeth clenched, the spasms of his muscles traveled through Betty's palm. Beads of sweat popped out on his brows. But he didn't mutter a sound of protest.

Betty hugged his arm to her chest wanting to ease his obvious pain.

"So mote it be." When Galeta recited those words, Betty's skin tingled and all the fine hairs on her body stood up.

Gerard dropped her hand. Betty wanted to ask him what had just happened. She'd seen it, but she'd understood nothing. But he was like a live wire. Anger spit off him like exploding bits of hot shrapnel, and Betty winced, not wanting to draw his ire in her direction. His eyes were flat, hard, and almost black, burning into Galeta with murderous intentions.

For her part, the fairy seemed completely oblivious. Or uncaring, which was more likely the case. She turned and held the necklace out to Betty. "It's yours. Enjoy it." As she made to pass it to Betty's outstretched hand, she snapped her wand out and pointed directly at Gerard's manhood. "*Mortuus*!" she boomed, and a bright burst of blue engulfed the lower half of his body like flames.

"Gerard," Betty cried when he fell to his knees with a loud grunt.

"Galeta, by the goddess," Danika screamed, "what have you done?"

Gerard's back bowed so hard Betty thought his spine might crack. His bellow of pain shook the frame of her house.

Then the light died and Galeta smirked. "Vengeance is sweet." She turned glowing eyes on Betty and tossed the pendant at her. Betty jumped out of the way, fearing the thing might burn her. Instead she wrapped her arms around Gerard's back, he heaved, and like someone experiencing electroshock therapy, his every muscle twitched. Betty grabbed his face. A grayish pallor tinted the lines around his mouth.

"Look at me," she cooed, trying to get him to focus on something other than the pain, "ssh, that's good. That's good." She petted him in a soothing up and down motion on his back. Finally lucidity stared back at her instead of pain.

He gripped her wrist.

"Pathetic," Galeta whispered one final word of hate before vanishing in a puff of blue smoke.

"I'm fine," he said, jaw tight and working back and forth. "Fine." He stood, leaning heavily on Betty's shoulder, and Danika hovered in front of them.

"What just happened?" Betty snapped her frustration. Danika winced.

"The petite *chienne* neutered me," he spat and then coughed.

"What the hell? Neutered?" Betty looked at Danika, heart trapped like moth's wings in her throat.

Danika squeezed her eyes shut. "I feared she'd do something like this. I feared and yet she still took me by surprise." She shook her head and looked hard at Betty.

"What does that mean exactly?"

"Means I'm done having sex," Gerard growled. He stepped away from Betty and without looking back at either of them marched back down the hallway.

Betty gazed at the empty door for a second before turning back to Danika.

Danika gripped her finger. "Betty Hart, there is a way. There is a way to undo this curse, but you are the key. Hear me, girl, and hear me well. Galeta has sought to put Gerard down for ages. There's a vendetta between them, old but deep. I don't know what it is, but I feared when I discovered who'd head his hearing, she'd find a way to exact revenge."

Comprehension at this point was nil. Betty had zero idea what the fairy rambled on about, in fact she could barely understand what'd just happened. She shook the little fairy off. As far as she was concerned, this one could be just as bad as the nasty piece of work that'd just left. There wasn't a single reason to believe a word of what Danika said.

The necklace hung in the air as if suspended on wires, Betty eyed it like one would a snake ready to strike.

"Oh, dear me," Danika sighed, grabbing her chest, "what a fine mess. Oh, my dear, truly I'm so sorry."

Had any of that been real? And yet she only had to look at the glowing red pendant to see proof positive that she'd not totally lost her mind. Not to mention the bruise she was sure she'd have on her shoulder tomorrow morning, the muscle still throbbed where his fingers had dug in. And then of course there was the matter of fairy dressed in tree bark and covered in dew, yeah, all pretty convincing examples she'd not gone nutters.

"Who are you, what is that, and who is he?" Betty turned, glaring at the tiny fairy whose smile wobbled.

"Sit," Danika gestured to the couch, "this might take a while."

After an hour, many questions, and lots of groans, Betty was beginning to understand the sheer magnitude of her situation.

"Please tell me," she eyed the necklace she had no intention of wearing, "that is not what I think it is."

Danika started swishing her wand, probably from a case of nerves, but Betty had seen how powerful that thing was, and didn't want it swishing anywhere near her.

"Please don't." She pointed to the wand and Danika blinked as if she hadn't realized what she'd been doing.

She tucked it into her pocket and threw her hands up with a dramatic sigh. "You must understand, it was the only way. I had to tell them you two were mated in order to spare his life. In Kingdom we're not allowed to kill those who've truly bonded. Too cruel."

Betty laughed. "Oh and neutering a grown man like he was a dog, isn't?"

Danika wrinkled her nose. "That should never have happened."

"Then why didn't you stop it?" Betty glared.

Danika sucked in a sharp breath, her jaw trembled, and it was obvious the tiny thing was close to tears. Betty's heart softened against her will, not that she really knew a thing about Gerard, but seeing him suffer like that… for some personal vendetta-- and she could only guess it had something to do with being jilted (no woman ever went that crazy unless it involved a matter of the heart)-- it was wrong. Danika was a fairy too, she should have stopped it.

"Short answer is, I cannot." Danika shook her head, sending her fat curls bouncing. "She is the Head Mistress of Fairy Inc. and we cannot raise a hand against her. But besides that, my power is no match for hers. I cannot undo what she has wrought."

"Then tell someone who can!" Betty shouted.

Danika's look was sad. "Would that I could, lass, truly. But that is not the way of it in fairy, Galeta wouldn't let me close to anyone powerful enough to tell." Her small frame shook. Danika took a moment to gather herself, and with a deep breath, gave Betty a calm smile. "But this is where you come in. You can fix this, Betty Hart." Danika grabbed the necklace that still floated and traced the glass pendant with a soft sigh. "This is the pendant of Veritas."

"Truth." Betty nodded, recognizing the Latin word immediately. "What truth?"

"Yours." Danika pressed her lips together. "In essence he's bound to you for a month. The pendant is a recording, not of what happens in a physical sense, but rather a recording of the heart. At the end of the month he will stand trial one final time, the pendant will either glow for him or not."

"What does that mean exactly?" Betty bounced her leg up and down.

"I told them you were his mate, but obviously they did not believe me." She held up the locket. "However, if the pendant glows then he'll be set free."

"Oh," her eyebrows shot up, and then quickly turned into a frown. "Oh. And if he doesn't pass the test," she waved her hand, "he has another test or something?"

"No, not exactly, dear."

"Then I don't understand."

Danika's wings fluttered a nervous rhythm. "If the necklace fails to glow, he'll be killed. That was their verdict. To be freed you must fall in love with him, that is the condition."

She sucked in a breath. That was impossible. That big, virile man, in danger of losing his life if she didn't fall in love with him. "That's… that's barbaric."

Danika shrugged. "All things considered, he's lucky."

Betty chewed on her thumb. "And if I fall in love with him? Does that mean he stays?"

"He'll stay." Danika glanced at the wall opposite her.

Betty tilted her head. The way the fairy had said it, more like a question than a statement of fact bothered Betty, but it didn't really matter because Betty had no intention of falling in love with him. Though she wouldn't think about him dying either, there had to be a way around that. No way would she be responsible for sending someone to their death. No way. Betty was plenty smart, she'd figure this out. "What about the other thing? The thing Galeta did to him?"

"Put this on." Danika handed Betty the necklace.

The thin chain felt as heavy as a five pound dumb bell on her finger. She could barely stand to look at it. "I'll put it in my jewelry box. I don't want this thing on me."

"Doesn't work that way, dear." Danika swished her wand and unclasped the ring. "Move your hair."

"Why? I really don't want to wear this."

"Because if you want to save his life, you must wear it at all times."

Betty wanted to refuse. But she shoved her hair off her shoulders instead and tensed as the necklace wound around her neck as if by invisible fingers. The moment it settled against her chest, warmth flowed from the pendant through her skin. Her entire body throbbed with liquid heat, from the tips of her pinky fingers to her toes. It was hard to describe, but it almost felt like the gentle swell of an ocean tide lapping against her breast. Her eyes widened and her mouth parted in an 'o'.

Danika patted the pendant and sighed.

A rush of dizzying euphoria took hold of her, drove Betty to her feet, and she paced back and forth with restless energy. "I don't want this. I've been burned. I don't want to deal with another egotistical jerk and what... Oh no, wait a second." She stopped on a dime, as another thought become painfully obvious. "He's gonna have to stay here with me, isn't he?"

"Well--" the fairy wheedled, eyes scrunching in her face.

"Oh jeez. Just wonderful." Betty shook her head.

"Get to know him, lass. If anyone can bring out the best in that man, it's you. It's there, just hidden. Make him see you."

"Why? What if I don't want to?" After James, Betty had zero desire to begin another romance. She was tired of dating, tired of men, and so far Gerard had done very little to make her feel in any way romantically inclined toward him. The man could kiss like nobody's business, but that was just sex. Betty wanted all or nothing, and refused to ever settle again.

"Because you are his perfect match. Only you can awaken the shriveled mess of his heart, only you can break the curse Galeta planted on him."

Betty shook her head. What did the fairy possibly see in her to even make her think that? She and Gerard were oil and water. They didn't mix, barely even got along. There was nothing there, chemistry maybe. But anything of any substance-- not a bit.

"I can't keep him here," she crossed her arms.

"He's got no place else to go. Betty, you are it. His last hope. Love, that is the most powerful magic of all." As she said it, her body began to grow translucent. "Love, it can move mountains."

She was fading, and Betty was still confused, still full of questions. "But what Galeta did. How do I break that?" she yelled at the barely there shadow.

"Love conquers all..." The last words quivered on the air like the silken strand of a spider's web.

Chapter 8

A knock sounded on the bathroom door. Gerard didn't move off the toilet seat. "What?" he growled.

"Gerard, its Betty," her soft voice made his heart clench.

"Go away." He glanced back down at the dragonfly rug on the floor, dizzy with the reality of what'd just happened.

How could Galeta have neutered him? Being bound to a woman was punishment enough, within the month they'd learn she did not love him and execute him posthaste. But now, now he'd never again know the pleasures of a woman's body beneath his. Galeta might as well have killed him now.

Galeta had warned him years ago, after he'd rebuffed her advances, that she'd make him pay. And she had. First with the twisted parody of 'his' story and now this. The muscles in his forearms locked with the strain of holding himself back from punching a hole through Betty's wall.

"Gerard, you need to come out. I think we should talk."

Women-- a pox on them all.

He eyed the door and shot to his feet, slamming his open palm against the white paneled wood. "Come to gloat, to demand your due? What? What do you want from me?"

His blood rushed hot in his ears. Gods the humiliation. Forced to do her bidding, knowing he could never feel another moment of pleasure again unless with her, and only if she fell in love with him. As if that could ever happen. She hated him already.

Gerard pressed his forehead to the door. A sound, like the tapping of her fingers grated in his ears.

"I'm sorry."

His fingers twitched. Why would she apologize?

"Open the door, please."

He didn't know what possessed him to open the door, but he flung it wide and her mouth parted on a wordless scream as she fell forward.

Grabbing her under her arms, he righted her, and then glowered. "You asked me to open, you should have been prepared instead of tripping into me like a drunken whore!"

Betty blustered, shoving strands of hair out of face. That's when he noticed her spectacles. They were tipped at the corners, reminding him of cat eyes. Hideous things, but on her they looked adorable and he was shocked to note his pulse racing. That's also when he realized he did not become hard, and the anger returned, sizzling hot through his gut. Growling, he walked out, forcing her to press up against the wall so as not to be run down.

Gerard had no clue what to do. He felt lost and helpless, and those feelings so vexed him, he walked to front door intending to head out to the nearest bar and pound the first male face he saw.

"Gerard Caron, you stop right there!" Betty demanded.

Shocked, he paused with his hand on the knob.

"Firstly," she grabbed his shoulder and twirled him around, "you're naked, do you have any idea how much trouble I'd get in for letting a crazy Frenchman walk the streets of the bible belt like that?" She gestured at him, a becoming pink flush rose high on her cheeks.

He glanced down at himself and his lips twitched; nudity bothered her more than him. Though he did not care for the fact that her eyes lingered on his flaccid cock. He squeezed his eyes shut, wanting to shout that if he could, he'd be hard and ready for her.

"Secondly," she said slowly, drawing his attention back to her, "I'm so sorry this happened to you."

"Why do you care?" he asked after a hearts beat.

She smiled, and when she moved closer, the hair slid off the nape of her neck, exposing the fluttering beat of her pulse. She was nervous? Of him? Of the situation? He wished he knew. Betty grabbed his hand and led him back to her living room.

"We need to talk," she said again, "Danika told me parts of this story. But you really have to give it to me straight. It's not just you anymore. We're in this together now."

She tucked her long legs underneath her bottom, and Gerard clenched his eyes shut. He couldn't look at her, seeing her and knowing he could do nothing to quench his lust was as a dagger in the heart. Torture.

"And maybe you should put this over your lap," she smiled, tucking a fluffy pink blanket around him.

He almost chuckled, relieved that even unmanned as he was, he still managed to make her want him. That was, until he saw the large face of a cartoonish cat staring back at him. "Gods *mademoiselle*," he curled his lip, "so much pink."

"Hey," she punched him lightly on the arm, "I'm a single girl. If I want to rock the Hello Kitty theme, then it's my prerogative. Now stop stalling and talk."

"Go change," he ordered gruffly, scrubbing a hand down his jaw.

"What?" her brows gathered and she looked down at herself. "I'm perfectly fine."

"Betty Hart," he growled, "you wish to talk, fine I'll oblige you. But change, I cannot focus for want of you, it is a small torture to see you and know I cannot have you. Change."

"You couldn't have me anyway," she huffed, crossing her arms underneath her chest and his mouth watered seeing the rounded globes inch higher.

"Now," he gritted and clamped his lips shut, choosing to ignore her jab.

Betty narrowed her eyes, but after a tense moment, she finally stood and marched back into the hallway.

Gerard leaned his head back, rubbing his throbbing temples, wondering how he'd ever last around her. His curse could be lifted, if she fell in love with him.

Hell of a turn his life had taken. He'd tell her the truth, in all its unvarnished glory. She'd never believe him anyway, what did it matter?

Her shuffling feet made him lift his head, and he laughed when he saw her glower. She wore a thick white jacket that covered her down to mid calf.

"There," she snapped, "better?"

Still laughing, he nodded. "Much."

"Look at me," she walked slowly to the chair opposite him, "I'm not even going to sit next to you."

He bit his lip, delighted to note her breathing hitch ever so slightly. Gerard slouched, stretching out his legs.

"Ugh! You made me change, I really wish you'd do the same for me. I gave you some clothes earlier, why aren't you wearing them?" Her nose did a cute wrinkle when she grumbled.

The jacket might as well have been a big marshmallow on her. But even so, with her mussed hair and sexy glasses, she made him ache for a touch of that supple flesh beneath. For another one of those kisses that had stolen his breath only hours earlier.

"They've been worn by other men. I don't share," he said, and her eyes widened. He licked his teeth, knowing she'd caught his double meaning. "What do you wish to know, shrew?"

Her lips thinned. "For starters, Danika never could tell me why Galeta had a hard on for you. The she demon had revenge on the mind and I want to know why."

"Oh gods..."

"Ah." She held up her finger. "You promised."

He rolled his eyes. "*Enfer*."

She lifted a brow. "Oh hell is right. I'm waiting. In fact, I'll wait here all night. Out with it. I'm involved in this now too, I need to know why. Danika gave me very little and call me--"

"A nag," Gerard supplied with a grin.

She stuck her tongue out. "Whatever. I don't care. You owe me. I think I just saved your butt from the fire, and I want to know that it was worth it. So start talking, mister."

"Because she tried to seduce me, I spurned her, and she's never forgiven me for it." He waited, knowing she'd laugh.

She laughed. "Oh man, that's rich. You, the guy with sex on the mind twenty four seven, expect me to believe that. How long were you guys bumping fuzzies before you decided to move on to greener pastures?" She lifted her brow.

He had no idea what the hell that meant, but he was pretty certain he got the gist of it.

"Gerard, you're stuck with me for a month. I've got nothing but time." She tapped her fingers rhythmically on her arm.

"You don't know me, Betty. You know nothing of me. Yes, I like sex. In fact, I love it. I know you do, any red blooded creature does. I won't deny it." He drilled her with his hard gaze, defying her to deny his assertion.

After a moment she blinked and looked down at her feet.

"I did deny her. She's rather terrifying as far as females go. Those fangs," he shuddered, "nasty creature that *fee*."

Betty nodded. "I noticed those things too. She's pretty scary for being barely a foot tall."

"You're taking this very well." He cocked his head. "I'd have expected most mortals to deny what they'd seen. Run in terror, something."

Betty plucked at her jacket. "I'm not most mortals." She chanced a fleeting glance at him, her brown eyes huge and warm in her beautiful face.

What was it about the woman, the more he looked, the prettier she became. It was odd, and not altogether pleasing. Gerard frowned, shifting around. The blanket slipped, and like a laser her eyes zoomed to his lap. He patted it back into place. Her face flushed crimson, but she nodded in silent thanks.

She swallowed and then looked directly at him. "I swear I'll kill you myself, Gerard Caron…"

The way his name spilled from her lips with her strange accent made his blood hot.

"But I'm a card carrying geek."

"A what?"

Betty ran her finger along her jaw line. Why had he never noticed the shimmering green of her sculpted nails? She had such delicate fingers, long boned and finely wrought. What would that hand feel like on him? His blood hummed and his body tingled. Those fingers caressing his balls, running long and slow down his hard length.

He clenched his jaw, and glanced quickly at the wall. Gerard might no longer be able to harden, but the desire hadn't waned. And if he didn't watch it, he'd keep himself in a perpetual state of phantom arousal and pain.

"Oh jeez, I never talk about this." Her eyes narrowed, and with an embarrassed twist of her lips, she got up, grabbed her bag off the kitchen counter, and then plopped back down on the couch next to him. She dug around the brown purse. "No laughing. You swear."

Did her voice shake just now? And why was that so damn adorable? He nodded. "No laughing."

Betty bit her bottom lip, and Gerard licked his own, wishing it were his tongue on her instead. The jacket was doing nothing to dull his desire. For the first time in his life he realized just how often he'd focused on sex and sex alone. Now that he couldn't have it, he'd have to learn new ways to seduce and woo. The moment he thought it, he knew that's exactly what he meant to do. He'd win his freedom by making her fall in love with him.

It might be harder without the benefit of his skills in bed, but he'd succeed. He had no choice. Mind made up, he turned to her, deciding then and there he'd focus fully on her needs, wishes, and wants.

She handed him a yellow card. Betty nibbled on her thumb, her anxiety so palpable his pulse quickened.

Gerard glanced at the card. A cartoonish picture of two men engaged in a fierce sword battle stared back at him.

"Hello my name is Betty Hart, librarian by day, and Manga superhero slash anime fanatic by night. I'm a member of the guild of Bleeding Heart Rebels and go by the name Eclipse. I've even been known to larp in college," she squeaked out the last, wincing as she stared at him, looking like a frightened colt of what he'd think.

Based off her reaction, he was fairly certain what she'd just admitted to was as heinous an embarrassment as they came. Gerard scratched his chin. "And that means what?"

She covered her face with her hands. "You were supposed to be talking to me about this stuff, and here I am the one suddenly on the spot. Look," she peeked out at him from between her fingers, "if you're real nice I'll show you what I mean some other day. Can we just get back on topic?"

"But this is on topic," he grinned, enjoying her sudden display of shyness as much as anything else. "I asked you why you're so okay with all this, and I'm not sure what this," he lifted the card, "has to do with that."

She snatched the card out of his hands and shoved it back into her purse. "That's only part of it, the other part, and I guess the most relevant, is that Daddy was an astrobiologist."

Again he shook his head. "And that means?"

"He believed in life on other planets. In fact, he was so sure of it, he wrote several books based on the truth behind popular mythos and the science of the fall of alien man. I guess you can say I came by my geek status honestly. Daddy taught me all he knew, and when I grew up, his words still made sense." She shrugged. "I went to college, got a degree in psychology which I put to zero use, and discovered my dad wasn't crazy, but brilliant."

"What made you certain he wasn't simply a raving lunatic?" Gerard asked, genuinely intrigued. This woman was so different from what he'd known, gorgeous yes... but stimulating as well.

Her smile was brilliant as she bounced up again and ran back down her hall. She came back seconds later with a large leather bound book in her hands. Gerard's heart flipped when she opened the book and handed it to him. She pointed to a spot on the page. "Read this." She fairly vibrated with enthusiasm.

He glanced at the black smudges, nodded as if he had a clue what it said, and closed it. "Yes."

"Yes! That's it. That's all you have to say about that? It's amazing, it's true, and my Daddy knew it all along. The Fermi paradox, space is so vast... surely we're not the only ones to exist in it. Out there, beyond time and matter were other civilizations, peoples." She pointed to him. "You." She clapped her hands and he had the sudden sick feeling that she viewed him more as a bug beneath a viewing glass than a man all of a sudden. "Riddle me this, Gerard. Did you happen to travel here through a worm hole?"

He lifted a brow. The woman was insane, he was still stuck on the Fermi-whats-it paradox thingy, and she was talking wormholes... and what the hell was that anyway? A giant worm eating holes in air? Why the devil would that make her so excited? He brushed his fingers through his hair. "I've not a clue. Danika swished her wand, and I was yanked through."

She laughed. "Was there a tunnel?" Her brown eyes glittered. She'd the fevered look of a wolf snapping in for its kill. "Did it shimmer? Swirl? Glow?"

Gods she was gorgeous, skin all flushed and dewy pink. If he could somehow mute her voice, he could stare at her all day. But she was giving him a massive ache in the back of his skull. Gerard squeezed his brow.

"It was blue. What are you saying, *mademoiselle*?" he grumped.

She rolled her eyes. "Isn't it obvious?"

Suddenly memories of another woman-- just as lovely as this one-- intruded in his mind. Belle had wielded her sharp wit and keen brain better than any blade. More than once he'd suffered the knowledge that she'd thought him beneath her. Heat stoked the glowing embers in his gut to an incendiary level and his nostrils flared as his fingers clenched.

"There's life in other planets, dimensions... whatever!" She clapped her hands and laughed, a full throaty sound so sexy and alluring he couldn't help but lean in to her, even while still fueled with anger. Her brown eyes sparkled, and then she cradled her face in her hands, and sucked in a sharp breath.

"Oh my gosh, I did it again, didn't I?"

"What?" he grumbled, scooting back on the seat, trying to maintain some distance between them.

She grabbed his wrist. "Oh, Gerard, I'm sorry. Trisha gets on me all the time about how rude I come off sometimes. I'm sorry, I... I just, jeez. How lame. I love science and science fiction and all the weird stuff girls shouldn't like, which is why I work in a library, and I hope you don't think I was talking down to you. I swear I wasn't. I just get wicked excited."

Not once in all the years he'd known Belle, had she ever apologized for making him feel intellectually inferior. Had Betty truly not meant to offend him? Was her enthusiasm for a subject he found mind numbingly boring, truly that exciting to her?

Betty flicked her hands. "Look, truce okay? Let's start over here. You're stuck with me for a month. Let's try to make it pleasant." She stuck her hand out. "Hi, my name is Betty Hart. What's your name?"

Her smile was pure innocence, and his heart tripped when he took her hand. The woman was nuts, and yet she excited him on a level he'd never known before.

"Gerard Caron," he said. "Good to meet you, *folle*." Her skin was so soft, he didn't want to let go. The feel of her small hand in his large one, the way she looked at him with a mixture of awe and shyness-- he wanted to see her like this always.

"I guess I am kind of crazy." A good natured laugh spilled from her.

Something strange happened in the center of Gerard's chest. A tickling flutter of weirdness he'd never felt before, mainly because he'd only ever looked at women with one desire in mind. He couldn't do that with her, it made her different. But he wasn't sure yet how.

"There's something I'm dying to know," she continued, and he noticed she seemed as content to hang onto his hand as he was to hang onto hers. He thumbed her knuckles.

"What?"

"Danika told me about Kingdom."

He nodded.

"How it's a realm full of immortals of legend. What we here on Earth call fairy tales."

Gerard let go of her hand and squirmed, knowing where this line of questioning was headed. "So why have you never heard of me?" He pierced her with his steely eyed gaze. "Is that what you're wondering?"

Her lips stretched into a crooked smile as she nodded.

He sighed, and placed his elbows on his knees, staring at nothing in particular. Again she touched him, her fingers grazed his jaw and he jerked.

"You don't have to tell me now," she said softly, "not if you're not ready."

He shook his head. "If I tell you, you'll not believe. None do."

"Try me."

She'd told him that once before, he hadn't trusted her then. Still wasn't sure he could now. The soft glow of lamplight washed across the top of her head, highlighting the natural gold in her hair. It made her appear almost angelic. Gerard glanced down at the beige carpet.

"She was the youngest of three. Daughter of a merchant. Stories would have you believe she was all that was kindness and grace. The girl was a *demone*. Breathtakingly beautiful with her soft brown eyes and chestnut colored hair." He looked at her. "You look a little like her. Although I think I prefer the black of your hair to hers."

Betty's lips twitched.

He sighed. "I was young, and a fool. I fell hard, and did anything she asked of me. Kill the neighbor's dog for digging up her sister's garden." He clenched his fist, staring at his knuckles. "Hit the town drunk for daring to look at her wrong." Gerard squeezed his eyes shut, the hated memories pressing in on him like a wall closing in.

"Are you talking about Belle, Gerard?" Betty's soft voice was a gentle caress. "As in Beauty and the Beast?"

He nodded.

"Wow. But, there was never any mention of a Frenchman in the original book, and the one in the movie..." She grimaced, letting her sentence die off.

"Wasn't me. That," he pointed to the empty case sitting next to her television, "is the perverted version Galeta pandered about. My name is Gerard. I never tried to kill the Beast, he was an idiot that deserved that cold blooded, money hungry *chienne*. The Beast detested my love for her, when it came time to pen our story to tale he had coin enough to sway Galeta's black heart. Wasn't hard, she hated me enough as it was." He laughed, a bitter, scornful sound. "I can never escape the witch, no matter how hard I try. Did you know she's the fairy of the arts as well?"

Betty shook her head.

He snorted. "The bitch has ruined me. I'm forever a joke in Kingdom. Congratulations, Betty Hart, you're stuck with me."

"But, I don't understand--"

"What is there to understand?" he snapped.

"I just want to know you better--"

He stood, uncaring that the blanket dropped, that she got a good eye full, let her. Her eyes widened, and she glanced quickly away. Gerard was tired of talking about it. "Don't. Where am I to sleep?"

"Gerard, please understand..."

"*Non*." He sliced the air with his hand. "If you'd rather, I'll find accommodations elsewhere."

Betty's smile was sad, soft. She pointed down the hall. "Take the guest room. It's always made up for Briley whenever he wants to have a surprise sleepover."

The tip of Gerard's tongue danced in his mouth, words like-- *I'm sorry, it's not you*, settled like a heavy weight. Turning on his heels, he strode down the hall, breathing hard from words left unsaid.

Chapter 9

Betty shouldn't have pushed him. She'd seen his chest heaving, his nostrils flaring... classic flight or fight response to something unpleasant. And why she continued to goad him into telling all was beyond her.

She put the car in park and grabbed the ShopMart bags from off the passenger seat, slamming the car door behind her. The night was still, the maples surrounding her town house towered like hulking shadows. Past two in the morning, she was probably the only idiot still up at this time of night.

Not afraid of the dark, but slightly creeped out by being so alone in the dead of night, she jogged to her door and ran inside. The moment she stepped into her darkened hall her heart rate slowed to normal.

The plastic bags crinkled loudly through the quiet of the night. Her tea cup shaped wall clock tick-tocked. Its metrical rhythm only helped to increase the intensity of her already frazzled nerves.

She leaned against the door, glancing at the hall, knowing he slept in her house. Tonight had been a revelation. She still didn't know Gerard, but she wanted to. They were stuck together for a long time. Ignoring him was no longer an option, besides, she'd done a pretty lousy job of that anyway. Kissing him, letting him kiss her back, imagining his lean naked body pressed tight to hers... heat zipped down her spine and she clamped down on a moan.

Trisha would die, and that thought made her smile. Never in her life had Betty imagined she'd find herself in this situation. Harboring an alien from some alternate dimension, a hot, sexy one at that. Martian ManHunter had been her first crush growing up, though she'd always assumed her alien would have green skin and oblong shaped eyes. As an adult the green skinned freaks had long since lost their appeal.

But Gerard looked so human-- so purely masculine-- that had she not experienced the fairies and magic herself, she'd have thought him as mortal as her.

She rubbed sweaty palms on her legs, the sound of the bags disturbed the peace of night and she cringed. Betty had driven for hours, vacillating between running to Trisha's-- kicking whatever piece of man meat out of her house and dishing all-- or keeping Gerard's secret to herself.

Of all the people in the world Gerard could have met, she doubted many would be as accepting of what he was. Betty had been primed from the moment she could talk, to believe in life beyond Earth. But even her brother, raised by the same parents in the same house, rejected any and all notion of aliens.

She sighed and grabbed the pendant that had ceased feeling like a weight. It pulsed against her skin like the warmth of a sun's ray. The lights swirled in and on each other like a wave tumbling onto shore. Betty straightened her shoulders and headed to his room.

She didn't bother to knock, knowing if he said to go away she do it. Instead, she opened it. A slice of moonlight cut across his body like a silver blade, highlighting the flat, corded muscles of his stomach. Betty swallowed and licked her lips.

"*Cherie?*" his deep voice brushed the night like a master painter's stroke. Her lashes fluttered.

Betty gripped the bags tighter, knuckles flexing tight as she held on to the bags like a life line. With quiet resolve, she pushed away from the door, she'd come this far, she wasn't going to wimp out now.

"You're awake?" Duh, of course he was. Betty frowned, wishing for a do over, a smoother more sexy entrance. One she'd imagine Trisha doing.

He sat up, the white sheet dropped even lower, and though she'd glimpsed his bit of male flesh already, it still made her dizzy and slightly breathless. The man was gorgeous. Gorgeous, and in her house. Two words not normally synonymous in her life.

"Betty," his smooth whiskey voice made her stomach churn, "is something amiss?"

His hair was mussed, the whiskers on his cheek more pronounced than this morning, and jeez... could her heart beat any harder? She dropped the bags on the floor.

"I bought you some clothes. Nothing fancy. Just some jeans, you looked like a size 32... so I got 34's just in case and a pack of large ribbed shirts. There's some..." she blushed, thankful it was so dark, "underwear. I didn't know your size so I guessed. So um, yeah... goodnight, then."

Her hair snapped like a band behind her head as she turned sharply on her heels.
"Betty."
She stopped, spine rigid, breathless. "Gerard?"
"I'm not happy about what's happened."
Betty turned back around, concern for him easing her fears immediately. "Is it me?"
He shook his head.
"If I could take it off." She yanked on the necklace that she'd tried on the drive to divest herself of, only to learn it wouldn't come off.

"I can't sleep," he grumbled. "Slept better last night on that damn table. I just keep thinking."

Betty took a step, and then another and another, before she knew it, she stood by the edge of his bed. With the lights turned off and nothing but moonshine to see him by, he looked vulnerable-- no less sexy, but much more approachable.

She fingered the edge of the sheet. "I can't sleep either," she finally admitted. "I've been driving for hours."

"I heard you leave." She drowned in the depths of his eyes as they roamed her face. "I'm not a man used to talking. To telling so much of who I am. I'm still not sure I want to."

Betty gripped the sheet, inching it higher. "I'm not asking you to, Gerard. But I think this can at least be fun. Now that sex is out of the equation, maybe you can view me not as a body but as a person. Get to know me. I'm not all that bad."

His lips twitched. "You've still the tongue of a viper about you."
She rolled her eyes. "And you're still a Neanderthal, but I forgive you for that."
"Gods help me," he moaned, and his smile was so boyish, so silly, Betty's nerves completely fled.
She tugged on the sheet.
His eyes narrowed. "*Cherie*, are you trying to slip into my bed?"

Her heart jerked. "No," she said a bit too swiftly, "why, are you asking me to?"

His brow rose, and his lips spread into a slow curl. "Do you want to?"

Yes. "Why? Do you want me to?" Pulse pounding so hard she tasted the adrenaline, she waited. She should just say it. It was obvious. But again, this wasn't something she'd ever do, but anytime it came to this man she found herself doing and saying things outside her comfort zone.

He crossed his arms as if waiting on her to say something.

She lifted her chin, recognizing his challenge and responded to it. "Fine. Yes, I want to cuddle. I'm tired, but I can't sleep. We're in this together and I feel sort of bonded to you because of it. I trust you not to manhandle me in the middle of the night, and it's been a long time since I've cuddled anyone. Call me a slut if you want but--"

"*Enfer, Cherie.* Too many words." Gerard threw the sheets back, and he was so naked and she was so not, she felt hot and twitchy all over again.

"Oh jeez, Gerard. You're gonna have to put on some night pants or something. I... I can't."

"Have you ever lain with a man before, Betty?" his deep voice rolled over her skin like warmed oil.

"Many times. Tons. Lots."

He snorted and got up. "Give me clothes then, woman."

Betty tripped over her feet, and dived into the bag, feeling around for the soft fabric. She grabbed the black sleeping pants and tossed them at him. "There."

He laughed and slipped them on. He held his arms out. "Better?"

Not really. Because the pants tapered to his slim waist like the finest silk, hugged his hips and thighs, teasing her with what lay beneath. She bit her lip.

Gerard hopped back into the bed, crossed his arms behind his head and reclined. "Well?"

"What?"

His brow rose. "Your turn. You can't sleep in all that."

Betty glanced down at her jeans and shirt. She narrowed her eyes. "I'm not afraid of you, Gerard. I'm not a prude."

"Prove it." He crossed his heels, wearing a cocky grin.

"This is so stupid," she said, lifting her shirt above her head, tossing it at his face. She always wore an undershirt, so if he'd hoped to see the color of her bra he was S.O.L. "Not like you can do anything, why put yourself through the torture?"

He sniffed her pink top, and her stomach swirled with dancing butterflies, she'd spritzed herself with orange blossom perfume before she'd left and couldn't help wondering if he liked it. Her toes curled, digging into the carpet.

"The trews," he said, and she licked her lips, pulse fluttering as the butterflies climbed out her stomach and up her throat.

Betty touched the button of her jeans and channeling her best Marilyn Monroe meets Xena warrior princess sex kitten vibe, snapped it open. Her fingers shook, but thankfully he didn't seem to notice as she pushed the jeans off.

"You've the shapely thighs of a gazelle, *sorciere*."

His voice sounded hoarse and hearing him call her a sorceress, knowing he implied she cast a spell on him, it filled her with a sense of womanly empowerment. Betty smiled and hopped over her pile. "See, not afraid of you."

He scrubbed his jaw.

But the second she got in bed with him, and his arm stretched across her shoulder, the fear came back like a splash of ice water to the face. She tensed.

Gerard didn't speak either, but his fingers rubbing her cold upper arms soothed her, and before she knew it, she was shuddering out a deep breath, body liquid and languid.

Briley hated covering his window with a curtain, hated blocking out the stars he said. Now she knew why, Gerard's big body cradling hers, her head on his chest-- lulled by the steady beat of his heart-- and the beauty of a million twinkling lights, was better than any sleeping pill. From one breath to the next, Betty slipped into the peaceful oblivion of dreams.

***

Gerard stared at her, entranced by the soft lift of her chest, her warm breaths against his skin, and wondered why he'd never taken the time to watch a woman sleep before. Watch the shadow of dreams race across her face, see her face twitch and hear her gentle moans. T'was a wonder he'd never want to miss out on again.

He couldn't understand her. Understand why she was okay with this. If it'd been him, and she'd fallen into his lap, he'd have screwed her senseless, then walked away. He'd not have cared for her plight, it wasn't his problem. And yet here she was, snuggled up to him, with her leg wrapped around his and her tiny hand splayed against his heart, and he couldn't understand it.

His lips twitched. She rambled, a lot. Nonsense he often couldn't make out, but it didn't bother him. Not even the sharp tongue of hers did anything other than make his blood hot and his brain crazed with a consuming need to know her.

Maybe this wouldn't be so bad after all. But the one month limit told him one thing… the tribunal had not believed she was his mate. This was a test, one he was sure to fail.

Though he'd bedded many women, Gerard had never been able to make one truly fall in love with him. With his body… yes. With his skill to illicit passion unlike any they'd ever known, beyond a doubt. He'd do everything in his power to make Betty fall in love with him.

Because he knew this was Galeta's final attempt at revenge. If within the month Betty didn't fall in love, she'd be freed, and he'd be sent back and destroyed.

She twitched and he brushed his fingers across her forehead, tucking her hair back.

Gerard had fallen in love once before, deeply. Truly. He'd loved Belle like no other before or since. He'd sworn off love after her betrayal, after she'd left him for a beast with money. He'd grown callused, cruel. He'd do the same to Betty, he always did. Gerard couldn't love anymore. It simply wasn't in him.

"Betty Hart, I'm sorry." He whispered and she smiled, snuggling in deeper. "You shouldn't know me. I'm no good. Don't fall in love with me, *Cherie*. Guard your heart, because the moment I'm free, I'll leave you. I always do."

Chapter 10

"Good morning, *mon petite*."

Betty lifted a brow, never a morning person she shuffled her way toward the coffee maker and smiled when she smelled the roasted aroma of Arabica beans. "You made coffee?"

He grinned and a tingle of appreciation zipped down her spine, making her fingers clench around the handle of the coffee pot. She'd known it-- he was even more delicious looking in the morning with the scruff and the heart melting smile.

His smile held and the air around them tightened, prickling her flesh as he ever so slightly moved in. "I thought you might need some."

Betty licked her lips. He was shirtless, chiseled pecs flexing under her hot gaze. She snapped her eyes back to his face, but it wasn't much better. Blue eyes the color of hottest flames popped in the morning light. How had she ever thought them black?

She shook her head. *Get a hold of yourself, Hart*! Clearing her throat, she turned abruptly and with shaking fingers, grabbed a coffee mug out of the cabinet above her head. "That was nice."

She poured a generous amount of the black brew into her cup and with it still steaming, gulped a mouthful. It burned the sensitive skin on the roof of her mouth and brought tears to her eyes, but the pain helped her think about something other than his yummy delectableness. Was that even a phrase? Either way, it completely applied.

"There's milk on the counter," he said and turned back to the stove.

"I drink it black," she murmured, then frowned. "What are you doing?"

He shot her another one of those killer grins. "Making your breakfast." Grabbing the carton of eggs off the counter he asked, "two or three egg omelet?"

"One, and you don't have to do that."

He shrugged and cracked two eggs, then started to mix them. "It takes no effort. You're putting up with me for a month and I've nothing else to do, *Cherie*."

How in the world had he learned her kitchen so quickly? Betty hardly knew it and she'd lived here three years. There were days she'd open a drawer and rediscover a gadget she hadn't seen in months. To say she wasn't much of a cook was a stretch.

He padded around the kitchen with smooth efficiency. Opening drawers, grabbing a utensil, beating the egg, moving to the refrigerator and pulling out tons of vegetables and a bag of generic shredded cheese-- all of it with an effortless grace that let her know the bedroom wasn't the only place the man felt confident.

Before she knew it the room filled with the scent of buttery veggies. Betty inhaled greedily, used to only smelling this when she went out to eat-- which was usually never thanks to a measly librarian's salary.

Not wanting to get in the way, she sat down at the breakfast bar, crossed her legs, and sipped her still piping hot brew.

"When do you work today?" he asked with his back still to her.

Betty drummed her fingers on her warm mug, admiring the flex and sway of his muscles as he poured the egg batter into the pan. The sizzle made her mouth water and her stomach growl.

"Nine. I've got some shelving and paperwork to do before I open the doors."

He nodded. "Grab two plates, *s'il vous plait*."

Betty got up and took two plates to him. With a deft flick of his wrist, he sliced the omelet in half and slipped one end on her plate and the other on his. He handed her a plate.

The omelets were the fluffiest, yellow things she'd ever seen. Normally if she made one, and those attempts were rare, the egg would be just shy of black and the cheese tasting of rubber. Picking up a fork, she sliced through the creation and popped the steaming forkful into her mouth. Moaning in ecstasy at the incredible moist and lush flavors of roasted peppers and onions and gooey cheese, she beamed at a proud looking Gerard.

"Oh my, wow," she breathed, tongue throbbing from the hot bite and not caring. "This is amazing. What did you do?"

With a nod toward the table, he guided her to her seat of the night before.

He took a bite and nodded. "Butter, vegetables, salt. The only things truly essential for a fine meal."

Betty ate, each bite tasting better than the last. She smiled and he returned it.

"I hope the coffee is not too bitter. We tend to prefer tea in Kingdom, though Jinni's got an affinity for the coffee. I learned from him." He pointed to her now empty cup.

Strange that this should feel so perfect, so cozy. They hardly knew each other, and it was amazing how she'd gone from terrified and suspicious of the man, to comfortable and fully at ease. Betty rested her chin on the hand holding the now dangling fork. "You know this is feeling domestic. I'd ask you what you're up to, Gerard." She lifted a brow.

He chewed the last of his omelet and then sighed. "As you said last night, we're stuck with each other for a month. Let's at least try to get along, no?"

Betty nibbled on the last forkful. Even cold, the food was great. It'd been fantastic last night too. The man knew his way around the kitchen. Made her curious what else he knew his way around. Her stomach fluttered with that thought.

"You said you learned from a woman. Who was she?"

He licked his teeth. "Sure you want to know?"

"Why not." Probably some skank he'd slept with.

"Bar maid I slept with."

Yup, she'd known it. Betty chuckled.

He tipped his jaw. "Why do you laugh?"

She rolled her eyes. "I don't know you at all, and yet there's times where I feel like I've known you forever. Although I gotta say..." she gave a melodramatic sigh, pushing the plate away, "your cooking is amazing. If I had to get stuck with someone for a month, I could have done worse. I want more."

The moment the words left her lips, a strange silver glow shimmered in the air between them like smoke. The necklace she'd still been unable to yank off flared hot. Gerard's face tightened, he cracked his jaw, and shot to his feet.

Mechanical footsteps took him back to the stove where he grabbed an egg.

"Gerard?" Betty frowned. Why was he acting so strange? His movements seemed forced, not at all graceful like before.

"What?" he snapped, and beat the egg to within an inch of its life, the fork pinged off the glass bowl with such force she feared he'd shatter the glass.

"What are you doing?"

"Doing your bidding," he snarled, and slopped the egg into the pan.

It took a second for the truth to dawn on her (had she been more awake, she might have recognized what was happening sooner), she'd compelled him. Or rather, the power of the necklace had.

"Stop!" Betty held up her hands. "I was kidding."

Suddenly he stopped. The tense muscles of his back visibly relaxed, and he turned around then, his breathing was labored. Gerard planted his hands on either side of the stove. His eyes sparked fury, betrayal.

Betty shook her head. "I had no idea I could do that."

"Didn't you?" his eyes narrowed to twin slits. "They told you, I'm yours to command. To enslave," he spat, and a lump wedged in Betty's throat.

"No," she denied again with a firm shake of her head. "No. I'd never want that kind of power over you." Betty glanced down at the necklace. She yanked on it, more desperate now than ever to take it off.

What had the fairies done? What a wicked, vile magic, and to make her be the one in charge of something so absolute. To have this much power over anyone, to tell him to jump off a cliff and know he'd have to do it. It was wrong. Betty could never hurt a fly and though it'd just been eggs this time, in a moment of anger she could forget herself and make him do something awful. The enormity of the responsibility slammed into her, and she tugged harder, the silver chain tore into her neck.

Then his fingers were covering hers. "You'll hurt yourself," he whispered.

He smelled so good, like soap and coffee, and he was looking at her not with anger, but firm resolve, and she wanted to cry. "I will never, ever, ever do that to you again. I swear. I'm sorry, Gerard."

Gerard smoothed his hand against her hair and nodded. "I believe you, *Cherie*. Forgive me?"

She nodded, though there was nothing to forgive. He grabbed her empty mug and refilled it, then settled her back in her chair.

"Drink," he ordered.

Her grin was wobbly. "Touche."

Gerard winked. "Turnabout, you know how it is."

Betty drank the entire cup before she started to feel more like herself again. "You should know, I'm not usually such a wimp. I don't cry at sappy love stories, or even when boyfriend's break up with me. Except for the first day, okay maybe the first month… but I'm not a wimp."

Why was she telling him that? It's not like she had cried, although he must have seen the sheen in her eyes. Heart in her throat, she snuck a peek at him. He had his arms crossed behind his head, studying her with a contemplative gleam. "They meant to unman me, *Cherie*. I apologize for taking my anger out on you."

She nodded and tapped her pointer finger in the center of the table. "Then let me lay some ground rules now."

He lifted a brow.

"To prove to you I can be trusted, I will never boss you around."

"Good."

Her lips twitched. "Unless it involves making sure the toilet seat goes back down, and changing the toilet paper roll when it's empty." She shrugged.

"Agreed," he said.

She met his gaze, but instead of laughing and glancing away, he held her look. As the seconds ticked by her pulse sped, heat spiraled down her legs and the terry cloth robe she wore felt suddenly too heavy and scratchy against her skin. His eyes went from playful teasing, to glinting with smoke and snapping with flame.

Heat rose up her neck. Betty grabbed the edges of her robe with nerveless fingers and closed it tighter around her waist.

He laughed, stood and grabbed their dishes. "Are you satisfied? More coffee, toast, juice?"

Again, he seemed completely unaffected, which rankled. She was hot, itchy, and desperate for something. Something she shouldn't want-- a taste of him. Of his body, his lips, his touch, but it was impossible now.

"No, I'm good." Betty stood and ran to the bathroom.

***

Gerard gripped the kitchen sink, breathing hard as shivers pulsated throughout his frame, the remnants of trembling muscles slow to burn out. The magic had been strong, demanding, and he'd seethed with hatred for Galeta... even with Betty herself. He'd thought she'd done it apurpose. But then he'd seen her eyes, the quiver of her soft pink lips, and his fury had vanished.

If he'd been fully a man-- fully himself and able to get hard-- he'd have grabbed her and kissed her. Letting Betty taste the passion of his lust before disrobing and screwing her senseless on the kitchen floor. She'd looked so vulnerable, gorgeous. Black hair all mussed from sleep, luscious mouth tipped in a frown... vulnerable to him then.

Though his arousal raged hard in him, he couldn't get it up, and so he'd kept his distance. Knowing touching her would only make his lust worse, not better.

Gerard slammed his open palm on the counter, rattling the dishes in the sink. Breakfast had been a brilliant idea, she'd responded as he'd hoped. But then he'd growled and acted a baboon, scaring her. If he had any hope of freedom, of leaving a free man, he had to make her love him, not fear him.

"You can do this, Gerard," he growled, "you must."

Chapter 11

Already a week had flown by. Betty brushed some bronzer on her cheeks. Why she was primping when they were getting ready to go fishing on the lake? If Daddy had taught her one thing about fishing, it was that real fisherwomen didn't wear makeup. It would just melt off in the heat of the day. Usually she listened, but this time Gerard was coming with her and she wanted to look nice.

"Betty," he knocked on the door, "you almost ready, *Cherie*? Too much longer and the fish won't bite."

She dropped the brush and swiped her mascara up. "Just a minute."

The past week had flown by in a whirlwind. Trisha suspected something was up, Betty knew. Especially because she kept asking Betty to go out to the bar, have a late night drink, to which Betty stoutly refused. The moment the clock struck seven she was out the door, heart somersaulting in her chest, knowing he was home, and waiting on her. Trisha wasn't dumb and would soon start poking around, but right now, Gerard felt like her guilty secret.

It sort of made Betty feel bad, not sharing such a huge thing with her best friend, but this entire situation was so bizarre Betty felt an inexplicable need to keep mum about it and him.

In fact, this was her first day off in a week-- Trisha's too. Which meant in another hour Trisha would probably show up looking for her and would immediately see why Betty hadn't wanted drinks.

The phone rang.

"Betty?" Gerard called.

"Let the machine get it." It was probably Trisha. She blinked, blotting out the excess black glop from the corners of her eyes.

The machine whirred then beeped. "Listen you whore--"

Betty's heart stuttered the moment she recognized the voice and she threw the door open, running to the machine on legs that were suddenly heavy and clumsy. She tapped the red button on the machine to stop the recording.

Gerard's nostrils flared, his fists clenched, and he looked at her through slitted eyes. "Who was that?"

Pulse still racing, she squeezed her eyes shut and pinched the bridge of her nose. "Nobody."

It'd been over a week since Gretchen's last phone call-- long enough Betty had almost forgotten about her completely.

"Didn't sound like nobody to me," he said, his thumb grazing her chin and tipping it up. Betty huffed, giving him a weak smile.

"It's nothing."

His eyes were so blue this morning, deep and bottomless. Dangerous eyes, because if a girl wasn't careful, she could fall and lose herself in their hot depths. Something Betty could never afford to do. Though when he looked at her like that, all kind and searching, it made heat race through her limbs-- turning them to jelly, and making it hard to remember why she shouldn't jump in headlong.

He grinned, and rubbed his thumb across her cheekbone. "You've a smear on your eye. Grease, I think."

She chuckled and pushed his hand away. "Makeup. Let me go finish up. Did you pack the sandwiches?"

He pointed to the cooler. Amazed yet again by how efficient he was in her home, how well he knew her place already. How normal and comfortable it all felt, them sharing a home, cuddling each night in bed. Her stomach fluttered.

Betty turned, and he grabbed her shoulder, his large hand gripping gently. "You sure you're okay?"

She patted his hand. "I'm fine, Gerard."

As Betty padded back to the bathroom the phone rang again. Her spine stiffened. This was insane, when would Gretchen understand she wanted nothing to do with James? As if! Especially now with Gerard in the picture, it was like comparing boring apples to exotic passion fruit. Betty marched back, intending to hurl some of her own insults at the woman, when Gerard picked up the phone and growled, "What?"

The mask of anger he wore was quickly replaced by a lifting of his brows and a pulling of his lips. He held the phone out to her. "Somebody asking for you."

"If it's Trisha, I'm not here," she whispered and waved her hands in front of her face.

"It's a boy. I think."

Only one boy would call her at home. Smiling now, she grabbed the phone. "Hello, monkey butt! What's crackalackin'?"

Gerard gave her a strange look, and she giggled, clutching the receiver with both hands.

Briley chuckled. "Hi, Aunt Betty. You're weird," he said in that high pitched voice of his that never failed to elicit a smile from her. "I want to see you today."

"Aww, monkey. That's sweet. Where's your dad?"

"Dad!" he cried. "Aunt Betty."

Betty licked her lips. Gerard leaned against the counter, his arms crossed over his chest, and wearing an amused grin. "What is crackalackin'?" his deep burr resonated with a hint of laughter.

She opened her mouth to answer, when her brother got on the line. She held up a finger.

"Betty?" Kelly asked.

"Hey, K, you pulling a shift tonight?"

"Yeah."

Betty heard the exhaustion in his voice and could almost picture him running his hand over his head. Poor thing. He was working too hard, and now that it was summer vacation Briley would be out of school. Pulling long shifts was tough enough, but pulling long shifts and having to pay for special child care was even tougher.

"Let me take the kiddo today," she offered.

"Oh man, would you. That would be great." His relief rushed over the line in a loud whoosh. "I've got to head out in about twenty minutes."

"Yep," she nodded, "I'll be there. See you."

They blew air kisses and hung up.

"Are we not going fishing today?" Gerard asked.

Betty ran to her hall mirror and grabbed a tissue off the end table, dabbing at the black smear. "No we are. We're just making a pit stop first."

Once she was satisfied she no longer looked like a raccoon, she grabbed her keys and purse. "Well let's go."

Gerard picked up the cooler and followed her into the car. Betty climbed in, turned the ignition, and backed out of the parking lot.

"I guess I should warn you, I'm picking up Briley. He's going fishing with us."

She bit the corner of her lip. Hoping he wouldn't mind. She'd not thought to ask him, mainly because she didn't assume he'd care. But then again some guys weren't kid people, and if he in anyway made Briley feel unwelcomed, she'd have a serious conniption. Betty drummed on the wheel.

He didn't say anything for a moment.

"He's a good kid. Quiet. A little angel. Really, you'll like him."

"What is crackalackin'?" he asked finally.

"What?" Betty laughed, thrown for a moment by his question. "Umm, well, nothing really. It's slang. Means what's cracking. What's happening." She turned right at the light, heading down the country road toward Kelly's house.

The countryside was awash in sprays of gentle pinks and soft yellows, the gloom of night still held court at the very tip of the sky as the sun slowly crested the horizon.

"Then why don't you simply say that?" he asked.

She laughed. "Who knows. It would be easier wouldn't it?"

He nodded.

Betty gripped the wheel tighter. "So do you mind?"

"*Non, Cherie.* I do not."

He seemed so relaxed this morning. Nights spent in his arms, talking about stupid stuff like which superhero movie was better (he'd seen every Spiderman and Superman, and so far thought the superhero customs much too girlie for him-- but she'd promised he'd love Iron Man), or how to make the perfect soufflé without causing the top to sink in, had only made her feel closer to him. Apart from the first night, they'd not discussed the fairies, the pendant, or any other part of his past. It was the elephant in the room both refused to broach. She wasn't stupid, eventually they'd have to talk about what happened after the month, but not now.

Now was a time of discovery.

Each day was a new surprise. Like finding he was a closet metro. Though, that wasn't really all that surprising. Even now, just to go fishing, he had his dark brown hair slicked back, he'd chosen the pair of jeans with cross stitched pockets and a dark burgundy shirt. In no way did he look comfortable, unlike her in a pair of cut off blue jeans and ribbed tank top. Then again, she was wearing makeup... bit of a pot/kettle moment there.

But there were other things, cool things she bet only she knew now. Like the fact that he loved to have the shell of his ear rubbed right before bed. That his favorite color was gray-- though not the dreary gray of a cloudy morning, but the lavender gray of twilight. If he'd been born on Earth he'd have been a master chef, that apart from sex, the man also had a true passion for cooking and was damn good at it.

In turn he put up with her Manga obsession, watching one episode of Dragon Love

Spell after another, long into the night. Discussing why overly dramatized facial expressions conveyed a truer sense of emotion as opposed to the Americanized drawings, and how Xena could have kicked any gladiator's butt. A point he hotly denied.

"I'm going to have to introduce you to my brother," she said.

He brushed the pad of his thumb against her neck and the touch was electric, snapping her nerves to life and making her every cell hyperaware of his proximity. She breathed, tasting the scent of his woodsy cologne on her tongue.

"I was beginning to wonder if you'd let anyone else know I existed." His tone was teasing, and the deep tenor of his accent made her roll down a window, suddenly hot and shaky.

The cool breeze caressed her flesh, helping her to think clearer.

"He'll want to meet you because of Briley." She nibbled her lip. "Have you ever been around someone with down syndrome, Gerard?"

"What is that?" he asked, cocking his head.

Spying Kelly's white farmhouse in the distance, she slowed down to twenty miles per hour so she could finish their talk.

"It's a chromosomal disorder. Makes kids slower to learn and develop. But they're smart as a whip." She jerked to look at him, nodding hard. "So don't you dare treat him bad, or be mean. I'm serious, Gerard. I'm very careful who I let around my nephew, so if you've got a problem now, you tell me."

His eyes widened, and he held up his hands. "Peace, *Cherie*. I'll not harm the boy. I confess I know nothing of that disorder, but I'll be on my best behavior." He crossed his heart and she was pretty sure hers melted.

"Okay, well come on then." She pulled into the gravel driveway and parked the car. The moment she stopped, the red door flew open and an adorable blond headed child waved at her.

She smiled.

"Is that Briley?" he asked.

"Yes."

"Aunt Betty," Briley was halfway down the steps and running full tilt toward her, his arms open and wearing his hunter's green fishing jacket. A tan piece of fabric bulged from his hand. "I'm ready. I'm ready. I'm gonna catch lots of largemouth bass."

Then he slammed into her with the joyful exuberance unique to him. She hugged him tight, squeezing hard and peppering his forehead with kisses. "Missed you, monkey butt. Golly, it's been a long time. Well let me look at you."

She pushed him back to arms length, putting on a show of studying him. His warm brown eyes glowed, the exact shade of melted chocolate, they always sparkled with life. He giggled. "You saw me three weeks ago."

"No way," she shook her head, "because I swear you grew an inch. No five!"

"Aunt Betty," Briley giggled and hugged her again.

She ruffled his hair. Kelly clapped her on the shoulder, his other hand full of fishing rod, tackle box, and a Spiderman book bag. Betty looked up. "Oh jeez, K, you've looked better."

The man didn't just sport a five o'clock shadow, more like a ten, and his brown hair had been finger brushed, if that. His blue scrubs though were sharp and wrinkle free as always. "Too many shifts, not enough sleep, and now Jennifer drops him off late last night..."

Betty rolled her eyes. "Another get rich quick scheme convention?"

"Something like that," he growled, forking his fingers through his hair. "I've got the rest of the week off, but today." He grabbed his hands as if in prayer. "You're a life saver."

Betty kissed his cheek, his gray-black stubble rubbing her cheek. "Anything for my, big bro."

Gerard cleared his throat, and Betty jumped guiltily, she'd almost forgotten him. "Gerard, this is Kelly and Briley." She clapped Briley's back.

Kelly stepped forward and grabbed Gerard's hand. "Who are you and how do you know my sister?"

Gerard straightened almost imperceptibly, meeting Kelly's hard gaze head on.

"I'm--" he started.

"My boyfriend." Betty smiled at Gerard's startled expression and nodded at Kelly. "New boyfriend." She grabbed Gerard's hand.

Kelly cocked his head. "And why am I just hearing about this now? Does Trisha know?"

Betty ignored Gerard's burning look. "No, she doesn't, and besides when did you start getting so chummy with Trisha? As I recall you burned her in high school. Minor miracle she and I stayed friends after that." She arched a brow.

"Jeez, Betty, chill." Kelly rolled his eyes. "She was calling looking for you last night, apparently she called five times and went straight to voicemail each time."

"Hot date." She winked at Gerard, who suddenly seemed to understand and wrapped his arm around her shoulders, giving it a gentle squeeze. Whoa, did her stomach just flutter? Sheesh, she felt sixteen and unsure again.

"Aunt Betty, is he gonna be my uncle?" Briley asked, brown eyes creasing into a deep frown. He stepped behind her back.

"No, monkey butt," she said.

"Maybe," Gerard said.

She shot him a venomous look. He didn't need to get into character that much, no need to give Briley hope. They both knew that wouldn't happen. His smile faltered.

Already the sun grew warmer on her back. Betty wore a green tank top and hadn't yet slathered her desperately pale body with sunscreen, she needed to get her butt in the car before she turned into a lobster.

"Okay, who wants to go fishing?" she raised her voice to an exaggerated pitch, trying to regain the happy vibe of only a moment ago.

She snatched the fishing rod, box, and bag from Kelly's lax hands and gave him a weak smile. "So yeah, I'll bring him back safe and sound tonight."

Kelly still looked like he was trying to work his way through her weak explanation, and if she hung around too much longer, her brilliant brother would see it for the white lie it was.

"Welp, k then!" She kissed his cheek, grabbed Briley and Gerard's hands, and dragged them to the car.

"Bye, Daddy!" Briley waved happily.

Once in the car, and all buckled up, she waved again and pretended she didn't see Kelly mouth: Wait!

"Boyfriend?" Gerard's deep barrel voice did weird things to her insides, made them feel all tingly and fuzzy. She squirmed in her seat. "Hmm…" He sounded amused and heat bloomed on her cheeks.

"Hush," she whispered, she didn't want Briley hearing she'd lied. After all, she always told him how bad it was to do that, if he found out she'd lied, he'd hound her about it all day long.

Gerard's jaw clamped shut with an audible click. His nostrils flared, and her eyes widened when she realized what she'd done. The pendant flared hot against her breast.

"And I mean that in a totally independent non-bossy way."

He took a deep breath and glared at her. "You swore you wouldn't."

She peeked at Briley in the backseat. He was oblivious, staring out the window with a happy grin.

"I'm sorry," she hissed. "I forget sometimes. But…" she pointedly looked at the mirror and jerked her head, "not here. Cool?"

Gerard thinned his lips. "*Non*, I'm not cold."

She frowned and then laughed. "No, I mean is that okay?"

"Why don't you just say that then?" he grumped.

"It's called a colloquialism. An informal expression used in common speech and you're right, it's total nonsense. Unfortunately I speak a lot of nonsense." She bit her lip and tapped his forearm. "Still friends?"

The world stretched out like an endless horizon of trees and sky. The robin's blue sky held barely a trace of clouds.

Gerard nodded. "Cool?" His brows furrowed, seeking her approval.

She fought the grin and nodded. "Good enough."

"Aunt Betty," Briley chirped. "I want music."

"Well, you're in luck." She popped ol' faithful into her radio and cranked it up loud.

Briley clapped his hands and started singing loud and clear. "I love you-"

Her heart soared as she crested the hill. "You love me," she joined him, her warble strong, but uncaring how badly it cracked. Briley thought she had the voice of an angel, and Gerard, sticking his finger in his ear with a wince, wouldn't stop her from making her little man happy.

Chapter 12

The fish had stopped biting hours ago. Although the mosquitos were still going strong. Betty smacked her leg and sighed.

Briley laughed, a glop of peanut butter coated the corner of his plump pink lips. "Should have brought the bug spray."

She rolled her eyes. "You're totally right, Aunt Betty is a dunderhead sometimes."

He giggled, wiggling his rod in the algae tinted water. Bugs danced ripples across the placid lake. Bubbles surfaced next to their boot. A minnow had been teasing Briley all day, stealing his worm before jumping off the line. Briley was determined to catch the thief.

"Don't bob the line, *garcon*," Gerard touched his rod, stilling Briley's excited movements. "You'll scare the fish."

"Garcon ain't a word," Briley laughed and shook his head, blonde wisps of hair slipped into his eye, but he did stop jerking the rod. Gerard only smiled.

This morning she'd feared Gerard might do or say something wrong to Briley. But the man had been as patient as a saint. Threading Briley's hook with one worm after another. Or when he snapped the hook off on a piece of drift wood, he'd rethread the hook again. He smiled and laughed often and Briley had complemented his superior sandwich making abilities-- looking shyly at Aunt Betty and stammering he might love her, but her food tasted really yucky sometimes. To which she'd blustered and pretended to be offended until he crawled over the wooden seat-- worrying her for a split second when the small paddle boat rocked precariously-- and gave her a big hug. After that hug (two hours ago) she'd been chopped liver, it'd been Mr. Gerard this and Mr. Gerard that, and Betty's cheek muscles were sore from smiling so hard.

Briley held the rod absolutely still, barely breathing, his excitement palpable. Gerard reached into the cooler and took out a piece of ham. He ripped the lunchmeat in half and dropped it into the water with a small plop.

"What are you doin'?" Briley asked.

The ham bobbed on the surface for a moment before sinking slowly in. A silver flash streaked through the water. Briley shrieked. "The minnow. It's back. Give me a net," he demanded.

Gerard reached for the green net, and with a swift flick of his wrist, slipped the unsuspecting fish into it. It flipped and flopped, thrashing violently.

Briley cooed and dropped the rod. It thunked on the bottom of the boat. His hands shook as he reached for the net. "It's so little." He giggled, and tickled the silvery fish's belly.

The thing was no bigger than Betty's pinky finger and she knew they'd have to toss it back.

Gerard nodded. "I think it's ticklish."

Briley snorted. "Fish ain't ticklish, Mr. Gerard."

Gerard's eyes widened into a shocked expression. "*Non*? But see it is dancing under your touch."

"Naw," Briley jutted out his jaw, "it's gaspin' for air. Here now," he patted the teeny fish one last time. "I just wanted to say hi. Now it's time to go back." He dipped the net back into the water and the fish slid out, taking a moment to right itself before zipping off, disappearing beneath murky waters.

He dusted his hands on his mud stained jeans and grinned, exposing the small gap between his front teeth. "Aunt Betty, I got my costume," he said, so matter of factly it took Betty a second to follow, then she clapped her hands excitedly.

"Me too! MoComic-con, baby!" They sang in unison and Gerard groaned.

"Next weekend. You're still taking me, right, Aunt Betty?"

"Yup." Betty shoulder bumped Gerard. "What was that groan for?"

"Is that not the geek stuff you'd mentioned earlier? With the two men in spandex on your yellow card?"

"Oh yeah," Briley fist pumped.

She nodded, grinning hard. "And you're coming."

A large black bird swooped from one tree branch to another, knocking some fat brown seed pods off the tree. It landed with a loud plop into the water. The ripples reached out to their floating boat.

Gerard groaned louder. "I thought you'd say that."

"Daddy bought me my Spiderman custom already," Briley said.

"Amazing or Symbiote?" she asked.

Gerard's face scrunched into a confused mask.

Briley must have noticed, because he clapped Gerard on the shoulder and very patiently explained that Amazing had bright red and blue colors, and the symbiote suit was covered in black slime from outer space that made Peter Parker kind of crazy.

"Indeed," Gerard said, then peeked over Briley's shoulder at Betty with an help-me expression in his eyes.

She covered her mouth to ward off the threatening giggle. But as Briley continued to explain the entire history of Spiderman, and Gerard's eyes started to glaze, she finally decided to put him out of his misery.

"Monkey butt, time to read. You know you have to get in at least thirty minutes a day."

"Aww, Aunt Betty, do I have to?" he sighed, and set his lips into a heavy pout, hanging his head.

"Well, I guess it wouldn't hurt to read to you." She crossed her arms. "But only if you brought the adventures of the amazing boy wizard."

He nodded, and grabbed his book bag, digging around. "Yup. But I want Mr. Gerard to read to me."

"*Non*!" Gerard sliced his hand through the air. "I don't read."

"Aww, come on," Briley shoved the massive tome into Gerard's hand. He pointed midway in the center of the page with his chubby finger. "Chapter 14. I did a lot...," he stressed the word with a roll of his eyes, "of reading last night. 10 whole pages!"

Betty clapped, but she was no longer smiling. Gerard was staring at the page with a look akin to horror. Even his breathing seemed rapid and hard. He'd done this the other night when she'd shoved her book into his hands.

Briley sighed. "I'll start then. *The friends*..." Briley tasted the word, pronouncing each slowly and precisely, stuttering over particularly hard ones.

"Pha... pha--tom..."

Betty peeked. "Phantom."

"Phantom." Briley nodded and took a deep breath, half parts relief and half exasperation. "Your turn, Mr. Gerard." He thrust the book back onto Gerard's lap.

Briley had taken five minutes to read the first paragraph. In that time a white ring had spread around Gerard's mouth, and the instant Briley turned the reigns over, the vein in the side of his neck jumped.

Betty chewed on her lip. He couldn't read. Why hadn't she picked up on that before? Maybe because the man was plenty smart. She didn't want to humiliate him, and opened her mouth to tell Briley he must do it, but Briley spoke up first.

He looked at Gerard with a thoughtful look. "You can't read, can you, Mr. Gerard?"

The muscle in Gerard's cheek ticked. Betty held her breath, gazing at him, hoping he'd look at her. But he refused to acknowledge her.

Briley's smile was huge. "I can't read real good neither. Tell you what, Mr. Gerard, how 'bout we try my favoritest book ever." Gently he took the book from Gerard's tense hands.

Gerard sat silent as stone, blinking and licking his incisors, still refusing to look at her.

Briley pulled another book out and sat it on Gerard's lap. He opened to the first page and pointed to the word. "My teacher says you gotta taste the sounds." He puckered his lips. "*A little steam engine*," he began, "*had a long train of cars to pull*." Briley paused. "It don't work if you don't say it with me, Mr. Gerard."

Swallowing hard, Gerard finally looked down at Briley and repeated his words-- slowly, methodically. His mouth forming the letters with hands visibly shaking.

"*I think I can*," Briley said.

"*I think I can*," Gerard repeated.

"I know you can," Betty whispered, heart trapped in a throat burning with tears.

Chapter 13

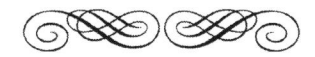

Her soft body wrapped around his like a warm hug. Gerard hadn't wanted her in his bed tonight, hadn't wanted to remember the humiliation of revealing he couldn't read. Of knowing she viewed him as less than, just like Belle had.

Her breaths were soft on his bare chest, tickling the hairs, and he rubbed her back. He'd not talked the rest of the day and she'd not forced him. After they'd dropped Briley off he'd gutted the trout they'd caught and prepared their dinner in silence. Once they'd eaten, he'd cleared the dishes, and she'd walked off. Betty hadn't asked him to watch yet another one of her awful Manga cartoons, and he'd left for his room, knowing this night she'd not join him. An hour later he was almost asleep when she crept into his room, pulled the sheets back, and snuggled up to him. That'd been three hours ago.

Why would she come? He was beneath her, intellectually inferior. His chest ached.

"I'm not stupid, *Cherie*."

She rolled over. Wide guileless eyes stared at him. "I never thought you were."

"You're awake?" he sighed, sitting up when she disentangled herself. He propped his head against the pillow, and stared out the window at the full moon that lit the room in its silvery glow.

She brushed her fingertips against the corner of his lips, forcing him to look back at her. Betty smiled, full lips curving into a sexy tilt, and he clenched his jaw, not wanting to want her. Not wanting to know her anymore.

"I know you're not stupid," she said softly.

He shook her hand off. "I never needed to learn. Where I'm from, where I live, it's not expected and generally frowned upon. A man is to be out hunting, providing for his family. One who sits and reads is considered vain and lazy."

She shook her head. "Gerard, I'm not judging."

"She did!" He snapped, shoving his face into hers. In some way wanting to see her eyes fill with fear, wanting her to leave, to run off, to forget he existed. That all the humiliations, one heaped upon another, would cease when she forgot him.

Betty jerked his chin. "I'm not her. I'm Betty Hart. I don't judge."

He snarled. "Of course you do. You judged me from the moment you met me."

"Hey," she smacked him on the chest, "probably because you were trying to play tonsil hockey with me, makes a girl jumpy."

He shook his head. "You make no sense."

She sighed. "Gerard, I didn't know you. But today, seeing you with Briley, how patient you were, how gentle…"

The pendant on her chest began to glow, bands of deepest indigo swirled like newly cut amethyst in the sunlight, and his pulse jerked hard, blood rushed to his ears. She did not stop talking, did not seem to notice what he'd seen, what had stirred hope like a seedling shooting from within the earth. The pendant still glowed in red and gold, but now there was purple, and the anger abated with the knowledge. Betty was falling in love with him.

Remembering his goal, he channeled his focus, knowing he must forget his anger.

"…you made him feel special. It's not often he gets to teach a grown up to read. Thank you." Then she kissed him.

A chaste peck on his cheek, but it was the first time Betty had ever initiated a kiss. Her touch burned fire, and he wanted to rub the spot where her lips had pressed against him.

Black hair tumbled around her pale shoulders like shadow. Like a moth drawn to its glowing demise, Gerard touched the silky strand lying across her breast. She shivered, her mouth parted, and the world around them melted into oblivion.

Gerard wanted to freeze this moment, remember it always. The way her pink belly shirt exposed her navel, how her nipples puckered-- presenting themselves like jewels to his waiting mouth. He licked his lips, wishing he could do more than touch her hair.

"Would you like to learn?" she asked, her sultry voice made him tremble.

He nodded, not knowing why he wanted to, only knowing he needed to. Needed to feel whole, needed to feel she saw him as more than an ignorant brute. "Yes, *Cherie*, I wish to learn."

Chapter 14

Betty pointed to the book-- at the picture of the little girl smiling at a running dog. "*See spot run*," she repeated slowly.

"Dammit," Gerard growled and flung the book off the kitchen table. "This is stupid."

Betty sighed and walked to the spot on the floor he dumped the book, she picked it up and opened it again. She wasn't angry or even annoyed with him. It was humiliating for him-- she knew-- for her to see him this way. A man like Gerard couldn't bear her thinking him weak. Not that she saw him that way, but perception was reality, at least in his mind.

"Gerard, it's how you'll learn. Trust me. Simple repetition, learning how to properly stress your vowels. It's how we all learned to read."

"It's a kids book. Nursery rhymes. I'm a man," he pounded his chest. His very bare, naked chest. The man seriously had a thing against clothes.

Then again, when they looked as yummy as he did, clothes were definitely optional. Betty grinned, and patted his hand. He gripped her fingers, giving it a tender squeeze and her heart tilted.

"You put that brilliant mind to good use and hurry up and learn then." She picked up his mug of tea and took a sip. He narrowed his eyes. They'd fallen into strange habits lately-- Betty taking swigs of his breakfast tea, and he eating her leftovers. She kind of liked it-- no scratch that-- she loved it. Loved seeing him in the morning, cuddling up to him at night, Betty was growing way too used to it, and didn't want to think about what would happen when their month was up. Thankfully, that wasn't for another two and half weeks and fourteen hours.

Not like she'd been keeping count or anything.

"I've gotta go to work." She checked her watch. "How do I look?" She twirled, her pastel flower printed dress hugged her calves and made her feel sexy. Lately her wardrobe had taken a huge upswing from jeans and sweaters, to dresses and hip hugging skirts.

He looked her up and down, a slow perusal that made her thighs tingle and her nipples harden.

Gerard smirked. "You are fortunate I cannot drag you to the bedroom, *mon petite*."

Stomach taking a serious nosedive, she tripped over her feet and headed to the door. Wishing like hell he could. She wasn't fortunate at all, because at this point she felt just as cursed as him.

"I'll be back," she called over her shoulder, running from him, from the temptation of a forbidden fruit and the very real knowledge that when this was all over, she'd be lucky to have a still beating heart.

His laughter floated behind her.

***

Betty missed him. She kept sneaking glances at the wall clock. Two hours left. She wanted to call, just to hear his voice. But what would she say? 'I miss you. You're so hot. Let's have wild sex.' Which of course could never happen.

"I swear time goes slower when you keep staring," Trisha's sharp voice penetrated through her pity party.

Betty dropped her head into her hands and leaned against the desk. The library was empty. Only one customer in four hours. Why stay open when no one bothered to come anymore?

Or course she shouldn't think that because this place paid her bills, but seriously.

Trisha's green gaze bored holes into her skull. Betty pried open an eye, unable to ignore the mile long stare anymore. "Yes?"

Full red lips set into a stern line of disapproval. "Dish. Now." Trisha planted hands on her hips and tapped her high heeled foot on the carpet. "Who is he, and when did you meet him?"

Hmm… to tell the truth, or not tell the truth, that was the question. Trisha was in a fighting mood, her small hands were balled into tight fists, and a hurt look glinted in the depths of her malachite eyes.

Not truth. Definitely, not truth. Betty stood. "What are you talking about, Trisha?" She pulled a drawer out and rifled through it, pretending to suddenly be in desperate need of a sticky note.

"You are the worst liar in history," Trisha flattened her hand on the desk, "you know I know, so let's stop playing, and just tell me. I can't believe we've been best friends for twenty years, and you can't trust me with this." Her words were sharp and sliced Betty deep, she winced, knowing she'd been a bad friend.

Betty sighed. "I didn't tell you because I knew what you'd do."

"Do what? What can I do when I don't know anything?" Trisha threw her manicured hands high, shrugging with exaggerated anger.

"I kept him," Betty whispered, pulling out the yellow sticky note and doodling on the pad, anything to keep from looking up.

"Him?" Trisha questioned, and then sucked in a breath when understanding dawned. "The hottie from the library?"

"Mmm." Betty bit her lip.

"No you didn't!" Trisha slapped her arm. "The dude that was all busted up, the French dreamboat that gave me a serious case of--" she stopped talking when Betty glanced sharply at her. Trisha cleared her throat. "That guy?"

Betty rolled her eyes. "Yes, that guy. Now tell me how stupid I am." She grabbed her throbbing pendant, the thing hadn't stopped pulsating since the fishing trip yesterday. It was just this side of warm, almost hot against her breast. And she'd noticed in the mirror this morning that it now shone with more threads of purple than red.

"You're stupid!" Trisha growled. "He could be dangerous."

"He's not," Betty asserted with a swift shake of her head.

"How do you know?" Trisha lowered her voice into a sharp hiss.

The bell above the door pinged as the second customer of the day-- an elderly man-- walked in and headed straight toward the civil war era section.

Betty waited until he was well out of earshot before answering. "I just do, okay."

When Trisha got really mad, she'd grab her hair and twist it up into a tight bun. The more tight it got, the madder she was. She wound her hair so tight, her eyebrows pulled back. "Next you're gonna be telling he's asked for your hand in marriage." Narrowing flinty eyes she said, "he hasn't, has he?"

"No. Jeez, Trish, what do you take me for?" Betty gripped the edge of the desk, while her pulse beat a staccato tattoo in her skull.

"Are you sleeping with him?" Trisha asked the question like an accusation, and Betty's blood boiled, the one percent threatened to rear its ugly head.

The man appeared for a second, glancing at them with a concerned frown before quickly scooting down another isle.

"I don't see how that's any of your damn business," Betty snapped.

"But it is my business!" Trisha pounded her fist, her words ringing like cannon fire in a still forest.

"Keep your voice down," Betty pleaded, jerking her head in the direction of the book shelves.

Trisha gulped air until her breathing calmed and then smoothed a hand over her blond head. "You want to know why it's my business, Betty? I'll tell you why." She pointed to her chest. "I can sleep with a man, and it's not personal. It's fun. I don't expect more than that, but you can't. You sleep with a man and you're in love. And let's face it, honey, your track record sucks."

Betty slapped Trisha's finger off her. "How dare you? This is exactly why I didn't tell you. I knew you'd act all stupid, and crazy, and silly. Look, yeah, it wasn't the smartest thing to take him home with me, but as I recall it you told me to."

"No." Trisha's blood red fingernail drove like a spike through the air. "If you recall, I do believe I said take him to Kelly, or drop him off at the shelter. What part of that did you not understand? The man could be a rapist, a murderer…"

Try none of the above. But Betty couldn't tell her that, and Trisha wouldn't believe it anyway. She huffed. "Yes, he could have been. But he's not. So why do you care? He makes me laugh. He makes Briley laugh. I lo…" She jerked, realizing what she'd almost said.

Trisha's eyes widened. "Love him? Is that what you were about to say?"

"No," Betty shook her head, "I like him."

"That's not what I heard." Trisha crossed her arms.

The man came up to the counter with two leather bound books in his hands. His rheumy blue eyes studied the girls. "I could come back later if you're busy," he said in the thin, scratchy voice of a man well beyond his prime.

Betty sighed, and plastered on a smile, though inside she wanted to cry. Why couldn't Trisha just be happy for her? Betty wasn't going to fall in love with the man, it wasn't like that. She didn't have a choice in the matter anyway. Yeah, so she'd almost used the word love. But not love-love, more like the way one loved a favorite pair of shoes, or a puppy.

She took the books, grateful her hands didn't shake too badly. "No, now is fine. Library card, please?"

He pulled a well-worn card out of his pocket. The picture showed him, maybe ten years younger, with the horseshoe hair, but brownish instead of gray, and without the frizzy tufts poking from his ears. What would Gerard look like when he aged? Would he age? Thoughts scrambled through her head as she checked the man's books into the computer.

Trisha paced behind Betty's chair like a restless tiger in a cage, and Betty flashed him an apologetic smile as she handed him back the books. "Due back in a month, Mr. Adams."

He nodded, grabbed the books, and sprinted as fast as his old legs would carry him out the door. Betty sighed, swiveling in her chair.

Trisha gripped the sides of her chair, pinning Betty in place.

"Listen, sweetie, if you think I'm being mean, I probably am. I miss you. But more than that, I'm worried about you. Can't you see he's a rebound guy? And not a good one. Yeah, he's incredibly delicious, and if I were you I'd probably slather his body in warm chocolate and lick it all off."

"Oh jeez, you're so disgusting." Betty scrunched her face.

"But, I'm telling you now, the man is a pig. A player. He's another James, except prettier. He's playing you, girl. He's having his fun, but I swear to you, he'll leave. Just like all the rest."

"You don't know that," Betty mumbled.

Trisha smiled softly, stepping back and nodding. "Yes I do, sweetling. Because he's just like James, just like high school quarterback Carter, and he's just like me." Her voice trailed off sadly. She hugged her arms to her chest.

The words were a fist hammering through her heart. She looked at her friend, as if seeing her for the first time. Trisha looked pretty today. Hunter green top and woodland brown pencil skirt-- a luscious figure on a petite frame. Compared to her, Betty might as well have been an ogre. Tall and gangly, awkward and a nerd to boot.

"We're all fun, but zero substance, honey. Just guard your heart, Betty. Promise me. Because when you get hurt, I get hurt, and I don't want to see my best friend turn into a puddle of crying goo again. Not over a player." With that, Trisha turned and walked to the back of the library.

Trisha was right. Gerard would leave. Either she fell in love with him, or he'd die. Neither choice was particularly appealing.

If she fell in love, he'd leave. Only she had to love him to save him, he didn't have to love her back. Which meant his heart was free to beguile and seduce someone else. Someone more like Trisha-- perfect, sexy, a blond bombshell-- a someone Betty could never hope to be. But if she didn't love him, they'd kill him. The thought tore Betty's heart into a million tiny pieces.

Love sucked.

Chapter 15

"You promise not to laugh?" Betty's voice came out small behind the bathroom door.

Gerard sat on the bed, drinking his morning brew, breathing in the bitter vapors, anything to try and get more alert. "I'll promise no such thing, *Cherie*. Spandex looks awful on anyone."

"You're not helping."

Today was the day he'd been dreading all week. Comic-con. She'd woken him at an ungodly hour, stars still thick and heavy in the sky, with the fevered excitement of a child at Yule. She'd tried her damndest to get him to dress in character too. No chance in hell. Blue jeans and a shirt were good enough for him.

"Just come out, Elliptical," he growled.

"It's Eclipse, and I'm not gonna come out unless you're nice," her voice trembled.

Gerard chuckled, tapping the side of the ceramic mug with his thumb. "Fine, fine. Come out please."

The knob turned.

First thing he noticed was a shiny pair of black thigh high boots with heels so high she seemed to tower in the doorway. A black and navy blue cape fluttered behind her, hanging well past her knees.

He swallowed, tongue thick, as his gaze continued the slow slide up. Silvery black spandex covered her torso and chest, reminding him of a bustier. His fingers flexed hard around the ceramic. The top pushed her breasts up and out, her exquisite mounds, plump and firm, and begging for a man's touch. His touch.

Betty's hair hung long and loose around her shoulders, framing her heart shaped face. But it was the silk mask tied around her eyes that made his pulse race and knees tremble for want of her. Glowing blue eyes stared back at him from behind the mask, as electric as a hot bolt of lightning. He'd have laughed at the ridiculous circlet on her head, the two circles-- one golden, the other black-- had it not been for those eyes.

What had she done? What magic had she used? "Your eyes, *Cherie*?" he said, his voice sounded thick to his ears.

She smiled, and for the first time ever, he noticed a slight dimple curve a sickle shape in her right cheek.

"It's contacts." She tossed her head, sending her curls flying behind her. "You like?"

Gerard shot to his feet, gripping the cup like his life depended on it. For a moment, one moment to be free of Galeta's bloody curse, he'd throw Betty down on the bed and make her sing for him. "I like."

The heart pendant sparkled deeper shades of Indigo. Did she know? Could she sense the change? Gerard's only thought was of his freedom, saving his life. He ground his molars-- confused if that's really what he wanted anymore.

He could hardly breathe around the heat of her gaze. The room grew thick and cloying, filled with an impossible tension. Like stepping out in a storm only seconds after a lightning strike-- ozone laced air still shivering with raw volts of power.

Betty walked to him, but he couldn't move. His heart beat a painful rhythm in his chest, demanding he do something, demanding he take control as he'd so often done before. But he wasn't in control, she stripped him bare, made him forget who he was, what he was. All he knew in that moment, was that Betty was the most divine creation he'd ever seen.

Her fingers grazed his, and for a moment he thought she'd push him down on the bed. But instead she yanked the cup out of his hands and with a saucy wink, drank.

Her throat worked as she swallowed, and he shifted toward her, moving like shaved iron into her magnetic pull. "You know I like that."

Ruby red lips curled up into a slow smile. "Like what?"

"Your lips and tongue touching the same spot mine did. It's like a kiss, *Cherie*."

The cup visibly shook in her hands, sloshing the drink. "This is coffee," she said it breathless, voice hitched and strained.

He nodded, stealing the cup back and setting it on the night stand. "I've developed a craving."

"For coffee?" her whisper feathered across his lips like a caress.

Gerard grabbed her face, the softness of her skin like silk against his rough palms. "So soft. *Mon ange*." His angel, and she was that. Then there was no more talking, only tasting.

He moved his mouth against hers, the smooth friction made him groan. Her lips were the softest satin. "Open for me, *Cherie*."

Betty's fingers found his shirt, she bunched the fabric in her fists and moaned, it was enough. Gerard licked, tasted, and suckled. Her tongue tasted of mint and coffee-- both sweet and bitter. She clawed at his head with the frenzy of a woman desperate for more, he slipped his tongue into the warm recess of her mouth, their tongues dueled. A mating pantomime-- each seeking dominance, each expressing with moans and guttural sounds how much they'd longed for this.

Too soon she broke away. Gerard was left panting, his forehead pressed against hers, willing his body to stop trembling.

"Briley," she said her nephew's name with a regretful sigh.

Gerard didn't want to stop touching her, he rubbed his bristly cheek against her smooth one. Betty's hands crawled under his shirt, her nails scratching lightly at his back, and gods he didn't want to leave this room. He wanted her all to himself, all day, all night.

But this was important to her.

"This isn't over, *Cherie*," he promised, his thumb tracing the plump swell of her bottom lip. "Not by a long shot."

***

"I'm Spiderman!" Briley made small *shwing* sounds, pumping his fist at groups of people, some of whom were dressed in the most ridiculous costumes Gerard had ever seen.

Briley's was bad enough, black, silver, and white, with a large spider at its center, but even that was preferable to some of the others. There'd been a lime green thing of fur that snarled and limped along on six cloven legs, a fat lizard like tail dragging along behind its enormous ass. Several silver painted bodies, eyes glowing much like Betty's. But where Betty's made Gerard hot and eager to touch and fondle, these made him uneasy and flexing his fist with a need to smash in noses, especially when one (a male by the sound of its deep voice) moved in close to Betty and attempted to pat her rear.

That ass belonged to him for the next week, and he'd not allow a soul to fondle it but him.

"Eclipse!" a shrill, highly feminine voice screamed her name.

Betty was bent over a booth, looking at comics when she stilled and turned. Her cape whispering behind her impossibly lean legs, and Gerard desired nothing more than to steal his harpy tongued wench far from the chaotic milieu.

Betty squealed, she then grabbed one of his hands and one of Briley's, and shoved her way through the crowd to the still waving female headed their way. She dressed similar to Betty-- blue and silver cape and black spandex-- but her plump form didn't elicit the same sort of passion for him.

Her chubby face was splotchy and sweaty, green hair frizzed wildly about her head, and the bustier (a size too small) seemed painted on the way it bulged at the seams.

"Nightmare," Betty said, dropping their hands.

The moment Betty acknowledged the other hero, the plump one dropped to her knee, genuflecting almost fully to the floor, and held her hands out in supplication. "The Bleeding Hearts have gathered, my Queen," she said solemnly. "We await your directives."

Gerard snorted, covering his mouth and tried hard not to laugh. Betty turned a hard stare on him, then raked the air with her clawed hand, before turning back to Nightmare.

"Arise, noble hero. Your Queen welcomes you," Betty modulated her voices an octave deeper, and the sultry sound of it shivered down his spine.

Nightmare stood and grabbing her face, Betty rubbed noses with her.

"Ms. Lydia," Briley squealed after the apparent ceremony finished.

Lydia (Gerard refused to even think of her as nightmare anymore) grabbed Briley in a tight hug and ruffled his head, even though his hair was covered by a full mask. "Heya, squirt. Havin' fun?"

Briley nodded and sought Gerard's hand. "Mr. Gerard bought me lots of candy and we saw Xena and Lady DragonSpell and I got to take a picture with Spiderman!"

Gerard stiffened, glancing at the boys chubby fingers within his own. Betty sucked in a sharp breath, her hands over her mouth. Gerard's eyes grew wide, knowing something had just happened, but not understanding what.

But Lydia leaned in to whisper, killing the moment. "You should know, Eclipse, the Rockers have a booth next to ours. The bastards…"

"There is a child present," Gerard growled, feeling oddly protective of Briley, an astonishing thing considering he'd never particularly been fond of kids. Though he found he kind of liked this one.

Betty again whipped around to face him, this time a smile crooked her lips.

"Oh my bad." Lydia zipped her lips. "Sorry, squirt."

For his part, Briley seemed completely oblivious as he happily sucked away at a lollipop he'd dug out of his bag. He'd pushed his mask half way up, it now bunched around his cheeks, his lips were coated with the red candy.

Betty pulled some wet wipes from her pocket to clean up his face, and then gestured for Lydia to lead the way. Gerard barely held his groan in check. Were it not for the fact that Betty looked damnably delicious in the costume, he'd demand they head back home now. He hated the crowds, hated this world, and wanted her attention all to himself.

They walked to a booth well in the back of the monstrously large building, a gaggle of silver and blue bedecked 'heroes' gathered around it, reminding Gerard of a flock of geese. Some short, tall, fat, slim-- but all deferring to Betty. Bowing and pontificating about how wonderful it was to see her, and 'all hail the Queen', then they each took turns rubbing noses. Honestly, Gerard found the entire affair ridiculous, but he couldn't deny watching her smile and laugh flooded his body with a warmth that ripped through him like a spear.

"Mr. Gerard," Briley looked up at him, the candy dangled from his hands. "I'm tired."

He sighed. "Me too, *garcon*." Spying a row of white fold up tables, he pointed. "Let's sit."

The moment they sat, Briley went back to sucking his candy, and Gerard watched her. What was happening to him? Acting like a girl the way his eyes constantly sought her out, watching her every move like a man entranced. Pulse quickening when she laughed, when even the tinkle of her laughter reached his desperate ears.

Drumming his fingers on the table, he shook his head. The pendant had very little crimson in it now. She was falling for him, but it still wasn't enough. Because no matter how much he wanted to slide his shaft deep into her willing, hot body, he couldn't harden. If he couldn't harden, she didn't love him, and if she didn't love him, he'd die.

One week. T'was all they had left. What more could he do? What hadn't he done? He cooked for her, listened to her, watched her repulsive cartoons, and still something inside her resisted him. Should he attempt a seduction? Would that push her over the top?

"Do you love, Aunt Betty?" Briley's small voice broke his musings.

"What?" he growled, staring down at the boy.

Briley licked his lollipop. "I said--"

"I know what you said, boy," Gerard snapped, grabbing his pounding skull.

"Then why did you ask me to repeat myself?" Briley rolled his eyes and gave him a goofy grin.

Gerard snorted, it was very hard to stay aggravated with the boy. He was completely unfazed by anger. "It's not as simple as that, *garcon*."

"Yes, it is." He nodded and snatched his hood off. The sweaty strands of his blond hair stuck to his forehead. "I love her." He shrugged. "Easy."

Briley's fingers glistened with pink stickiness. On the next table an almost empty bottle of water sat alone. Gerard snatched up a napkin, and uncorking the bottle, wet the tip of the napkin. Whoever left their water shouldn't have.

He cleaned the boy's hands.

"I like her," Gerard reluctantly admitted, and shifted on his seat. Saying it, acknowledging it, didn't help his dilemma. It only made it worse. Because he would still leave. He had to. She was of Earth, he of Kingdom. What if she didn't like it there? He couldn't stay in Earth forever, he loved his world, and whoever he wound up with had to love it too. What if she didn't want him?

He frowned, the thought making him rough as he rubbed harder at Briley's hands, using yet more water to get the worst of the mess off.

"You're going to leave aren't you?"

Gerard stopped, and turned his face to the boy's. Clever brown eyes studied him, not the eyes of a dullard, but a human who saw more than others would, or could, ever know.

"Who told you that?" he growled.

Briley shrugged, yanking his hands back and licking what Gerard hadn't taken off. "Because you didn't say it."

Gerard wadded up the disgusting napkin and tossed it into the garbage. When he looked back at her, it was to see her smiling at him. His heart clenched, like an ogre had taken a ham fist and smashed it in. He jerked and turned away.

"Who are you?" A rough masculine voice pierced his skull.

Gerard looked up. A massive beast of a human-- muscles bulging on top of muscles-- stared down at him from behind a full mask. Green eyes, like deepest moss, pinned him hard to the chair. Blond hair hung long and loose down the things back.

"I said, who are you? What class do you belong to?"

Gerard had heard the greeting all day. Though not directed at him. Dressed as he was, he might as well have been invisible in this circus of freaks.

The Green thing (as it was dressed entirely in green from its patent leather boots, to its green halter top) flattened a work roughened palm against his chest. Then the voice turned husky, throaty.

"Only the guild can walk these halls, mortal." Blunt fingers walked up his chest, toward his neck. "State your business. Or…" the voice hit an octave lower, going even more throaty. Was this creature attempting to seduce him? Bloody hell. "Have you come to visit, Gargantuan?"

Full red lips curved into a large grin.

Gerard couldn't decide whether he spoke to a male, female, or a creature of Kingdom itself. He'd never encountered anything so masculine and yet at the same time, feminine.

He narrowed his eyes. Betty had taught him much of her language. "Notta chance," he said calmly.

"Mmm. Really. Never heard of you, Notta." The fingers traced his jaw, sexual light flared hot and bright from Gargantuan's eyes. "What is your guild?"

"In hell."

The hands stopped moving. "Get out of here, only heroes are wanted back here, puny mortal!"

Betty's hands clapped onto his back. "He is my slave, Gargantuan. You are not to molest my toy." Her voice cut like a blade, breathing hard Gargantuan looked between him and Betty and then stomped off.

Betty's laughter was a balm to his rattled nerves, she kissed his cheek nonchalantly, and then flew to Briley's side and did the same. Her kiss excited Gerard, sizzled electric, rocked him to his core and pissed him off all at the same time. Gerard didn't like this, didn't like wanting her in this way. As a dying man desperate for water.

"That was hilarious, Gerard," Betty's electric blue eyes touched off a firestorm in his blood. "I've never seen her so pissed! I'll remember that forever, stupid Gargantuan, always throwing her big, fat weight around. Serves her right."

Briley frowned. "You said a bad word, Mr. Gerard."

"Sometimes a bad word is the only thing you can say, Briley." Gerard grumbled, but it was impossible to resist Betty's teasing light, or Briley's infectious laughter. Gerard laughed, and for the next two hours forgot just how badly he wanted to maim something.

***

Betty curled around him. The room danced with shadow, starlight shone in the navy canvas of sky, and Gerard felt his world closing in on him. He'd read to her for hours, his throat raw from repeating over and over stupid nonsensical phrases of 'See Spot Run' and 'Run Jane Run'… though he knew his abilities were improving, it was slow and irksome all the same. And though the very notion of cuddling had induced a riot of bile in his gut before, he found this was the part of their day he most enjoyed.

"That was fun today," she said, her smile evident in her tone.

He rubbed her back and she moaned. "Glad you thought so. I found it a detestable act of nature."

"Oh, it wasn't that bad," she giggled and sat up, her warm brown eyes seared him, and his heart clenched. Her skin was so silky soft, so smooth, sliding along his hairy one. He squeezed his eyes.

"Why do you work in a library, *Cherie*?"

She tilted her head. "Where did that question come from?" Her fingers framed his face.

"You're so smart. You have a degree. I know what that means. Why are you stuck here? Why do you work for so little, when you could have so much more?"

She thought for a moment and then smiled. "Briley. That's the simple answer. When Kelly got divorced I knew he'd need help. Our parents died years ago, we only have each other. He needed me and I came." She shrugged.

Why could he not find one flaw in the woman? Why was everything about her so good, so nice? It would be so much easier to leave if there were even one thing wrong. "Didn't it make you angry? To be forced to put your life on hold? Resentful?"

She shook her head. "It hurt. I worked hard to get that degree. But all I've got to do is look in Briley's wide guileless eyes and I know I did the right thing. I'd do it again."

She said it so matter of factly, and he knew he'd never be half as good as her. Hadn't been. Gerard was a beast, a man who got what he wanted, when he wanted it, and he wanted her. Now.

"Tell me about your world, Gerard," she asked hesitantly.

He sighed, knowing for some time this conversation would happen. "What do you wish to know?"

She smiled. "Do you know the Beast?"

He growled. "Dog face, *oui*, I know him. Next time I see the arrogant bastard I'll punch him in the face."

She laughed. "Okay, let's not talk about dog face then. Who else do you know?"

Gerard thought of the bad five. She might as well know the crowd he ran with. "I'm particular friends with Hook, Jinni, Hatter…"

Her eyes widened. "Oh man, that's awesome, tell me more!"

Gerard chuckled at her child-like enthusiasm, and wanting to continue seeing her smile, told of some of their raunchier exploits. Betty cried with laughter at some of Hook's debauchery, winced in sympathy at Wolf's unfortunate problem, and sighed happily when he'd told her of Hatter's successful mating. They talked for hours, and the more they talked, the more aware Gerard became of her. The way she sighed, how she would unknowingly curl closer to him, how her tiny hands touched him constantly, her scent, her warmth-- Betty Hart flooded his senses and his mind, and he could no longer remember stories.

"Betty," he said, urgency lending a hint of violence to her name.

She shivered, as if sensing his mood. "Yes?"

"I need you." The words tore from his soul. Vulnerable, exposed, Gerard sat up, pushing her away. "I cannot touch you each night, and pretend it isn't so. I want to slip inside you, *Cherie*. I want to lick you, touch you," *make love*, he refused to say the last.

Her eyes widened, as her breathing grew ragged. "I want that too," she admitted softly.

With a groan, Gerard rolled on top her. Grabbing her by the waist, digging his fingers into her firm flesh, he pulled on her blouse with an impatient tug until her breasts popped free.

Her moans spurred him on.

She had the most amazing breasts. His hands shook a little as he traced the swell of each one. Pink tipped nipples poked like tiny daggers into the air. Leaning down, he blew a moist breath across one tip. The darkened skin puckered and her legs spread. Gerard lay between her spread legs, even through her shorts, the warmth of her body speared his.

He trembled, never remembering a moment he'd ever felt this wild, this crazy with wanting.

"Gerard," she moaned. "But I thought…"

"Shut up, harpy," he moaned and dipping his mouth, suckled her nipple. The sweet jewel tickled the roof of his mouth and he groaned at the salty, flowery scent of her nude skin. His tongue swirled and danced over and over, head dizzy and swimming with thoughts of Betty.

Only Betty.

His beautiful, harpy-tongued shrew.

She rocked on him. "Oh yes," she moaned, "so good. Love..."

Gerard smashed his lips on her mouth, cutting off the lie. Knowing it for what it was because his cock was still a limp noodle. He didn't want lies, he wanted truth. Just this once, just this night.

He coaxed her mouth open with his tongue, slipping in when she parted on a tiny pant. His hand slid down her flat belly, slipped under her shorts and found the wet center of paradise.

She grunted, pushing down, and he couldn't think anymore. Gerard slipped a finger in.

"Harder," she shoved down.

He slipped in another digit, stretching her, filling her. Wishing it was his cock, and not his damn fingers. Her earthy scent tickled his nose. He inhaled deeply letting it fill his lungs. "*Mon belle, mon belle,*" he murmured.

Her nails scored his back, but it felt good. So damn good. He pumped harder, and she writhed on him. "So good," she cooed, and then her body seized, and a delirious expression wreathed her face.

Her soft center rolled with her orgasm, squeezing his fingers as her rocking slowly subsided. She laughed, kissing his chest, his neck, his face. But he wasn't done with her, not by a long shot.

Gerard pushed her shoulders back onto the mattress.

"Gerard?" she asked, her voice shaking.

"Open your legs, *mon belle*," he said, voice thick with his need.

Her breathing stuttered, but she dropped her legs open, and with a deft flick of his wrists, slipped her small shorts off. The sight of her swollen pink nub made his head reel. He touched her with just the tip of her finger and she surged up in response.

"Gerard…"

Breathing hard, Gerard bit and nibbled his way up her thigh until he reached the apex of her pleasure. "Betty," was all he could choke out before he drew her nub into his mouth and sucked hard.

She screamed, her thighs immediately clamped to the sides of his face. Gerard pulled harder, a low aching spiraled through his gut, made him woozy and weak. He wanted this woman, wanted to slam his cock into her slick warmth, and never come out again.

He rolled her nub around his tongue. Her scent flooded his mouth, better than any wine. She tasted of tart strawberries.

"Oh, Gerard," she moaned over and over, making his blood heat to a fevered frenzy.

Her thighs shook, and he lapped at her like a cat with cream, then he shoved two fingers back inside her and flexed so that his fingers massaged the center of her pleasure, and she yelled his name as she ground her hips hard against his face.

Moaning, twisting, she pumped on him up and down. Her thighs shook violently, but he didn't dare move, accepting her gift, only wishing her could give her so much more.

After what seemed an eternity, she flung her hand across her face and laughed, pain flooded his testicles and he hissed, needing desperately to relieve the ache of being pent up for so long. But relief would not be his, and the reminder of the curse pissed him off, cleared the fog of lust, and brought with it an agony of searing pain.

"Gerard, that was…"

He jerked back, and with a withering glare, stalked to the bathroom, shutting the door. Shutting her out.

He slammed his fist against the wall. His flaccid cock offered him no release. His blood sang, his head swam, and the throbbing was excruciating. His balls were tight orbs against his body, pulsing hot and hard down his legs, making him weak in the knees.

"Gerard," her soft voice echoed hollowly through the door.

Gnashing his teeth, he slammed his fist into the wall again. He wanted her. She'd called him her slave earlier, and gods he was. He hated himself. Hated her.

"Go away, Betty. Just go the hell away."

Chapter 16

Betty stuck a book on a shelf.

"Betty! Wrong shelf, for like the thousandth time!" Trisha snapped Betty from her mournful thoughts.

"What?" She frowned.

"This is a medical reference book," Trisha dangled the red hardbound book in front of Betty, malachite eyes bright with annoyance, "so why the hell are you putting it in with the Encyclopedias?"

Eyes burning, throat working hard not give in to the tears threatening to let loose, Betty could only stare.

Trisha's eyes grew wide. "Betty?"

The question in her name tipped her over, and leaning against a bookshelf she covered her eyes. "He's leaving, Trisha. It's all over tomorrow."

Trisha grabbed Betty's arms. "He dumped you?" she snarled. "That low down, worthless pathetic..."

"No," Betty shook her head, "no, he didn't dump me. I just, I can't even. Oh Trisha, I'm falling for him hard and fast, and I can't stop this, and I don't want to." She stared at her friend, knowing her eyes were blood shot.

Since the night Gerard had given her the best orgasm of her life, he'd been ignoring her. Refusing her entrance to his bed at night, refusing to let her even touch him. He still cooked for her, but left her food on the counter, no longer eating with her.

Betty didn't know what she'd done wrong. She'd tried to talk with him several times, but he would turn cold and distant, and she refused to humiliate herself further. But if he wouldn't talk to her, she couldn't help him, and why she even still wanted to... let her know just bad she had it for him.

"I don't understand then," Trisha's lips turned down in a plump frown.

Betty gave her a weak smile, and wiped up the tears gathered at the corners of her eyes. "It doesn't matter. It's just... he's got to go home, and I'll probably never see him again."

Trisha's lips tipped. To her credit she never once told Betty I-told-you-so, just enfolded her in her warm arms, and patted her back. "I've got a date tonight. We're headed to Charley's. Why don't you guys come?"

"I'll ask him," Betty sniffed, knowing he'd say no.

***

The moment the front door opened, Gerard shot to his feet. He'd sat in her favorite arm chair in total dark thinking all day long, longing for her return. He was an ass, he'd ignored her for days, and not because he wanted to. But because being near her was a pain beyond any he'd ever known. She still didn't love him, and that bothered him, not because it meant he'd die, but because it meant she didn't feel for him what he did for her.

If all he had was tonight, then he'd enjoy it.

She stood in the door, and his greedy gaze devoured her luscious form. The tan pencil skirt hugged her slim hips, the white shirt outlined every beautiful, perfect curve of her body.

"I'm sorry," he whispered, and she stuttered.

He frowned as her face scrunched up. Then she was sobbing, great heaving cries that gripped his soul. Betty ran to him, wrapped her arms around his neck and nuzzled him. She was warm, and smelled of vanilla, of flowers, and…

"*Cherie*, I'm so, so sorry." The words trembled from his soul.

He let her cry, patting her back until her heaving wracks slowed down and her breathing became calm.

"Me too," she finally whispered.

Gerard grabbed her fingers, kissing each one. "*Non, me petite Cherie*. I'm a huge ass and do not deserve your tears."

She hiccupped, hypnotic brown eyes holding his fast. "But, but… you're still not free. I feel so much for you. I burn for you, ache for you, and you're still not free."

He rubbed his knuckles along her velvet cheek. "This is enough."

She smiled, and he returned it, though his heart ached and shattered in his chest. Tonight was all they had left.

"Trisha wants to go out for drinks," Betty said, "I don't want to stay out long, but maybe--"

He kissed her lips, wanting to linger on them, savor them. But now was not that time. Tonight, when the world was all theirs, then he'd show her and tell her what she meant to him.

"Yes, *petite*. Let's go."

Three hours later, they were laughing. Country music lingered in the background as around them dancers swayed and groups talked. Betty nursed the same glass of white wine. His little featherweight. Her laugh was free of the cloud of pain, of the heartache sure to face them in the morning. Trisha's date was an engaging sandy haired man who seemed wild about the waifish blond. But Gerard was having a hard time focusing. He chugged his fourth tankard of beer and sighed. He wanted to take his woman home, tell her finally how he really felt.

"Let's dance," Trisha touched Bill… Bob's… Harry's?… (whatever his name was) arm. They left, leaving Gerard and Betty alone, finally.

He knuckled her cheek, needing to touch her. She sighed, leaning into him. "You want to go home?" he asked.

Funny how he now thought of that two bedroom place his, no longer could he see it as a prison. Wherever she was, he was home. Simple as that.

She nodded, brown eyes growing liquid with an unnamed emotion that made his chest ache.

Just as they stood to go say their good-bye's to Trisha, a female shoved into Betty shoulder. At first Gerard thought her a drunkard wobbly on her feet. But when Betty's eyes widened and she sucked in a hard breath, he tensed up.

"Gretchen?" Betty's voice was sharp. "What the hell do you want?"

"You know your girl's a whore, right?" The red headed woman with the most enormous pair of breasts he'd ever seen leaned around her shoulder to look at him. "She's been sleeping with my fiancé."

He recognized the caustic shrill tone of that voice, and instantly his nails dug into the palm of his hands. If she wasn't a woman, he'd punch her. He pushed Betty behind him. "You're the, *chienne*, always calling. Stay the hell away from her."

Her blue eyes scrunched up. "The who what?" her country accent grated on his nerves, and he hated the woman, hated looking at her, hated having to share a space with her.

"Do not call. Do not talk to her. Do not," he shoved his face right up to hers, "even look at her. She is mine!"

The woman's jaw trembled, then a man came and slipped his arm around her shoulders.

"What's going on?" he growled, then his eyes widened. "Betty?"

"James." She stepped out from behind Gerard's back and sneered. "Why don't you warn your little dog away from me."

"Aww," he grinned, and Gerard's gut clenched as the blood rushed to his head in a red haze, "she don't mean nuthin' by it. Do you, G?" He chucked Gretchen's jaw, and she grinned, popping a piece of gum, seeming more confident now that her man was in the picture.

James looked at Gerard, his upper lip curled. "Who's this?" he jerked his chin at him.

Gerard closed his eyes, on the verge of pummeling the man. His anger so hot it oozed off him.

"Screw you, James," Betty grabbed Gerard's hand. "Let's go, baby."

His heart tripped at her endearment. She'd never called him anything other than Gerard, occasionally pig, or bastard. Never baby, never something so obviously loving.

And he might have forgotten James and his slut, if James hadn't grabbed Betty's elbow, jerking her to a stop.

"Hey, you can't even talk to an old friend?" he snapped, and Gerard didn't think.

He slammed his fist into the bastard's face. Hot blood oozed from the crunched nose, and James dropped to the ground with a shriek. "He punched me!" he squalled, sounding like a pathetic baby crying for its *maman*.

A large man walked up to them, his arms crossed over his barrel chest, lips thin as he glared at Gerard.

Betty stood in front of Gerard. "We're leaving. No worries." She yanked on Gerard's hand and walked outside. The moment the cold blast of night hit him in the face, she shoved him against the wall and laughed, a deliriously joyous sound that shivered across his skin.

"His face, did you see it?" Her brown eyes sparkled. She grabbed Gerard's face and leaned in, planting a soft kiss on his lips. His legs grew weak and he tightened his hold on her waist, wanting to slip inside with his tongue, tasting and nipping at her delicious lower lip. Her breathing was a feather soft kiss on his lips. "I love you, Gerard Caron."

The moment she said it, the pendant blazed deepest amethyst, there was no red, no gold, it was solid purple. He peppered her brow with kisses, her lips.

"Betty Hart," he said.

"*One month's up. You are mine, Gerard!*" Galeta's sharp voice exploded around them, then a blue hole tore through the air, and a phantom hand yanked on Gerard's collar, stealing him back to Kingdom.

"No! Gerard stay!" Betty cried.

He reached for her. "Betty, I lo…" But he never finished the thought, and she never heard what he said, as he was sucked into the vacuum of space.

He rolled head over feet, over and over, at a dizzying, alarming speed. Lights flashed by in a blur, and then his face smacked into something hard and all breath left him on impact. It took a moment for the stars to clear from his vision.

"Stand, Gerard," Galeta's gruff voice pierced his throbbing head.

"He cannot stand," Danika's gentle words, hovered above his head, "he's in shock." A gentle swell of fairy magic netted him in warmth, lifting the fog, the pain, and giving him the strength to stand.

Danika's smile was crooked and strained, but her eyes glistened with joy, and he knew he'd passed the test. But instead of joy, he felt only pain.

He was in the fairy hall of justice. The checkered tile glistened alternating shades of onyx and mother of pearl. The head fairies sat behind an imposing polished bench of speckled marble, the room glowed a deep hued magenta, radiance that emanated from within the fairies themselves.

Galeta cleared her throat. He looked up and she waved the still glowing pendant. "You have passed," and the way she said it, she was none too happy about it. "You are free." The moment the words left her lips, a rush of heat centered on his cock, and like a cork popping free of a bottle, he sprang to life. His cock became thick and painfully hard for his woman, his Betty.

Galeta snarled. "Well go!" She jerked her head. "But know this, Caron, I'm watching."

He shook his head. "*Non*. You owe me a gift."

She curled her lip. "I owe you nothing."

"*Non*?" he lifted his brows, looking at the silver haired fairy to Galeta's right, "should I tell them of your breach of magic then?"

Nina the White jerked and looked at Galeta. The silver of her eyes turned a creamy spiraling white as she gazed through her third eye-- her spirit eye-- at Galeta. "Sister?"

Esmeralda the Green's voice mimicked her sister's, her voice rang with the strain of bells. Green vines crawled from the tip of her green wand, inching slowly toward a visibly shaking Galeta. The thorns of justice would be all the fairies would need to convict Galeta of improper use of magic. But Gerard was no longer interested in revenge, all he wanted was his Betty, but he needed something first, and he wouldn't leave here without it.

"So?" he narrowed his eyes. "Have we a deal?"

Danika gripped her wand, worrying her bottom lip, and jerking her gaze back and forth between him and the tribunal.

Galeta's thin lips compressed into a hard line. "What is it?" she asked between clenched teeth.

"I want you to make me the mate."

Nina the White sucked in a sharp breath. "Think long and hard what you ask for, Gerard Caron. For once the soul is bound it can never be unbound."

He held his chin high. There were no doubts, she loved him, that's all he wanted. "I know what I ask, *fee*. I want my soul, and my life forever bound to hers."

Esmeralda turned her black alien like eyes on him. "So mote it be."

The air shivered with the use of such powerful magic as the tiny fairy covered in vines glided down toward him. "Your heart is pure, Gerard, your wish is granted."

In an instant Danika grew to human height and threw her arms around Gerard's waist. "I knew it, boyo. Knew she was the one. Did I not say?"

Gerard's grin was proud, grateful. "*Oui, fee*. You knew." He hugged her back.

She stepped back, her blue eyes twinkled with joy. Patting his cheek with a motherly fondness she said, "I must needs be off. I've a wolf to satisfy. But I wondered if you could give Betty a message for me."

Gerard tilted his head. "What?"

Danika smiled, her form became vaporous as a glowing blue tunnel spun behind her. "Tell her to tell Trishelle I said hi, and I'll be seeing her very soon." And with those cryptic words, she vanished.

***

Three months later and Betty still cried herself to sleep sometimes. She'd hoped and waited, expecting stupidly Gerard would return for her, would return to confess his love. She'd known, even as he'd slipped through the tunnel, that he'd meant to say those words back. Had seen them trembling on his tongue.

She loved him. The pendant had glowed, he was free, which meant he'd left, just like Trisha said he would. Just like she'd known he would.

She drank tea at her kitchen table, hating that she'd developed a taste for it, and using a red sharpie to circle yet another potential roommate in the paper. She couldn't live alone anymore, come home to the unbearable silence of an empty house. He'd spoiled her in so many ways.

She glanced at her half eaten plate of frozen waffles and sighed.

Betty had an appointment in another ten minutes, a girl in college. They'd talked over the phone, and the references were good, at this point, she didn't much care. She should get out of her robe, the girl was gonna arrive any second now.

Pushing away from the table, she walked to her bedroom when the doorbell rang. "Dammit," she looked down at her scrubby robe. She turned back. If it was a guy, she'd change, but she just didn't feel like it now. She had a hot date with a Hagaan Daaz after the appointment, and he sure didn't care.

Betty opened the door and then screamed when Gerard's smiling face looked back at her. She slammed the door, trying to close it on him, he shoved it open.

"*Cherie*, hear me out."

"Screw you!" She stomped back to her room.

He swung the door shut and ran after her. "Betty, wait."

"Why?" She stopped and turned, fists clenched tight by her sides, knowing if she didn't… she'd clock him. All the anger, pain, humiliation, and angst bubbled to the surface at once and she was dizzy with it all. "I told you I loved you, and you bailed out on me. Now three months later…"

"Three months?" He forked fingers through his hair and her heart flipped, why couldn't he have at least been uglier than she remembered? His face was still as drool worthy as ever, the five o'clock shadow scruffy and framing a jaw seeming chiseled from granite. His blue eyes crinkled at the corners, then he groaned, slapping a hand over his face.

He grabbed her hand, leading her to her room. Betty dug in her heels, trying to push his iron grip off her wrist. "If you think you're gonna get lucky now, buddy--"

He grinned, and the flip in her stomach was almost physical pain.

"I will get lucky, *Cherie*. Very lucky." He bit his lip, and she tried to smack him. He swatted her hand away as if she were no more than a pesky nuisance. "One day in Kingdom is one mortal month on Earth. We've very long days, *petite*."

They were in her room now. Gerard closed the door and locked it, the sound like the boom of gunshot in her ears, and she swallowed hard. Then his large hands were on her robe, slipping the sides down and she moaned.

"You can't just come in and out of my life like this and expect…"

"Shhh." He pressed his warm finger to her lips. "You talk too much, harpy." Then his lips covered hers and with a tiny moan of desperation she returned it, pouring her hate and her need into it, tasting his lips, his tongue. Her tears mingled in their kiss.

He pulled back, frowning. "*Mon belle, mon belle*," he traced the line of tears falling free from her eyes.

Her heart broke hearing him call her his beauty, all she'd wanted for three months was to hear his sultry French tenor whisper love in her ears, and now that he was here, it hurt so bad. Opened everything up, all the wounds that'd finally started to heal were once again fractured and cracked.

"I brought these." He lifted his hand, and she gave a quick sob. Her still glowing pendant chain dangled from his hand, along with another one. Similar, except the other pendant was in the shape of a square. Less feminine, but definitely a matching set. But where hers was purple, his was the familiar red and gold color of before.

She grabbed her pendant, the hearts warmth almost seeming to pump in her grip like a real heart, warmth seeped into her palm. Betty looked at him. "I don't understand."

The sultriness was gone from his eyes, truth-- unvarnished and raw-- stared back at her. "This is the mate. If I put this chain around my neck, and you do the same with yours," he handed her the chain, "our souls will be bound. You will never age, you will never die, your mortality will be forever striped from you."

Her hands shook as she stared down at the pumping, beating heart.

He covered her hands with his. "This is what took me so long to come back. Galeta didn't want to. She procrastinated the entire time…"

Her entire frame trembled. "Gerard?"

He stopped talking, his eyes were large, and she sensed his nerves. She'd never seen him like this, so vulnerable. It made her want him more.

"Are you talking marriage?"

His jaw clenched. "I'm talking much more than that, *Cherie*." He forked twin fingers through his hair, reminding her oddly of the man she'd seen that first day in the library. Disheveled, slightly devilish, and incredibly alluring. "I know what I ask might be overwhelming, frightening even. But I swear to you, my love, I've never felt like this before. You're it. And I'll prove that to you if I must…"

Betty shushed him with her finger, her eyes burning with unshed tears. "You talk too much."

He grinned, taking a nip at her finger. His bite shot warmth straight between her legs, heating her blood to a fevered frenzy. The anger melted into something full and impossible and so deep she knew she was drowning, but didn't care.

"May I?" he asked, easing the necklace from her hands and unclasping it.

She grabbed his and did the same. "Yes."

They put the necklaces on each other, the moment the heart touched her chest it flared to life and burnt her skin. She hissed and Gerard trembled.

"My life with yours…" he said, and then the red of his pendant flared crimson for the briefest moment before completely being overtaken by purple. Swirling veins of glittering sapphire skated through the lava like movement of color. "Forever."

The pain in her chest vanished, and when she looked at her pendant, it too glowed with ribbons of blue. He grabbed her face. "You're mine. Forever."

She smiled, and was pretty sure she'd never be able to stop now that she'd started. "How old are you?"

A devilish grin curled his lips. "Old. Ancient." He leaned in so close she tasted the mint of his breath. "You're stuck with me now, *Cherie*. So long as I live, you live."

But then she stopped thinking, because he scooped her up, walked to the bed and laid her down, his hard body sliding along hers. It took only seconds for him to bare her skin to his touch. His eyes burned hot on her body as he looked her up, then down.

He licked his lips. "Hungry, *Cherie*. I'm starving."

Empowered, she thrust her chest up and sucked in her stomach, assuming-- what she hoped to be a sexy pose-- and beckoned him with a curled finger. "I'm waiting, Caron. And I hate waiting."

She laughed as he literally tore himself out of his clothes. His body was magnificent, lean and hard. But it was his manhood, the piece of him she'd seen soft for so long, standing hard and ready that made her mouth water.

"I'm sorry, *Cherie*," he moaned, crawling on top of her. "Fast now. I must feel you."

She was so wet, her thighs were already soaked, the moment he slid into her body she squeezed her pelvis down around him. Betty was home, in his arms. Gerard kissed her, pumping hard, twisting his hips in an infinity motion, hitting her G-spot over and over.

Betty cried out, her legs jerked, as her entire world faded to black. "I'm so close, baby," she grunted, and with one last shove, they howled in unison, falling into the hardest orgasm she'd ever known.

Then it was her turn to show him how much she loved and needed him. She pushed him onto his back, much the way he'd done her so long ago, and took his still hard cock fully into her mouth, still tasting herself on him. He moaned long and hard, his large hand framing the back of her head as she pumped up and down, humming low in the back of her throat.

"*Cherie*, my love. My heart," he murmured a constant stream of endearments, his hips flexing into her mouth. His smooth skin like satin on her tongue, and then his body stiffened. "I come, my love."

Betty took all of him. The taste was salty, but sweet. Not bad. She smiled and he grinned.

"Turn over," he commanded, and her eyes widened.

"You're not too tired?"

He laughed. "I'm not like one of your mortal men, Betty. I'm the best lover you'll ever have."

She shivered at his words and flipped over, her heart beating uncontrollably in her chest as he slipped into her still slick warmth from behind, pumping hard. Their sweaty bodies slapping together loud in the quiet of their room. Her body tingled with fire, with heat and Betty screamed when the final orgasm rocked her. The fullness of him stretching her from behind made the orgasm seem to last forever. Then he turned her over and cradled her, whispering in French in her ear. She was his beloved, his love, his lover, his everything. Kissing her cheeks, her neck, his hot tongue dancing across first one breast then the next. Betty had never felt more in love, or more loved, and he worked his magic, her tired body came to life for him again.

He made love to her throughout the night. Soft and slow, hard and fast. She tasted him, he tasted her and neither one came up for air until hunger finally drove them apart.

Betty cuddled into his side after downing a full pint of coffee ice cream, she smiled as he rubbed her back. She'd never felt so spent, so wonderfully in pain in her life. Tomorrow would be impossible to walk, but she couldn't even muster up an iota of care. She was a contented kitten lapping at a bowl of cream. Life was good.

His heart beat a steady song in her ears, lulling her to sleep.

"Oh, I forgot," Gerard said. He gave her a tiny shake.

Betty glanced up at him and couldn't resist tracing the lines of his stubbled jaw. "Hmm…"

"Danika asked me to tell you 'hi' and to please tell Trishelle she'd be seeing her soon."

Betty scooted to her knees, her eyes bugging as she wrapped the sheet around her breasts.

Gerard frowned. "What, *Cherie*?"

She laughed. "Oh man, that's hilarious!"

His lips quirked. "Do share?"

She planted a kiss on his lips, even knowing they had forever, she didn't think she'd ever get tired of her brutish man. He was so perfect for her, so wonderful, and love settled deep roots into the soil of her heart. "Trisha's going to be set up with one of your boys."

It took him a second to think it through. "*Non*."

She nodded. "Oh yeah. Definitely. Which one do you think? Jinni?"

Gerard's crooked grin had her toes curling. "*Non*, he prefers dark meat."

"Wolf?" she scrunched her nose, trying to imagine her impetuous friend doing the nasty with a shape-shifting werewolf.

Gerard snorted, his fingers gently caressed her shoulder. "I'd imagine Red would have something to say about that."

They gasped at the same time. "Hook!"

"Oh my gosh, poor Trisha," Betty giggled, only imaging how impossible that awful pirate would be.

Then she had another thought. "Gerard?" She grabbed her pendant.

"Hmm?" His fingers stroked her lower.

"Now that I'm with you, can I visit Kingdom?"

His smile was huge. "Would you like to?"

She nodded. "I've always wanted to see Neverland."

He scoffed. "My hamlet is infinitely better to Neverland. Anytime you want, *Cherie*, tell me. Danika can take us between realms. I'd love to show you my home." His blue eyes blazed. "Our home."

Her heart trembled and she nodded. "Though I'd still really love to see Neverland. I'm curious what Hook looks like. Just so I know what to tell Trisha."

Gerard shuddered. "I've a nude, beautiful woman in my bed. The last thing I want is to think about that ugly pirate. Come here, harpy," he growled, pulling her in for a kiss and when he slipped inside her, he moved slow and sure, filling her body and her soul.

"I love you, Betty Hart. Forever and always," Gerard said and proceeded to show her just how much the rest of their long lives.

Gerard's Luscious Salmon Fillets:

Ingredients

Citrus Glaze:

- 3/4 cup fresh orange juice
- 1/4 cup fresh lemon juice
- 1/4 cup fresh lime juice
- 1/4 cup chicken stock
- 1 garlic clove, minced
- 2 tablespoons orange marmalade
- 2 tablespoons soy sauce
- 1 tablespoon rice wine vinegar
- 1 tablespoon light brown sugar
- Pinch kosher salt and freshly cracked black pepper

Grilled Salmon:

- Extra-virgin olive oil, for brushing
- 4 (6-ounce, 1-inch thick) salmon fillets
- Kosher salt and freshly cracked black pepper

Directions

Glaze: Bring all of the ingredients to a boil in a medium-sized saucepan over medium heat, stirring to melt the preserves and to keep the mixture from burning. Reduce the heat to a simmer and let the glaze reduce until syrupy, about 15 to 20 minutes. Adjust the seasonings with salt and freshly cracked pepper, to taste.

Salmon:

Heat a grill to medium-high heat.

Brush both sides of the fillets with olive oil just before grilling, then season with salt and pepper, to taste. Grill the salmon for about 4 minutes per side, brushing with the glaze during the final few minutes of cooking. Transfer the salmon to serving plates and brush them with the remaining glaze before serving.

Red and Her Wolf

by

Marie Hall

Red and Her Wolf

Copyright 2012 Marie Hall

Cover Art by Claudia McKinney of www.phatpuppyart.com Copyright June 2012

Photographer, Teresa Yeh
Model, Danny
Edited by C. C., Lea Griffith, Jennifer Blackstream, Marie Hall

Formatted by L.K. Campbell

Smashwords Edition

This is a work fiction. All characters, places and events are from the author's imagination and should not be confused with fact. Any resemblance to persons, living or dead, events or places is purely coincidental.

All rights reserved. No part of this publication may be reproduced in any material form, whether by printing, photocopying, scanning or otherwise without the written permission of the publisher, Marie Hall, except in the case of brief quotations embodied in the context of reviews.

This book is licensed for your personal enjoyment only. This ebook may not be resold or given away to other people. If you would like to share this ebook with another person, please purchase an additional copy for each person you share it with. Thank you for respecting the hard work of all people involved with the creation of this ebook.

Applications should be addressed in the first instance, in writing, to Marie Hall. Unauthorized or restricted use in relation to this publication may result in civil proceedings and/or criminal prosecution.

The author and illustrator have asserted their respective rights under the Copyright Designs and Patent Acts 1988 (as amended) to be identified as the author of this book and illustrator of the artwork.

Published in 2012 by Marie Hall, Honolulu, Hawaii, United States of America

Acknowledgements:

First and foremost to my fans for sending me awesome notes, asking when Wolf would finish, how much you love Kingdom. To you guys, you rock. Second, I could never have done this without the help of many, many wonderful people. Sonya, C.C., Joyce, and Jennifer… you all are always awesome and a real encouragement to me. To some very special fans: Gaele Hince, Livia, and Katie at <u>Curse of the Bibliophile</u>. You girls went above and beyond, I'm grateful to know you.

Dedication

To my fans, this one's for you guys…

Red and Her Wolf

'Bad boys need love too...'

Long ago there lived a beautiful child. Her name was Violet. Fair of skin, with blonde hair and large blue eyes. Born of wild magic, she was a woman with a child's heart. Innocent and lovely, but not at all what she seemed--you see Violet went by another name: The Heartsong.

She was the child of fairy magic, the physical manifestation of all fae kinds unbridled power. Cosseted and pampered, she grew up in isolation, never knowing who she really was, or why there were those who'd seek to harm her.

Ewan of the Blackfoot Clan is a wolf with a problem. He's been sent to kill the Heartsong, but the moment he lays eyes on the blonde beauty he knows he'll defy the evil fae he works for to claim Violet as his own.

This is the tale of Little Red Riding Hood and the Big Bad Wolf, as it really happened...

Table Of Contents

Prologue:
Chapter 1
Chapter 2
Chapter 3
Chapter 4
Chapter 5
Chapter 6
Chapter 7
Chapter 8
Chapter 9
Chapter 10
Chapter 11
Chapter 12
Chapter 13
Chapter 14
Chapter 15
Chapter 16
Chapter 17
Chapter 18
Epilogue
A word from the Author:
Sneak Peek: Jinni's Wish
Other Books written by Marie Hall:

Prologue:

Long before the Hatter met his Alice, or Gerard his Belle... a Wolf claimed his mate...

Weak light spilled through the twisted forest. The sky, a wash of orange and pink, threatened to give way to night. Violet shivered, hugging her cape tight around her body. Strange sounds whispered on the breeze. The call of night owls and the squeak of tiny field mice played a gentle melody in the background.

But there was more--something slithering, creeping like the cold hand of death slinking slowly behind her. The wind whipped through her hair as she tried to brush it back. Her heart pounded a chaotic rhythm in her skull as she swallowed the bile working its way up her throat.

Grandmother hadn't been feeling well. She gripped the handle of her basket, fingers clenched until her nails gouged her palm. Violet never strayed from the safety of her home, never farther than the river. Grandmother had taught her years ago that beasties of the worst sort lurked beyond.

She glanced up at the massive trees that towered above her. Skeletal branches twisted gnarly fingers heavenward. It was easy to imagine the forty foot behemoths might at any moment open sappy maws to suck her up.

Shivering harder, she picked up her pace, nearly running. Lungs heaving now with the effort to climb the steep hill leading back to the safety of her river. Night was closing in quickly. Already the colorful splash was giving way to the inky blue of a silver studded sky.

A raven cawed and ice skated down Violet's spine. She swallowed hard, first noticing the bird back at the apple orchard. Yellow apples--almost golden the way they shone in the sunlight--a prize worth escaping the temporary safety of her grandmother's home for. The gift should make her ailing Gran smile again.

Bushes rustled behind her.

Violet didn't look back. She wouldn't. To look back might make the fear manifest. Ignoring the knot of dread in her gut, she yanked at a dangling root and hoisted herself over the hill. The river was finally in sight.

A black blur brushed her cheek. Fear slithered down her throat. The raven circled back around, and with a loud *caw*, dove for her again.

Violet marched.

***

"Och." Danika--fairy godmother semi-extraordinaire--sailed through the breeze with her fairy friend like a graceful swan cutting a swath through a placid lake. "I swear that Gerard will be the death of me. He has a thing for the maids of the sea now." She shuddered, eyeing Miriam the Delighted.

Miriam's large white teeth flashed at Danika as she grinned. "The man's useless,

Danika. Truly, ye should give him up as a lost cause."

"No," Danika shook her head, zipping high and low, dancing through the air with the joy of a fairy with ample time on her hands. "I'll find him his match, you mind my words."

Gathering her fairy dust, Miriam threw it at a pitiful looking bloom of a rose, its red drooping petals gleamed a deep ruby red when the golden dust settled upon it. The flower gave a happy chortle and waved on its thin stem back at them.

Miriam snorted. "Are ye sure of that now? Wouldn't ye rather seek my boon, I could tell ye quite simply who she is."

Danika scoffed. "No, Miriam, I work alone. I've told you time and again I'll not be needing the use of your boon…" Danika narrowed her eyes, a flash of red sailed past her vision. She stopped flying and gripped Miriam's elbow. "Did you see that?" Danika whispered, heart pounding forcefully against her chest.

Miriam's swirling lavender eyes scanned the valley below. Just at that moment, the last of the days light winked out like the pitiful flicker of candle glow. Kingdom was bathed in a sea of black and blue, making it hard to discern much of anything at the moment other than shadow and sound.

"See what?" Miriam's brown and white speckled moth's wings flitted slowly behind her back.

Danika frowned; sure she'd seen a flash of red. She licked her lips; rumor had it the Heartsong had been hidden here centuries ago. Unlimited power in the form of a beautiful girl, a conduit for any fairy, and power so tempting she'd had to be hidden. In the care of the only fairy known to be truly pure of heart: Jana the Green.

Or at least that's what the tales said, but all within Kingdom knew never to believe such nonsense. Fairy tales rarely held a grain of truth to them, and if they did, it was stretched so thin as to be transparent.

Danika laughed. "I thought I saw-"

A surge of power rolled forcefully through Danika, she screamed as every limb locked in place, and she hurtled straight toward the ground. A loud buzz the only thing she heard as the ground rushed up to meet her face. Danika had only a moment to throw her arms in front of her, bracing for impact, when a strong pair of hands clamped onto her vest and halted her fall only inches from the ground.

The whites of Miriam's eyes were large, and her breathing stilted and heavy. "Danika, what happened?"

Danika trembled, slow to regain feeling in her limbs. "My muscles. The power, t'was overwhelming…" the words died on her tongue as the flash of red brushed by mere yards to her right.

Miriam gasped, dropping Danika in her shock. Danika landed with a thud, air left her body on impact, and she glared at Miriam who was now visibly shaking.

"We must needs leave, Dani," Miriam whimpered, and Danika might have asked why, had she not just seen for herself the cause of Miriam's distress.

A large red wolf, stalked the maiden wearing the red hood. He padded on silent feet, moving like shadow behind her. The girl hummed, but this was not a relaxed song--more a nervous melody that vibrated through the woods haunting and eerie all at the same time.

Miriam landed beside Danika and yanked her to her feet. They were barely a foot tall, and well hidden behind a thick gooseberry shrub, but Miriam gulped and shivered as she pointed to the large beast. "The mark, Dani," she hissed, "the beast wears *her* mark."

The wolf's ears twitched, and though he did not look their way, Danika knew he'd heard Mir.

Danika clamped her hand over Miriam's mouth, urging her friend to silence. Then another wolf loped out from behind the woods and this one was bigger. A full hands length taller, the creature more resembled a hound of hell, than a wolf. Its black shaggy coat covered the muscular form like a bear's pelt, lush and thick, gleaming like onyx in a flame. Its hackles were raised, and it too bore the mark.

A chain hung around its thick neck, with a small golden medallion embossed with a dragon in battle hung in plain sight. The mark was a sign of loyalty to Malvena the Black, the worst of all fairy kind--she'd turned her back on truth and light centuries ago, and though her reasons had at first been understandable (even honorable), they'd morphed and twisted into something dark and macabre.

Seeing the mark, knowing to whom they belonged, Danika knew the flash of red she'd seen had been very real. Malvena had one goal, find the Heartsong. All fairies scorned and mocked the black hearted fae, knowing her quest impossible. The Heartsong did not exist; she was a myth, a legend, nothing more.

The black wolf growled long and low, and birds shot from out tree branches into the air with a loud squawking cry.

Danika's body still crackled with surging pockets of power, making her teeth clamp down hard.

"Come, Dani, we must leave," Miriam tugged at Danika's elbow. Danika hadn't realized she'd begun walking toward the girl until Miriam stopped her.

Danika hugged her wand to her chest, frantic with an overwhelming need to go. Not to run away, but rather, to go to the girl.

"Dani," Miriam groaned again, the whites of her eyes large in her face. Danika turned, ready to growl at Miriam to hush her mouth, but then Miriam started jerking. Her entire body shook, and a low moan vibrated from her chest.

The black wolf's ears twitched, and Danika flicked her wand, casting a protective net around them to prevent any more sounds from reaching sensitive ears.

"Miriam," she cried, grabbing her friend by the shoulders as she slumped to her knees on the ground.

Miriam's head snapped up and Danika's eyes widened because the eyes staring back at her were a solid white and the voice that came out sounded as deep as a man's. "*The Heartsong must be saved.*"

Goose flesh skittered down Danika's back, Miriam was in full 'sight' mode. It could take hours to snap her from these trances and Danika couldn't let that happen. Miriam was vulnerable and exposed when using her third eye.

But if they had any hope of saving the Heartsong, Danika needed to wake her friend up.

"Mir?" Danika shook her gently. "Wake up, dear."

"*Save the Heartsong,*" Miriam intoned, heavy inflections undulating against the translucent bubble like waves crashing upon a rocky shore.

"Oh bloody damn, bloody, bloody, bloody damn…" Danika muttered, slapping a still mumbling Miriam on first one cheek, then the other. The skin turned crimson and still Danika slapped her. "Wake up, you gnatty old fool. You want us to save the chit; wake the bloody hell up!"

Miriam's head lolled around, but the whites of her eyes remained. The wolves were gone, the girl... who knew where, this couldn't be happening. Heart thundering loud, Danika grabbed a handful of dirt and threw it at Miriam's face.

The fairy coughed, but still did not cease her rambles.

Quivering, on the fine edge of desperation, Danika did the only thing she could think of. "*Incendio!*" she cried, pointing her wand at Miriam's feet.

Thick waves of amber encased Mir's bare feet, and a shriek that made Danika's ears ring, sprang from the brunette's mouth.

"My feet!" Miriam cried, blinking big lavender eyes up at Danika accusingly as she stomped the flames off, "What have ye done?"

Danika flung her arms around her friend's neck. "I'll tell you later, we must find the Heartsong, Mir, she's in grave danger."

Mentioning the girl almost seemed to make Miriam forget her momentary anger. "Yes," she said, "we must."

There was a resolute tone to her voice, no longer fear, but knowledge of something deep and powerful.

"Follow me," Miriam cried, and streaked in a blur through the air.

Danika followed, large blades of grass slapped their faces. Her pulse pounded a furious tempo in her ears. They had to make it. They must make it in time. The Heartsong must not be killed. Though Danika had only ever thought of her as myth, all knew to kill the Heartsong was to release the dark magic that beat within her soul. It must never happen.

Up ahead a thatched roof cottage came into view. A silver plume of smoke curled like a beacon through the air, then a scream that rang with pure and primal fear, blasted all around them.

"Inside. Hurry!" Miriam cried, her wings beat faster as she streaked, a golden bolt of lightning cutting a straight path through the navy blue sky.

Sweat dripped down Danika's back with the effort to keep up, yet still she urged her wings to pump harder. Faster.

They sailed through the half opened door and the scene within was chaos. On the ground Jana the Green lay dead, her wand dangled limp from lifeless hands. The Green had assumed the form of an elderly woman; her silver white hair was long and tangled, partially covering one eye. Her pudgy face forever frozen in a soundless scream--a big black wolf lay on the floor, savaging her, ripping off her hand, spitting it out, and then ripping off the other and doing the same. Fleshy parts of the Green were everywhere.

The Green--one of the *Powerful Ten*.

Shock rooted Danika to the spot, scrambling her brain, her ability to reason or think. The slaughter of the Green--so shocking, so unbelievable, Danika could hardly breathe. Of all the fae in all the world of Kingdom, none were more powerful than the *Ten*. That the wolves could destroy her with such ease... Danika's gut clenched--insides revolting at the earthy, metallic stench of so much blood.

Backed into a corner of the wall, the Heartsong screamed and screamed, quivering within the folds of her red cape. A basket lay by her feet, yellow apples rolling like heads on the packed dirt floor. The red wolf Danika had spotted earlier, stood in front of the Heartsong, growling with its hackles raised. Ready, it seemed, to pounce and tear the girl limb from limb.

The big black wolf lifted its shaggy head, glowing yellow eyes swiveled toward the girl and he gave a long, low whimper.

The red wolf growled and snapped its fanged jaws.

The black wolf's nostrils flared, as if scenting. His head bobbed up and down, his tail thumped excitedly on the ground. He whimpered again.

The other wolf growled louder, taking a menacing step towards the girl. His gums pulled back, revealing wickedly long incisors.

The black wolf shot to his feet. A rumble tore from his chest, spilled up his throat, and dropped from his tongue. But Danika was dazed to note the black did not eye the girl, rather he eyed the red wolf.

The girl whimpered, refusing to look at anything.

"Oh no," Miriam said.

"What?" Danika asked.

The red wolf vibrated, and then pounced so quickly Danika couldn't follow his blur. He sailed through the air, mouth open and teeth inches from the huddled girl's neck. Danika and Miriam finally found their senses, and pulled their wands out of their sleeves, hot pink power crackled upon its tip, ready to blast the red wolf into oblivion, when the black jumped on red's back and sunk his teeth into the other wolf's neck. The sound of a spine cracking blasted through the eerie hush and then the red wolf dropped like sack cloth to the packed dirt floor.

The black wolf breathed heavy, mad glowing eyes stared intently at the girl who still refused to look at him. Danika raised her wand.

"No!" Miriam cried, slapping the wand from Danika's hands. The pink bolt of power arced into the air, shooting off the roof, and burning a black hole through the thatch. The scent of burnt grass was everywhere.

"What the bloody hell?" Danika yelled in bewilderment, turning wide frantic eyes toward the beast. Miriam had slapped her only source of power from her hands.

Black's head jerked in their direction, his long pink tongue lolled out of his mouth as his ribcage flexed in and out. The red wolf wasn't dead; a small whimper escaped his fanged jaws.

"**WHAT HAS HAPPENED HERE**?" The voice could belong to no other. It cracked through the room with power, all the fine hairs on the nape of Danika's neck stood on edge, then a blue blast of light poured through the room in a wave.

Everything paused. The wolves stopped breathing, the girl stopped whimpering, even the wind stopped breezing through the dank confines. Time itself held its breath.

Galeta the Blue--Head Mistress of Fairy, Inc. and Ruler of all Fae--appeared ghost-like within the blue radiance. "I felt the disturbance of my song, where is she? Where is the Girl!" she demanded, sharp fangs standing out in shockingly bold relief compared to the doll like innocence of her young face.

Her ghostly head turned, and a sharp gasp escaped, then glacial blue eyes locked first on Danika, then on Miriam. A sneer curled her tipped nose. "You!"

Miriam winced.

"I should have known you'd be here, you coward. You swine. What have you done?"

Danika flew before her friend. Galeta had never much cared for Miriam. Not since the day of the Summoning; the day all fairies were received by the oracle and told what their ultimate destiny would be. All knew Miriam's kith descended from greatness. Every one of Cherry Blossom stock went on to rule the Kingdom as head Mistress. Every last one, that was, until the Oracle told Miriam she was destined to rule and Galeta was to be muse of the arts. Though Miriam had rejected her course, and chosen instead to be untethered and a free fairy, Galeta had never forgotten, or forgiven.

"She's done no wrong," Danika quickly asserted. "We were feeding the flowers when we came upon the scene. What is this, Galeta? What horrors have transpired this night?" Danika wrung her hands, still not sure what she'd witnessed. What had happened.

Galeta held her chin high, but the light of fury slowly dimmed. "The Heartsong's been discovered." She stared at the unmoving bundle draped in red on the floor. "What did you see?"

Danika barely had a moment to digest the news that the Heartsong did in fact exist. Not like she hadn't already put the pieces together, but to hear Galeta admit it as truth was… shocking. "Like I said, we were too late, Mistress. We entered to find Jana already dead and the black," she pointed to the large wolf, frozen, and staring at them with hollow gold eyes, "attacking the red."

A green glow began to emanate from within the savaged remains of Jana's broken body. Galeta pursed her lips, eyebrows raised. "We haven't much time," she said cryptically. "I need to access the black wolf's mind."

The moment she said it, the wolf's limbs unlocked, he wuffed, shook his shaggy head and then growled.

"To me, wolf," Galeta snapped her fingers. Though Galeta was not with them in form, her power was such that the wolf had no choice but to spring to her ghostly apparition, head bowed and breathing heavily under the influence of forced magic.

"Esmeralda," Galeta cried over her shoulder, a moment later a second figure emerged from within the blue fog of light.

Esmeralda--fairy of justice and truth--was a lovely counterpoint to Galeta's sharp cruelty. Fair of skin, with forest green eyes, she was the ideal representation of what most mortals believed the fae to be. "Yes, sister dear," she said in a flute like voice.

"Enter the hut, discover the truth," Galeta ordered.

"As you wish." Esmeralda bowed her head.

The sound of chimes rang loudly in the air as Esmeralda emerged with a loud pop (like an object escaping a bubble) from within the swirling mercurial radiance. Her full pink lips tipped up into a grim smile. The air turned crisp, smelling of morning dew and clinging ivy.

"Well met, Godmother," Esmeralda nodded her chestnut colored head respectfully toward Danika. Then her eyes widened as she finally took notice of the scene before her. "What has happened here?" Her tiny voice trembled, her gaze unflinching and focused as she stared at Jana--or, at least what was left of her. Bits of the Green were scattered throughout, but her trunk and legs were now glowing a deep hued moss. The magic, a fairy's very soul, would soon erupt from the body, seeking a new and suitable host.

Danika trembled at the thought of so much power. To be one of the *Ten*, could she do it? Would she want to? She gripped her wand tighter, palms sweaty as her heart beat hard. Who would the magic take?

Galeta rolled her eyes, her mouth set into a tight line. "That is why I've called you here, Ese. The wolf knows, his memories must be revealed."

A change overcame the lovely fairy then. Esmeralda's head tilted as a helix of black bled through the color and whites of her eyes. No less beautiful, but alien and frightening as she turned that penetrating gaze on the black wolf who was now eerily silent.

"Wolf," she said in that same flute like voice, "show me the truth."

Whining, but unable to resist the command, the wolf looked at Esmeralda.

Wind ripped and roared through the tiny thatched cottage, stirring dirt and brambles, making Danika's hair whip into her eyes painfully. Wincing, she narrowed her eyes, trying desperately to keep them open so she could see the vision unfold.

A scene stirred like a ripple in a pond. Slowly at first, largely blurred at the edges, but tightening at its center, forming a picture.

Galeta narrowed her eyes when a healthy Jana came into focus. Her long white hair flowed well past her waist, nearly to her knees. And though she appeared a fragile woman with liver spots and wrinkles covering her from head to toe, her eyes gleamed like the glint of steel in flame. A nasty smile curved her lips as she spoke, not in terror, but calmly to the black wolf.

Jana pointed a gnarled finger--the sharp nail long and curling downward--at the door.

Danika's eyes widened. Why was Jana not fighting the wolf? Why did she not attempt to defend herself?

The scene shifted again when the Heartsong entered the doorway. Her eyes moved between the wolf and Jana. At first with fright, but then her facial features dropped and something akin to horror flickered in the depths of her eyes.

The red wolf leapt into the picture, creeping in behind her. The wolves had set a trap and Jana was smiling.

"Bloody, bloody hell!" Galeta spat as Danika's heart sank to her knees.

How could this have happened?

Then Galeta spun that arctic stare on both her and Miriam. "None must know of this night. Should Kingdom ever discover what has transpired here, our world would cease to exist as we know it. Swear it!" The power of her words rolled like shifting lands, stealing the very breath from Danika's lungs.

She gulped, but nodded. Miriam nodded too, but closed her eyes. She had her arms wrapped around herself, and Danika knew her friend was not well.

Galeta's nostrils flared. Esmeralda blinked and the black of her eyes were no more, they'd returned to the vibrant green of a tree's canopy.

"Sister," Esmeralda said, pointing to Jana, "she glows."

The green light encased Jana's remains like a tomb, lifting what was left of her high into the air. The room grew heavy with the sharp nip of ozone. Bolts of lightning streaked from within the corpse itself.

Galeta pursed her lips. "The magic will find who it will." Then she turned her hawk like gaze back on the wolf. "Destroy them all. Malvena must never know how close she came this night."

Miriam's head shot up then. "What? All? Even the Heartsong?"

The Headmistress snarled. "How dare you speak to me? I've given the order. Kill them all!"

Danika's head seemed completely independent of her body at that moment, turning this way, that way, following each harshly spoken word with a lump in her throat.

"**NO!**" Esmeralda cried, one eyebrow rose as she studied Galeta with the look of a fairy who would do bodily harm if ignored. "You may not kill any."

"You cannot stop me--"

Esmeralda crackled as she flitted towards Galeta's projection. She planted small hands on her hips and spread her legs, a shower of dust dropped from her wings as she spoke. "I am truth, Galeta. Do not forget it."

Miriam flew to Ese's side and nodded forcefully. "I've had a vision, Galeta. 'Tis true. Tonight's actions will determine the fate of our brethren for an eternity. The Heartsong must not be killed. Nor can the black wolf."

Danika felt suddenly useless. She'd never seen such a forceful side to her friend and did not know what to do. Though she was infinitely grateful there'd be no killing tonight. She turned toward the blond girl, still suspended in time--huddled under her red hood--*poor thing, such a tragedy to befall one so young*. Her life would never be the same.

A muscle in Galeta's jaw ticked. "Malvena will surely know otherwise. The Heartsong is no longer hidden. If we do not kill the wolves and the girl, word will spread. The girl's identity has now been exposed. We must kill her in order to cast a new body for the Heartsong."

The sparks shooting off Jana's body were now pinging off the walls of the room.

The black wolf lifted his nose, sniffed the air, and then with a low growl fell to his belly. A blinding white light encased his body, flaring so bright that Danika had to shield her eyes as tears stung the corners.

When the light faded, a man, long and lean and thickly muscled with shaggy black hair, jumped to his feet. Galeta's gaze roamed the length of him, slowly, methodically, taking in all the twisted cords and muscles of his body.

T'was common knowledge Galeta loved men. And this one was a sight beyond most.

"What do you want, black wolf?" she sneered finally.

His chiseled jaw set into a tight frown. "Ye speak of killing me. And yet ye saw my truth, ye know I meant the girl no harm. Can ye not guess why?"

Miriam flitted to his shoulder, lightly tapping it. "Ye are Violet's mate," she said softly.

Danika gasped. Could the night get any stranger? "But…but, he works for Malvena."

He looked at her, with eyes hollow and flat, more animal than human. "Yes, for the sake of my starving clan, I did. She offered to feed us, I had no choice. But I could never harm my mate."

Danika looked at the girl.

But she was so young.

Or perhaps not. A youthful face in Kingdom was no indication of age. Danika should know.

Miriam nodded. "He does not mean he's mated her yet, did ye not notice on the vision what happened when he saw her, Danika?"

Danika scratched her jaw, remembering vaguely the flattening of fur around his neck when he'd first gazed at Violet. "She will not want you," Dani told him, "surely you know that."

"It matters not," he growled, "*she* is mine."

Galeta lifted her hands. "She belongs to me, black."

"The name is Ewan of the clan Black Foot," his rich throaty burr made Danika's heart quiver. Aside from the small crook to the bridge of the man's nose, he was the most magnificent creature she'd ever beheld.

"It matters not at all to me," Galeta shook her head, blue ringlets bobbed attractively around her head. "What does matter is that you are now a problem. You cannot return to Malvena, and it seems we cannot kill you. So we are at an impasse. Though," her lips curled, exposing glinting baby fangs, "I hear it's quite hard to kill one of you. Perhaps the Jabberwocky would like a bit of sport later."

"Give him to Danika!" Miriam cried.

Danika's eyes widened. "Miriam," she squeaked. What in the bloody hell was the matter with her friend?

Miriam nodded, never glancing Danika's way. "She's always going on about the reformation of the bad boys. The big bad wolf is as bad as they come, no? Give him to her."

"I cannot be given to anyone," Ewan thundered, nude body twitching with barely suppressed rage.

"Mir," Dani squeaked again. "Are you mad? Shut up, now. I couldn't possibly hope to hide him from Malvena's spies."

"Have you ever switched forms in front of the Black fairy, Ewan?" Miriam asked, still ignoring Danika's protestations.

Galeta and Esmeralda peered on in thoughtful silence. Danika jumped when a bolt of Jana's power rushed past her bare legs, singing the hair off, and making her yelp from the immediate flare of pain.

In all the commotion of secrets exposed she'd forgotten the power bubbling like brew behind her. The cottage was in grave danger of imploding, and yet--she looked around--no one else seemed to notice.

"We should leave. Quickly," Danika whispered.

"Nay," Ewan said with a swift shake of his head, drowning out Danika's words, "I'm much more dangerous in wolf form."

Danika's pulse fluttered.

"Galeta," Miriam turned back to the ghostly image of their Mistress, "it is perfect. Danika can keep him hidden, if he keeps his nose clean."

Galeta nodded. "And the red wolf, what of him?"

"I'll supply him with new memories." Esmeralda stepped in, laying a silencing hand on Mir's shoulder. "I'll make it so that he believes he killed not only Jana, but the black as well."

Galeta narrowed her eyes. "And the Heartsong? She must not be discovered again."

"Give her to me."

An echoing laugh filled with both shock and disgust fell from Galeta's pearl pink lips. "To you? Miriam. The Shunned."

Danika inhaled sharply at Miriam's new name. No longer was she Miriam the Delighted. The air shivered with ribbons of static as Kingdom responded to Galeta's authority. Miriam's lavender eyes grew huge in her face, and shone with unshed tears. But she nodded bravely. "Aye. To me. I'll take her someplace safe. Someplace Malvena will never find her. I'll teach her all she needs to know, make her strong enough to return and set it right."

Flying to her friend's side, Danika gripped Mir's arm, and gave it a gentle squeeze. Miriam patted her hand and nodded.

"Yes." Esmeralda nodded. "Yes, just so."

"Nay!" Ewan roared.

But this was clearly a day when no one meant to listen to another.

"Then it is settled," Galeta nodded, "the girl must never again be found. Which means you can never return to fairy. You're an outcast. A ghost. Nothing."

The last word settled into Danika's heart like a dirk. The head mistress' image disappeared from within the mercurial portal.

Esmeralda turned. "You do understand what you've done, Miriam?"

Heart clenching, Danika looked at her friend. "Take it back, Mir. Don't do this. You can't. You mustn't. I cannot lose you forever."

Miriam nodded. "Aye, I do," she said, ignoring Danika's pleas.

Then the room erupted into chaos. The ground rumbled, Jana exploded, and the power that'd begun seeping from within now shot like a streak toward Danika.

"*Finis!*" Miriam held up her hand, the undulating sphere of green stopped mere inches from Dani's body. "Ye are not for her," she whispered to the ball.

Sweat poured free down Danika's neck, her entire frame shook. She'd been chosen to be a *Ten*. She was powerful.

Then she frowned. Why had Miriam sent it away?

The ball gathered into a tighter knot and then blasted itself into Esmeralda who shrieked, the sound like a banshee's wail as flames licked at her flesh, consuming her in a net of sparkling green radiance.

"She's dying!" Danika cried, rushing to retrieve her wand, ready to extinguish the flames. But Mir stilled her.

Within moments it was over. Esmeralda slumped on the ground, panting and breathing heavy. Clumps of ivy slithered from her pores, covering her body in a lush and living drapery. It took a second for her to stand. Her hair curled in becoming waves down to her waist, ivy threading throughout. It moved as a snake, sliding slowly down her neck, sheathing her body down to her legs. Her eyes were no longer green, they were black as night.

She nodded toward Miriam. A silent exchange passed between them.

Esmeralda opened her broad monarch stained wings and flitted first to the red wolf, passing her wand lightly along the length of his body. Pops and snaps sounded as his bones shifted, reformed, and became whole again. She then turned toward Violet and made to touch her forehead.

"No, Ese," Miriam shook her head. "She is mine. I will strip her of the memories myself."

Ese turned with a sad smile. "As you wish, Miriam."

A scent of lavender and sage traveled in the new Green's wake as she flew past them. Then she turned, and looking directly at Miriam, whispered, "I will not forget." With those cryptic words, she left.

"Forget. Forget what? What has happened?" Danika could barely understand anything of the night. Where was her timid friend? Who was this new fairy, commanding such powerful creatures around? Even Galeta had eventually given in to her.

Miriam closed her eyes. "I'm leaving, Danika. I must take the Heartsong far from here."

"No!" Ewan roared again, and rushed to the still frozen side of the huddled mass draped in red. "Leave her in peace. Give her to me, to heal, to love. I will protect her."

"Ye will get yourself killed," Miriam snarled. "Ye will do as I say. Ye will go with Danika, ye will stay in human form for fifty years. Fifty years. No less. After that time it will be safe to resume wolf form, Malvena will no longer care if ye're discovered to be amongst the living."

"Mir," Danika pleaded, grabbing hold of her friend's arm. "Please, what has happened to you? Was it that vision you had in the forest?"

It felt like her entire life had just been turned on its head. This was her friend, from the moment of their birth underneath a moonlit rose garden, they'd been inseparable. Why would Miriam leave? Forever, no less. This couldn't be happening. Surely they could find a place to hide them within Kingdom, a place Galeta would never think to look. "Tell me, Mir. Please."

Miriam shook her head. "I ken what ye're thinking, sister. Galeta has a track on me. There is no place to hide in Kingdom. I wish I could tell ye all, but I canna. Not now. I will, I swear it. But not yet. She must be safe. Time is quickly fleeing. Take him and go, Dani. I'll find ye again."

A distant rustling sound alerted them to the presence of something.

Even in human form, Ewan growled. He had Violet in his arms--she was still frozen as death--keeping her close to his heart.

"Go, blast ye!" Miriam cried, and then cast a net of magic around Danika and Ewan, throwing them through dimensions just as the pounding of feet poured through the thatched cottage.

Ewan's howl was a melancholy tune as he reached fruitlessly for the mate stripped violently from his arms.

Chapter 1

Present Day, Alaska

"Aunt, M, I'm going," Violet called over her shoulder.

A spry woman, looking no older than middle age with salt and pepper hair, stuck her head out of the kitchen door. Clearing her throat, she wiped her hands on a blue rag and padded on bare feet into the living room. "Where to, honey? Isn't it kind of dark?"

Her aunt eyed the window, nothing but black and stars as far as the eye could see--the occasional tree breaking up the monotony of a monochromatic world.

Violet sighed, giving her aunt the same smile she always did. After five hundred mortal years it no longer bothered Vi that her aunt was always such a worry wart. "It's always dark here, you know that. But not to worry, I think the dancing lights will be out soon. I'll have plenty of light." She winked, cleaning a pear on her winter jacket and took a huge bite of the sweet fruit. Juices dripped down her chin before she could wipe it up.

"Aurora Borealis, Vi, and don't laugh." Her aunt pursed her lips. "There's wolves, bears, wolverines--"

Violet rolled her eyes and hand mimed talking. "Oh, c'mon now, I think I can handle myself just fine." She patted her jacket, reveling in the familiar hardness of the six inch blade. "But," she crossed her heart, "I promise to be safe."

Her Aunt meant well, truth was, this had become more of a routine than anything else. Violet loved her space and her aunt knew it. There was something about the outdoors, of walking alone through the trees, and inhaling the sharp sting of the cold winter night (actually day, it literally was dark in the middle of the day this far past the equator), that made her feel alive. Violet hated confinement of any sort.

No longer tasting the fruit, she tucked it into her pocket. It would freeze within minutes outside.

Miriam walked up to Violet, her unusually colored eyes so different than Violet's own. She traced Violet's cheek, a sad smile on her face. The glow from the lit fireplace shaded her aunt's face, making her seem in that moment distant and faraway.

"Be safe, my love." Her aunt embraced her in a rough hug, squeezing tight, and Violet frowned, patting her back gently.

Lately her aunt had been acting weird. Different. More touchy. Violet's lips thinned.

With a small shake, her aunt nodded. "Okay, then. Dinner's at six."

Violet snorted. "I'll follow the shadows."

Miriam chuckled. "It's all your favorites. Roast beef, new potatoes, and peach cobbler."

"Wow. I feel so honored." Violet sniffed, stomach grumbling as the scent of rosemary and thyme in a beefy brine tickled her nose. "Sounds like a last meal."

Miriam's smile was frozen in place. "Be on time, Vi."

Violet frowned. "I will."

"Good."

Violet left, closing the door softly behind her. Shutting out the soft blues and pastels of their decorated home, walking deep into the woods, uncaring of the howls echoing long in the distance. She shrugged deeper into her parka, taking deep breaths, letting the cold pierce her lungs like a blade.

Stars twinkled like brilliant jewels above. Somewhere a snow owl hooted, seeking a meal to devour, and Violet laughed. There was magic in the woods. In the quiet serenity of nature, it hummed all around her, through her, even her blood sang with it. Fluttering with something more powerful than herself.

She and aunt Mir had arrived at this remote part of mortal realm a hundred years or so ago. Before that, they'd moved often, always running in the middle of the night. Her aunt had said that it was because she had an adventurer's heart, but it didn't take long for Vi to figure out it had more to do with them running away than seeking adventure. Eventually she'd stopped asking why and just resigned herself to a life of solitude. Never allowing anyone too close, never really making friends. Intuitively knowing it was verboten. Now, the lifestyle was one she preferred. She just wasn't much of a people person.

Violet ran, zipping in and around twisted trees. Snow drifted in lazy curls through the breeze, kissing her nose. She didn't care, her legs were strong and her body sure.

A gray cloud streaked slowly through the navy sky.

Her aunt always wondered about Violet's forest romps. But now it was getting worse. Actually, for a year Miriam's worry had increased. To the point she had even followed Violet on more than one occasion.

Lungs heaving with fire, legs burning, Vi pushed on. She was almost there.

The worry had probably started the moment her aunt noticed her drawings. Sketches really. When they'd first come to Alaska, Violet could barely remember her past. Her aunt had called it brain trauma. From what, she hadn't known, and Miriam hadn't explained. But large snatches of time had been lost to her.

A hundred yards ahead she spied the tree. Heart galloping with glee, she put on an extra burst of speed--uncaring that she sank into thick snow; nothing would stop her this night.

It'd frustrated Vi for years that she simply couldn't remember a childhood, a point where she wasn't grown. She'd asked Miriam countless times to tell her of her youth, but her aunt was always tight lipped and easily aggravated when the subject came up. So Vi had stopped asking. Her life was good now, and though it was strange to move so often, she didn't think much of it. She loved her aunt and trusted that her best interest was in Miriam's heart. But like a fuzzy television screen getting signal back, things had begun to take shape recently.

An image of an old woman. Then more.

Apples.

Rolling like heads on a packed dirt floor.

Lots of them.

Her lip curled. She hated apples.

Innocence.

She'd been that once. Pure joy. The old woman--her grandmother--had once told her she lit up her life with her smile.

Violet's heart gave a painful squeeze and she blinked back hot tears.

And then the nightmares came and the wolves with them.

A thin pine branch slapped her cheek, but Violet barely felt it. She was panting hard now, huffing from the exertion. She wondered if the tracks were still there.

Her body tingled, a slow hum at first, but the closer she got to the tree the harder it pulsed. The tracks were here, she still felt its magic. She smiled.

In her dreams, the wolf was black. Big. Frightening. And she hated to admit, even to herself, how absurdly drawn to the beast she was. She was fixated. Obsessed. Sketching his image over and over. Most of them were of him kneeling over her, over her grandmother, with a shocking spill of scarlet bathing the ground all around them.

Violet grabbed her chest, panting when she finally reached the tree. She took a moment to calm herself and then looked down.

Large paw prints circled the tree. Her entire body flared to life when she brushed her finger over the impression. It was close.

Biting her lip, she glanced both ways. Was it watching her? She cocked her head, listening for the faint disturbance of movement. All she heard was silence. But not the dead silence of fearful animals, the silence of nature at rest.

He wasn't here. Yet.

Grabbing hold of the lowest branch, she hoisted herself up. Climbing from one branch to another, delicately, gently… trying to disturb nothing. Knowing her scent would be all over the place and hoping it would attract him.

When she got as high as she could, she sat and waited, scanning the horizon for any movement.

Minutes ticked past, and then an hour. Two. She didn't move. Barely breathed. He would come. She knew it.

They would always come for her.

Long ago Violet had suspected she was special when she didn't age, when Aunt Mir didn't age. Time stood still for the two of them, whatever damage had been done to her brain was now gone. Because, last night, Violet remembered everything. In her sleep she'd heard the growls, the screams of her grandmother being ripped apart, fear closing her throat and making her numb, stupid, and weak. Huddled under her red robe like a child thinking if she closed her eyes they wouldn't see her, couldn't hurt her. Violet knew who she was now.

She was the Heartsong, the manifestation of wild fae magic. She wouldn't age because she wasn't mortal.

Vi tore a sturdy twig off her branch and toyed with its sharp edge, dragging it along her palm. Time had been good to her. She wasn't only strong of mind and body, but she'd learned to do something even grandmother had said was impossible.

She rammed the twig through the palm of her hand, entranced as the pool of blood--black because of the night--welled up and began to spill. The pain had been absurdly delicious. Strange to think of pain that way, but for her it was more euphoria, a drug-like high of adrenaline and cutting pleasure.

But that wasn't what she'd learned.

Violet focused on the twig, watching as it slowly worked its way completely through her hand before dropping to the ground below.

Grandmother had told her she was magic, but she could never do magic. But grandmother was wrong.

Violet raised her hand up to her face. The hole went completely through. Then she kissed herself, right where she'd shoved the twig through. A small sphere of light escaped her lips, like a golden drop of dew, it entered her wound. Flesh and tendon knit themselves back together again.

Something snapped.

Violet jerked her head up and smiled as a massive loping beast emerged from a dense thicket of bushes.

The creature was easily nine feet long, with its massive shoulders and gigantic paws, there was no mistaking the thing for a normal wolf. Its grey coat was muted in the moon glow. It stopped, taking a moment to sniff the air before padding slowly to the tree. She'd noticed it last night, the first wolf roaming these woods that wasn't quite a wolf. Just like the wolves from her past.

Something gold glinted around its neck.

It was one of them.

Not the black wolf that'd almost killed her. But just like it, close enough she could pretend it was the big, black wolf of her nightmares. Close enough to make her thrill with the sharp desire of ripping into him, of watching his blood spill like he'd watched her grandmother's.

She was easily twenty feet up. Violet smiled. "Looking for me."

The wolf growled, looking up, its hackles rose and mouth pulled back revealing impossibly thick canines.

Violet withdrew her knife and jumped. All breath left her on impact, needle sharp stabs of pain clawed through her thighs. She'd not broken any bones, but there would be bruises later. Snow drifted in a flurry around her face, blinding her for a brief moment. The wolf pounced, its claws gouged her legs, her stomach, and she laughed as the power of hate rose up inside her. She wielded it truer than any blade and slashed mindlessly, feeling a rush of strength she'd never known before surge through her muscles. She was strong. Powerful.

There was blood everywhere. On her arms, her hands, her face. It coated her tongue, but she didn't stop stabbing. Over and over again. The wolf lay still, no longer fighting. Little more than a carcass and still she savaged it.

"Down with the Big Bad Wolf," Vi hissed, stabbing her knife down the gut of the beast; smiling as the blood painted the white snow crimson red.

Chapter 2

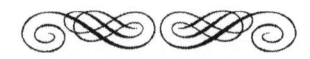

Danika--fairy godmother extraordinaire--waited until the sun set fully, the last warm rays dissolving behind the sharp blue sky. All around her, the woods sang with the song of fairies deep in sleep. Actually, sang was a nice word for what they were doing. They were snoring. Like banshees. All of them. They'd fallen soundly asleep, dropping like flies the moment they'd left her home. Some were leaning against the wall, half slumped forward, and others were spread eagle upon rocks and mushroom caps.

Why?

Danika whistled, patting her pocket that at that moment concealed a glass vial full of eau de dragon. Or in laymen's terms, dragon fart. Crude yes, but effective. One whiff of a dragon's fart, especially of the sea variety, (let's not get started on just how impossible it is to bottle a dragon fart underwater... Danika shivered remembering) and a fairy was as good as drunk. Something about the noxious odor of the fumes mixing with a fairies magical make-up, and boom... a fairy was out for the count.

The serpentine dragon's smell had been so powerful; it'd brought tears to Danika's eyes, even though she'd placed an invisible pincher upon her nose prior to the tea. She'd worried a fairy might realize she was breathing through her mouth during all of tea time, but thankfully she'd been spared.

Her heart clenched when she heard a noise.

Bianca--fairy godmother of toads--scratched her tiny bell shaped rear, let out a belch and sighed happily, sinking even deeper within the grassy field. Grabbing her chest, Danika leaned against her door, awaiting the signal.

She hated to poison her friends. And normally she'd never dream of doing anything so awful. But she did what she must. Orange blossoms began to open, their perfume thick in the air, as they yawned loudly. It was a beautiful night and the flowers would soon notice there were no fairies to dust them. No amount of squawking or crying would wake the fairies at this point. They'd inhaled a potent amount and would be out of it for at least another hour, none the wiser, and suffering no long term effects.

Enough time for Danika to make it to her meeting.

Fireflies came in droves then, doing their nightly dance ritual; zipping and spinning through the mushroom homes of the fae. It was precisely eight thirty. Time to go.

Rubbing her arms, Danika eyed the motley assortment of snoring fae one last time, just to ensure they were all well and truly out. Satisfied, she sailed into the air. Wings buzzing like a hummingbird's as she flew to the edge of the woods. She zipped and sailed, dodging tree limbs, heart speeding with the aftereffects of her fear, but also joy.

She smiled when she finally sailed clear of the woods. Peering through the darkness, she looked for her marker: a series of boulders in a helix formation. Finally spying it, she dove. It took only a moment before landing on gray rock. Glancing both ways, she tapped out a quick sequence of sounds on the stone face.

Tap. Taptaptaptap. Taptap.

Danika nibbled her lip. She was much too exposed. *What if the keeper had left? What if he'd been discovered? What if...* Squeezing her eyes shut, she blocked out the incessant questions and tapped her foot.

He'd come.

A groove in the rock, little more than a jagged edge, shifted. A narrow pinprick of an opening soon grew into a hole large enough for her to pass through. Cool air emanated deep from within the earth, brushing past her face and making her break out in goose pimples.

"Who goes there?" A voice, hollow and deep, boomed from the cavernous depths.

"Goblin, it is I, Danika of the fae," she said, proud that her voice did not quiver. Though the same could not be said for her knees.

"Danika," the goblin growled, "tribute first."

She clenched her teeth. Of course he wouldn't care that she was exposed. That any moment Malvena might discover Mir's whereabouts; which every moment she stood outside, threatened not only herself, but the whole of Kingdom.

None of that mattered though, because the stupid goblin must have tribute.

"Fine," she muttered, yanking her wand from her sleeve and with a swish and flick produced a mound of rotten, stinking silver streaked fish. "There, you putrid, slimy toad. Now let me pass!"

"Proceed," the disembodied voice poured through the hole, blasting her face with the fetid stench of decay.

Wrinkling her nose, she covered her mouth, and flitted inside, following a winding staircase down deep into the heart of the rock. There was no light. But there didn't need to be. Danika knew the path well; she'd met Miriam here many times.

Her pulse rate decreased the deeper she went into the shelter of the earth. Quickly, she ran down the steps, smile growing wider with each step, until finally she spied the mirror.

Well, mirror wasn't the right word. It was a looking glass of sorts, though in no way resembled a mirror. Long ago she'd learned to hide the amulet by altering its true form. If anyone, let alone the *Ten*, knew she still communicated with a shunned fairy, Danika's life as she knew it would be over. She'd be thrown into the fiery dungeon and stripped of her wings.

She shuddered. She was rather partial to her wings. Thank you very much.

Still, the fear of reprisal didn't stop her from her monthly check-ins with Mir. Glancing both ways--habits died hard--Danika rubbed her hand across the golden genie lamp.

Immediately an image flickered, and then a grim face stared back at her. "Oh, Mir," Danika gasped, "what has happened to you?"

In the span of a month, Miriam had gone from looking fleshed out and rosy of cheek, to gaunt and withered. Her eyes were sunken in and rimmed in purple. Her hair was lackluster in color, differing shades of gray and brown. And though every fairy could change their true form, all fairies could see through the magic. This was Miriam, as she really looked.

"My friend. My friend," Danika patted the cold metal screen. "Och…"

Miriam gave her a weak smile. "I'm tired, Dani. Aye, verra tired. No more, no less."

"What has happened, my dear?"

Mir closed her eyes for a brief moment and rubbed her nose. "Times have gotten worse. Malvena," she shook her head, "I donna ken how, but she's found us. I've killed three wolves now already, not a fortnight ago."

Danika tsked. "Does Violet know?"

"Nay," Miriam shook her head, "I've been careful. I don't think she's seen one yet. But it's only a matter of time. Her memories return clearer every day."

Danika sighed. "Was that wise, Mir? Allowing her memories to return? What if you just kept her hidden longer?"

"How long?!" Miriam sneered, thin nose curling up. "We run, always the same thing. I'm tired, worn down. So is she. We cannot keep this up. But she is strong; I see the magic building in her. Soon she'll be strong enough to hunt Malvena herself."

Lips thinning, Danika rocked on her heels. "You know the *Ten* will not like this. Galeta said you were never to return. It--"

"Galeta knows nothing of the truth. Esmeralda saw it, years ago, she knows. It is time, Dani." Miriam's brows drew together sharply.

"Yes, but is this wise, dear one? Did we go about this the wrong way? Should we have told Violet everything? Maybe if we had…"

"Nay, my friend. She must discover the truths on her own, only then will she make the right choice. In the end, the choice is hers. The safety of Kingdom rests in the palms of her wee hands."

A chill breeze caressed Danika's cheek. She glanced up at the wet black rock, remembering that awful night of long ago. So many choices they'd made since then; keeping Ewan from her, never letting Violet know the truth, allowing her to believe a lie. Had they made the right choices?

"Aye," Miriam whispered, "we did."

Danika smiled, her friend knew her so well. "Are you sure, Mir? Ewan grows madder each day for want of her. I've sent him on wild goose chases all over Kingdom, letting him think his Red's been spotted, when the truth of it is, he's never even been close. He grows weary himself. And yet if I tell him, I know he'll force me to take him to her, exposing her location again. Galeta would surely discover his visit, she'd kill him… maybe even me. Not that I care about myself, but I still have my other boys to consider." She shook her head, curls bobbing forcefully around her face with her frustration.

A faint smile feathered across Miriam's thin lips. "In order for Violet to challenge Malvena, she must learn the truth, and there's only one to tell it to her."

"Ewan will be so angry at me for keeping the truth all these years," Danika's words were soft, echoing with the faint trace of bitter laughter.

Mir cocked her head. "Aye, he will. But in the end, he'll know the truth, why it had to happen that way."

Danika snorted. "Such trouble we find ourselves in all the time."

Laughing, the sound almost like what Danika remembered, Miriam nodded. "Aye, and that is the truth of it, my friend." She glanced over her shoulder quickly. "Violet will return soon, I must go, but first… how fare your boys?"

Smiling, Danika sighed happily. "Hatter is mated. Alice is wonderful, crazy herself, in fact, I visit them often. Quite fond of Alice's cupcakes." She patted her stomach. "Gerard and Betty are doing well, vacationing in the Bahamas I believe. Wedding present, you know how it is."

Miriam nodded. "Good. Good. And Jinni?"

"Worse." Danika frowned. "He's fading quickly. There are days when he's little more than a bodiless voice. I can barely see him."

"His mate is coming; she's not quite ready yet, Dani, cheer up. He too shall have his happily ever after."

A rustle sounded, like a door knob turning, Mir's eyes widened and she squeaked. "I must go now, I'll contact you again. Love you, sister dear."

And then she was gone.

Danika swallowed when the lamp went black. Her friend was gone. Again. And though they talked once a month, it was still hard; and getting harder. Miriam was a sister to Danika, her only true friend, and she was desperate to get her back from mortal land. No matter what it would take.

Even if it took angering the Big Bad Wolf to do it.

"I do what I must," she whispered, and nodding decisively, went in search of her moody prince.

Chapter 3

Ewan howled, stamping his foot like a bull's against the very edge of no man's bluff. He hated visiting Jinni. Why the bloody fool insisted on living here baffled him. Jinni's home, (and even calling it that was a stretch) was little more than a cave at the rock's edge.

The exiled genie was more ghost than man now. The curse had long since stripped him of his body; he was now nothing more than an insubstantial mirage.

The Seren Seas whipped forcefully into the cliff, gale winds clawed through his fur pushing him back and threatening to rip the skin off the pads of his feet.

He howled again, long and low, knowing the bloody bastard could hear him. It was time to hunt. Ewan would not leave until Jinni had joined him.

Period.

After the fourth howl, a vaporous shape manifested before him.

Pulsed as a dim blue, before coalescing into a tight shape of arms and legs, torso, and head.

"What?" The Persian lifted a fine dark brow, his nostrils flaring as he glared at Ewan.

Ewan shook his head, pointing his nose in the direction of the Mad Hatter's woods- where the Jabberwocky roamed. Few were brave enough to enter, but Ewan was close and Jabberwocky or no, he'd not be detained again.

Last night he'd heard an echoing cry, haunting and so achingly familiar his body had broken out in a sweat. For the first time in years, he'd heard her. Jinni he brought along not for the help, the miserable man was terrible company anymore, but rather out of a sense of loyalty.

He was fading fast. Never had Ewan seen one so determined to release his spirit to the Great Wolf in the sky.

"Not today, Wolf," Jinni said, turning to go back.

Rain fell like shards of ice; pricking the sensitive tip of Ewan's nose and making him sneeze. Already Jinni was dematerializing. With a huff, Ewan called the change to him. *Unbecoming*, as easy to him now as breathing. In moments his bones had shifted, his muscle lengthened, and he stood on two legs, attempting not to flinch as the rain pelted his sensitive flesh.

"Jinni, ye damn fool. Ye're coming with me. I've need of yer assistance," he growled, the weather making his words sharp and raspy.

Jinni had never been a gregarious sort, but it wasn't hard to see the twinkle in his once vibrant brown eyes turning a dull shade of gray. He was disappearing, becoming nothing more than a pale imitation of his former self.

"For what?" Jinni asked. "I'm no use to anyone anymore."

Ewan had to strain to hear over the wail of the winds. Black sky ripped open with a jagged streak of yellow light, thunder exploded in their ears.

"To scare away the Jabberwocky should he come." Ewan cupped his mouth to be heard.

He rolled his eyes, crossed his arms over his chest, and said, "And how am I to do that? Cry *boo*?"

When Ewan had first come to Danika, he'd hated her. Hated his life. To have found his mate and have her stripped away on that very same night; it'd driven him to madness. Hatter had been useless, his lunacy more than Ewan could bear. Gerard and Hook, neither one could be counted as friend. But it'd been Jinni, who'd brought him back from the brink. He still wasn't sure why the genie had done it for him, but he was grateful. Those had been dark days, dark times. He trembled remembering.

"Have ye seen your face lately, ghost? 'Tis a frightful sight. Ye'd scare anyone with a glance."

Jinni snorted, but something of the old twinkle came back to his face. "I'm not good company today, Wolf. Leave me be." He turned, clearly intending to disappear once more into the goddess forsaken excuse he called a home.

Ewan snarled. "I'll howl the entire bloody night, be a constant source of irritation in yer miserable existence. Ye will come. Now, or later, but ye will come. Decide, Jinni." He narrowed his eyes at the still visage of his floating friend.

Seconds ticked past, then a minute, two. Jinni didn't turn, didn't move or even flinch, for a moment Ewan considered he might have to put his search on hold just to make good on his threat when the specter finally heaved a loud sigh of disapproval.

"Lead the way, filthy mongrel," Jinni said, but there was no heat behind the words, more a detached acceptance.

It wasn't in his nature to be particularly thoughtful of the feelings of others, especially another male, but Ewan worried at this rate the genie may not be around another year.

A particularly strong gust barreled into Ewan just then, nearly knocking him flat and forcing him to shove thoughts of genie aside. He needed to *become* the wolf again; next gale might drive him below sea. Gods forbid that should happen, t'was nigh impossible to extricate oneself from within a sea maiden's clutches for at least a fortnight should she catch you. Lustful wenches they were.

Calling his power, he shifted, content to be back in wolf form. Sounds were sharper, smells richer, and his senses more keen.

He shot like a bolt away from the cliff's, not worried about going slower. Jinni could follow with a thought.

The moment Ewan entered Hatter's woods the landscape shifted. Trees, once tall with trunks thick and brown, were now contorted monstrosities painted in rainbow hues. Some were speckled, others striped. Leaves the color of rust reached out on twisted limbs, attempting to wrap their snake like ends around his tail.

The magic in these woods distorted and twisted everything. Anywhere else in Kingdom a tree was just a tree, but not here. These trees did not bear fruit for others, nor were they attractive to gaze upon. They were carnivores, seeking easy prey to devour.

But that was only the beginning of the surprises to be had within the mad realm.

Birds and insects flitted by, resembling that which they were named after. Horse flies whinnied at his passing. Wolf could not stop, and would not look back. Only the unschooled did so. Before Alice, the woods still held an element of the arcane, but it'd been tame, innocent, and not nearly so dark.

Since her return, the woods were full to bursting with the Hatter's mad magic. Trees that'd seemed mundane in years past were once again treacherous and capable of killing an unwary soul.

Pollen dusted his nose when he ran headlong into a thicket of posies and thorns. Ewan sneezed, clawing at his nose, but never stopping. Not when the hooked thorns tore into his side, nor when Jinni laughed.

"Your obsession with finding your mate is not worth this, surely, Wolf?"

Ewan ignored him.

Morpho butterflies erupted from the brush, filling the sky with their electric blue shimmering. Pads of butter squirted from them, coating Ewan's fur with the sweet hint of clover. He curled his nose, hating when they did that.

A distant howl rang through the woods and the fur around his neck stood up. Lips curled back, teeth gleamed as he growled low and pushed harder, kicking up dirt in his wake. Demonic laughter zigzagged all around him. High, low, in the sky, in the ground. A crescent slice of teeth materialized in his sights.

"Whom, do you seek?" Cheshire asked. "Oh wait…" A tiger striped face manifested within a plume of smoke. "We all know the answer to that riddle, do we not? Big. Bad. Wolf."

Snarling, Ewan plowed through the image, huffing as he inhaled the brimstone fumes.

Eyes, independent of one another, bounced inside Jinni's chest. Blinking, opening wide, and then narrowing into slits.

Jinni rolled his own eyes, but apart from that, gave no other indication of annoyance.

"Hmmm…" Cheshire's ghostly voice returned.

The floating eyes turned its glance on Ewan--who was now coated in sweat, pulse hammering wildly as he tried to reach the edge of the woods with his sanity intact.

A branch rushed out, latching onto Jinni's ephemeral ankle. But Jinni phased through it, the tree shuddered and shook a wooden fist at him.

Just a little further.

Ewan sailed clear of a tree root lifting up from the ground.

"I could tell you where she's at, Wolf." The cat smiled its ghostly smile up at him with pointed teeth sharper than his own.

Blood rushed through Ewan's ears, his heart thumped hard against his ribcage. The cat lied. He always lied. He was a trickster, a deceiver, better to tune him out.

But what if he knew?

Blinking furiously, panting even harder, Ewan shook his head. How could the cat know? Not even Danika knew? T'was impossible, the cat toyed with him again.

Pain ripped through his sides as he ran harder, using every ounce of energy left to exit the woods quickly. Ahead he saw the glimmering wave of twilight, the edge of Hatter's forest. Warmth seeped from his padded feet, he'd cut himself somewhere. Almost as if the thought conjured them, gnats descended in a black haze, attracted to the scent of his sweat and blood, they nipped at him.

"Don't you want to know?" Cheshire floated fully in front of him, relaxed and licking one paw. "Aren't you even the slightest bit curious?"

"Go away, cat," Jinni said sharply, his vaporous hand streaked through the tabby, who only laughed as if he'd been tickled.

Squeezing his eyes shut for a brief moment, Ewan tried to recall where he'd heard her cries. Yesterday hunting along the border of the woods, he'd heard her faint call. She'd whispered 'wolf' and his heart had clenched. For the first time ever he felt hope, hope that his ordeal would soon be over.

He looked around him, at the still black night, at the trees that were now returning to normal. Somewhere a raven cawed. He licked his teeth. Malvena had spies everywhere.

Miriam had been right all those years ago. Malvena no longer cared whether Ewan lived or died, but that did not mean she'd left him in peace. It'd been years since he'd worked for her, but Ewan knew her mind, knew the mystery of that night ate her alive. No doubt, Patrick the Red had been killed. He might have felt a flicker of remorse, but Patrick had tried to end his mate's life, sadness was simply not in him. If Malvena hadn't done it, caution be damned, Ewan would have. He'd have found a way to slink back to his clan just so that he could rip Patrick's still beating heart from his chest for daring to lay one claw on her.

The cat floated at the edge of sanity and reason, a creature of madness and lunacy unable to go further for fear of losing himself beyond the safety of his magic forest.

Ahead the land rolled like the soft swell of a rolling sea. Stopping, Ewan panted, catching his breath, waiting for his heartbeat to return to its normal rhythm. Jinni floated by his side, gazing up at the bejeweled sky with profound longing painted on his face.

"The fairy has lied to you, wolf." Cheshire lifted a brow, the perpetual grin curving higher like twin sickles. Cat's voice was low, filled with hubris. "The girl is not here. She never was. She's on Earth. A place called, A-Laska."

His chuckle grated on Ewan's nerves.

Popping his eyeballs out, Cheshire juggled them in the palms of his fuzzy hands. "Ask me how I know, dog."

"The cat lies, Ewan," Jinni hissed. "Do not listen to his madness."

"Do I? I did not think that I did." He tossed the eyes higher into the air with each pass, until finally he threw them so hard, they blazed a white streak through the night.

A memory floated to the very edge of his consciousness, so brief it'd almost slipped by unnoticed. Ewan latched onto the image. Danika had mentioned something at the table the night she'd promised Hatter his mate; their mates were from Earth.

His nostrils fluttered. He'd dismissed her words as unimportant, all knew Red was his, and hidden somewhere within Kingdom. Danika had been talking to the others, not to him.

But what if she hadn't been? What if she'd slipped and he'd been too stupid to realize it? Was Red on Earth? And if so, why had Danika sent him on chases all through Kingdom for years with 'sightings'. Surely not. His godmother wouldn't lie to him? Not like that.

But what if...

Calling the *unbecoming*, Ewan ignored the sharp sizzle of snapping, sliding bones, and strutted to the gloating cat.

"What do ye ken, Cheshire?" His voice shook from the depths of his belly.

Balls of white fell back to the cat's open mouth. He swallowed the twin orbs and blinking rapidly, readjusted his pale silver eyes before answering. "The birds talk. Talk. Talk. Incessant chatter; drives me simply mad."

He narrowed his eyes, tugged on the cat's scruff, surprised Cheshire let him. It didn't last long, the cat faded in a puff of smoke. Only his whisper remained.

"She's been found." Then he laughed, and the woods behind him echoed with the strain of a thousand eerie cackles.

"What?!" Ewan thundered, whirling on the only other soul around.

"He's a liar," Jinni said with a firm shake of his head. "Do not listen."

Fury ripped through his body, blanketed his mind with visions of death, and gore. "Danika!" Ewan thundered, roared her names to the heavens.

Hot air smacked his cheek, and with a crack of lightening, Danika hovered before him. Corn silk blue eyes were large in her pale face; wisps of gray blond curls framed her head in a halo effect. But he wasn't fooled. He knew what the fairies were capable of, had seen their savagery for himself.

Taking a deep breath, Danika nodded. "It is true."

Words escaped him, his mind went blank.

"The cat should not have told you. I came only just now to--"

Snarling, Ewan snatched her from the air, wishing her could squeeze the life from her fragile body. "How could ye? I've done all ye've asked and more. Trusting ye would help me find her, ye swore it. When I found Gerard that was yer promise. Yer oath…"

Her lashes fluttered, but gave no other outward sign of distress. "Three months ago Miriam told me--"

Trembling, Ewan dropped her, knowing he'd kill her if he held on any longer. "Miriam," he thundered, his brogue becoming deeper with his shock. "Ye've talked with the Shunned? How long, Danika? How long have ye known where to find my mate? How bloody long!" Spittle flew from his lips, but he didn't care. His vision swam in his head, out of focus, in and out making him dizzy.

"Since the beginning."

There was no longer heat in veins, but ice. It sunk its claws into his soul, turning him numb. "An eternity," he murmured and she flinched.

Memories crashed over him, rolling past his mind in a constant stream. Macabre visions of a desperate wolf mad with want for his mate. Bloody knives slicing through veins, rushing into the fray of battle as fiery arrows pierced his jugular, being forced repeatedly by fairy magic to return to the land of living. Dying slowly inside each day, soul shriveling down to nothing as the years rolled by one after the other. Returned from death so many times. Alive. But never whole.

She must have known, must have realized what the separation did to him. Danika had begun sending him on missions of hope. The flowers had spotted the Heartsong hidden deep within the Ogre's woods, atop Cloud Mountain, within the briny depths of Davy Jones' locker. Danika had sent him on fool's errand, knowing all along his mate was on Earth.

"How did you do it?" he asked, his voice dead, monotone.

Danika licked her lips, glancing at Jinni, then back at him. "You must understand, I did what I must. T'was for the good of Kingdom, for us all…"

He held up his hand, unwilling to listen to one more word fall from her viperous, liars tongue.

"Answer the question, fairy. How did ye make me hear her last night? Did ye throw yer voice? Bribe Cheshire with a bag of bloody hearts? HOW?"

As he'd spoken, she'd begun to look more and more confused, until finally shaking her head, she said, "You heard her? Are you sure?"

"Don't. Lie. To. Me." Each word, so full of scorn, made her flit back, as if slapped. "How did ye do it?"

"I…I didn't. I…" she grabbed her face, "dear gods, you heard her? Then it really is time. Miriam was right, the hour is upon us. You must save her, Ewan."

Hissing, he thrust his face to within inches of hers, forcing her to back up. Her dragonfly wings trembled violently.

"Where is she?"

She took a deep breath. "She is where the cat claimed. Alaska. Malvena's spies are close, Miriam has already killed many."

He made to go, but she reached out a small hand to stop him. Ewan shrugged her off.

Hugging her hand to her chest, she said, "This is bigger than you, or her, Ewan. The moment Violet steps foot in Kingdom it will be a race against time. Not only will Malvena sense the return of the Heartsong, so will Galeta."

"I don't care."

"You must!" she shrieked, face contorting, blunt teeth becoming momentarily sharp as familiar eyes bled with shades of red. The kind visage became for a moment, the true face of the fae. "I've not protected her all these years only to have her slaughtered because you feel the need to rut her like a mad fool. She is not what you think she is, Ewan. Aye, she's your mate, but she is much more than that. Much more than just fairy magic. Do you understand what the lass truly is?"

Grinding his jaw, he inhaled deeply. "Mine. That's what she is. I'll protect her--"

She scoffed, her laughter hollow and dripped with scorn. "Do you not wonder, for even a moment, why she's been hidden? Why I lied to you? I love all my boys. I always have. Especially you, you were never supposed to be mine. You belonged to the dark witch and I hated you for it. For choosing her, for fighting for wrong. But then I saw your heart and I hated myself for lying to you. The girl is powerful, but she's dark. Wicked. Her heart is full of hate."

"Because of ye and yer kind," he growled, unable to hold his tongue. Nails clawed grooves in the palms of his hands.

"Nay! Because it is in her nature." Danika's wand sputtered and crackled with energy, no longer did the wee fae tremble. "She is all the darkness that is within a fae soul. Thousands of years, legend states, that the *Ten* most powerful fairies in all of Kingdom divested themselves of their darker nature. Dumping that darkness into the earth. That blight took form. A beautiful babe emerged from the ground, swaddled in shadow. They should have killed it then."

He growled and her eyes shot to his.

"But they couldn't. She was a child, and the *Ten* decided Jana was the most pure of them, and would guard her, keep her safe."

Ewan remembered the day Malvena's crows sought out his clan. A muscle in his jaw ticked as the night turned chilly. "I ken what happened."

She nodded. "Aye, as do I."

"Why did ye keep us apart?"

Danika pinched the bridge of her nose, her features reflecting the innocence of before. "She must kill Malvena. 'Tis the only way."

"I could kill the Black. I know her weaknesses."

She shook her head, her curls bobbed hard. "No, it has been foretold, it must be the girl and no other. But to do it, she had to come into her powers and to do that, she had to learn to hate. Her powers are driven by darkness, Ewan. Not love. Not light. Keeping her safe and sheltered kept her weak."

"I need her back," he heard himself plead, hated himself for it, but he was desperate.

"She will hate you," Danika didn't blink, "but in order for her not to destroy herself, and all of Kingdom with her, she needs you too." She closed her eyes. "This will not be easy, Ewan. But I will do all that I can to protect you both and see you safely to Malvena's castle."

"I understand why ye did it, Danika."

Her eyes were wide, brimming with unshed tears, a soft smile flickered the corner of her rosebud lips.

"But I don't forgive ye for it. Take me to my mate."

A single tear spilled from her left eye. She didn't wipe it up. "Aye, Ewan. I'll take you." Glancing at Jinni, Danika nodded. "It is good that you are here, Jinni."

His lips curled into a tight grimace. "Deceiver. I hate your kind, I always have."

The old fire returned to her face and a nasty smirk crossed her lips. "You and I are not so different, are we genie? Or have you forgotten what brought you to me?"

His hand flexed into a tight fist.

"Aye, my friend, not so very different at all." She nodded toward Ewan. "You're to go with him. You've a purpose to fill in all of this." With those words, she swished her wand, a glowing portal opened before them and Ewan's heart sped.

There would be blood. Lots of it.

Chapter 4

The moment they stepped through Danika's tunnel, he smelled her. But she was different. Before she'd been fresh, like the sharp scent of verdant grass and new life. She still smelled of life, the warmth of the sun, and magic… but all of it edged in violence.

The woods were dark, shadows danced on trees, twisting them into shades of the macabre. Ewan ran, ignoring Danika's cries or Jinni's caution. Blood--particles of it-- tickled his sensitive nose, teased his brain with visions of slaughter. The metallic, iron rich scent flooded his synapses, making him go blank, think of nothing other than his desperate need to reach his mate.

After all this time, she was near. And though there was blood, the scent of her crisp scent reached out to him, shivering across his skin like thousands of massaging fingers.

Air, thick and white, puffed from his jaws as he urged his muscles to work harder, push faster. He swerved in and around trees, paws sinking into the thick fluffy snow. Sweat slathered his haunches, even as the cold brushed an icy caress against his face, threatening to freeze the air he frantically gulped into heaving lungs.

Ahead a wash of light beckoned like a beacon, he was a moth to its flame, drawn by scent and sight. She was in there.

His heart clenched.

There were wolves about, he smelled their woodsy musk. The stench of their mistress lay heavy in the woods, like oily residue it clung to his pelt, reeking of death and decay. Black beady eyes stared at him from within the shadows of the trees; he didn't need to see them to feel them everywhere. He'd worked for Malvena for centuries; he knew the way her twisted mind worked. The crows were here, they'd found her.

With a huff, he pushed fatiguing muscles to their limits, stretching his limbs to the point of pain, anything to reach her faster.

The light grew brighter, opening like a golden bloom, filling his mind and head. Was she safe? What would he find?

Roaring, he shouldered his way through the half open door, panting like a hound of hell come to devour a soul. His eyes scanned frantically, his nose lifted, scenting the eerie stillness of her home. Memories plagued him, bombarded his thoughts, so that he whimpered remembering the night long ago. The hated memories of seeing his mate curled within her red hood, shielding her body from him.

Calling the *unbecoming*, Ewan shifted. "Violet," he screamed, adrenaline flooded his tongue, his throat. Bile worked its way up, like a panicked horse spotting a snake on its path, dread surged within him.

"Violet, where the bloody hell are ye, lass? Answer me!"

He smelled her everywhere, blood so much blood, and yet there was nothing. Like his nose and his eyes worked independent of one another. He turned in a circle, there were wood carved chairs covered in colorful knitted blankets, threadbare rugs, a crackling flame in a hearth. All so peaceful, serene, but his nose knew truth. Violence had happened here.

He ran through the small cottage, following the confusing miasma of scents. Blood and sunshine. Where was she? There were three rooms, each white, each bare; with nothing to distinguish one from the other. All empty. Each time he opened a door, his heart pounded harder.

"Violet, lass, I ken yer around. Shew yerself," he said, brogue becoming so thick it was nearly unintelligible. Madness swirled through his veins, blanketed his vision. So close, closer than he'd been in years. He'd not be denied now.

He threw open another door. A bathroom; and here the blood was thickest. Viscous, coating the inside of his mouth with iron so thick he gagged. Gods above, someone had died. That was the only thing that could account for so much blood.

Then he saw it, a ripple like a wave in a placid pool, in the very bottom corner of the small room. And the moment he spotted the ripple, he felt the undulation of fairy magic move against his chest like a gentle swell. But though he knew magic covered the truth, he could not see through the casting.

"Violet," he roared, "I'll not harm ye, lass." Was his mate dying? Dead? He shuddered, unable to bear thought.

"Hush, now," a strong female voice shushed him, then a face he could never forget scowled at him. "Ye'll bring the wolves."

"Shunned," he warned, voice trembling with a rumble of violence seconds from erupting, "where is she?" His fingers clenched, unclenched, wanting desperately to smash his fist through something and watch the blood spill.

Miriam looked as if she wanted to say more, her lips thinned, and with a jerk of her head she pointed toward the living room. Immediately the mirage dropped, and the truth of what he'd smelled was now visible to the eye.

A trail of blood, black as night, saturated the carpets. Bloody handprints dotted the walls, as if someone had dragged themselves along.

Ewan jogged, it didn't take him long before he saw her. He wanted to savor the moment, the first time in years he'd seen her, was within reaching distance of his mate, but he couldn't. Her lips were blue, her skin lily white.

The blonde hair he'd remembered that curled so effortlessly around her face, now hung limp and crusted with blood. Her hand rested on her breast, not a muscle moved, her chest did not rise, and Ewan's heart slid to his feet. Suddenly he felt too heavy for his body, but somehow he was able to make his way to her.

A macabre vision of loveliness formed in his eyes. Finally able to give into his weakness, he dropped to his knees, not knowing where to touch her. A strange sound kept flitting in his ear, an annoying moan he couldn't place.

Gingerly, not wanting to further injure her, he hefted her slight weight into his arms. The moan grew louder, then voices sifted through his consciousness, but they were distorted--filtered through a long tunnel, low and hard to understand.

His hand was so dark against her pale, lovely face. Her neck was tilted at an odd angle, blonde hair rained down around her shoulders. The moaning grew louder, like the buzz of an angry wasp's nest disturbed. He traced the curve of her sharp cheekbone, gently, reverently. Following the line to her nose, so straight and perfect, her heart shaped jaw. Small, beautiful ears. She had freckles. He'd never known that. Flattening his fingertips against her neck he waited.

There was no pulse.

Blue lips did not part to utter protest at her lover's caress. She still looked as young and as angelic as he'd remembered, she'd aged not at all. Youth personified was his mate. Slowly, with measured ease, he slid his hand down the front of her still, cold body. Where was the wound? What had wrecked such devastation upon her? He smelled wolf, the stench of it lay thick in his nostrils--the musk of woods and upturned leaves, of bloody meat, and fatty marrow.

His hands slipped beneath her shirt. Maybe there was still time. Maybe the fairies could still heal her. Then his fingers found thick groves torn within her flesh, deep into the muscle. A sickening suction pulled at his digit and he shuddered, fire burned his throat. The sound cascaded all around him; the low moan was now an eruption of pain.

His chest heaved, his eyes swelled, and then he howled, pulling her beloved face into his chest. Crying out to the night; pain pouring out through his song.

Hands clasped onto his shoulders. Small ones, they squeezed. "Ewan," Danika began.

He hissed, jerking out of her reach, rushing to his feet; holding the lifeless body to his chest, as if he could somehow force his life's essence into her.

"Ye did this!" He snarled, the wild in him coming to the forefront, obscuring his reason or sanity. Only knowing the pain consumed and burned and he needed to release it or risk dying from the agony of his shattered soul.

Human size again, her eyes were huge, filled with sadness and unshed tears. "We must leave here, Ewan. There is dark magic about, the crows have surely reported to their mistress."

"I will not leave her." His words were vicious, sharper than a sword.

Miriam stood in front of Danika, almost as if shielding her.

"Move away, Shunned," he warned.

"Hear me, Ewan of the clan Black Foot," her words trembled with a surge of raw power, it crackled through the air like a heavy ball of static. "She is nay dead, though she may appear it."

Ewan wasn't sure he'd heard correctly. Afraid to breath, to believe, for fear it would turn out to be nothing more than a cruel joke, he whispered, "what do ye mean, nay dead?"

His tongue felt thick in his mouth; his throat in parched agony. Adrenaline flooded his brain, made him shake as his fingers dug into Violet's still chest, praying with all his soul the fairy spoke true.

Miriam looked around as shadows danced in her eyes; a pulse darted in her throat. She was nervous, she reeked of it. "We've been found a few weeks ago now. I've been killing the wolves and dumping their carcasses far from our home, hoping to keep the lass in the dark at least until I could arrange our departure." She closed her eyes, wringing her hands. "I'd thought I'd been so clever, keeping it from her. But she must have found out. She must have found one. She took him on, very nearly died. I've had to place her in a Sleeping Beauty spell. She is locked, frozen in time. In order for her to survive, we must return to Kingdom this night."

He swallowed the bile that'd lodged tight in his throat. She was asleep. Hands shaking violently, he brought her face to his, kissing her lips softly. Knowing the kiss would not wake her, this wasn't a fairy tale after all, but hope bloomed deep in his soul. She was alive, still here. He did not care if she hated him now, she wouldn't later. Ewan would show her the depths of his love, his devotion, and passion. Together they'd overcome Malvena. The madness of losing her faded slowly away. This he could deal with.

"The *Ten* will know if we sail into Kingdom, Mir, you told me that before. Remember? How can we sneak in?" Danika's words were rushed, full of fear.

Miriam smiled and hugged her friend softly. "Ssh, now. It matters not."

"How can you say that?"

Ewan rubbed Violet's back, reveling in his ability to touch her again. Hold her. He'd never let go, never again.

"I've been busy while I've been away, Dani." Miriam's old face and countenance transformed suddenly, she appeared younger now, and more spry as her hands flitted about wildly. "I've set up an underground network of spies and allies, they will usher us safely toward Malvena's keep." Miriam glanced at Ewan, the strange lavender eyes keen and sharp as she said, "we must split up. We cannot travel together. Dani and I will take one path, you with Violet..." she nodded, and reaching into her skirt pocket, extracted a rolled parchment, "will take another."

He grabbed the tan roll from her hand, knowing it to be a map of some sort. Glancing at it quickly, he looked back at her.

"Read it, learn it, then burn it." Her gaze bored into his, hot and demanding. "If anyone discovers this trail, we're ruined."

Danika licked her lips and Ewan's pulse thumped.

"We've one chance, Wolf. One, to right the wrongs of a night long ago. Can I trust ye to keep her safe?"

His nostrils flared, anger burned through his veins like a shot of poison. "None will harm her, I vow it."

She exhaled; her small shoulders sagged with relief. "Good. Good." Miriam grabbed Danika by the elbow, leading her away. "The moment the lass passes through into Kingdom, Sleeping Beauty's spell will dissolve. Do not contact us for any reason, the map will lead ye. Stay to the course. I've got a tracker on Violet, but it's not always reliable. Do yer best." She shook her head. "Goddess be with ye, Wolf."

Her words still quivered with worry. Ewan frowned. "I'll guard her with my life, Shunned."

Miriam's mouth turned down. "Be wary of her, Ewan, she is not what you think." With those cryptic words, she walked away.

Danika hung back. She looked the same aged sprite he remembered, slightly pudgy, face filled with a goodly light, but there was tension now where there didn't used to be. Perhaps she had tried to do best by him, but the wound was still too fresh, too raw to forgive and forget.

She nodded, as if she understood his thoughts. "I'll open a portal for you both, it won't last long. I smell the wolves all around us. Jinni," she looked at the silent, nearly translucent ghost of a man. Dark eyes burned with some unnamed emotion. "You are not to accompany us. You must stay here in Alaska, go due north. Several miles out, there'll be a flat clearing with a star in it. Wait there."

The ghostly jaw worked from side to side. "How long?"

"Until it's time." Inhaling sharply, she nodded, and left.

Ewan had seconds. He turned to look at his friend, the only one of the bad 5 who'd ever treated him with an ounce of friendship. He held out his hand. "May the sun shine upon you, my friend."

Morose eyes stared back at him. A cold shiver passed through him when Jinni's hand phased through his own. Goose pimples rode the length of forearm. "And you, Wolf."

With a nod, Ewan ran from the demons creeping closely on their heels.

Chapter 5

Ewan stood within the safe embrace of the spiraling tunnel, scanning unfamiliar surroundings. Night sang all around him, the whistle and whisper of the wind telling its secrets on the gentle breeze. Cicadas hummed, the bejeweled sky glinted so bright as to seem a sort of twilight.

Ewan hefted Violet higher in his arms, cradling her limp head against the firm beat of his heart, willing her to open her eyes. They hadn't yet crossed the threshold into Kingdom, his heart thumped hard at the thought of finally getting to introduce himself; know her, have her know him. Cursing his clumsy human form, he scented the impossible stretch of dun colored sand dunes, trying in vain to detect friend from foe. He'd committed Miriam's map to heart, surprised at the many stops they were to make before reaching Malvena's keep, he'd had no flint to burn the scroll with, so he'd dropped it somewhere within the channel of light that'd transported them here.

Twin planets, glowing a hazy bluish-lavender, filled half the sky. Kingdom was massive, beyond imagining. Ewan had never left the comfort and safety of the western borders; this was eastern lands, Jinni's territory. He could have used the ghost now, though Jinni would likely have thought Miriam crazy for bringing them here.

In the distance, beyond rolling hills, lights flickered and danced. That was the first of many stops for them. Gathering his courage close and Violet closer, he kissed her cold brow and stepped beyond the threshold.

Pulse rushing through his ears, drowning out all other noise, he watched and waited for the first flickering of the spell to dissolve. The breeze caught a streamer of blond hair, wrapping it like a coil around his wrist. He wasn't sure how much time passed as he waited; a buzzing noise forced him to glance up. The green iridescent body of a large scarab beetle sailed past his periphery.

There was no time to waste, outside, they were exposed, his feet took them where his mind dreaded to go. Sand caught between his toes, rubbing them raw the farther he walked. The lights that'd seemed so close before, mocked him, seeming to move further and further away the more he walked. One hour slipped by, then one more. Soon, he'd lost track of time completely.

In a trance like state of shuffle, step, shuffle. Sweat and sand irritated his skin, made him growl and burn from the constant friction. But he couldn't stop; they had to get to safety.

The planets cast long shadows, almost obscuring the moon's glow. T'was hard to know precisely how much time had passed, but his muscles ached. This would be so much easier in wolf form. This land was nothing but an endless sea of sand. Why hadn't the fairy dropped them off within the village?

Eventually, even his thoughts ceased, caught up in just getting there.

Biceps and thighs trembling, he climbed the long hills. Up and down, down and up, one after another, landscape never shifting or offering surcease. A brutal test of his endurance, alone he could climb hill after hill, but holding onto dead weight while doing it in his weaker human form, coated him in a thick sheen of sweat. Hair clung to the back of his neck, wet and uncomfortable.

The abrasive sand rubbed his feet raw, a suspicious wetness gathered on his heels.

"Red," he whispered, lungs heaving for relief from the humid night, "wake, my love. We're in Kingdom."

She did not respond, but he would not lose hope, because now her lips no longer resembled a permafrost blue, but the rosy pink of health. The spell had begun to lift.

"Ye are so lovely, Vi," he inhaled, "and I ken ye have nay knowledge of me, but I promise ye this… none will ever hurt ye again."

Preserving the remnants of his energy, he stopped talking or thinking about anything other than the beckoning flames. Ewan urged his shaking legs to top the crest of yet another hill and this time, the lights were there. Not twenty yards ahead. The village moved with life, people moved in and out of houses shambling around in random patterns.

Smiling grimly, he stopped, taking a moment to rest and study the quaint mud brick village. The night so well lit, he could make out the beige hue of the bricks spiraling up like coral from a seabed. A massive gate and walls surrounded the city; he'd have to figure out a way in without alerting any to their presence. He did not know this land, nor whom to trust. He wasn't even certain he could trust the spy Miriam led them to.

A graveyard was their assignation point. Ewan did not know who the spy was, but it filled him with dread knowing where he was to find the individual. Few dared to dwell within dead man's land, and those that did, were never friendly.

A gaggle of drunken men stumbled out from an oblong door, small children dressed in cream toned clothes raced between homes kicking a ball. But no matter where he looked, he could not find any sign of the graveyard.

Then a chatter of discordant voices reached his ears, men carrying torches suddenly filled the dirt streets. He narrowed his eyes, instinct telling him to crouch.

Guards were kicking in doors, cries of alarm rang out as women were yanked roughly from their homes and thrown to the ground. Children screamed and cried, running to their mothers even as the guards kicked them, demanding to know where the Heartsong was.

Ewan sucked in a sharp breath when a movement from one of the guards exposed a glint of gold around his neck. Malvena's spies. Here. Already? Danika had worried they'd know, but he'd felt no disturbance in the air, no shifting of the land.

"Bloody hell," he snarled.

His nostrils flared as he looked about wildly for a cave, a hole, anything to hide them in.

A low growl seeped from his belly, where was the bloody grave? He closed his eyes, trying to remember the map. The image of the village sprang up in his mind and behind it, outside the gates, a small x.

Ewan licked his lips, and glanced over his shoulder. He'd have to go back down the hill, travel horizontally, and hopefully would be able to avoid any eyes that might be on the lookout for his mate. As he was deciding this, a soft whimper made him jerk. Glancing down at his mate's face, he caressed her blood encrusted hair.

"Be easy, Red." He hungered to kiss her, taste her, mark her and make her his finally… soon, once they were safe.

It took several more hours; Jinni had always said the nights were blessedly long, and Ewan was thankful the shadows kept their secret. His neck prickled, as if eyes watched, burning a hole through him.

Glancing over his shoulder, he noticed a bright green jewel walking slowly toward him, then another, and another. He cocked his head when he realized they weren't jewels at all, but beetles. He'd stumbled onto a nest. Not odd in the desert. Shaking his head, he shoved them from his mind.

The scent of jasmine grew redolent; a gentle breeze caressed his sand encrusted body. But he couldn't allow himself to relax, the clang of steel and cries of the dying was a melancholy song. Goddess help them, he could only hope Miriam's ally would give them shelter.

But the further he walked; the sweet scent gave way to a musty odor, sickly and putrid. Violet moaned, and ignoring the spasming ache in his arms, he nuzzled her soft cheek. "We're almost there, Red. Calm yerself."

Curling his nose, Ewan resisted the urge to vomit. The smells were ghastly, rotten and thick, clinging to his nostrils, forcing his eyes to water as he tried desperately to ignore the sneeze filling his throat.

The moment he stepped around the dune he saw the graveyard and the thick gray fog that shaded its perimeter in gloom. The smell was stronger, noxious. Like meat that'd set out in the baking sun for days, festering and boiling over with maggots.

"Bloody fairy," he spat, knowing now who the ally was. Glancing at Violet's twisted face, he worked his jaw from side to side. She was covered in blood, a beacon to this monster.

While he studied her, he did not notice the amorphous black fog coiling around his ankles until it yanked him off his feet, the ground tore into his nude flesh, scraping him raw. Grunting, he was able to still cling to Violet's body.

"*Sssoo much blood*," the sibilant voice rang with greed and perverted joy.

Then a hot tongue, tough as a cat's, licked the soles of his feet. Ewan kicked at the oily claw wrapped around his ankles, but it was useless. He thrashed even as a demonic mask coalesced within the inky vapor.

"*It's been sssoo long. Sssoo hungry.*"

Blood pounding, Ewan twisted away from the fanged teeth. Horns sprouted from the face and jaw, a curved bony protuberance latched onto Violet. Scrabbling for purchase, his hold on her precarious, Ewan grasped a crooked gravestone and grit his teeth against the sensation of his legs moments away from being torn off him.

"Miriam sent us," he shouted not caring if Malvena's guards heard. Avoiding imminent death at the hands of a blood thirsty ghoul of far greater importance at the moment.

Instantly the hands dissolved. "*The Ssshunned?*"

"Aye, ye bloody fool," Ewan snapped, anger throbbing through his skull as he spat blood and grit from his mouth.

Violet moaned.

Ewan sat up, every muscle in his body ached as he hugged her tight to his side, dizzy and breathless with the reality of how close he'd come to losing her again.

The deformed creature slithered up to them, red eyes glowing like embers as it stared first at him, then her.

"Get away from her," Ewan growled, he had little strength in him at the moment and he knew the demon ghoul knew it, but he'd die protecting what was his.

The red eyes stared at him briefly before turning to her, ignoring Ewan's warning, the ghoul sniffed.

The face looked to be chiseled from stone, cracked and splitting from age. The gray pallor of the ghoul's body nearly indistinguishable from the tombstone's all around. Kingdom granted immortality, of a sort. One could not die of old age or disease, but death by battle or monster had taken many lives.

"*She smells of deathhhh, violence, chaosss,*" the ghoul intoned in the deep heavy inflections that made Ewan's skin crawl and ice heat his veins. Then the eyes returned to him and a long black tongue licked cracked and bleeding lips. "*A tassste?*"

Growling, Ewan scooted back on his heels, the stench of the creature nauseated him. "She is mine, ghoul. Safe passage, that was the bargain struck with The Shunned, was it no?"

The ghoul snarled, curling his lips. "*Yesss,*" he spat it like an insult.

Calling his wolf, Ewan let the animal spill in his eyes and growled low, "Then leave off."

With a bird like hiss, the ghoul backed away.

Heaving a sigh of relief, trembling with a rush of adrenaline, Ewan closed his eyes. The villagers surely knew of the ghoul within the grave, the guards must know it too, meaning none would dare investigate here. But that didn't make it safe.

The beast was hungry. Soulless, and with a desperate taste for flesh, its appetite was bottomless and unceasing. To be here for any amount of time, vow of safe passage or not, was lunacy.

The creature knew one thing. Hunger. The graves' held nothing but bones, which meant he and Red were the only meat around. He needed to find the ghoul feed, and there was only one place to do it. Despising the choice, Ewan closed his eyes and whispered, "Many have died this night within the village…"

The words had barely left his mouth before the ghoul cackled with glee and became mist once more, a haunting laugh fluttered behind him.

Shuddering, Ewan kissed Violet's cheek. Tonight she was safe, and the ghoul would gorge, hopefully for a few hours at least. His stomach roared, twisting and churning in his gut, demanding food. But the stench of death was everywhere and even if he had food, he'd never get any of it down.

Ewan settled against a headstone, eyes staring blankly at the rows of stones all around them. Finally sleep called, and her lure was impossible to ignore.

***

Fire raced jagged claws through his veins. Pain exploded in his brain, and Ewan's eyes snapped open.

"Move, and I'll slit you gullet to throat." The dulcet voice so at odds with the cold press of a blade in his gut.

Chapter 6

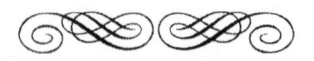

She straddled his hips; knife gripped so tight in her hand, her knuckles ached. "Who are you?"

Last thing she remembered was tearing the wolf to bits, slicing through his gut, and then stumbling home, blood leaving a scarlet trail for any predator to follow. In her lust to kill the beast, she'd not known how injured she truly was. Aunt Miriam had dragged her to the bathroom, trying to staunch the constant flow streaming from her belly where the wolf had sliced her repeatedly.

Then Aunt Mir had promised she'd be okay, grabbed her face, and told her to breathe. The rest was blank. Until now. Until him.

His hands shifted and she shoved the knife in deeper, lips curling when she heard his hiss.

"Easy, lass. Easy. I'll not harm ye." He held up his hands in entreaty.

Those words spoken in his deep Scottish brogue made her lashes quiver and her thighs tremble. There was no denying the man was beautiful. And the first male she'd touched, ever.

Something about his voice, the way it moved against her body like a soft caress… she'd heard that voice before. Distantly. But how could she have? She'd never have forgotten the face.

It was hard, chiseled, as if by a sculptor. His jaw sharp and well defined, his nose equally severe, and with the slightest crook at the bridge. Dark shaggy brows framed a pair of liquid gold eyes filled with flecks of amber. The epitome of male beauty, save for the scar that curved from his eye to mid-point on his cheek.

Her spine tingled with a rush of appreciation even as anger heated her blood. "I'll not ask again," she said, cursing the natural sweetness of her voice, wishing for once she could growl and threaten like the wolf she'd killed earlier. "Who are you?"

He was nude, his muscles lax, his body still, trying to not appear threatening. But she knew it for the sham it was. Felt the hardness of his thighs beneath hers, the flex of muscle as he shifted, slowly lifting his hands. His bronzed skin gleamed with pearls of sweat, adding a luminescent sheen from the sky's eerie lavender glow.

"Yer mate," he said, so slowly she wasn't sure she'd heard correctly.

The ropes of his stomach flexed as he tried to sit up, she dug her knife in, briefly casting her eyes down as a thin crimson ribbon appeared where smooth skin had once been.

"Red." His voice rang in warning, she narrowed her eyes. "Put the knife down."

It wasn't a request.

She leaned in, hating that his scent of sweat and musk attracted her so, filled her head with dizzy longing for something she didn't understand. "My name is not, Red, and I am not your mate."

Looking up, she studied her alien surroundings. The sky glowed orange with streaks of pink; the land a monotonous shade of beige with a smattering of green palm fronds swaying in a gentle breeze. Magnificent twin orbs, took up a huge section of sky. Large, gray rings surrounded them.

"Where am I? Where have you brought me? Where's my Aunt?" Panic rushed through her veins, her mouth tasted of cotton and her throat felt raw and parched.

He closed his hypnotic eyes and she could breathe again; when those eyes were on her face, looking at her with heat, it was hard to remember who she was. The strangeness of those foreign emotions made her angry.

Quicker than she could blink, his hands gripped her wrists, and then his hard length was on top of hers, pinning her beneath him. Bucking and screaming, she fought to free herself.

"Stop yelling, lass." He shoved his face so close to hers, the heat of his body became second skin.

"Get off me," she wheezed, trying to pound her fists on his hard as steel chest, but she couldn't move her hands even an inch. Furious, terrified, she did the only thing her wild mind could think of. She bit his forearm.

He hissed as her teeth sank in so deep, the skin broke.

"Lass," he growled, and she envied the fire in his voice, the deep timbre that flooded her brain with desire and rage, "doona make me hurt ye. Release me."

Shaking her head, she bit harder, blood pooled on her tongue and the taste of him saturated her senses. It reeked of death, earth, dark power, and wicked nights. A wolf! He was a wolf. Fear slammed her like a wave, and with it came the hate, that sharp flinty passion that consumed her mind like poison and engulfed her body with adrenaline. Wild, crazy to get out from under him, she yanked with the preternatural strength she'd used to massacre the last wolf she'd fought.

He grunted, but his hands released her. She curled her fingers, dragging her nails down his cheeks, leaving welts behind.

Then he had control of her again. "Damn ye, lassie. I dinna wish to do this yet."

Light filled his eyes; they glowed even as his mouth curled back like a dog's muzzle. Large fangs dropped and… her heart was going to explode in her chest. His bite was not savage, but it was deep. He bit her collarbone, making her whimper as his fangs sank in.

There were moans, deep and trembling with a need that bordered on desperation. She was doing it. Alive, consumed by passion, tremors wracked her frame as she panted through the liquid pleasure. Lit with desire, her sanity screamed at her to get away, but her traitorous body could only undulate as the pleasure overwhelmed her with its violence.

"Violet," her name dropped like a prayer from his lips and that was the catalyst she needed to snap from her stupor.

She shoved him for all she was worth. He was so much stronger than her, he barely budged. A heavy sigh tickled her ear before he kissed her neck so softly it was almost a whisper, he scooted back.

Finally free of the blinding, all-consuming craving for more, she gripped her neck. Blood stained her fingertips, but not as much as she'd thought there would be.

"What did you do to me?" she demanded, lungs still heaving for air, scooting back on her heels until her back was plastered against a gravestone. Traitorous body tingling, not with anger, but with desire so consuming she had to claw her nails into the dirt to keep from crawling back for more.

His eyes were shaded, thoughtful… haunted?

"I've marked ye."

"You what?" Her brows lowered, and she fought a swell of dizziness as she shoved to her feet, slipping her hand casually into her back jean pocket.

Kneeling, he glared up at her. There wasn't hatred, or even anger, but a sort of shock, as if he couldn't comprehend what'd just taken place between them. He seemed completely unaware of the vicious bite wound in his arm still oozing blood.

They stared intensely at one another for several moments, she with fury, he with a dawning understanding. He broke first. Standing, he took a step toward her. But this time she was faster, and pulled her pocket knife out, slamming her thumb on the button to release the three inch blade. It wouldn't kill, but it would hurt.

"Red," he warned with a shake of his head, "stop and listen."

Every hard line of his body flexed as he moved closer. She didn't want to notice that about him. She didn't want to care. Fact was, she'd sever his beautiful head from his neck if he came one inch closer.

"Stay back." She held the knife out, swishing it from side to side. "I've killed your kind before, I'll do it again."

He stopped walking, jaw working hard from side to side. "Ye canna harm me. T'was the purpose of the bite, lass. I've marked ye, a mate canna harm their own."

"Liar," she spat. "I'd never whore myself for a dog. I'm not your mate and so help me, you'd better tell me where I'm at before I cut that," she pointed at his big, stiff, ugly… thing, "off."

"Bravo! What fun," a roughly masculine voice trembled with laughter as he clapped.

Startled, Violet twirled on her heels. A brightly clothed peacock of a man waggled his brows at her.

"I am Kermani," he said in a strangely accented voice not all together displeasing, melodic, almost mesmerizing. She wasn't given much time to ponder it before he'd rushed her and grabbed the knife blithely from her hand, hiding it efficiently within the voluminous folds of his turquoise colored pants. She hardly had time to register it was gone, one second it was firm within her grasp, the next she held nothing but air.

"Give it back," she said.

He wagged a finger. "Within my walls, there is peace. No weapons allowed."

And yet, it didn't escape her notice that he'd held onto it.

A short man, slight of build with burnished umber skin gleamed in the early morning light. He bowed theatrically with one arm tucked beneath his waist. "I'm sorry it took me so long to make my acquaintance known, but I had…" his black eyes narrowed shrewdly, "matters most urgent to attend to."

Face creasing into a friendly smile, he winked. The large golden hoop in his ear gleamed with several large ruby settings.

Violet frowned.

"And ye are?"

Just the sound of the dog's voice made her wet and gnash her teeth, damn that bald headed thief for taking her only knife.

"My apologies, I'm your ally."

The wolf cocked his head. "I thought the ghoul…"

Kermani hopped onto a jagged piece of tombstone, crossing his legs. Tan pointed shoes bouncing to and fro. The colors he wore were amazing. Like he'd taken the brightest jewels and spun them into fabric, from the deep red of his strange shirt, to the orange striped scarf he'd wrapped around his waist.

"The ghoul works for me. You have been given safe passage, therefore…" He waved his hand, letting the rest dangle off. "Anyway, come. We've food, clothes," he eyed the wolf with a slight sneer, "and company. Come, come. Even eyes have walls. Or is that, walls have eyes? Hmm…" muttering to himself, he jumped from the crumbling stone and hooked his finger, never glancing back to see if they'd follow.

Crossing her arms, Violet stood where she was. Harmless as the strange gypsy looked, she didn't trust him. She didn't know what was happening and until she did, she'd not leave this spot.

With a growl, a strong pair of hands hooked onto her arm above her elbow. "Come." One word, but it made her body shiver.

Violet had led a sheltered life, but that didn't mean that she was stupid to the ways of the world. She'd lived a long time, had hidden herself away from prying always, but always watching and learning.

Many years ago, she and Aunt Mir had settled in England, during the days of the Ripper. Violet had been fascinated by the world around her, the constant fog that bathed the gas-lit city and made it impossible to see more than five feet ahead. She'd moved as a wraith through the streets, even at times within the hidden underground network of tunnels and sewers that crisscrossed the underbelly like a giant labyrinth.

The walls had been made of brick, the water foul smelling beneath her feet, everything coated in a thick sludge of unmentionables. Hygiene, or the lack thereof, had killed many. But she'd been sure of her ability to not age and had learned the impossible maze, had even reveled in her ability to be outside of her home, watching the world sing around her, knowing she'd never be caught.

That's what this place reminded her of. Kermani had surprised her when he'd touched a brass knocker on the wall surrounding the graveyard. A crumbling gravestone had moved silent on oiled hinges, revealing a long staircase that descended into the earth's bleak darkness. Placing a finger against his lips, he'd headed down the stairs. She'd no fear of the dark and the things that hid in them, but she didn't want to be so close to the man who'd claimed her as mate.

The wound of her neck chose that moment to throb, stoking the flames of her anger. But not just because he'd bitten her, mostly because she hadn't wanted him to stop.

Her captor dragged her behind him, his grip still as sure as before, but more protective than commanding. The heat pouring off him felt nice compared to the chilly damp caressing her cheek. Though she hated to admit it.

Kermani grabbed a lit torch from off the stone wall, and smooth as silk, the gravestone covered them, hiding its secret once more behind its ruined façade. Once all light from the outside ceased, Kermani turned to them, the ever present smile lurking on his face.

"We've much to discuss. My wives will attend to the girl."

"The name is Violet," she said with a glower.

"As you say," his silky voice could not hide his disregard. "You and I have much to discuss," he said, to the wolf.

The man only nodded, gripping her arm tighter. "We'll talk, but nay without her."

She hissed, yanking her arm out of his hold. "I don't need you to babysit me, whatever your name is."

"Ewan," he answered.

She shrugged. "Whatever. I can see to my own self. I want to be taken back to my aunt, and you to just get the hell away from me, mongrel."

His face did not shift, but a subtle movement in his gaze let her know the slur had found its mark.

"She's the one who sent me to ye, Violet."

It was her turn to flinch. "You lie," she flung the accusation at him.

"Yes, yes, we're all liars down here," Kermani rolled his eyes, "leave the bed sport for later, we've matters to discuss."

Though the man was small and upon first impression, not worth a second glance-- there was an edge of steel to his voice that implied he lived beneath no man's land because death did not bother him.

Ewan made to grab her elbow again, and she reared back, ready to plant her fist through his nose. But powerful pressure gripped her arm, immobilizing it. As if it was set in concrete, she couldn't move it toward him, though she had no problem lowering it.

Laughter twinkled through his expressive gold eyes. "Canna harm me."

Doing her best snarl, she plowed past him, following Kermani who was now several steps ahead. What was wrong with her? She traced the edges of her bite, the ridges were still there, the pain--nothing more than a gnat's bite--could wolves leak poison?

She didn't feel ill. In fact, she felt alive, energetic. Strong.

So why was she so aware of him?

Of his breaths in and out, the waves of heat rolling off his body like fog on a bank. The way his stride was long, his footsteps nearly silent, save for the small creak in one knee. And the scar. She trembled remembering the smooth line of it. In no way had it detracted from his beauty, only heightened it, turning a model into a warrior. There was a hard edge to him that appealed to the fire within her heart.

And then there was the nagging feeling that she'd seen him before. But when? Something about his eyes, the shape of them. The almond slant and the vivid gold, she'd seen his eyes before.

Hadn't she?

She nibbled on the corner of her mouth, desperately trying to conjure up the memory.

"Here we are." Kermani's words broke her thoughts, he stood by the edge of a hollowed out section of stone made to resemble a door. He gestured within. "Enter, please."

With a glance at his face, alert to any treachery, she reluctantly stepped through and was amazed to discover the beauty within. Silk splashes of color bathed the red rock in every hue of the rainbow. There were flames tucked within the walls at spaced intervals, well lighting the interior. Finely spun rugs covered every inch of floor, pillows covered in gold and deepest purple were scattered throughout. Black wrought iron chandeliers inset with colored glass hung from beams above, throwing splashes of color everywhere.

She'd watched a movie long ago of a Turkish bazaar. This was exactly like that and she couldn't stop her grin. It was wonderfully exotic. A crimson curtain was tossed aside and a large woman with the most amazing head of hair stepped out. She bowed to Kermani, clasping her hands together.

"Welcome home, Master," she said.

He tenderly traced her round cheek, lifting her face for his kiss. There was much restraint in the greeting, but Violet shivered and looked away, aware of the hunger that simmered just below the surface.

It didn't help though, because Ewan was way too close. It didn't matter that the welts on his cheek were still swollen, or that his body was covered in sand burns, those hungry eyes were all she could see. She knew he was stripping her of her clothes. Heat crawled up her neck, bloomed in her cheeks. Tension arced through her shoulders, down her spine.

"Look away," she mumbled, barely even forming the words, urging her brain to snap out of the stupor keeping her dull and unable to think beyond needing to watch him with the same intensity he watched her.

A slow curve of his lips let her know she'd not been as quiet as she'd hoped. He lifted a hand, the movement agonizingly slow.

Her throat was dry, her breathing hard. Then his knuckles brushed her cheek and her body zipped with a strange heat in the lowest part of her belly.

"So bonny," he breathed and her lashes quivered.

A throat cleared and finally, finally she could think again. Jumping, she hissed and stepped back. The woman's soft hand covered hers. "Come with me, Heartsong. My name is Marika."

She had kind eyes. Large and doe like, with an expression of warmth and innocence Violet could not help responding to. Nodding, she followed, and refused to look back.

***

Marika scrubbed harder, and Violet knew she stripped the skin. She clucked and fretted, while below Violet's feet the water ran pink.

Covered in suds, and skin scalding from the almost too hot water, Marika scrubbed and scrubbed. Beneath her breath bemoaning Violet's state of unwash. Holding her arms tight to her breasts, she tried to pretend some woman she didn't know wasn't currently bathing her.

No matter how many times she'd pleaded that she could do it herself, Marika had insisted, stating it was custom, and that if she didn't allow it, Kermani would demand justice for the humiliation heaped upon his household. True or not, Violet had finally conceded. But it wasn't fun, and she wasn't enjoying it--even if the natural hot spring felt amazing against her raw and torn flesh.

Marika's skilled fingers set into her hair, again scraping the hide off her scalp as the nails dug in. "What happened to you, daughter?" Marika huffed. "You look like you fought with a sandstorm and the sandstorm won."

It felt like her brain was rattling side to side, as Marika maneuvered her none too gently.

"I guess sort of. I can't remember."

"And the blood? All over. What did that wolf do to you?" Warm brown--almost black--eyes peered at her. "Did he try to eat you?"

Chuckling despite herself, she shook her head and tried to wiggle her head away from the kneading fingers of death. But it was no use, the woman's fingers were as tough as steel and could probably crack walnut shells bare-handed.

"I did fight a wolf. But not that one." She frowned, covering Marika's fingers and stilling them for the moment. "Why am I here? Who is that man?"

Marika's full lips turned down into a frown. "You mean he did not tell you? Surely, the Shunned--"

She shook her head. "No, my aunt told me nothing. And to be fair," she rolled her eyes, "I didn't really give him much chance to either. I was kind of busy trying to slice him into a bloody ribbon when Kermani found us."

Marika's lips twitched as her fingers resumed a more gentle lathering. "I don't know much, daughter. But I overhead Kermani talking with Sherbia the second, that the wolf is your transport to the Black witch's keep."

Twisting around--state of undress forgotten--Violet gripped Marika's wrist. "Why? Why him? Why am I going to Malvena's--"

Marika shook her head, placing a finger against Violet's lips. "Hush, daughter. It was a secret I was not supposed to know, sadly I know no more. Now hush."

Grabbing Violet's shoulders she turned her around, and didn't utter another word, quickly bathing her and then pointing to a folded red sheet upon the pale woven mat beside the spring. "Do you know how to dress in the Hadashek style?"

Violet shook her head, wringing the water from her shoulder length hair.

Marika grabbed the jonquil fold at her waist and unwrapped--what had at first appeared to be a dress--from off her body. Violet looked quickly away from the large boned Marika who was surprisingly firm given her size.

"Nudity means nothing to us here, were it not for the flesh eating power of the sand, my people would walk nude constantly. Now watch so you may learn," her voice was patient, but carried an edge of annoyance.

"Well I'm not used to it. I hope you plan to give that wolf clothes too."

Marika chuckled and her large breasts bounced with the movement. Violet desperately wanted to look away again, but trained her eye on Marika's face and ignored the rest.

"He has a fine body. Surely you've noticed. Much better than my Kermani," she quickly touched her breast, "though I would never claim so to him."

"I don't think he does. He's disgusting."

A sly smile curved the corner of her full lips, coal rimmed eyes narrowed with a knowing glint. "Have you never known the touch of a man?" Then her fingers briefly touched his bite and she winced. "Ah, but you have. Haven't you?"

She clenched her jaw. "I don't want his touch."

Marika's fingers toyed with the bite, fingers fluttering softer than she'd thought them capable over the bump. "A wolf's mark. He's claimed you as mate. I hear the bite is better than sex."

She shuddered, remembering how she'd felt every cell in her body flaring to life, as if they would splinter apart with pleasure. "He had no right to do it."

"A wolf cannot claim what is not his. The fact that you bear the mark means you belong to him."

"I belong to myself," Violet pounded her chest.

"As you say." Marika lifted a brow and then proceeded to show Violet how to wrap the cloth around her so that it looked like the dress she'd thought it was earlier.

Getting out of the water, she dried off with the large white puff ball Marika handed her. It felt like cotton, but much more absorbent. Anywhere the white fluff touched it sucked up the water. Clumsy fingers tried to do what Marika had made look so simple.

The beautiful fabric hung on her like a large sack.

Marika gave a throaty chuckle and soft shake, her fat curls bounced becomingly around her head. Frustrated, Violet threw out her hands and those nimble fingers of Marika worked their magic once more.

"You're quite a bit smaller than myself," Marika muttered, "must fatten you up."

There was a large swath of fabric at her neck, eyeing it with a frown, the large woman snapped her fingers and then gathered it and lifted it to cover her head like a hood.

"Come look."

Leading Violet to the back of the steaming room she paused before a smooth black rock that gleamed with light from the inside out. The moment Violet stepped in front of it, she gasped. The rock became a mirror and she could hardly believe she was the same plain Violet.

Marika's eyes glinted. "Do you never age, Heartsong?"

She shook her head. "No. I've been stuck at this age for a long time."

Sun burnished skin touched her pale cheeks. "You're a woman, look like one."

"I don't know…"

Grabbing a blunt piece of black rock, Marika brought it to her face. "Close your eyes," she ordered. Something smooth and soft brushed against her eyelids, and then Marika said, "perfect."

The liner gave her a smoky eye effect, making her look much older and more like a woman than she'd ever thought possible. She smiled, admiring the long line of her neck and column of her throat, seeing her image like it was the first time. Violet smiled softly.

"His heart will stop when he sees you."

Her jaw jutted out and she turned her back to the rock. It didn't matter how many times she screamed that that man was not her mate, Marika would insist he was. Whatever. She hadn't learned much, but if he was leading her to Malvena's keep, then she had a purpose and a direction. Kill the witch, and all the wolves. Including him. She'd find a way around that spell he'd placed on her.

Bowing, Marika smiled.

"It was my pleasure to serve you." Then she turned on her heels, as if she planned to leave.

"Wait." Violet rushed up to her elbow. "Where are you going? Are you leaving me?"

"Sherbia will come to get you for dinner. Relax," she pointed to the pillows beside the rock mirror. Then she was gone, leaving Violet with her thoughts.

The dress and makeup was beautiful, but why did they insist on pampering her, dressing her up like some doll. For what? To whore herself out to the wolf? Kermani? She shuddered. Goddess forbid.

She plopped onto a large turquoise pillow and plucked at the hem of her dress. Wiggling her toes, she felt suddenly ridiculous, and missed the comforting weight of her knife.

Why hadn't Aunt Mir told her the truth? In all the years she'd traveled with her, she'd never known her aunt to be anything but loving. So why the secrecy? Where was her aunt now?

And why him? Why would her aunt send her with the wolf as a guide? She knew, Aunt Mir knew her hatred of the wolves. She was there that night when two had slaughtered her grandmother. Aunt Mir had nursed her back to life, given her a loving home to heal in.

Her aunt wasn't a stupid woman, or even naïve.

Growling, she yanked the bit of charcoal off the counter Marika had used to paint her eyes with and began aimlessly doodling on the ground.

Violet licked her lips, not really looking at what she drew. There had to be an answer. Something she was overlooking. She wasn't sure how long she sat there, aimlessly drawing, when she finally heard another voice.

"Daughter?" A gentle sound, much more timid than Marika's, intruded into her thoughts.

A beautiful woman stepped in, draped in dark greens and gold, she jingled from the gold chain around her waist as she walked. A golden stud adorned her nose and ink black hair fell in soft waves around slim shoulders.

For a brief moment, Violet experienced a swift pang of jealousy. Large eyes narrowed with fear, and then the woman dipped her head, never looking back at her.

Her reaction was strange and Violet frowned. Surely the woman wasn't afraid of her.

"My name is Sherbia," the dulcet voice whispered, "you are to come to dinner."

"Okay," she said slowly, unsure of protocol. Violet dropped the charcoal and stood. "My name is Violet," she thrust out her hand.

"I know who you are. Follow me," Sherbia said, and turned, leaving Violet to stare at her back in bewilderment.

Confused, she glanced down at her feet for a second and finally saw what she'd drawn on the red rock floor.

The Big Bad Wolf, and the eyes staring back at her were a beautiful almond shape.

Chapter 7

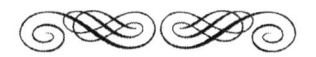

Ewan growled, tearing into the thin baked bread with animal aggression. She was beautiful. Gorgeous, and draped in red silk, so reminiscent of that night. And she wouldn't look at him, wouldn't return an answer to a simple question.

She was all that was kindness to their host, but him… he might as well not exist.

Pale blond hair peeked out of the hood, heating his blood, making him angry with need and desire. She felt it too, he'd seen it her glance earlier. Red wanted his body as much as he wanted hers.

Incense curled a sinuous path through the cozy stone room. Candles and lanterns spun light everywhere.

"Do you not like the food, daughter?" The one named Marika leaned in to whisper in Violet's ear.

She'd not done much other than pick at her food, pushing the red curried lentils from side to side with her wedge of flat bread. She smiled and shook her head. "I do. Very spicy. Good. Just not very hungry."

Marika patted her arm with a motherly smile.

Kermani lifted a brow and shoved the last bit of stewed meat into his mouth. "Dancing, that is what we need."

He reclined back, stomach bulging, and clapped his hands. Children entered from a side door, they scampered around, collecting the empty serving bowls.

"Bring my hookah," Kermani commanded a wide eyed youngster, nodding, she jogged back toward the silk partition and disappeared once more within its voluminous fold.

Ewan licked his fingers and then downed a large tumbler of water, drinking slowly of its coolness to help take the sting of heat off his tongue. Sweat trickled down his neck.

"The lamb was delicious, I thank ye," Ewan clipped his head, grateful for their host's hospitality. He'd been washed by two maidens, dressed in a strange wrap below the waist, and fed until he'd gorged.

He'd worried Violet might take offense at the thought of strange women bathing him, but it'd only been a passing thought. The chit hated him. T'was fairly obvious to him she'd not come willingly or eager to his bed. Clenching his jaw, his stomach fluttered recalling the hard press of the blade against his bollocks. She'd meant to do it; he'd seen it in her eyes. Inhaling sharply he wondered how he'd get through to her.

Looking at her, he felt anger and grief. It shouldn't be this way. She was laughing, blue eyes twinkling at something Marika said. If only he could have been there for her that night, held her and nurtured her back to health, things would be so different now.

"Have you had a moment to read the scroll I gave you earlier, wolf?" Kermani asked as the small child laid a gilded silver hookah before them. Reaching out, the slight man grabbed one hose and handed him another.

"Sheesha?" he asked, shaking the hose at him.

Ewan had smoked a time or two with Jinni and never found the taste appealing, but he took the tube and nodded. "A little."

Kermani inhaled and reclined back once more, a look of contemplation drawn across his brows. "Have you read the scrolls yet?"

His countenance and voice were modulated, polite. But a greedy gleam burned like flame in his dark brown eyes.

Ewan shook his head, pulling in a small amount of the perfumed tobacco. There was a taste of ripe cherries, slightly bitter and astringent on his tongue, but better than the stuff Jinni forced him to inhale.

The scrolls Kermani referred to were the ones he'd handed Ewan the moment Violet had been taken to the bath. His second set of directions from Miriam, and though curiosity burned him, he wanted to study the document at his leisure. "Nay," he said around a puff of water laced smoke.

"How many stops have you?"

Something about the way the slight man asked gave Ewan pause. Rather than answer directly he shrugged and said, "several."

"Ah." Kermani nodded, rubbing his jaw, eyes glinting with something akin to fascination. "Indeed."

Talk ceased after that as a troop of women covered in sheer red and purple gauzy linens entered the room, heralded by the sounds of bells attached at their hips and ankles. Their laughter was effervescent as they swished and swayed, moving with the casual grace of a jungle predator. A seduction meant to tease, but nothing more.

Ewan glanced at Violet and this time, she was looking at him. Cold, violent hate glittering in the depths of ice blue eyes.

***

Grabbing his forehead, Ewan leaned back against the cold wall of his room. Again there were nothing but pillows scattered everywhere. A thin, rough mat would serve as his bed. He looked at the weathered scroll beside his foot.

Kermani had insisted he'd not read the letter, but, something about the way he'd asked with that avaricious gleam in his eyes made Ewan wonder.

Where was she? Soon after the dancing ended, Violet had been spirited away, and save for that one moment when she'd glared at him with unconcealed hatred, she'd never acknowledged him.

"Bloody hell," he growled rubbing at the ache spreading through his left temple.

Maybe he'd imagined it all, Kermani's look and Violet's distaste.

He snorted, she was safe and his mate. The rest would come with time, for now, he must focus on the task at hand, seeing her safely to Malvena's castle.

Breaking the wax seal with his thumb, Ewan opened the scroll. It was blank. Flipping it over, he was shocked to notice it was blank also.

"What is this?"

The moment the words left his lips the scroll flew from his hands, hanging suspended before his face. Pearlescent light danced across its surface and then Miriam's soft voice filled his room with a distant echo.

"Greetings, my wolf. I am happy to know ye've made it safely to the thief's den. A word of caution before I proceed, trust no one. Tell nothing of your trek. We can all be bought for a price. Kermani is a good man, but caution is always best..."

Frowning, Ewan glanced around. There were no doors, but he was all alone, in a separate section of the underground home. Kermani had thought it indecent to allow him to sleep too close to his harem.

He licked his lips.

"I'm sorry I couldn't tell ye more before, there was no time. I hope ye've destroyed the map I gave ye earlier, there are spies everywhere. Dani and I will travel a circuitous route, our hope is to arrive at the same time ye do with Violet. Ye and the girl will travel by dream stone, I've hidden them along the way. Press the stone and a portal will open to yer next location. Do not engage Malvena until we have arrived. Violet is strong, but she is young and untried. I did my best and raised her with all the love I could..."

The scurry of feet caught his attention; he glanced down to notice a mouse scuttling through a small hole in the wall opposite. Hyper aware and sensitive to his surroundings, he prayed Miriam's message would be brief.

"It is time to tell ye of yer mate, of the darkness that keeps her soul captive..."

Like a fist had punched through his heart, he sat up straighter, desperate to learn more.

"She was conceived of dark magic, as I'm sure Dani told ye by now," the voice turned distant and thoughtful, *"perhaps it was wrong, to keep her naïve of her past. But it was the only way I knew to nurture the hate. Ye see, her magic cannot be worked through good. She is powerful, very powerful, but it is only through hate that her magic can work. So I let her hate ye. For that, I'm sorry..."*

His jaw clenched so tight, his molars began to ache.

"But I would do it again, if I had to. She is the key to Malvena's undoing. Only she can stop the Black. Violet's power can take many forms, some benign and useful, but most dark and terrifying. I doubt she knows most of what she can do. But her truest power and darkest art, is that she is an eater of souls. It is within her to devour the very essence of the divine..."

Brows lowering, he glanced back at the curtained door, gripped by a powerful urge to seek her out and hold her. His fingers clenched.

"I've followed her for years out on her treks, many of which she didn't know. I can say that she's only just discovered herself; her knowledge of what she can do is still very much in its infancy. That is why I've set up a test at yer next location. She must engage and defeat Hansel and Gretel's witch."

Blood spilled on his tongue and he winced, only realizing he'd been chewing on it. Breathing heavy, clenching his hands, on the verge of violence he attempted to slow his pulse by taking deep breaths.

"I'm aware ye must not like that, but it is the only way. We haven't much time to train her, ye canna help her defeat the witch. But once she has, ye must extract the soul from her body. Ye are her mate, and that is yer duty..."

"Duty," he snarled. Why hadn't the damn fairies remembered that in the first place? Surely there was another way to harness her power than by forcing her hatred of him to grow like a slow malignant cancer. But the voice did not stop speaking.

"Let instinct guide ye, ye'll know what to do when the time comes." He could almost picture the smile in her voice now. *"You are her perfect mate, and more than able to bring her back from the blackness I was forced to allow to fester. That is why the time is now; she is still at the brink, able to be redeemed. If Jana did one thing, it was to show Violet true love in the beginning. The child of darkness was brought up in light."*

He spat, Jana had tried to kill Violet. She'd done nothing good, and he for one was glad he'd butchered her traitorous body.

"Though we both know now she kept Violet in a happy state to suppress her powers so that killing her would be simple, in the end the lesson was learned. Violet is capable of love. She remembers the emotions and yearns for it again. If anyone can drag her back from becoming a monster of legend, it is ye. Her powers have been channeled, now refocus that hate, and she can be won. If however..."

He sucked in a breath, gut clenching, knowing instinctively he would not like what she was about to say.

"I never arrive at Malvena's, should I die along the way, ye must kill her."

"How dare you!" he roared, despairing at the thought. Uncaring if anyone heard, he'd never do it.

"Ye may think me cruel, but in fact I only want what's best for her. She must not engage Malvena without me, because if she does, she may not kill the Black witch and then she'll be haunted forever, she'll never stay with you or anyone else. If, however, she does kill Malvena, that level of toxic power will destroy what remains of her sanity and reason. She will be forever lost and beyond all hope of redemption. Either way, she loses."

Ewan slammed his fist into the wall and the dirt foundation fractured; sending a shower of silt to cover his bed.

A heart shaped pendant manifested from within the scroll and floated to him.

"That is the pendant of truth; I've spelled it to reveal the truth of the events of that night. She will need to see it to know the truth. She blames ye for all that happened that night, I deliberately blocked Jana's deception from her mind. Violet will hate me, as I'm sure ye now do. But even so, I would ask ye to pray for our safe travel. I love my girl, and only want what's best for her, and ye. May the goddess bless ye."

The scroll suddenly caught in flame, the heat creeping off its green tinted hue burned his eyes. Within seconds, nothing remained of it save a fine black powder.

Ewan snatched up the pendant, heart racing, mouth dry, and wondering if any of that was true. But knowing deep in the depths of his cold, bleak soul that it was and he be damned if he'd let her die.

"I've only just found ye, lass. I'll not let ye go, nay till I'm cold in the grave." He curled his fingers around the dark purple stone and held it to his heart.

Sleep did not come for many hours.

***

A shadow stirred in his doorway. Ewan jumped to a crouching position, hearing the rapid breathing of a female. His female.

She smelled of jasmine, rich and earthy and his blood stirred, heating his veins and making him instantly alert.

"Red?" he asked as gently as he could, but couldn't disguise the need trembling heavy in his brogue.

"It was you," she said in a voice as dead as the ghoul's.

He frowned. "Wha--"

"That night."

She stepped inside the door, and though in human form, his eyes were sharp. He drank in the sight of her like a man parched. Still dressed in red, she was as a lovely wraith with her pale luminescent skin and large blue eyes.

"You're the black wolf." Her eyes were vacant, cold. "You killed her."

He touched the jewel resting against his chest; he'd fallen asleep with it on. "Aye, I killed her, but it's nay what ye think, Red."

She didn't even flinch. "I can't even hurt you. I stood here in the door for an hour and you're magic wouldn't let me enter. Want to know why?" Such a sweet, soft voice. So at odds with its deadness.

Lifting the pendant over his head, he tried handing it to her. "This was given to me by Miriam, it's the truth of that night. Come here, Red. Come."

He beckoned her; an uneasy tension slithered up his spine, made the back of his neck tingle.

"For years I've thought of you. Obsessed about you, drawing your picture over and over. Always your eyes, they haunt me the most. And I knew when I met you, I'd seen you before. And I was right."

He blinked. "Lass... please."

"I hate you. I came here to kill you, to end your miserable life."

Her words chilled his blood, froze the breath in his lungs. "I would never harm ye, lass. I vow it. I've searched for ye, loved ye then and now..."

She didn't acknowledge his words, only pulled her hands from behind her back. Opening her hand, she showed him what she held. A thin silver hairpin, innocuous, and yet he knew it was more than a hairpin to her. It was long and sharp looking at its tip.

"Lass, what are ye--" He twitched, every muscle screaming at him to pounce on her and throw it away.

She looked at her palm. "What hurts you the most, Ewan?"

Her name on his lips, first time she'd ever called him by his birth name, he should have rejoiced. Standing, he inched toward her. Slowly, like one approaching a wild, scared animal. "I've the proof, lass. I can show ye what happened that night. Let me."

Violet's eyes blazed, the first time she'd shown any type of emotion. "Answer my question."

He searched her face, every line, every lash seared into his brain. "You. Nothing could hurt me, but losing ye."

She closed her eyes. "You took my ability for revenge, but you gave me another instead."

Moving faster than he'd expected her to, she raked the pin across her wrist. He was on her, wresting the pin out of her fingers, but it was too late. She'd cut deep, blood welled from her pale skin like a dark bloom.

Ewan's heart seized. He grabbed her by the shoulders, crashing down to the floor with her, his brain unable to comprehend what she'd done. Why she'd done it.

"Red," he stuttered, pain caught in his throat, threatening to claw itself out, "nay, nay."

"Hate... you... so... much," she sobbed and her tears became his.

Grabbing her wrist, Ewan brought it to his mouth. Wolves could heal, they weren't fast at it, or very good, but good enough. He licked the blood, savoring the sweetness of her, even as his tears mingled on his tongue. Rocking hard, covered in blood, he licked and licked, passing whatever healing he could to her, praying to whatever god might hear him.

"I love ye, lass. Please don't leave. Don't leave me again."

Chapter 8

Dreaming, Violet roamed somewhere between awake and asleep, haunted by images she couldn't understand.

Her grandmother Jana, standing inside the doorway, alive and aged. Her wrinkled hand beckoning to Violet with hurried gestures.

"My, what big eyes you have, grandmother." A ghost of a voice whispered.

Jana's grin widened, the sharp rows of fangs glinting with a coat of something clear, yet thick.

"My, what big teeth you have, grandmother." The same voice, soft and unsure.

Jana's eyes were black, full and alien like. So different than the kindly green they'd once been.

"The better to kill you with, my dear…" A sharp, brittle laugh punctuated the small hut and then two wolves jumped out. One red, one black.

The red stalked her, slowly, methodically. Licking its muzzle as its eyes blazed with hunger.

Violet stood, a specter in this vision, watching her past self huddle and cower in the corner; screaming with a bottomless pit of terror that'd blinded her to the truth.

The black wolf wasn't moving. Its belly heaved as its slitted pupils dilated, then its hackles rose and it jumped Jana, tearing her limb from limb. The red wolf had turned, growling and moaning, as if seeking to understand what'd possessed the black wolf.

Over and over the vision played and she was helpless to its thrall. Wetness coated her face and soft moans rumbled through her chest, for hours she lay, replaying the past, seeing what couldn't possibly be.

He hadn't saved her. Ewan had killed her grandmother. But then the visions swept in like a tidal wave and each time she watched it, she knew it was true.

The mystery of that night was finally solved. The last piece of the puzzle she couldn't remember, her soul accepted and believed, her mind screamed. Everyone had lied to her. Her aunt, Jana, everyone.

But not him.

No!

She trembled, something strong and firm gripped her hard. It was comforting, warm, and she was ashamed and confused.

"Wake up, Red," the thick brogue whispered in her ear, a caress so soft and sweet. "Open those big blue eyes, look at me. Ye can hate me all ye want, just live, Red. Please."

The last word was choked out and strained, scratchy and full of something deep and profound, but she couldn't make sense of it.

Finally the dreams relented, and like a fog being lifted, she opened her eyes. Immediately she noticed a heavy sensation against her breast. Glancing down, she saw a purple pendant pulsing against her bare flesh, his hand pressed tight to it.

His mouth was covered in dried blood; looking like he'd feasted. She hissed, glancing at her wrist, suddenly recalling the demonic anger that'd taken her last night. The pure hatred that'd burned brighter than the sun at its zenith, her need to kill him, end her agony, only to discover there was no way around the enchantment he'd woven with his bite.

She swallowed and didn't push away when he nuzzled her hair, inhaling her scent deep into his lungs, muttering nonsense she couldn't understand.

"Let me go," she finally croaked, voice raw and scratchy, as if she'd actually been screaming throughout the night.

He set her aside gently, and crawled back on his knees, moving like an animal would. But instead of disgust, she found beauty in the motion. A perfect symmetry and balance to it that left her awed.

She was still angry, but wasn't sure anymore if she should be. Not at him. Violet covered her breasts, hugging her arms to her body.

"What happened?" She rubbed her smooth wrist, tracing the length of the faint pink line.

He scrubbed his face. "Our saliva can heal, I… goddess, lass. What? What can I do?! How can I prove to ye I'm nay the devil ye take me for?" He was yelling, chest heaving, his golden eyes wild. Looking like the wolf she'd seen in the dreams.

Violet tucked her knees to her chest. "What did you do to me?" She pointed to the necklace in his hand.

Throwing the necklace against the wall, the stone cracked. He was angry, his body vibrated with it. He wouldn't even look at her as he began to pace, rubbing his jaw so hard she was afraid he'd scrub the skin off.

"It was the truth I'd tried to show ye last night. I didn't ken if it would work in yer sleep." He turned his back to her, staring at the wall. The muscles in his back rippled as a shudder took him. "Ye glowed, yellow. When I licked ye, I tasted the essence of sunshine and wild fae magic. Do ye ken who ye are, lass?"

He turned, and she sucked in a sharp breath. His eyes, so human before, were now pure wolf. Tawny, with a vertical black slit. Breathtaking, but oh so dangerous. Her body thrilled even as her heart raced with forbidden desire.

"No," she shook her head. "No one tells me anything." Looking at her feet, she nibbled on her lower lip. "Was that true? Was all that true?"

He knelt beside her, his finger under her chin, forcing her to look at him. She flinched, but held his gaze, spellbound by him.

"Aye. All of it." His whisper was a caress against her lips.

Her lashes fluttered. "I've hated you for so long. I'm scared to stop."

Alien eyes searched hers. "Why?"

"Because," she swallowed hard, "then it means everything I knew was wrong. My grandmother hated me, my aunt lied to me."

Blunt fingertips feathered across her cheekbones and the touch burned a path straight through her body, filled her legs with heat and longing.

"I haven't, and I won't. Yer my mate."

She closed her eyes. "Please don't say that."

His hand left and his warmth went with it. She yearned for more, but didn't know how to ask, how to plead for something that her brain said was so wrong. It was hard reconciling fact with fiction, knowing how wrong she'd been. It made her sick, fueled an anger that now had no release.

"Did you come to kill me too?" Her voice sounded childlike.

He was standing by the wall again, his eyes hooded. "Aye."

It was a knife to the heart.

"I would have ripped yer throat out and never looked back. I didn't know ye, and I dinna care to know ye."

She ground her molars, picking at her blood stained dress. "But you couldn't because you found out I was your mate, is that it?" Panting, she let the anger take her, felling her limbs grow sure and strong, her blood pulse with adrenaline.

"Stop trying to find reasons to hate me, Red. I'm nay the one ye must fight."

She snapped her head up, glaring at him.

He lifted a shaggy black brow. "Going to deny it?"

Nostrils flaring, it was on the tip of her tongue to tell him to go to hell. But a small voice she rarely heard, and never heeded, called her bluff. She was still trying to find a reason to hate him.

"How do I let go of something that was my constant companion all these years?"

"One day at a time." Grabbing the knotted section of fabric wrapped around his slim waist, he tugged, releasing the wrap and standing fully nude.

Goddess he was beautiful. Every part of him was sculpted perfection. Blushing, she glanced away.

"I hear footsteps headed our way, it's time to go. I do not wish to say goodbye, or be caught. Kermani showed me the dream stone that would open the portal last night. Keep to the shadows."

White light flared from every pore, burning so bright she had to cover her eyes. When the light died, a big black wolf stared back at her.

Chapter 9

Ewan studied the woods, while alternately glancing at Red's shadowy form hidden behind a large barrel shaped tree. Since leaving the Eastern realm six hours ago, they'd made their way slowly through a forest unlike any he'd ever known.

Crushing the dream stone beneath his paw, he'd opened the portal, able to leave before any eyes spotted their departure.

The incident last night had left him shaken and disturbed. Who was this woman? His mate? She was violent, ancient, yet in so many ways still young and naïve, untried in the ways of the world.

Tasting the wind, he plucked through the miasma of scent laden breeze. There was gingerbread, peppermint, and even the faintest whiff of molten chocolate.

Violet had stared in wide eyed wonder when they'd arrived at their next destination. Quiet and much more subdued than the day prior, as if she was thinking, sorting through thoughts, more likely wondering about not only him, but herself. Who she was and where she fit in this strange new world.

Again he glanced at her wraith-like form; pride bloomed in his chest seeing her move between the trees. Stealthy and silent, it was obvious to him she'd done this before. Her movements barely disturbed the gum drop leaves scattered upon the cookie crumble forest floor.

The sky was edged in bright washes of lavender and tangerine, a moon--not two planets--rested pregnant in a sky ready to descend into darkness.

Every so often her scent would tickle his nose, there was light, but like Miriam had warned in her letter… there was darkness too. Something malignant and foul that lingered in her blood. Huffing, blowing the stench from his nostrils he padded silently forward.

These forests were a macabre and intentional design. Within these woods lived a witch who preyed on the young. Every tree, every rock was made of sweets. Luring the children in deeper, making them forget the safety they'd left behind.

It would be good to rid Kingdom of the crone, but her death wouldn't come by him.

Licking his muzzle, he glanced at her yet again. They'd not spoken a word since leaving his room. Ewan knew this form bothered her, saw it in the way she glanced at him when she didn't think he was looking.

She was afraid, and he wished he could tell her not to be. That in this form he could kill, smell and see better than in his weaker human one. That he could, and would protect her from any and all harm. But the tradeoff for strength was his inability to communicate with her.

The path led straight and unswervingly forward. Many times his stomach grumbled, demanding protein. But to touch anything here was to alert the crone to their presence.

He wasn't sure how he felt about Red being the one to take her on. Miriam had called her a soul sucker, but hadn't explained what that was. How to use the 'gift'. The crone had killed many, Violet had killed one wolf, and had very nearly killed herself in the process.

He swallowed hard.

A thud sounded like a loud pop in his ears and he spun, the hairs on the back of his neck rose as he growled low in his throat. Nothing lived in these woods of horror. There were no land animals, no birds, no gentle hum of insects.

The crone had eaten them all.

He wasn't sure what he'd find, a hidden trap, some beast let loose. Perhaps Red had begun nibbling on a tree branch. He should have warned her, he hadn't thought she might not know the land as he did.

But it was none of those things. She was on her knees, head bowed, the red cowl covering her entire face. Calling the *unbecoming*, Ewan exhaled through the change, breathing through a transformation that pulled at bone and skin.

"Lass?" He trotted up to her and knelt by her side, heart clenching violently when he noticed the fat drops spilling from her cheeks.

"Who am I?" She sobbed, finally looking at him, blue eyes streaked through with red veins, as if she'd been rubbing them for hours. "What am I?"

Lips twisting, he looked over his shoulders, studying the unnatural calm of the woods. The witch wouldn't come tonight; he'd not smelled her rot and Violet needed him.

Sitting, he crossed his ankles, and studied her. She didn't blink.

"Who am I?"

Needing to touch her, to comfort her anyway he could, he grabbed her hand. Expecting she'd yank it away and hiss at him, she flinched, but didn't pull back.

"Yer the Heartsong."

Gathering a corner of her hem, she dabbed at her eyes. "But what is that? Can you help me? Can you tell me the truth?"

For just a moment he understood why everyone had lied to her, because he was tempted to tell her nonsense himself. Perhaps to spare her feelings, or just because he was a coward and didn't want to face anymore of her hate. He sighed, and tenderly rubbed her knuckles, amazed she let him.

"I don't know all of it," he began, and her eyes grew hopeful, "but yer the result of fairy magic."

"Grandmother told me I was born of fairy magic, that it made me kind and gentle.... and…" she frowned when he shook his head.

"Jana was a liar, lass."

She looked away. "I keep forgetting. That."

She looked so fragile, weak. Her face eternally youthful, it would be so easy to see the package and forget that beneath the large blue eyes and innocent smile lurked madness and death. He'd witnessed it for himself last night.

"Do ye ken who the *Ten* are?"

"The high fairy council?" she asked, and he nodded.

"Aye. They were too powerful, and Kingdom feared that unless they weakened themselves, one could become bloated with greed and a thirst for power."

Her breathing grew shallow, slow, as if she feared moving or in any way distracting him from talking.

Continuing to toy with the soft flesh between her thumb and finger, he talked. "They agreed to bleed off the darkness. All of them, even the Black Malvena. The night of the purification ritual, they all gathered beneath a large moon on a grassy plain. But Malvena dinna come."

"Why?" she whispered.

He looked at the tree, absently noting the rough texture of the gingerbread bark. His stomach groaned, gut twisted in knots with hunger. "Because two days prior, her daughter Rose had died and a seed was born in that dark heart. Reanimation. Bringing the dead back to life."

"Isn't that forbidden?"

"Aye. It is. And the only way to do it is to use dark sorcery. But on her own, she is nay strong enough. The other nine dinna bother with her, they proceeded on with the purification and dumped their darkness within the land."

Her eyes looked sad and haunted. "That's when I was born. I wasn't born of light at all. I'm evil."

He grasped her chin, not allowing her to break eye contact with him. "I killed, maimed, and tortured. I'm a wolf. Not born to be evil, and yet, I was."

Red glanced away and he sighed.

"Just because yer born a certain way, doesna mean that is who ye are."

"Maybe it does." She pulled her hand back and jerked his thumb off her chin. "Why have you brought me to the witch's woods?"

What should he say? *Yer aunt told me to come here so that ye can kill the witch by sucking out her soul? But I swear to ya, yer nay evil, lassie.* Bloody hell, he hated the fairies at this moment.

"Tell me the truth, please. I can handle it. I just can't handle anymore lies."

Bathed in moonlight, she looked ethereal and lovely. Maybe this was how he'd get her to trust him, truth at all cost, even if the telling of it pained him to do so.

"She called ye a soul sucker."

Her face scrunched. "A what?"

Ewan shrugged. "I don't know, Red. That was all she said."

"So I suck out souls? That's my magic?"

"One of."

Grabbing her stomach, she leaned forward. "I think I'm gonna be sick." Her face looked splotchy and pale. "I only thought I could heal. Jana told me I couldn't do magic. I never…"

"She lied, about everything. Jana was a wicked, evil woman. Doona try and make sense of anything ye knew before, especially when the truth is so much different.

"Also…" he rubbed her head, tucking her hair behind her face in case she expelled the meager contents of her stomach. "If yer going to puke, try not to puke on the candy. Ye might alert the witch to our presence."

"What?" She laughed, and instantly the sickly pallor on her face lightened. "Oh gods, this isn't funny. None of this is."

Then she laughed even harder, the musical tinkle of her melodic voice made his lips twitch in return. It took a moment for her to get herself under control.

"Thanks, Ewan, I needed that."

Everything inside him stopped. She'd used his name, but this time it'd sounded hopeful, alive, and the sound of it was almost as good as tender caress. Heat nestled in his gut, filled his loins. He scooted back, hiding the evidence of his desire, knowing she wasn't ready for him yet. Nudity never bothered him, it simply was the way of the wolf, but he wished for some clothing now, if only to make her comfortable.

He nodded. "Are ye tired, Red?"

She nodded. "A little. I didn't sleep much last night."

"Neither did I." His lips tightened, trying to forget the reason why. "I don't smell the witch, we're safe to stay here tonight, rest while ye can. I'll keep watch."

"Okay." Glancing around, she spotted a thick cluster of gumdrop leaves and settled upon it.

Planting his hands behind his back, he listened to the eerie night. There was nothing save for the gentle breeze, her soft inhalations, and the steady gurgle of the chocolate stream in the distance.

Enough time passed he'd thought her asleep, when she said, "I'm scared."

Her face was covered in shadow, her red dress looking like a sea of blood upon the ground.

"I know. Me too."

"Why?"

"Because I've waited so long to know ye, the thought of losing ye now is more than I can bear."

She didn't answer, and he didn't think she would. Maybe he shouldn't have said it, but truth at all costs…

"Are ye going to try to kill yerself again, Red?"

A second ticked by, then another, until finally she shook her head. "I'm sorry for that. I didn't really want to kill myself, I knew I would heal from that wound. I didn't actually cut my vein, just cut deep enough to make it bleed really bad." She sighed. "I wanted to hurt you."

"Don't do it again," he gnashed his teeth, letting the pain leak out, letting her hear the depths of his plea.

She didn't say anything, but their gazes locked and he knew she understood. Her lashes gave the barest flicker before she turned and rolled onto her side. Eventually she fell asleep, leaving him alone with his thoughts. Several hours later he noticed her shivering, drawing her legs up to her body and wrapping the dress tighter around herself.

Calling the *unbecoming*, he got up and trotted to her side. Scooting in as close to her body as he could, he shared his wolf's warmth with her. She sighed, her fingers ran through his pelt and his body trembled.

***

"I don't like this place," Red grumbled as she knelt by the thick viscous stream. "There's no water to wash myself with. Nothing but this chocolate I cannot even touch."

He grinned. "I donna think this place was created for the likes of us."

She glared at him, her blond brows drawn into a fierce scowl. "Food everywhere and I can't even have a bite. I hate sweets, and right now I think I could gobble an entire tree." She stared at a gingerbread elm longingly.

Grabbing her hand, he helped her stand. "Trust me, lass, ye dinna want what the witch has to offer. All is not what it seems."

She curled her lips, huffing, and dusting sparkling bits of sugar off her luscious rear. "I'm hungry and irritable. Let's go find this stupid witch, before I forget myself and dive head first into that chocolate river."

Red stood there, staring down at the stream with a sad, pitiful expression. She'd barely eaten the day before, only picking at her food. Ewan wanted to provide for her, but to do so would mean backtracking, which he could not do.

"C'mon, Red," he tugged on her finger. "Doona look. Walk away."

Sighing, she turned her back on the stream and he gave her a swift tilt of his lips. Calling the *becoming*, Ewan quickly switched forms. They resumed walking, Red within the forest itself. She seemed possessed with a natural instinct to shy away from being easily spotted. Preferring to traipse through the rougher terrain, so as not to be exposed to the elements of the unprotected trail he walked on.

Not that he didn't want to join her, but he sensed keeping his distance for a while might help her better acclimate to not only her strange surroundings, but also him. Ewan wanted to ravish her, take her, drive into her and roar to the heavens that she was his mate. It wasn't easy controlling his baser instincts.

Huffing, he attempted to appear nonchalant. Tongue lolling out the side of his mouth, looking like little more than a stupid dog that had wandered down the wrong path. His size was a dead giveaway that he was definitely *not* a dog, but he hoped the act would keep the witch from immediately going on the offensive once she spotted him.

He knew Red was supposed to be the one to take the witch on, but it was ingrained in him to at least help ease his mate's way into the battle. Give Red a little time to study the witch before the witch noticed her.

Hopefully.

The closer they got, the faster his heart pumped. He glanced at her from the corner of his eye, she was so small and the physical scars of her encounter with the other wolf hadn't fully vanished yet. Faint and pink, bisecting her belly and breasts, he couldn't help noticing them the night he'd pressed the stone of *veritas* (truth) to her chest.

Red's stare was wide and panicked, her pupils dilated. Even in the shade of the trees, he could see her pulse beating frantically upon her pale throat. Forcing a calm he did not feel, he shook his head and pressed on, giving her no choice but to follow. If he pretended all was well, maybe she'd panic less.

Before long a gingerbread house crested the horizon, a faint plume of gray smoke undulated like a charmed snake through the air.

The home itself was a cornucopia of treats, an enticement to come and gorge and feast upon. It all nauseated him. He'd not be sad to see the crone dead.

Suddenly he realized Red did not pace him. He stopped and spotted her several yards back, gripping the trunk of a gingerbread tree with a white knuckled grip.

She looked at him. "I… I can't."

He whined, and jerked his head toward the candy studded home. The chimney, made up of big, fat gumdrops--a bright brilliant red--shimmered like rubies in the sunlight.

"No." She turned her face into the tree. "I don't know what to do."

He huffed, knowing this would not be her first kill.

She scowled. "No doubt you're thinking about that wolf I killed. Well, it was easy because in my mind it was you. But…" she swallowed hard, "it's all different now."

Dropping his shoulders, he sat. Miriam had said it was hate of him that had fueled her power. He knew what he'd have to do. Though the thought pierced his heart with thorns.

"I… don't know if I hate you anymore. I'm not sure I like you, but…" She blinked. "Ewan?" she cried, finally noticing that he'd begun to barrel toward her. Her eyes were large, round, and filled with terror.

He ran, powerful leg muscles bringing him to her in less than a second. The growl tripping from his throat was the deep throaty inflection of a wolf on the hunt.

Hating to see the fear in her eyes, he willed himself to ignore it. If killing the crone would help her kill Malvena, he didn't have a choice.

A white ring surrounded her lips and her breathing grew harsh, she pressed her back against the tree. He advanced, predatory. Menacing. Hackles raised and gums exposed. Her breaths were short and choppy.

Then he jumped and she screamed, throwing her hands over her face and glancing to the side.

Ewan sank his teeth into the thick branch beside her head, ripping out a chunk of gingerbread. It settled like rotten meal in his gullet. He knew what these woods were really made of.

A cackle erupted, chilling and foreboding, and then a door slammed open.

"Come here, my pretty," the ancient voice beguiled, wrapping a breeze like hand around his throat and squeezing hard. The power of the crone, deep and darkly disturbing rushed through his veins, slammed into his skull. He winced against the mind numbing moment of terror.

She was still in the house, but she knew they were here.

Dark clouds gathered high above them.

Her terrible magic was strong. Even he suffered the urge to run away from the cannibal crone.

Red jerked, holding onto her chest. She glanced at the house, then at him. Dangling bits of gingerbread caught in his fur.

"You called her to me?" she accused as he nosed her thigh, urging her forward. She slapped his nose, making him sneeze and lick at the tingling burn. "No," she gritted out.

Ewan nosed her harder, using his front paw to propel her out of the shelter of the woods and onto the path.

"No," she hissed.

But he was too strong, he kept bumping her forward, until finally she stumbled onto the cookie path.

The path was empty. The house of candy and cakes stood silent and still. Then he blinked and the old crone appeared, fluidly, like a vapor rolling across water.

She was bent nearly in half, her stooped shoulders large and yet withered by age. The crone stood fifty yards in front of them. Her beaked nose was hooked at the end, warts covered her cheeks and jowls, and the hands she beckoned to them with had thick black claws attached to each fingertip.

Red curled her finger into his nape, tugging so hard on his fur he knew she'd ripped some out. But he didn't move. Adrenaline seeped from her glands, rushed out her pores and settled on his tongue, thick and bitter.

"Come here, girl."

There was a quality to the crone's voice that bespelled the listener. He found himself leaning forward even as his feet tried to turn away.

Black beady eyes turned to him, and the thin mouth curled into a tight little smile. "If it isn't the Big Bad Wolf," she laughed, and the sound of it rolled over his body like slithering maggots on rotten meat. "Which means, you..." she glanced back at Red, "are the Heartsong."

Her fingernails tapped a jarring rhythm against one another.

Violet's breathing was as rapid as hummingbird's wings, if she didn't breathe soon, she'd pass out. Ewan whined, nuzzling her thigh.

She took in a deep breath.

When he turned back, the crone was even closer. She did not walk, or float, she moved as silent as thought.

Sounds, threatening and violent, seeped from his lips.

"You mean nothing to me, mutt," the crone spat by her bare, arthritic foot. "I'll make mincemeat of you. But you," she hooked a finger toward Violet, and something dark and twisted encased Red's body, lifting her off the ground.

He yelped when her fingers left him.

Violet screamed. Twisting, she tried to reach out to him. Ewan latched onto the edge of her red dress, tugging hard, but succeeded only in shredding off a long piece. He jumped, attempting to latch onto her arm, but a tingling shudder ran like a bolt through him, locking him in place.

"Malvena, told me to call her, bring you to her. But I'm so very hungry, you see." Her dirt stained green robes brushed the ground as she reached out toward Violet who was now much too close. Cloudy blue eyes filled with an avaricious gleam.

Fear clawed at his brain, Ewan urged his legs to move, to tear the crone limb from limb as he'd done Jana, but he was frozen. Locked in place and unable to do more than howl as the crone dragged Violet closer to her side.

The black miasma circling Violet pulled in tight, forming a thick shadow, so that he could no longer see her. The crone laughed, devilish eyes glinting with glee. Then her hands were inside the shadow and she began to inhale. Every color of the rainbow seeped out from the shadow and the screams of terror turned to moans of horror.

"So much power," the crone murmured in ecstasy, eyes rolling to the back of her head.

Seeing the crone pull Red's soul out, Ewan finally understood what Miriam meant when she'd called Vi a soul sucker. He needed to tell her. Straining, heaving against the invisible barrier, Ewan prayed as he called the *unbecoming*. His lungs had barely shifted, before he was roaring. "Breathe her in, Red. Breathe her in."

He wasn't sure she'd heard him, he screamed it louder, hoping to penetrate the fear riding her soul.

But then the scream turned different, higher pitched and frantic.

"What are you doing?" It was the crone and the impenetrable fog that'd bathed Red lifted, pulling back inside the emaciated witch.

Vi was pale, skin almost blue, as she reversed positions and latched her hands into the crone's twisted body.

Violet breathed, inhaling through her mouth, lungs expanding as the crone began to twist and wither. A wave, every color of the rainbow oozed from Red's body, wrapping them in a kaleidoscopic hug.

A pale red miasma bleached Violet's blonde hair pink, her skin turned to swirling bands of green, blue and purple, her lips a bright yellow. The *Ten*--represented by their individual colors--bled out of Violet, making her shimmer with a fiery and icy glow.

Entranced, Ewan watched the dance of death play out. Macabre as the crone's dark soul poured like black venom from her mouth, and yet the swirling colors… so, so lovely.

The witch's mottled skin turned to paper, nothing but a husk over bones. Her black soulless eyes blazed fear, as she twitched and shook. Soon even that stopped. The screams reverberated long after the crone was gone.

Violet dropped the husk, the green robes fluttered like a dead leaf to the ground. The barrier holding him back lifted, and Ewan was finally free to run to her side.

But the moment he touched her, he felt the stain of that dark soul. It clung to his flesh like a leech sucking on blood. And when he looked in Red's eyes, only black stared back at him.

"Ewan," she sobbed, "something's wrong with me." Then she dropped to her knees, and retched, but nothing came out. Sweat peppered her brow, her back, her skin blazed fire.

The colors she'd bled while killing the witch, pulled back inside her body. Once it did, he was able to see how pale she'd become. White as freshly turned snow.

"Red," he gripped her face.

"It hurts," she screamed, "oh goddess, it hurts so bad!"

Going stiff in his arms, she seized up. Shaking violently.

Desperate, he glanced around. Where was the antidote? Miriam had said he'd know what to do. But he didn't know.

Bringing her hand to his lips, he licked her thumb. But there was no wound and nothing to heal. So he licked her neck, still she screamed.

Licking her jaw, her cheek, he finally came to her mouth and the moment his tongue touched her lips a sickly sweet substance clung to him. It was a parasite, gripping on, sliding down his throat, the acidity burning sores into the skin of his mouth.

Startled, he jerked away as the sickness spread through his belly. The screaming had stopped. Whatever he'd just done, it'd worked. Bracing for what was to come, Ewan sealed his lips to hers, slipping his tongue deep into her mouth.

The poison latched on. It was thick and dark and filled his gut. He swallowed more and more, all of it. Gagging, he forced himself to keep it down and out of her. Her nails dug into his cheek, she was kissing him back with passion, twining her tongue with his.

But it was too much. Ewan wanted her. Wanted to taste her, to hold her, but the acid spewed hot in his gut, with one final pull he felt it coming back up. Pushing her away, he ran to a tree and retched.

Black blood spewed from his lips, covered the ground in gore. Up it came, with no end in sight. His body broke out in chills and then burned with fever. It felt like hours, but must have only been minutes when he sank to his knees, spent and panting, feeling as if his soul had been torn from his body.

"Ewan, I…"

Her soft hands were on his shoulders, rubbing gently. Expressing thanks with no words.

The world spun and shifted around him. There was nothing left in his gut, but still he felt the need to give up more. He grabbed his stomach, moaning. Black spots danced in his vision.

"Ewan," her voice held a frantic edge to it, "you gotta come." She tugged on his hand. "The land is dying; we gotta get out of here."

It took everything he had to crack open eyes that felt full of sand and busted vessels.

The woods were melting. The trees ran with blood, branches were now skeletons, their limbs interlocked into a macabre structure. Sightless eye holes peered at him.

The crone's dirty secret revealed. All the sugar drop trees and gingerbread rocks had been nothing more than past victims spelled to appear as sweets.

If he hadn't already thrown up, he'd have done so again when the stench of decay assailed his nose. The breeze was alive with the rotten scent of flesh hung out to dry. Toxic waste ran where the chocolate river once flowed.

"Please, Ewan, come on." She tugged on him, snapping him from his stupor.

"We must hurry," he said, voice rough and scratchy. Shaking his head, attempting to right his vision, he called the *becoming* to him. The shift had him howling, his body too weak to handle the change.

But her tiny hands, and soft pleas of encouragement, spurred him on, drove him to ignore the desperate ache filling his limbs. They ran, trying not to slip on the thick sludge beneath them. Violet cried as her feet gave out beneath her. She landed on her butt in a thick pile of something foul and sticky.

Dizzy, vision blurring with spots, Ewan nudged her to sit on his back.

"Are you sure?" she whimpered, biting her lip.

He grunted, barely able to hold his head up. She didn't hesitate again, quickly straddling him.

Adrenaline was the only thing that kept him running.

Chapter 10

She shivered, hugging her arms tight to her body, wondering if she'd ever be able to sleep again. All that blood and gore. The knowledge of where it had all come from… she swallowed the bile trying to work its way up her throat.

Night kept their secrets, held them within her dark arms, making it impossible for Violet to see too far beyond their camp.

Ewan's back was to her, his chest heaved hard and though he'd feared starting a fire, the moon was bright enough that she could see the gray pallor tinting his skin. She sighed.

"Are ye okay?" His deep voice was a caress, and her lashes fluttered like moth's wings against her cheekbones.

"I should be asking you that," she said with a half snort. He was the one that'd risked his neck to save them, and yet he still asked after her welfare.

Finally he rolled over, his liquid gold eyes sliding slowly along the length of her body. She shivered again, but this time it had nothing to do with the chill nip in the air. She bit her bottom lip as her lower stomach dipped with a sudden rush of nerves.

"Ye are my mate, Red. I'll always worry after ye. Now are ye okay?"

A lump lodged in her throat, the kindness in his words, the deep timbre of his voice, it did something to her. Confused her more, made her care. It was hard to speak, so she nodded instead.

His eyes closed and a look of relief swept over his patrician features, making him seem softer, more approachable, and a million times more sexy. Her fingers twitched as a lock of midnight black hair flipped over his left eye.

"Good," he smiled and her heart dropped. "Get some rest when ye can take it, Red. I doona think we'll have too many more nights like these soon."

"Are we close then?" There was a sort of quiet detachment in her question, maybe she should have felt fear. Any sane person probably would, but so much of this felt surreal. It's not that Violet hadn't known about the wonders of this world, she'd lived here once, long ago. But to see the stories of the mortal world open up before her eyes, to battle the cannibal crone and walk through a forest made of literal candy… sometimes it was hard to believe that all this wasn't a dream.

"Aye, we're close." He nodded, and then giving her a grim smile, stood. "My bones ache this night, I must turn to wolf. It helps me heal properly, shake me if ye need me."

She watched as his magnificent body became engulfed in a bright flare of white light and suffered a momentary pang of regret. He was much nicer to look at in human form, and the wolf still disconcerted her.

The large black beast padded out of the light, gave her one last lingering look, settled down close enough to her that she could feel the waves of his body heat, and let out a long puff of air. Violet studied him in the soft moonlight. He must have felt worse than he'd let on, within seconds he was sleeping, but somehow she sensed should another predator approach he'd snap awake. His muzzle was long and lean, the fur dense and so black it blended in with the shadows all around.

He'd saved her, and she wasn't sure how she felt about that.

A rushing tide of blood and bits had nearly taken them; the crone's forest had tried to consume them just as its mistress had consumed so many others. The moment they'd passed the witch's boundary, he'd collapsed. So still, she'd feared he'd died. Violet had sat with him, not knowing how long he'd remain that way. He'd come to an hour later, dazed but not quite so miserable.

He'd shifted and her heart had flipped. Something was happening to her. Something scary; but not altogether displeasing. He was gorgeous to look at; it was hard to pretend he wasn't anymore. Her hate hadn't been able to blind her to his charms, and now... well, now things were different.

Ewan had led her to a thicket of bushes, growling and fumbling in the dirt for thirty or so minutes, before finding what he'd sought. Another dream stone. He'd pressed his palm against the stone and the blue portal had opened wide for them.

Here they were now, sitting in another grove. This one was slightly different. The trees were full of fruit and she'd nearly sobbed with joy. Didn't matter that it was an apple, nothing had ever tasted sweeter.

They'd gorged until they could barely breathe, but beyond the chat of seconds ago, neither had talked. Which should have suited her fine; except now she wanted to talk to him. Wanted to know everything he knew about her past.

His past.

Glancing at her clothes, she frowned. She was still covered in slaughter, her dress beyond ruined. Where were they headed now? To another monster, something even more insidious than the crone?

Violet shuddered, remembering the slithering feeling of that dark soul sliding down her throat. The wash of pain that'd blinded her to everything, and then the sweet, sweet lips consuming the evil within.

She brushed her fingertips against her lips and closed her eyes, his soft steady breaths a lullaby in her ear. Leaning against the tree she wiggled her toes, reveling in the warmth of his fur brushing against them.

An owl hooted and she shivered. Growing up, she'd led a sheltered life. Never able to stray farther than grandma's territory; the apple trees the farthest she'd ever dared to go. But she'd known in her heart that there was more to Kingdom then the small valley she'd called home.

After much pleading and begging, grandmother had finally bought her maps, many of them. She'd stayed up into the wee hours of the night, reading and memorizing each wiggle and line by candlelight.

She'd been happy and content, but there were times she'd wished she could have seen them for herself. As a child she'd drooled at the thought of a forest made of cookies, but the reality was so much different than her childhood fantasies. The thrill of seeing a world she'd never thought to return to was still there, but tempered now with the knowledge that there was bad in this world.

Violet rolled her eyes, snorting. "You're bad too," she whispered.

What she'd done to the crone. The power that'd filled her body, spread through her like a dark cancer, sweeping aside reason or kindness. In its place had been something all-consuming and vile and she'd gloried in it.

The rush of all that power made her heady and wanton, desperate for more and ashamed of it all.

Until the pain.

But then Ewan had kissed her, and that kiss swept the evil aside, like a gentle swell lapping the beach. And she could breathe. Think.

Her head had swum with visions of a full moon, running and sweating, and howling. It'd been freedom, wild and untamed. And she'd wanted more.

Violet sighed, heart twisting painfully in her chest as she glanced at his still form. She should be sleeping, just like him. But her brain wouldn't stop working. A side of her, smaller and smaller every day, still thought it was wrong not to hate him.

When he'd pushed her out onto the path, forced her to confront the crone, it'd flared to life. But then she'd seen him desperate to get at her, and had known he was trying to help.

But why?

Did he really think he was her mate?

She touched his bite mark, feeling nothing. Her flesh was smooth. Violet licked her lips. Was she his mate?

Was that why she'd obsessed about the big black wolf for so long? Not because she wanted to kill him, but because she needed him?

She shook her head, not wanting to think about any of that right now. It was too much to process. She wished he would have told her where they were headed to next.

Glancing up at the trees above, she tried to remember the landscape. Recall the maps she'd learned by heart so long ago. These woods looked… familiar.

Well, not so much these, but the ones to the left. The forest she and Ewan camped within seemed mundane, but not a stone's throw from where they sat was a copse full of twisted, thick bellied trunks. Limbs splayed out like crooked fingers, and the silver mist encasing those woods… something about them teased the edge of her consciousness.

But the thought was fleeting, the faint memory indecipherable. Huffing, she stood and dusted her butt off. She needed to stretch and take care of some business.

Ewan growled, yellow eyes piercing hers. A question blazed in their depths.

"I need to relieve myself," she admitted, cheeks blazing. "I thought you were asleep."

He shook his furry head.

"I won't take long." She pressed her lips together, humiliated beyond belief.

He sighed, and laid his head back down.

Violet moved silently, aware of her surroundings, but moving far enough away that he'd not hear.

Finally satisfied, she did her business and wondered when she'd stopped thinking of him as the big bad wolf.

Moonlight bathed everything in a pale blue glow. She'd not realized she'd gone so far, until she noticed the silver fog circling her legs.

"Little Red Riding Hood."

The cultured voice wrapped itself around her throat, making her feel like she suddenly couldn't take a breath. She didn't feel like dealing with another monster right now, especially not without Ewan by her side. She turned, and started trotting back to their campsite.

"I suppose I should be offended at your running off so soon."

Far from sounding threatening, the voice was inquisitive, which made her curious enough to stop and glance back. This time a face materialized with the voice. A floating orange head gazed at her, the cat's sickle shaped smile revealed wicked long fangs.

She smiled, delighted. "I know who you are."

He lifted a brow, and then the rest of his body materialized. A large fluffy tail whipped gracefully back and forth. "Oh, do tell. I often forget."

"You're the Cheshire Cat."

Large brown eyes widened and then he nodded. "Ah yes, indeed I am."

The fog was thickest where he floated. His fur was so silky looking, so soft. She had a strange urge to pet him, but curled her fingers by her side instead.

"That must mean these are the Hatter's woods."

"A biscuit for the lady," he smiled, and licked his paw.

His coat of fur gleamed like somebody had taken a torch and infused the mesmerizing colors within it.

"You're beautiful," she murmured, and then jerked, wishing she hadn't said that.

His eyes rolled down his nose, the whole time studying the length of her. "I wish I could say the same for you. Who did you eat tonight, Heartsong? You made quite a mess."

She curled her nose; the description wasn't that far off. "The old crone."

"Oh my." He seemed surprised, eyes popping back in their sockets. "No more kiddies for breakfast, eh? How terribly mundane."

"That's a terrible thing to say."

He shrugged; his body hovered between two trees, never coming closer. She nibbled her lip, obsessed beyond reason with feeling the texture of his fur.

"You want to pet me." It wasn't a question.

Hesitantly, she nodded. "I've never seen fur like yours."

He kept licking himself, fluffing the fur higher, drawing her eye like a dragon's to a gem. "You can you know. Just come… closer."

"Why don't you come here?"

He inhaled deeply. "Do you see the fog?" He nodded. "That is the demarcation point between my world, and that one." He curled his nose, long whiskers twitching.

"What do you mean, that one?"

"The one you stand in. Of course."

She frowned, looking around. The trees on this side did seem more normal than the behemoth's lurking on his side. "Have you ever come on this side?"

"How do you think I found my way in here? I came from that goddess awful place."

A shudder rippled across his shoulders, down his spine and through his legs. It was a strange sight.

She lifted a brow. "Which means it won't kill you."

"Mmm. Debatable. It might as well, because you see, my dear girl, if I step one itty bitty paw beyond this boundary I'll become *normal*," he drawled, disgust dripping from his tongue.

Laughing, she said, "You make it sound like a fate worse than death."

"Isn't it?"

She stopped laughing, glancing down at her feet. "I don't think normal is all that bad. Sometimes, I wonder what it feels like."

"Red?" he said, a question in his voice.

Violet frowned. "Why does everyone call me that?"

He hovered like a ghost between thick branches. "What would you like me to call you? Blue?"

"Neither. My name is Violet."

He tapped his jaw. "I prefer Red. Sounds more dangerous," he purred, the 'r' rolling hard off his tongue.

When she looked back at him, his fur almost seemed to triple in size. What was it about his fur? Ewan's didn't do that. Then again, she didn't really want to pet Ewan. Well, not his wolfy side anyway.

She licked her lips. "I think I would like to pet you, Cat."

He dropped to the ground and swished his tail. "Because I like you, girl. I'll let you do what few can. Come here."

She hesitated and he purred, that kittenish sound luring her in like a siren's song. The fog felt cold against her skin. She was right at the edge of the Hatter's woods, not too far in that she couldn't turn back in case this was a trap of some sort.

Her heart sped. Maybe she shouldn't do this.

"Now sit," he commanded.

His fur rippled and it was too hard to ignore the lure of it any longer. She sat, and the moment she did, he crawled in her lap. His big furry head rubbed along her chin. Sighing, she tickled him behind the ear and scratched under his belly.

"I'd forgotten how wonderful that feels," he purred, and she smiled.

"You're so soft. Like cashmere."

In the distance, birds cawed.

Violet petted and petted, losing track of time, until shadows began to dance between trees. At first she thought it was nothing, but when she turned back to pet him, she caught a dash of black out of the corner of her eye.

"Cat," she demanded, stilling instantly, "what is…"

The words died as the shadows took form. They were large, with big bellies, and covered in black and grey stripes. Black feathers adhered to their arms, and a long curved beak covered their nose and mouth.

"You've tricked me," her voice broke.

"And this is my cue," Cheshire said with a glint in his feral eyes, and then became nothing but a vapor. "Thanks for the rub down, Red," his ghostly whisper mocked her.

Her eyes widened in horror as the beings moved in.

"Stay back," she shot to her feet, "I can hurt you."

The heads cocked in unison.

"Not if you can't see us." The voice came out a tinny echo behind the mask.

But she didn't have a clue who'd spoken, and with the shock of seeing bird men advancing, came a complete lapse of reason. She stood frozen, a split moment of indecision that would cost her dearly.

"What?" Her pulse stuttered.

The bodies moved so fast they were little more than a blur. Finally, she remembered to move. She twirled on her feet, and started running back to the safety of her woods. "Ewan," she cried. "Help."

A black hood slid over her face. She screamed, clawing to get it off.

"Now sleep," the voice commanded and something tickled her nose.

She remembered no more.

Chapter 11

Ewan shot to his feet. He'd fallen asleep, he hadn't meant to. But purging the crone's soul from his body had seemed to drain his own life essence. He ran, pushing his limbs as hard as they'd go. Which wasn't hard, or fast enough. Running on jellied legs, he tried to ignore the fiery burn pounding away at his skull. Body be damned, all that was important was finding her.

His heart clenched when he picked up her fear laden scent.

And that of the cat.

Howling, he followed. She was deep in the Hatter's territory, but there were others with her. Birds.

Black feathers were scatted all around. And for a moment he feared the worst. Malvena's spies had somehow found her.

But there were so many feathers. Too many. Birds didn't molt for no reason. Had there been a struggle and she'd pulled some out? But one glance at the dirt spoke volumes. Red had barely turned to run before whatever had found her caught her.

Not only that, he did not smell Malvena anywhere. There was no stench of death, or waste of birds.

But that didn't mean she was safe. Something had taken her.

Dizzy with fear, he prayed he'd make it to her in time. Why hadn't he followed her? He should have followed her. She didn't know this land. He did, he knew how treacherous--this place most of all--could be.

Feathers were scattered everywhere, dropping off like someone had overturned a bucketful of them. Not only that, the kidnappers weren't taking her north toward Malvena's keep, they were heading in the direction of the Mad Hatter's garden.

It took a moment for the realization to dawn on him that even the trees did not attack. They sat, like great big giant bulwarks; almost appearing to be as benign as he knew they were not. No roots came up out of the ground to trip him, no branches made a grab for him. Even sappy maws remained closed.

This was not right. The land was only silent like this when…

His ears twitched when the crunching sound of a snapping twig reverberated through the desolate woods.

"Hello, Ewan," the sweet voice almost seemed to smile. "The girl is with us. Come quickly."

Turning, he saw Alice.

She wore a black silk dress that draped to her feet, the bodice tight on her waist; clusters of roses wove a trail from her chest down the left side of her body. Black paint, in a filigree pattern, framed her right eye. Flushed and rosy, she looked healthy and happy.

Alice gestured quickly. "Hurry, we spotted crows this morning."

Heart regaining its more normal rhythm, he nodded, and trotted toward her. She patted his nose when he neared, kneeling by his side, she grabbed his shaggy head and brought his ear to her mouth.

"Spies have been about these past two nights…"

As she spoke, she continued to stroke the length of his side. To the outside, it would appear like a woman petting her dog. Questions buzzed through his head. Why the subterfuge? How had the crows known? Where exactly was Red?

"Please accept our apologies for taking Violet the way we did. We meant no harm." Planting a quick kiss on the tip of his nose, she nodded. "Follow me, and try not to look so… wolf like."

Her pink lips twitched and he huffed.

Alice led him on a dizzying trail. She walked around trees, below trees, and even through them. Waving her hand in semi-circular motions as she mumbled nonsensical words, it was amazing to witness the land respond to her as it did.

He growled when he noticed the same purple polka dotted tree for the third time. Were they actually going anywhere?

She winked, waved her hand again, and then dropped to her knees. In a clearing lay a teapot, hidden by thick grass. Lifting the lid, she whispered inside the ceramic pot, "the cake please."

Suddenly a large slice of cake slid through the narrow opening. With a triumphant smile, she twirled and held out the slice to him. The cake itself was a deep yellow, while the frosting was the whitest, frothiest foam he'd ever seen.

After the crone's forest, the sight of it turned his stomach a little. He couldn't help but remember what her cakes had been made out of.

Brown eyes twinkling, she said, "Take a bite. A small one. Too much will make you cease to appear."

He'd only met Alice once before, she'd been beautiful, of course. But shy and withdrawn, he wondered if she realized how like the Hatter she seemed now. Speaking in his nonsensical way, dressing like him.

Would Violet be like that with him someday?

Careful not to take too large a bite, he barely tore a piece off the cake and instantly wanted to spit the bitter thing out. She held his jaw closed, and nodded.

"It's worse than awful, but it's the only way. Have you swallowed it?"

The offensive piece of carrion tasting waste rested on his tongue, and it was all he could do to choke it down, gagging and panting once it settled in his gut.

"Good." She tore a piece off for herself. "Upsy daisy now." She popped it in and grimaced. "Ugh, that's awful."

A wave of vertigo slammed into him and he winced, squeezing his eyes shut as the world around them became a giant's paradise. Ewan growled.

"I know, it's dreadful being so small. But it will only last for a while."

He looked back at the garden. It was lit, tables out and festooned with every sort of tea food imaginable.

Alice shook her head, her black hair fanning out like a blade behind thin shoulders. "No tea this time, Ewan. You're coming to our home. It's safer." She eyed him. "You will need to *unbecome*. I'll not be taking you through the world's my Hatter took me through when I first arrived, but the trip can be rather jarring. You'll need to hang on to my hand."

Calling the light, it took only moments for him to stand before her, and then to frown when her lips quirked and she quickly glanced away.

Alice cleared her throat. "I always forget it's not like the movies."

He glanced down at himself.

Smiling, she said, "As lovely as you look, you really should get dressed. I don't think Hatter would like it too much if you weren't clothed. He tends to go a little batty about those sorts of things when I'm around."

Ewan rolled his eyes. "Lass, I canna make clothes from air."

She looked at him, and lifted her brows. "Well lucky for you, I can." Snapping her fingers, he was suddenly clothed in tight jeans and a plain white shirt.

Alice laughed. "Hmm... Maybe not much better."

"I'm clothed, am I no? What's wrong now?" he tried, but couldn't get the irritation from his voice.

"Absolutely nothing. Now take my hand." She reached for him.

The moment their hands interlocked, she stepped through the tilted tea pot and a wave of vertigo slammed into him, making him lose his bearings. Everything was pitch black, and save for the tiny hand in his, he felt anchorless. An overwhelming desire to flail and find some sort of footing overcame him, but he clamped down on it, knowing this blackness to be merely illusion; though the knowledge didn't keep the sweat from beading on his forehead.

"I know this is kind of freaky. Just a little bit longer."

Her soft voice helped to calm the animal's natural instinct in him. He was not alone in this nothingness.

"Where's Red?" He finally asked.

"With Hatter."

He snarled and a small fist punched his arm.

"Not that Violet's not beautiful, but he's got me, Ewan. She's perfectly safe."

"So long as it's understood she belongs to me and me alone."

"Yes, yes," her voice was mollifying, "she's all yours. But just so you know, the caveman act really doesn't work for girls anymore. Just sayin'."

"Caveman?"

He was unprepared for the jarring transition from darkness to light and blinked back tears as a bright shaft of sunlight suddenly pierced his eyes, momentarily blinding him. A meadow spread out for miles in every direction. A placid pond sat next to a small thatched roof cottage. Dropping his hand, Alice gathered her skirts and started jogging toward the home. He kept pace beside her.

"It all looks so normal," he muttered. "I expected madness."

She looked at him, a fond smile on her lips. "Oh, it is, usually. But I told Hatter that we needed to make her as comfortable as possible. I wasn't too sure what she'd think of my fifty foot toad, so he made it all conform."

Ewan wasn't certain she was entirely kidding.

The bright red door was thrown open and Hatter--dressed in his customary suit brimming with pocket watches--stepped out.

Alice cried, and he smiled. Then she was in his arms and he was bending her over, giving her a passionate kiss, and suddenly Ewan knew Violet had been very safe. It was obvious, even to the deaf and blind, the passion that brewed between the two.

"I worried," Hatter whispered against Alice's lips after a while. "Did you have any trouble?"

She nuzzled his neck as he helped her stand, readjusting her skirts.

"No, but I think we gave Ewan a fright."

Dark eyes zeroed in on him. "Wolf," Hatter extended his free hand, the other was still firmly clamped around Alice's waist. "Forgive us for the necessity of it, but Malvena's spies are everywhere."

He nodded. "She explained. Was Red harmed at all?"

Hatter flashed bright white teeth. "No, though I think Tweedle-Dee and Tweedle-Dum gave her a terrible fright. She was reluctant to enjoy one of my wife's cupcakes, or even talk for that matter."

Alice touched the tip of his nose. "I think the poor thing needs a hot meal before a cupcake, Hatter. Ewan?" She glanced at him and gestured toward the door. "She's inside."

"Thank ye." He stepped in, taking a brief moment to adjust his eyes to the dim lighting within.

"Ewan?"

Her melodic voice made him weak in the knees and he wondered if she could hear the stutter of his heart.

"Red?"

Then she was in his arms, flinging herself into his body the way Alice had into her Hatter's. A wave of sunshine and wild magic engulfed him, and heat spiraled through his veins. She felt so good, so small, and perfect, and safe. Rubbing her back, he was reluctant to ever let her go.

She pressed her cheek against his chest, small fingers curling into the back of his shirt.

"I'm so sorry. I got tricked by that awful cat--"

"Cheshire?" His deep voice rumbled.

She shuddered. "Yes, he looked so fluffy and let me pet him--"

"He let ye pet him?" Ewan pulled back, chuckling. "The cat? That vile rodent? He never lets anyone pet him."

"He tricked me."

He kissed the pulse at her temple, wishing he could do so much more. Wishing he could taste her as passionately as Hatter had Alice. "It was a ruse Hatter and Alice orchestrated."

Blue eyes filled with confusion. "Why?"

"Because," Hatter's deep voice answered behind them, "Malvena's crows were spotted within these woods not two nights ago. We've much to discuss."

Alice kissed his cheek. "But not before dinner." She glanced at Violet. "And a bath. Jeez, Ewan… what in the world did you do to the poor thing?"

"Don't ask," he grumbled.

Red winced. "Can I take my bath alone?"

Alice laughed. "Of course. Did you think I was going to bathe you? Come on."

Violet turned to follow, and then stopping, took a deep breath and quickly pecked his whisker roughened cheek.

"I'm glad to see you," she whispered, and he swore the ground shifted beneath his feet.

Chapter 12

"So you're Alice, huh?" Violet asked, resting her hip against the mushroom cap shaped counter.

"That's what they say." Alice grinned, pulling a steaming foil wrapped pan from out the oven.

The aroma of roasted beef and vegetables made Violet drool.

Alice wiped her hands on her teapot apron and then lifted a corner of the foil, a thick jet of white steam escaped, tempting Violet to peek inside and sniff at it like a dog. Or a wolf. Like a big black one.

She shook her head.

"Thanks for my clothes." She plucked at her red knit sweater. "Though you know, you didn't need to get me red. It's not my favorite color or anything."

Alice pulled a silver thermometer out of the hunk of meat and covered the pan again. Crossing her arms, she leaned beside Violet. Alice had changed out of the dress Violet had first seen her in. She was now wearing a short blue dress with thigh high striped socks.

She was short and petite, not to mention Asian. So unlike the Alice of legend.

"I guess I shouldn't rely on fairy tales for the truth then," Alice chuckled. "You do know your story, right?"

Violet rolled her eyes, plucking at a bit of fuzz on her shirt. "You mean the one where Ewan ate my grandmother. Yes, I'm familiar."

Alice patted her arm. "He didn't really. Did he?"

Lifting a spatula off the counter, Violet flicked it through air. "Depends on how you look at it." She sighed, wanting to change the subject. "I thought you were supposed to be, you know, white. Blond hair and stuff. You look different than your story too."

Alice shrugged. "Well you're supposed to like red."

Grinning, Violet said, "Touché."

Picking up a piping bag full of fluffy white cream, Alice quickly piped it onto cooled chocolate cupcakes, topping each one with a chocolate covered cherry.

"It's Hatter's favorite," Alice murmured, tip of her pink tongue sticking out the corner of her mouth as she worked.

Fascinated, Violet watched as Alice swirled a perfect amount with artistic precision on each cake.

"He's really nice you know."

Violet's brows drew together. "Who? The Hatter?"

He'd sat looking at her on the couch, his dark gaze seeming to bore into her soul. She shuddered, that look had burned with a strange amber glow. Madness and sanity trapped within that hard gaze. Violet had no idea how he'd ever managed to hook such a sane person like Alice.

"No. Ewan." Alice sat her empty bag down on the counter and picked up a cupcake. "I always have to taste the first one. Thank goodness I don't seem to get fat in Wonderland." She laughed.

Violet took the portion Alice offered her. "I'm not too sure he'd mind. He seems infatuated with you."

Alice's dark brown eyes sparkled. "I know. Feeling is so mutual. And what about you?"

Violet squirmed, shoving the cake in her mouth to prevent having to talk or do girl time. She wasn't sure she was good at that. She'd only ever had Aunt Mir for the past few hundred years, and they weren't exactly chat buddies.

Notes of passion fruit and salty sweet rock crystals burst on her tongue. "Oh wow," Violet moaned, "so good."

Alice smiled. "Same reaction Hatter has. But you haven't answered my question. I can tell you're not totally comfortable with Ewan. Why?"

"I kissed his cheek," Violet said, attempting to defend her position.

Snorting, Alice popped a piece of cake in her mouth. "Yeah, and I kiss the March Rabbit's cheek, doesn't mean I wanna date him."

"You wouldn't understand," Violet grumbled, yet eagerly accepted another portion of cake.

"Try me."

Licking at the frosting on her fingertip, Violet shrugged. "Do you have any idea what it's like to believe something whole heartedly, only to find out you were dead wrong? But not only that, I developed a hatred for him that's so deep, I'm just not sure it's ever possible to truly let it go, even though I know it's no longer justified."

"Hmm. That sucks." Alice's lips twisted. "Danika didn't tell us much of the story. But I do know that what Ewan did that night was in defense of you."

Violet nibbled on the cake. Hard to stay angry when it tasted so good. "Yeah, but that's just the thing. I didn't know that. I was led to believe that my version of history was true. For over five hundred years I've lived with one goal in mind. Return to Kingdom so I could find him and kill him, except…"

"Except?" Alice lifted a perfectly sculpted brow.

Pursing her lips, a million answers flitted through her head. Except he was so nice. Except he kept doing things to protect her. Kept giving her looks that made her toes curl and her blood boil. That all she could think about was wanting to kiss him, even though at times an irrational hatred bubbled up and made her brain scream that it was wrong. That she should gut him like the stinky, filthy beast he was.

Instead she said, "He treats me like his property. Always growling at me and telling others I belong to *him*," she mimicked his thick burr. "It's annoying."

Laughing, Alice nodded. "I can see how that could be. But it's part and parcel of the wolf nature. And I hate to break it to you, Violet, but when one of the bad five sets their eyes on you; it's pretty much a done deal."

"Bad five?"

Alice flicked her wrist. "Another story for another time. Here's the deal in a nutshell. You're it for him. He'll never leave you, and I think a part of you already knows that. Maybe even thrills at the thought."

Even now her stomach felt like it was bottoming out; her thighs shook at the thought of feeling that naked flesh. Hearing him croon her name when in the middle of their passion. Of peppering the scar on his face with hundreds of kisses, discovering why her body ached with incredibe pleasure at the thought of his touch.

"Ugh, but how can he love me? We barely know each other."

Alice shrugged one shoulder. "I'm sure he doesn't love you yet. How could he?"

Violet's heart sank. It shouldn't matter. Hearing it said should only reinforce how stupid this whole thing was, but she'd be lying if she said it didn't bother her.

"It's all animal with him. Right now its pheromones, your scent, your look, everything. It all adds up to his perfect mate."

"That's ridiculous."

"No." Alice shook her head. "Maybe to you, because you don't understand it. And I barely do, but Hatter told me there were years when he wasn't sure Ewan would make it. It's a physical wound for a wolf not to have his mate once he's claimed her."

"What do you mean?" Violet felt like she was listening to Alice through a long tunnel, her heart pounding so hard as she tried to imagine what it'd been like for him.

"That's for him to share." She smiled. "You know I ran out on Hatter." Alice's smile grew sad, bitter. "I thought he didn't want me and I left. I didn't fight. Maybe I was too scared."

"But you guys seem so happy."

"Now. But then, I couldn't see beyond my hurt. My beliefs. It almost cost me everything. My life and my happiness. I love him, Violet, with every fiber of my being. These aren't the easiest guys to fall in love with, but I promise, if you let yourself, you'll never be happier."

"Mmm, I like the sound of that."

Violet jumped at the sound of Hatter's deep drawl. He'd poked his head inside the door, sniffing appreciatively. "Did you make the bread?" he asked.

Every time Alice looked at Hatter her entire countenance seemed to glow. "Why don't you turn your back and see."

Violet frowned when she glanced at the table in the dining area. There wasn't any bread on it. As confused as Violet was by the cryptic reply, Hatter was not. They shared a secret smile, a wordless exchange that transcended mere food.

"Minx," Hatter finally drawled. "Leonard grows impatient for his sustenance. Hurry it up, woman," he growled.

"You tell that rat, to be patient and wait," Alice huffed, but hopped off the counter and grabbed the pan. "Bring the salad, Violet," she called over her back.

She stood there for a moment, cold salad bowl in her hand. They had something and she desperately wanted it.

Was it really as simple as letting go?

Chapter 13

Danika and Miriam landed on the fattest branch the old oak tree had to offer and settled in, awaiting their midnight visitor.

So far the journey had been uneventful. Actually, boring would be a better descriptor. Danika wasn't sure what she'd expected, but it certainly hadn't been this. Miriam barely talked to her, hardly even looked at her. They'd shrunk themselves down to the size of a gnat, there'd be very little that could detect them in this form.

The moment they'd stepped through the portal she'd expected doom, winged monsters bearing down on them. Maybe even Galeta's fat rump making a showing. But nothing.

"I hope Violet and Ewan are doing well," she said, glancing from the corner of her eye at her friend.

Miriam stood as a sentinel, one arm wrapped around a thin vine, peering like a barnyard owl into the thick gloom below them. "Mmm," she nodded.

"Mir!" Danika stomped her foot. "Now really, this is enough. I'm your friend. You must talk with me."

Eyes covered in bright red veins turned to stare at her. Exhaustion leaked from every crevice of her body, wrinkles marred skin in a permanent patchwork of lines and age.

"Dani, it's better if ye doona ken too much--"

"Blast it all, you stubborn old fool. I'm your friend." She gripped bony shoulders and gave them a gentle shake. "What's happened to you, sister? How did you age so quickly? You look beyond your years."

Miriam pinched the bridge of her sharp, thin nose. "It wasn't easy, Dani. Living in that world. The constant use of magic to keep the humans away, making our home exist on fairy time. All of that's taken a toll. I'm tired. Worn out and…" she paused, mouth open as if she wanted to say something, but then finally shook her head and sighed. "None of which is your fault."

She patted Danika's arm, giving her a tight lipped smile. Gray frizz surrounded her head like a sort of aged halo. Even her moth speckled wings beat slowly, as if Miriam hadn't much strength for more.

"I'm worried about you." Danika laced her fingers through Miriam's. "You don't look well, my friend. Not at all. Fairy should have restored your youth, and yet you look little better than a hag."

Miriam snorted, some of the old light entering her eyes. "Ye've still a sharp tongue about ye, Dani, I'll give ye that."

The glen glowed silvery in the moonlight. A scuttle of tiny feet scampered up their tree, a bushy red tail disappearing quickly within a hole in the wood. The night was rich with the scent of hyacinth and lavender. Dark petaled roses opened their blooms, knowing the fairies were about and seeking a morsel of dust.

Miriam gently squeezed Dani's hand one final time before letting go. "I loved these woods. This place." Joy laced the longing in her words.

"You're back now. We can fly through here anytime we want."

She laughed. "That is until Galeta finds us. She will ye know."

Danika twisted her lips. "Did you see that in a vision?"

"Aye." Miriam nodded, not an ounce of fear in the word.

"Who's coming to meet us?" Danika asked, glancing over Miriam's shoulder, trying to catch a glimpse of their mystery guest.

"A friend that made me a promise long ago."

The wind picked up then, cool and sweet against Danika's gossamer wings. She inhaled, invigorated by the night. There was always something so magical about the woods at night.

"I love this spot," Miriam said again, this time there was a tremble of tears in her statement.

"You've already said that, dear." Danika frowned.

"Did I?" Miriam's eyes shone bright lavender. "I forgot."

Something was wrong. Very wrong, and it irked Danika that she couldn't figure it out. Miriam wasn't herself. But then again, she'd not been around her friend for far too long. Perhaps this was Miriam now. Distant. Silent. She was The Shunned, and perhaps it was more than just a title now. Perhaps her friend believed that's who she really was--an outcast and pariah within fairy.

Miriam pointed below. "We were born just there, do you remember, Dani?"

A small field of red roses waved in the gentle breeze. Most were snoring, though one was drooping, its petal dragging along the ground. Woeful eyes blinked at its sad petals.

"The moon was full and fairy song rang throughout. Aye," Danika nodded, a fond smile on her face, "I remember."

Miriam tucked a strand of hair behind her slightly upturned ear. "This is a good place. I could never be sad here, Dani." She looked at Danika. "I think I should like to stay here forever, beside the roses."

Danika gazed at her friend, trying desperately not to read more into the words, but her heart twisted in her chest with fear. "We're not going to die, Mir. None of us. We will defeat, Malvena."

"Though she be but little, she is fierce!" A bell like voice said, reciting one of Danika's favorite lines from Shakespeare's play.

Danika twirled, recognizing the voice instantly. Esmeralda stood on the limb they were on, cloaked in shadow; green vines slithered like a snake down the tree's bark.

Miriam nodded and smiled. "Hello, dear friend."

Ese stepped into the moonlight, ivy undulated upon her body. Her thick mane of chestnut colored hair flowed down to her waist. She was a vision of fae loveliness, save for the solid blacks of her eyes.

Miriam rushed up to her, moving faster than Danika had seen in days.

"I did as you asked, Miriam. I led Galeta on a goose chase, but I'm afraid…" She gathered her hands together, clasping her fingers tight in front of her.

"It is okay, this was good enough. I know what I must do."

"What?" Danika asked, though she really wanted to screech. She was so tired of being left in the dark, of knowing her best friend made plans without her knowledge. Why all the secrecy?

Ese glanced at Danika. "You should not have brought her, Mir."

"How dare you?" Danika puffed out her chest, ignoring the desperate desire to grab her wand and turn Ese into a green toad. "She is *my* friend. Not yours. And I will support--"

"Hush now, Dani," Miriam whispered, patting her hand in a soothing gesture. "She meant no harm. But you know as well as I do, Ese, that she must be here. It's been foretold. It will only succeed if we follow the plan."

Esmeralda glanced over her shoulder. "Galeta will be here any moment. Are you sure of this?"

"Wait. What?" Danika turned toward Miriam, tugging on the tattered sleeve of her blue dress. "You want to be caught? Miriam, have you lost your mind? We have time. We must go. What about the kids? We need to--"

Wide blue eyes pleaded with Danika to stop. "It is the only way, Dani. Galeta will find me now or later, I cannot escape her forever. I'm a fugitive."

"Of what?!" Danika finally did shriek.

"Of my law," Galeta's deep throated voice boomed like cannon fire. "You were never to return, how dare you?" The Blue crackled with bursts of flames as she flitted toward their branch, a tail of blue glow trailing like a shooting star behind her.

Sharp fangs gleamed bright white in her face. Her eyes were narrowed to dangerous slits. "I will deal with you later," Galeta said as she passed a contrite Esmeralda.

Miriam lifted her chin, her demeanor proud and almost arrogant. "Ye ken the prophecy; I've shared it with ye--"

Galeta's sneer was a mile long and dripped with malice. "Your prophecy. As if that's proof enough for me."

What prophecy? Why the bloody hell was Danika always in the dark about everything. She clenched her fists, digging her nails into the palms of her hand so hard she felt the skin break beneath. Her blood buzzed with fairy energy, like prodding an electric gate. Angry didn't even begin to describe how she felt at the moment.

"Lock them up," Galeta ordered Esmeralda.

As the fairy of Justice and Truth, Esmeralda had no choice but to do as Galeta ordered. Though she was one of the *Ten*, none had greater power than the Head Mistress. Galeta's word was law in fairy.

Miriam thrust her wrists behind her back. "We seek asylum and safe harbor through Kingdom."

"Ha!" Galeta threw her head back, blue hair swishing back and forth like a pendulum. "You'll rot in fairy flame. I'll never release you."

"But Galeta, surely," Danika stepped in front of Miriam, dragging the cold glacial stare to herself, attempting to remain calm and rational and not wail and shriek as she desperately wanted to do, "you must understand, we're going to kill Malvena now. In two nights we're to meet up with the Heartsong and her wolf."

A sharp blue brow rose so high, it nearly vanished beneath her hairline. Slowly, she turned toward Ese. "You knew about this?"

"Yes," Esmeralda said with a sharp clip of her head. "I knew."

"The Black grows stronger every day. The land sang when the Heartsong stepped back through, she will find the girl," Galeta mused softly, as if she'd forgotten her audience and spoke to herself.

"Ye ken the prophecy to be true, Galeta," Miriam spoke up. "I ken that ye hate me, and that's okay, but for the sake of Kingdom, ye must let our journey continue to the keep. Without me, the child canna win."

"Crows fly all about Kingdom, rats scuttle down my halls. The Black is desperate to find the girl." Galeta's nostrils flared, her words echoed with the faintest trace of capitulation.

"Have you been following Violet?" Miriam asked softly.

Galeta's jaw clenched. "We follow her traces. The dark magic in her veins is potent, it leaves its marker. We traced her as far as Hansel and Gretel's woods, but I lost her scent amongst the gore."

"Please leave her be. I've charted a course for them to Malvena's. They are headed there now. Do not arrest them, Galeta, please." Miriam closed her eyes. "We will kill the Black."

Scoffing, Galeta rolled her eyes. "And then what? Hmm? We all know the power of the fairy leaves the body when one of the *Ten* die. The Black power is too dark to contain, too deadly. It will be released and infect another unfortunate soul, and we'll be right back where we started. We cannot kill the Black, we must kill the Heartsong. It is the only way."

"No!" Miriam cried, her wings flapped so hard it stirred the leaves in the tree. "I ken how to stop that. That is why I must be there. That is why the girl must be allowed to continue the journey."

"She speaks truth, Galeta," Ese said, turning black eyes toward the Blue. "I've seen it. The Shunned will stop it."

Miriam's hands were clasped to her breast, her chest barely moving. Danika subconsciously mimicked that very stance, breathless to know Galeta's decision.

It took only a second. "Stop the Black. Then you're mine."

Miriam swallowed hard. "Aye, Galeta. Then I'm yers. But only me; Danika must not be harmed. Nor can Violet or Ewan."

"No." Danika shook her head. "She's done nothing wrong, Head Mistress. Don't imprison her."

Blue flames once more coated Galeta's body as she rose high into the air. "So mote it be," she said and the air charged with a swift current of spine tingling power. "Esmeralda, to me."

Esmeralda gave Miriam a grim smile. "Good luck, my friend."

Then they were gone.

And Danika could hardly believe any of it had happened. Nothing had changed. The air was still as sweet, the night rang with the quiet melody of sleeping creatures. Nothing had changed, that was, except for the greasy pit of dread curled like a ball in Danika's gut.

"You're not returning to her, Miriam? Please tell me--"

Miriam smiled. "No. I'm not."

Relief washed over Danika, and the tension between her shoulders immediately eased. "Thank the goddess." She laughed. "Good. For a moment you made me question your sanity. Galeta wanted nothing more than to ground you. Strip you of your wings; I couldn't imagine a worse fate." She shuddered.

"I can." Miriam said softly. "Leaving fairy."

"Oh, Mir, I'm so sorry."

She shook her head. "I'm back now, and I'll never leave."

"Good." Danika's wings buzzed, verve and joy bubbled through her body. "We'll hide and drink cherry blossom fire until we grow old and fat."

"That sounds lovely." Miriam hugged her swiftly. "Don't ever change, Dani. Never. Ye keep that joy, it'll take ye far."

"Us far. Us, right?" Danika hooked her arms through Miriam's, and then lowered her voice to a conspiratorial whisper. "Now, what is the real plan?"

Miriam withdrew her wand from inside her dress pocket and flicked it at a thick bunch of leaves, plucking them gently off the branch and forming them into a tight green nest. Once finished arranging the leaves, they flew to the bed and settled in, lying on their backs, they gazed at the stars.

"Do ye remember asking me why I dinna allow the Green's power to go to ye?"

Danika nodded. "Yes. I've always wondered that. Though, I must say you saved me that night. I couldn't imagine having to work with that inflated bag of blue poo day in and day out."

Miriam chuckled. "The truth is, Dani, yer a magnet. Ye draw powerful magic to ye, but the power isna meant for ye."

Danika sat up on her elbow, facing Miriam. "That's why I'm here isn't it? To draw the Black's power?"

For centuries Danika had wondered what that level of power would feel like, to be one of the *Ten*. Magic to rival even the Djinn's of the east. But never, in all her life, had she desired the Black's power. Malvena wasn't the first Black, she was third. Each one more terrifying and destructive than the incarnation before. That power was so dark it always corrupted, no matter how pure the heart started out.

"Will I have to absorb it?"

"Nay." Miriam shook her head quickly. "I'll destroy it."

"But, Mir?" She pressed her lips tight. Not wanting to injure her friend, but how did Miriam think she could destroy something so powerful? Miriam was only a fairy, not one of the powerful *Ten*.

"It could kill you, Miriam. Are you sure you're strong enough?"

"Aye, Dani, I'm strong enough."

Danika didn't utter another word, heart troubled and more than a little worried for her friend. Maybe they were on a fool's errand, because she just wasn't sure how Miriam would able to destroy something so malevolent.

She stared at the stars, praying to the goddess that somehow a miracle would happen, otherwise Danika knew, they'd all die. If Violet couldn't kill Malvena, if Miriam couldn't contain the Black's dark soul… none would survive.

Kingdom would be ruined.

Chapter 14

Just let go. Alice's words kept echoing in Vi's head. Ewan was in the next room, she'd heard his prowling this past hour. Pacing back and forth, muttering softly.

He was worried. All through dinner he'd stared at her, his eyes so sad, so haunted, and something inside her cried at the look.

This was all so scary and new. Life had been planned, it'd all made sense. Find the wolf, kill him then kill Malvena (maybe)… end of story. Live a happy, immortal, and boring eternity.

She hugged her knees to her chest, sinking deeper into the soft mattress. Moonlight cast kooky shadows on the wall. But she wasn't scared. There wasn't a lot in life that terrified her anymore. Violet had faced down a wolf. Yes, she'd nearly died, but the thrill of meeting her fears head on and surviving, had been euphoric. Although the old hag had creeped her out, but in her defense, she'd still totally laid waste to her.

Her heart hammered painfully in her chest as she dug her toes into the thick white comforter. She'd faced those fears, so why was she so hesitant to face this one? To walk up to him, to tell him that maybe she'd been wrong. No, that she *had* been wrong. That something inside her longed to know him better, learn who he was.

That she was lonely.

Needed him.

Wanted.

She squeezed her eyes and licked her lips. "Ewan," she whispered, so softly she knew he wouldn't hear through the wall. "I'm… sorry. I'm sorry for the pain I caused you. I'm sorry that I made you the bad guy and you weren't. I'm sorry for a lot of things." She rocked. "But mostly I'm sorry because I'm too much of a wimp to tell you to your face."

Her door opened on squeaky hinges.

She gasped and grabbed her chest as a dark shape slinked into her room. Golden eyes stared at her from within a wolf's face. Swallowing hard, she scooted to the head of the bed.

"Did you hear that?"

His tail thumped, gold eyes searched her face. Almost as if he could peer below the surface, exposing her soul, her strengths, her weaknesses, taking her measure, and giving it back. Letting her know he saw her, but didn't judge her.

His onyx colored fur gleamed in the moonlight. Like a dark flame, it fascinated. There wasn't a mark to mar his coat. His snout was long and regal, long whiskers hardly moving. But the eyes, the eyes that stared back at her sparkled with more than just the wild flicker of wolf, there was intelligence, humanity staring back at her.

Slowly, he crept forward, until she could feel the warm exhalations of his breath brushing against her cold fingertips. Her hand trembled as she reached out, touching the long scar that tracked down the corner of his left eye.

"What happened to your eye?"

He licked his muzzle, anxious energy radiated off him as he danced on his front paws.

This was a huge step for her, but she needed to let go. Not just for him, but for her sanity as well. Hating something for so long was exhausting.

"I don't mind if you switch forms, Ewan."

Suddenly the room buzzed with the tick-tock of several clocks, white noise she'd ignored, now blasted her ear drums. Kept tune to the beat of her pulse as his bright white light flared its feelers upon the walls.

When she could see again, he was kneeling. Big, beautiful body draped in shadow and gentle spills of moon glow. Those golden eyes were on her face, her body. Anywhere they touched she felt hot, exposed. Restless beneath her clothes.

"I canna sleep." His deep burr made her body flare with heat and need.

Violet squeezed her thighs, hoping the pressure might stop the tingles radiating between her legs. It only made it worse. Heart trapped in her throat, she could barely manage to whisper, "You don't need to kneel."

He stared at her, seemed like hours, but was likely only minutes, and then he was standing and she saw everything. The fine dusting of black hairs smattered along muscular thighs, abdominals so chiseled she was tempted to run her finger along it just to make sure they were real. Dusky skin with tight brown nipples. She saw other things too. A big thing, stiff and frightening looking. But even while it scared her, a part of her wondered what it might feel like inside her.

It couldn't be all that bad. There were too many people in the world.

Her mouth was dry.

The whole time she'd studied him, his eyes never left her face. She felt that gaze like an imprint, it bore through her skull. "Why do you look at me like that?" she stammered.

"Because yer fair bonny, Red, and sometimes I'm afraid if I blink, ye'll disappear like ye did before."

She tipped her head up to look at him. There was heat in his gaze, but there was more. So much more, she had no idea how to describe it. It made her feel warm, safe, desperate, desired. But mostly, it made her long.

"How do you know, Ewan?"

The mattress dipped as he sat so close the heat off his body emanated against her bare toes. Paralyzed with fear, she couldn't move, even though she desperately wanted to. She wanted to crawl to him, wrap her arms around his neck and beg him to help her.

All she could do was watch, and breathe.

"Know what?" he asked in that exotic scratchy burr and heat spiraled thick and heady through her stomach, resting between her legs.

It was on the tip of her tongue to beg him to go back to his room, that this was too much, too soon. That she still wasn't sure how to let go of the past--stupid as it was--but Alice's words were an echo in her ear, so she mustered the last sliver of strength and whispered, "That it was me?"

His fingers twitched, like he wanted to touch her, but knew if he did she'd flee.

"Because it is."

There it was, so simple, and so difficult at the same time. "Even knowing how I feel? What if I can't ever let this go?"

His smile was wistful. "Doesna matter. I'll never force myself on ye, Red. But I will always guard ye, protect ye with my life. That is what a mate does."

She chuckled and he cocked his head, brows drawn in confusion.

"You're a masochist. You would pledge your life to a woman who might never be able to touch you, or do the things for you a mate should."

He leaned in, full lips a feather's kiss from hers, irises narrowing to twin slits for a second. She went still, prey in the predator's sight. But it wasn't fear that rolled through her, it was desire. A yearning so intense she licked her lips.

"But I doona think, it'll come to that. Ye want me, Red. I smell yer desire all over ye. It's hot and potent and the wolf is hungry."

She hadn't realized she'd begun to lean forward until she almost fell when he pulled back.

He laughed and then standing, held his hand out to her. "Come with me."

Sweat trickled down her back, her neck. Violet was terrified to touch him, terrified because she feared if she did, she'd pull him on top of her and beg him to do things no man had ever done to her before.

"Where?"

"Yer hot, the Hatter is fond of his springs."

"A midnight swim?" She lifted a brow. "With you? Alone?"

"Aye. Aye. And aye."

He didn't give her a moment to think about it, latching onto her wrist, he yanked her off the bed. Within seconds they were down the hall, in the living room, and then exiting the front door. Violet glanced over her shoulder.

"Won't they know?" she whispered.

"Doona care." He marched briskly toward the pond she'd noticed earlier.

Heart racing, pulse thrilling at the thought of swimming with him beneath a large moon and no one else about, she almost skipped along. Then they were there and he was already naked and she knew he expected her to strip in front of him. She stared at the dark, burbling water. Fireflies twirled along the water, their lighted golden dance moving in perfect synchronization. Cattails swayed, and it all looked so magical, too beautiful for words.

It was pretty perfect.

"You shouldn't look," she said, cold fingertips under the band of her jeans as the anxiety riddled her gut, twisting it up in knots.

White teeth flashed. "Doona take long."

Then he dived into the center, a graceful arc that cut clean through the water, barely causing a ripple.

Violet kicked her shoes off and quickly shucked her jeans off next. Not sure how long he'd stay under; she stripped her shirt, bra, and underwear off. This was ridiculous. She was ridiculous. Hadn't she only been thinking mere minutes ago about the possibility of never being able to let go of the past?

But the thoughts were fleeting, she jumped in, bracing for the cold. Shocked when it wasn't. It was a hot spring, the bubbles were everywhere, tickling every inch of her bare body. Violet bobbed along the surface, turning and frowning when he didn't resurface.

Then a strong hand grabbed her ankle and yanked, she smiled as she slipped under for a second. Reveling in the warmth, but it didn't last. Within seconds she bobbed back up to the surface. She could never stay under long. But then his hands began a slow slide up her calf, her thighs, and the chill of the breeze was again replaced with heat. He moved so gently and expertly, that she couldn't stop the moan or the wash of goose bumps tracking her skin.

Something soft brushed her navel, and she was almost positive it was his lips. Her stomach flopped to her knees as he finally broke through the surface. Her hands brushed along his smooth broad chest and she gripped onto his biceps, latching her nails like daggers into the muscle. He didn't wince or flinch. The water ran in rivulets from his hair down his face, full pink lips parted and she bit her own, even while her tongue danced behind her mouth.

"The Hatter's waters are magical. Ye can breathe below. I tried to bring ye down to see his treasures, but ye bob, Red."

She nodded. "I know. I can't sink. I've tried." Violet continued to worry her bottom lip, she never talked about this with anyone, wasn't sure she should trust him. But she wanted to. She took a deep breath. "I've got bad blood."

Large hands framed her face.

"No, it's true." She grabbed onto his wrists, reveling in the texture of callused thumbs running softly along her cheeks. "I always wondered why. It's not normal. My Aunt can sink. Even Grandma could. But not me. Then I read about the Salem Witch Trials."

"Och, lass."

She shrugged out of his grip and bobbed backwards, feeling exposed and unsure. "That's how they tested if you were a witch."

"It was a failed experiment, Red." His black hair glistened, and her fingers twitched.

She loved touching soft things, wanted to touch him. But she felt vulnerable and that made her angry. "Because they weren't witches!"

"Nor are ye, Red." His eyes were kind.

"I'm something. I have dreams, horrible dreams."

Violet wrapped her arms around herself. The night was far from chilly, especially in the warm waters, but she couldn't stop her teeth from clacking.

He didn't come closer, which only annoyed her. What was wrong with her? She wanted him to go away, but yet she hated when he was gone.

"I dream about violence. Killing things." She was a dam, and the confession was the crack in that dam. She couldn't stop it now. Wasn't sure she wanted to anymore anyway. "I like cutting myself. The pain is pleasure for me. It feels good." Violet glanced at her open palms, smooth as a baby's butt. "I should be covered in scars. Do you know how many times I've done it?"

"Lass, don't--"

"No, you don't! I'm sick of never being able to tell people about me. Of always pretending like I'm okay, I'm not okay. I feel that darkness in me, it spreads through my body. It's already poisoned my heart. I want to hate you. It hurts that I can't. It hurts that I want to know you, touch you, feel you."

Ewan started swimming closer and she held up her palm.

"Don't touch me."

He swam closer.

"I mean it, Ewan, just go away. I'm a freak, I'm bad. You don't want me as a mate."

His hand grabbed hers, then his fingers softly slid between her own. He placed their closed palms against his chest. The firm beat of his heart a steady thump-thump against her hand.

She shuddered, heat built behind her eyes.

"Do ye ken what I see when I look at ye?"

She turned her face, and he turned it back with a finger under her jaw.

"I see eyes bluer than the sky after a good hard rain."

Her lashes fluttered.

Threading a lock of her hair around his finger, he gave it a gentle yank. "And hair more golden than Rumplestiltskin's straw."

He lifted their twined hands to his lips and pressed a firm kiss against the tip of her finger. It was like someone had connected a live wire to her brain, every nerve in her body flared to life. Humming and zinging against one another in a chaotic motion of desperate need.

Ewan kissed her next finger, and the next, until he got to the webbing between her thumb and gently sucked on it. Each pull tightened things down low, made her ache and want to cry.

"I'm sorry, Red. If I'd been there, I would have kissed it all away. Yer beautiful, lass. My heart aches to look on ye, to see that pain and ken I can do nothing for ye. Doona cut yerself again."

"But the urges…"

He shook his head, his eyes like a beacon in the dark, dark night. "Use me. I'm a wolf, I like being bitten."

She licked her lips as her teeth began to ache. What would it feel like to bite him? Could it possibly satisfy the urges she felt?

Ewan cocked his head to the side, exposed his neck. A large vein throbbed just beneath his skin. He touched the spot. "Do it."

Violet gave a self-effacing chuckle, humiliated at her desperate desire to do just that, work the flesh beneath her teeth, her tongue. "I… no. No, I can't do it, Ewan."

"Do it," he growled, his voice nowhere near as gentle as before. The wolf demanded and goddess she was so tempted. The vein pulsed, throbbed.

"I… I…"

His large hand gripped the back of her head, lowering her. There was a deep, rumbling moan and Violet had no idea if she'd made the sound or him.

She licked his collarbone, the slightly salty taste filled her head, her nose. He shuddered and then she bit him. Sank her teeth in, but unlike when she cut herself, she didn't break skin. She rolled him around in her mouth, her tongue tracing the contours of his taut vein.

"Lass," his deep voice caressed the side of her neck, stoking the flame.

His hands were on her waist, pulling her close. Her body melded with his, his heat hers and hers his. The thick length of him seemed to grow harder the more she bit and she moaned when his hands began to trace the curve of her back, up and down. Resting casually on her rear, before fingers tiptoed down its slope. Heat splashed between her thighs, she was wet and so ready. But for what? She didn't know what else to do, her body needed more, but she didn't know how to get it.

There was fire in her blood, her head, her veins. Panic clawed, screamed. She wanted this. Now. Now.

But… but…

She shoved him back, wiping the back of her mouth with her wrist. Thigh muscles twitched, her stomach ached. He was breathing hard, his chest heaving for air. His irises had slitted again.

"You liked that?" Her question came out an accusation.

He closed his eyes, trying, it seemed, to regain his composure. "Yer nay ready, Red. I'm sorry."

"I don't know what--" Her voice cracked and the tears that'd threatened earlier began to spill down the corners of her eyes, blinding his face. "I'm sorry, Ewan, I'm sorry. I don't know what I'm doing."

Quickly, she exited the water, scooping up her clothes and running back to the cottage with them pressed to her heart. It was gone. Her hatred. It was gone. She couldn't hate something she wanted so desperately, but the wanting scared the hell out of her.

Later in her room, when the rest of the world was silent as the grave, she punched a fist into her pillow and wondered what she'd say to him tomorrow.

How could she explain that she hadn't run from him, but from herself? From the madness spreading through her brain screaming that he was hers as much as he'd let the whole world know she belonged to him?

Violet stared out the window, at the sky bejeweled with silver stars, but all she could see was the memory of his golden gaze flashing with hurt when she'd run away.

Chapter 15

Ewan said goodbye to the Hatter and his Alice and then taking a hold of Red's elbow, guided her into the spiraling blue tunnel.

Last night had been a nightmare. He'd gone to bed harder than a rock. Her teeth on him, gripping him. Tiny nails clawing into his flesh, she mated like a wolf.

He glanced at Violet, she was silent, pale. They hadn't spoken after last night.

Sighing, he looked away. She didn't need to worry that he hadn't liked it. He'd loved it. Gloried in it. A wolf mated violently, it wasn't softness and rose petals. It was soul to soul, striped, bare, and raw. A melding of two like hearts. To an outsider it might even appear brutal, but it wasn't. It was passion at its very essence. Untamed and wild.

But she'd think he was lying, he knew that. Was coming to know her more and more each day. His Red was perfect for him, if only she could see that.

"Where are we going?" she asked, still not glancing at him.

He cleared his throat. "Beyond the Misty Isle, where the kraken roams."

She shuddered. "A kraken? My Aunt hates me."

Ewan laughed and was delighted to note her answering grin.

"Nay, Red. She only wishes to prepare ye."

Blue light sped past in a dizzying arc; millions of silver bursts studded the ever revolving tunnel of blue. It was surreal and yet lovely. Violet's gold blond hair almost seemed to sparkle.

She was trying to make peace; he knew this wasn't easy for her. There were dark rings beneath her eyes; she'd slept very little last night, if at all.

"So what this time? Do I have to suck that things soul out too? Because I draw the line at squid. I'm allergic to shellfish."

His laughter echoed hollowly, booming long and loud down the distant span of space and time. "Shellfish? Don't they have soft bodies?"

She shrugged and finally glanced at him beneath long, thick lashes. "About last night--"

He shook his head. "It shouldn't have happened. Ye were nay ready."

Violet placed her finger on his lips, stopping him. The soft weight of it tugged on his heart.

"If you keep talking, I'll lose my nerve, Ewan."

She took a deep breath, and all he wanted to do was pepper the tip of her upturned nose--covered in a fine smattering of freckles--with kisses.

"I like you. A lot." She licked her lips.

If he knew she wouldn't bolt, he'd lean down and taste her, lick at the seams of her closed lips until she parted for him.

"I like that you're always naked around me. I like that I can look as much as I want. I like that you want to be around me. I like that you're a killer. I like the darkness in you. I like that you're big and bad and scary. I like that you make me feel small and safe and special." She sighed. "I like you."

All the blood rushed to his head, making it hard to hear as his ears buzzed with the hot rush.

Her eyes were wide and frightened like a hare caught in a snare. The pulse at the base of her throat jumped, and it was all he could do to pretend her words hadn't given him a painful erection. One he'd barely been able to stop sporting a few hours ago.

"If I survive whatever comes with Malvena--"

"Ye will," he growled, knowing in his soul he'd do whatever it took to make it so. Even if that meant betraying all of his kind, killing them mercilessly and ruthlessly, he'd do it. He'd move heaven and earth to keep his Red safe.

She shushed him again. "If I do, then I think… maybe…"

Narrowing his eyes, his brogue grew thick when he said, "Aye?"

"Maybe…" She leaned up on tiptoe, their breaths mingling.

Tiny pink tongue darting out the corner of her mouth, so close, all he'd have to do was stick his own out to taste it. Small hands roamed the breadth of his chest as her nails began that delicious sliding scrape against his flesh.

He was only a man, a wolf one at that, she tempted him beyond reason. And all the promises he'd made to himself last night to be good, to keep his hands off--they melted into the ether. Ewan gripped her luscious bottom and lifted her, forcing her to open her legs and straddle him.

He hissed when the rough texture of her jeans slid along his shaft.

"Ewan," her voice broke, and then she claimed his lips.

Ewan had no idea where they traveled, they should have exited long ago, but none of that mattered. He couldn't think around the passion burbling through his brain.

She was wild, rough. Her teeth bruising his lips with each punishing kiss. There was no place for him to brace his back on, so he knelt, dragging her with him. Her nails gouged the back of his head.

"Can you make it stop?" she panted, nipping and clawing around his face and neck.

"Wha, lass?" he moaned, catching her lips between his teeth and sucking on its firm fullness, laving his tongue along its smoothness.

She moaned hard and pulled away, almost frenzied in her effort to touch him. Nibbling on his collarbone, his flesh broke out in goose bumps.

"The wanting, Ewan," she murmured. "The needing." She bit him and he groaned, balls so tight and hard to his body he was sure the pleasure would kill him. "I see you. All the time. I want you." She bit harder, sinking in so hard his skin very nearly broke.

Beads of sweat dotted his brow. He tugged on the shell of her ear gently, nuzzling the sweet scent of her neck, imprinting her on his heart. Ewan blew small puffs of air into her hair, her flesh, marking her with his scent. Letting anyone else know she was his and his alone.

"I can," he mumbled and then shuddered when his hands found her breasts. He palmed them, kneading and rolling the nipples expertly between his fingers.

She arched, moaning in wild abandon and pride bloomed in his chest. His touch did that to her, his mouth, his tongue. She danced for him.

"Touch me everywhere." She hissed when he rolled her nipples again, a rosy flush crept up her neck and settled in her cheeks making her blue eyes almost seem to glow.

"Are ye sure, lass?" If she ran away now, he'd go feral.

"Mmm," she mumbled, fumbling with the button of her jeans.

With a growl, he ripped the button off and then shoved his hand down her pants, fingers seeking the center of her. Pleasure swirled through his cock, made him grind his teeth with the pleasure/pain when his fingers became slick with her heat.

"Oh my gods." She flung her head back, arcing her neck and back, forcing him to brace her with his one hand, lest she slip from his grasp. "Yes, Ewan." Violet wiggled on him as he slid a finger in.

She was tight and when he encountered her virginal barrier his heart screamed with joy. The lass was untouched. All his, always.

"Red. Red," he moaned and then she gripped him in a tight fist and he jerked at the exquisite torture. The friction of no lubrication was nothing compared to the pleasure jackknifing through him.

"Too much clothes," he snarled, extracting his hand to pull her jeans down.

She kicked, trying to help. But only succeeded in getting herself tangled up in her pants.

"Calm yerself, Red," he murmured, and with a swift tug tossed the jeans aside.

"I don't know…" she said.

His heart almost stopped beating. Squeezing his eyes shut, panting harder than he ever had in his life, he rested his forehead against hers and ground through his teeth, "If yer gonna force me to stop, say it now."

His cock and balls ached so much; the merest touch of her hand against him would make him come.

"No," she moaned, eyes bright and feverish looking. "Oh, goddess no. I just don't know what to do. What do I do, Ewan?" There was a panicked edge to question.

He laughed, and then growled deep in his throat when he jerked against her hand. "Whatever the bloody hell ye please."

"Okay," she said, and then bit him at the base of his throat. Just like she had last night.

Ewan hissed, lights danced behind his eyes as the bliss rolled wave after wave over him. Drowning him in pleasure so deep he never wanted to resurface.

Wild, desperate, his wolf rolled just beneath the surface of his control. "I need ye. Now," he groaned, when she licked the tender flesh she'd just bitten.

"Yes, oh yes."

He needed to go slow. Though he wanted fire and passion, she was untried. Even a she wolf needed gentle when ripping through the barrier.

Clenching his teeth as sweat dripped into his eyes, he tugged on her panties, slipping them to the side and exposing the wet jewel beneath. He hissed.

"Gods, Red," he said, staring down at the thatch of blond curls.

She was breathing hard, looking dazed. "Will it hurt?" she whispered, no longer moving on him.

The muscle in his jaw ticked. "I'm big, lass. It'll hurt. At first, and only a little."

She swallowed hard, but nodded. "I trust you."

The words were a benediction in his ears. Grabbing her bum, he lifted her. "Spread your legs wide for me."

She did as he said and his stomach flopped at the sight of her. Legs spread wide, arms braced on his chest, as her wet center hovered just above the hard length of him.

"Hang on, and breathe," he advised.

Her blue eyes were wide.

Then he lowered her and the first touch of her wet heat on his cock, made him jerk. Ewan bit his tongue, forcing the wolf back. Control. He needed control, or he'd never last.

Inch, by glorious inch, he sank her down on him. It was slow, and agonizing. Her sheath so wet it slipped over him like a glove. Then he encountered her tight barrier.

She moved, and then grunted as he began the final push.

"Ewan," she whispered.

"Ssh, lass… almost… there." He kissed her lips, tasting her fears, her lust, and with one last surge, broke through.

Violet hissed, going completely still.

Ewan breathed through his nose, trying hard not to move when everything inside him screamed to buck. So tight. So warm. Perfect. His head swam.

After a moment she started to wiggle and slowly he pumped into her. In and out.

"Oh." She said and then started to move, finding the perfect rhythm.

Grunting, he pushed harder.

"Oooh," she laughed. "Ohhh, now I see why everyone does this."

Then there were no more words. Ewan wasn't going to last. "Red," he moaned, fingers gripped her waist tight. "Are ye close?"

She danced on him, her breasts bouncing beneath the sweater. Unable to resist, he released her waist and slipped his hands underneath, latching onto the plump globes.

Violet writhed when he pinched her nipples. "Something, it's building… so… ahhh," she threw her head back, exposing the beating pulse of her neck.

The same spot he'd bitten her before. Now smooth and unmarred. Growling, he licked at it. Pumping harder and harder. Then he bit and she screamed. "Ewan!"

Darkness spiraled through his gut, through his legs, out the tip of his cock as he unloaded his seed in hot spurts.

"Red. My Red," he moaned, slow to come back to himself. His head was dizzy, his legs like jelly. He pinched her firm rump.

She laughed, twining her fingers through his hair. A lazy gleam in her eyes. A fine sheen of sweat covered her face. "Sorry, about last night," she said.

"Ye can make it up to me later." He nipped the spot on her neck where he'd bitten her. Then kissed it tenderly, contented and at peace with his place in the world.

She kissed the corner of his lips, brushing sweaty hair out of her eyes. "I thought you said wolves did it rough." Violet punched his chest. "That wasn't bad at all."

His eyes widened and he growled low in his throat. "That was for yer benefit, Red. Nay mine. Now that ye've been broken in, I'll show ye just how rough this wolf likes it."

Her smile was shy, but gleamed brightly, until she glanced over his shoulder.

"Ewan," she whimpered.

There was no pleasure in the sound of his name, but fear, bright and instant. Violet scooted off him, rearranged her panties and looking around. "Where's my jeans?"

Ewan frowned, still in a lust soaked stupor when he turned around, only to stare into the smiling face of a brightly clothed Kermani. They'd exited the tunnel and he'd been too caught up to notice.

"Good evening, my friends. And may I just say, a much different reception than last time, no?" Brown, almost black eyes glinted in the waning daylight.

Jerking to his feet, Ewan shoved Violet completely behind him, shielding her body from the Easterner's view.

"What the bloody hell, are ye doin' here?" he barked, lungs vibrating with the deep animal growl of his wolf.

Kermani's walk was slow, deliberate and measured; his checkered colored pants distracting. "I truly hate to do this, as I consider The Shunned a true ally, but…"

Ewan's heart thundered as he scanned the horizon. There were no whipping seas, no violent gray skies, but there was a spiraling black gothic tower set against the backdrop of a twisted, skeletal forest. Malvena's keep.

"Ye sold us out," Ewan accused, his skin tingling with the rush of his wolf's hatred. "How did ye find us?"

"Oh." Kermani laughed, large golden hoop in his ear swished with his movements. "It's quite clever actually. The dream stone you used when you left my home, Malvena put a tracker on it. We very nearly had you in the Hatter's woods. But the bastard found you first." He rolled his fingers along his jaw. "Hid you well, but we knew you'd have to travel this road again."

Ewan's skin felt too tight, too hot. Fur rippled beneath his flesh, desperate to rip through, become the beast so he could tear Kermani limb from limb. But Red wasn't moving, barely breathing. He thought maybe she was in shock, and he didn't want to terrify her further.

"Then she heard a ghostly echo of Misty Isles." Kermani shrugged his shoulders, bunching his turquoise colored shirt. "It was a simple matter of rerouting. You were too busy rutting to notice."

His smile was lecherous, not at all open and pleasant as he'd been the last time. Fury was a hot consuming thing that threatened Ewan's sanity, his reason. He held on to the image of a quaking Violet as his tether, praying it might ground him, help him hang onto the last shreds of humanity.

But the shred was barely a sliver. His jaw felt thick, stretched, aching with the need to *become*. His throat burned with the pent up rumble.

"You've betrayed Miriam's trust." Ewan's fist clenched, nails gouging his palms, leaving behind a hot wet smear.

"I think you mean, I betrayed yours. The Shunned paid me, Malvena paid me more. My allegiance lies with my family. This is only a matter of business." Kermani shrugged. "No hard feelings."

Something cold and chilling brushed against his back, when a pulsation blasted through him. Dark and twisted, like a lethal blade, cutting into his flesh. Variegated colored smoke curled around his ankles.

Ewan didn't dare take his eyes off Kermani.

"Red," he growled in a voice more wolf than man, "are ye alright?"

Kermani's obsidian eyes narrowed to thin slits as he stared at a spot behind Ewan's head.

Breathing heavy, dripping with sweat, Ewan chanced a quick peek. But he was unprepared for the sight that greeted him.

Blue and red smoke billowed from Red's every pore, seeped from her nostrils, her mouth. Bled through her eyes, washing out the cobalt blue and turning them a deep indigo. She was looking dead at him, but not really. Her gaze saw beyond, into another reality. Blond tips of her hair danced like charmed snakes around her head as a wind he couldn't feel encased her body.

"Red?" Ewan sniffed the ash laden air; there was the scent of brimstone and fire. It clung its sticky fingers to his nostrils, forcing him to breathe through his mouth. She reeked of death.

"What is she?" Kermani hissed, his voice cracking just slightly beneath the veneer of cool.

She wasn't scared. She didn't cower. Which meant Ewan didn't have to wear the leash. He called his light, howling as his body stretched and contorted. Howling when muscles lengthened and claws ripped through his hands and feet.

When the white light died Kermani had a set of wicked looking daggers in each fist. "The Black will arrive any moment now," he warned, circling to Ewan's right.

Ewan snapped his fangs, pulling back his muzzle far enough to let the length of his canines show. The short man weaved in and out, his pants and shirt billowing like a silk curtain as he moved. Ewan kept him in his sights, never allowing Kermani too close to Red.

Then Kermani jumped, moving like a blur and drawing first blood as his blade carved a fine line through his ear. Ewan howled and twirled, but then Kermani was back. Over and over, taking a small slice out of him each time. A whirling dervish he could not see to defend himself against.

"YOU WOULD DARE!" Red's voice thundered, cracking through the air with an inhuman strain.

Then she jumped, pouncing on Kermani like a predatory cat with the thick smoke undulating around her. The slight man fell to the ground, slashing and cutting. Red screamed.

Desperate to get Kermani and his knives away from Red, Ewan barreled into the smoke screen. His eyes were useless, the smoke around her had increased. She was in color so thick it was like trying to look through shadow.

There were grunts and groans. The sharp slap of skin striking skin. Closing his eyes, Ewan scented the situation. But the brimstone was everywhere, disorienting him. There were elbows and hands everywhere, knocking into his side. But he didn't know who to bite, what to bite. Which one was Kermani?

Growling, panicked, Ewan bumped into a slight body kneeling upon another. He took several quick breaths, beneath the brimstone and barely perceptible, he smelled flowers.

Then there were screams, keening wails like the sound of a dying animal. What the bloody hell was happening? He needed to regain control of this situation, clamping onto the ankle beneath his paw (praying he hadn't bitten through Red's tender flesh), he dragged the body away from the cloying smoke.

Heart pounding, eyes wide, Ewan prepared himself for the worst. The second they escaped the dense shroud, he opened his eyes. And it was. It was brutal. Violent.

But not who he'd expected.

Kermani's lips were flopping open and shut, his dark eyes clouded with pain as he gasped for breath from a body whose ribs were sunken and cracked. Blood soaked through his shirt, turning it a dark shade of crimson black.

"Ewan," Red's voice was reedy and strained. He glanced up, she was stumbling out of the smoke. The breeze was clearing the haze, when she dropped to her knees, fingers curling into the ground.

Ewan ran to her as he called his *unbecoming*. Half man, half wolf, as he latched onto her with paws and hefted her to her feet. Fire sizzled through his veins, touching her was like touching a live wire. Power so strong rolled off her in waves, made him clamp his teeth against the scream trapped in his throat.

Dizzy with sweat, he gulped in air, trying to keep her steady on her feet. She swayed, blinking huge owl eyes back at him. They were still purple.

"Ewan?" she whimpered. "I'm scared."

"I got ye, Red. Stay with me. Listen to my voice." He patted her cheek, trying to get her to focus. But her head kept lolling side to side.

She was mumbling and he could only catch snatches of it. "…what did I do? Wicked… Dead?"

"Nay, lass," he shook his head. Trying hard to tamp down the stomach churning memory of Kermani broken and bloody, so that he could answer her with a calm, reassuring voice. "He will live." *Maybe*. "Yer nay wicked, Red. Now wake up."

There was clapping and the caw of several thousand birds and Ewan's heart sank to his knees.

"My big black wolf." Malvena's voice was bottomless, insidious. "And so we meet again. I thought you dead." There was a ghostly quality to her voice that was both lyrical and wickedly disturbing.

He shuddered, trying to keep Red firmly tucked within the shelter of his body. She was still mumbling.

Malvena stepped out of the shadows. She wore a robe spun of midnight and stars, it cut along the length of her body, exposing tantalizing bits of naked flesh beneath. Her red hair crackled like the flames of a chimera. Her rose red lips were curved up in a plump, luscious smile.

Crows sat on each shoulder, their beady black eyes drilling holes through Ewan's skull. Malvena petted one of them.

"Is baby hungry?" she cooed.

The crow snapped its beak with a loud thud. Malvena's deep blue eyes glowed with satisfaction.

"Why are ye here?" Ewan snarled, rubbing a soothing hand down Red's cold arm.

Malvena cocked her head. "That is none of your concern. You no longer work for me. Tell me," she ran her long red nail up and down the bird's back, "did you like being Danika's whore?"

His mouth curled.

She touched her breast, the slight curve of it peeking out beneath the robe. "When you could have had all…" She continued trailing her hand slowly down the peekaboo path of skin, down to the vee between her legs, hidden by the flimsiest bit of tassel. "This."

Then her eyes hardened and something dangerous flickered within. "Instead you choose to betray me!" Her voice grew deep, full of tempestuous hate. "Aero. Aria. Go."

The crows shot off her shoulders and she cackled as they bomb dived his head, their sharp beaks slashing at the back of his skull, drawing blood.

Ewan swatted at them, while trying to shield Red's body.

Then there were more. Ten. Twenty. Thirty. He was blinded by a choking cloud of feathers and beaks as blood poured into his eyes.

Red screamed, tiny fingers dug into his chest.

"Oh don't worry," Malvena sneered, "they were only sent to kill you, Ewan. Little Red Riding Hood and I have much to speak of."

Even though the cawing of so many birds nearly deafened him, he'd heard her every word. Chunks of flesh were picked off his body, too many birds to keep up with.

Malvena snapped her fingers, and with one final scream, Red was yanked out from beneath him.

"Violet!" Ewan roared, but there was no answer.

Malvena and Red were gone, all that remained were killer crows.

Chapter 16

One second she was in his arms, terrified, but safe. The next, she was bobbing in water. Teeth chattering, Violet rubbed her arms, coughing and sputtering as salty waves slapped her in the face.

The sky was a dark greenish-yellow and streaked with thick ribbons of clouds.

"The Heartsong. At last we meet."

Startled, Violet twirled. A miniature woman floated above her, broad black butterfly wings flapping languorously behind her. "Malvena," her voice cracked. "Where's Ewan? What have you done to him?"

The fairy flicked her wrist. "Oh nothing that I shouldn't have done ages ago. But tell me," her blue eyes sparkled, "was he as good in the sack as I always thought he'd be? He's got such a hard on for you."

"You're disgusting," Violet said, and then a wave smacked into her. She swallowed the briny water, coughing violently as she tried to expel it from her lungs.

"Oh, please don't tell me you didn't sleep with him." Malvena smirked.

The woman was mad.

Pulse ringing in her ears, spitting sea water out, Violet jerked around desperately trying to spot land, anywhere she could get out. Another long swell lifted her in the air, she stretched her arms, letting the wave drag her up. Where was the land?

"Don't bother," Malvena smiled, "you're in the middle of the Never Sea. There's no land for miles."

Violet opened her mouth.

Malvena tsked. "I wouldn't scream if I were you. You see, the Sea Hag makes her home here and she hasn't eaten in a couple weeks." Malvena laughed and whispered conspiratorially, "I wouldn't disturb her if I were you."

Panic ate at her brain and with the panic came the darkness trapped in her soul. It seeped up through her blood like a slow toxin.

A glint of something malevolent winked back at Violet and then Malvena inhaled, eyes rolling to the back of her head. The rainbow colored mist beginning to escape through Violet's body rolled toward the demonic fairy.

Violet jerked, sucking in a breath as a chill radiated through her bones, feeling as if her soul had just been leeched from her body. She cried out and wiped the back of her nose, a red streak marred the back of her hand.

Malvena clutched her chest and danced, wings flitting happily as she crowed loudly. "So much power."

Tiny fangs drew down from the fairy's mouth.

Her powers wouldn't work on the Black. Couldn't work on her. Malvena could suck her up too; clean her out like a vampire draining their victim's blood. The crone had done it too, but Malvena was much, much stronger.

Sea water stung Violet's eyes, mingled with the tears running down her cheeks.

Vi started to swim, anything was better than staying put and letting herself be eaten alive by the cannibal.

"I told you, swimming is fruitless." The voice no longer sounded feminine. "Come here, girl!"

It was like invisible bands wrapped around Violet's middle and yanked her back to where she'd been. She thrashed, but the bands were unyielding.

"You misunderstand me, Little Hood," Malvena smiled and then licked her lips. The serpentine forked tongue made Violet tremble and her stomach drop to her knees.

"You killed my crone, and made mincemeat of Kermani." She laughed with a sound like the demonic toll of Hell's bells. "You are not the same miserable, pathetic girl I searched for before. You are strong, powerful."

She flitted closer and Violet winced when the tiny claw dragged along her jaw.

"The hate, it burns in you." She inhaled. "You like killing, the taste of power. Embrace it, Violet, for it is our friend."

Violet jerked away, swimming backwards, kicking her feet to get away from the ten inch nightmare. "Why are you telling me this? Where's Ewan?"

Malvena smiled. "You like him," she laughed, "you do know he killed Jana."

"Because she was working for you!" Violet snarled. "She was going to kill me. He saved me."

"He worked for me too, little girl. Or did you not know that part of the story?"

The crux of it, the whole point of her anger toward Ewan, was that right there. He'd been sent to kill her. By Malvena. And he would have done so. Except she was his mate. And from that moment on, he'd done his very best to rectify his misdeeds. A soft smile pulled at her heart and tugged on her lips.

"I know it. I also know he's mine."

"Ohh," Malvena tapped her chin, "you've claimed him too. How very interesting."

Water moved rapidly beneath Violet's feet. She kicked, feeling the rolling balls of waves slap hard against her legs. Glancing down, she frowned at the muddy water.

"Then here's your choice, Red." Malvena held up a finger. "I won't kill you. I'll release you and give you Ewan as your lifelong mate," she rolled her eyes, "and in return all I ask is one itty bitty favor. You won't even miss it. Much." She shrugged.

Violet's heart clenched. "He's alive?"

Malvena nodded. "For now."

A small favor. Violet seriously doubted anything would be small with the Black. This was a devil's deal, she'd be stupid to make it. Everyone knew the devil always lied.

"What?"

"I want your soul." She didn't smile, laugh, or even twitch a brow. Malvena's words were sharp, clear, and unswerving.

Violet slapped her palm over her heart. "My soul? Why? Why do you want me?"

"Oh come, come." Malvena rolled her wrist. "Let's not get all theatrical about this. You don't even need a soul to live. You'll still be immortal, but with none of your wicked powers. And honestly, wouldn't it be a blessing to let go of that evil side of you?"

The way she said it, so calmly, rationally, Violet couldn't help but consider it. She didn't want to be bad. To crave hurting things. What would it be like to live the rest of her life without the darkness inside her?

She licked her lips.

Malvena flitted closer, holding out her tiny hand. "All you have to do is say… yes."

It was so tempting. So, so tempting…

Malvena's full lips curved. "I had a daughter once. She looked a lot like you. Blonde hair, green eyes, with a smattering of freckles along her nose."

Her words were soft, yearning. It made her seem less monstrous, more human. Violet leaned in ever so slightly.

Malvena settled on Violet's shoulder, her insubstantial weight barely felt as she tucked strands of Vi's wet hair behind her ear. Gently patting it into place.

"My reasons are entirely altruistic. I'm simply a mother who wants her daughter back. Can't you understand?"

In that moment, in that second, Violet didn't see a deranged or even evil fairy, she saw something that was grieving. Desperate to make right a wrong. How could she deny her that chance?

"STOP!"

The scream shattered Violet's thoughts, startled, she glanced up. Her Aunt flitted beside another tiny fairy. Miriam was grabbing her chest, heaving for breath. The traveling portal was little more than a sliver of a rift in the brackish sky.

"Get away from us, Shunned!" Malvena's voice was pure malic again, dripping with deadly intentions.

"Danika," Miriam pointed to Violet, her hand trembled, gray wisps of hair frizzed around her head with static power, "stop her."

A pink ball of light zoomed like a rocket toward them. Violet could barely understand anything that was going on. Then the pink ball crashed into Malvena and a scuffle broke out. They were clawing, gouging at each other. Danika's fangs became thick and long.

"She's mine!" Malvena screamed.

Then a tiny set of teeth pierced Violet's neck, breaking through the vein, and started drinking.

It was like being envenomed by a thousand wasps, prodded with ten thousand scorpion tails, and burned alive. Violet screamed as something cold and dark welled up from the pit of her stomach, leeching life and soul from her body.

Then the teeth were ripped out and blood leaked down her breast. Her head swam as the waves that'd calmed while Malvena spoke to her, now raged. Wracked with chills, she could barely move even though the water frothed and bubbled, churning with rage, lathered with fury. All around, it looked like the water bled red. Was she bleeding? Dying? There was so much blood, it was everywhere.

Violet's heart stuttered when a series of undulations rolled just below the surface; a green glint of scales beginning to peek through.

"Aunt Mir," Violet screamed, finally able to find her voice.

Her Aunt's arms were wrapped around her. She was back to normal size, but her skin looked worn, her eyes ragged. "Calm yerself, me love."

"Danika, have you got her?"

Something big and very rough brushed Violet's feet. She lifted her feet, tucking them beneath her bottom, even though the position forced more sea water into her mouth. There was something underneath.

"Help," Danika cried, her wand pointed at Malvena who--though her nose was busted and bloodied--wore a smile. The veins in her neck pulsed and twitched violently. No words escaped her lips, but there was a rigidity in her mummified stance that said she was fighting whatever enchantment Danika had thrown at her.

"I'm too weak," Danika said, arm trembling.

Aunt Mir withdrew her wand, a pink bolt of energy sang from its tip and Malvena's back arced, the robes were the only things that moved.

"This won't hold her long," Miriam cried.

"What are you doing?" Violet gasped as Malvena's eyes began to bulge from their sockets.

Aunt Mir was sweating, her nostrils flared tight. "We've bound her, but it won't last long. You must kill her, Violet."

Just then the beast that'd been thrashing the waters broke free. All Violet saw was a dog's face with tusks the lengths of her arms.

"Bloody damn!" Danika sputtered. "We can't stay here, Mir."

"I can hold her long enough for you to open the portal," Miriam cried, a shiny drop of blood dripped from her nose.

Aunt Miriam cried out when Danika moved to flick her wrist and open a portal. The dog faced hag swooped in, razor teeth grinding maliciously, its fetid breath bathing Violet's face when she was yanked by her collar through the portal. Taken to only the gods knew where.

Where was Ewan?

Chapter 17

His mouth was full of feathers and gore, his breathing was harsh and ragged. Ewan stood in the center of a pile of dead crows. Small black eyes unblinking, beaks opened, some with dangling bits of fur and flesh still in them.

He'd kill one and two more would take its place. Pecking, gouging, and tearing at him. His fur was matted with blood, mostly his own. One of the beaks had nearly pierced through to his lungs.

A soft wuffing sound happened whenever he exhaled. His muscles spasmed with each painful step he took. Blood clouded his vision, he licked his muzzle, but the thick liquid only ran harder when he broke up the clots.

Where had Malvena taken her? They could be anywhere. Anywhere. Dead crows littered his feet, Ewan threw back his head and howled. There was no scent, no trace of them.

Long he called, voice rolling up and down in a haunting melody of anguish and sorrow. But there was no answer. The woods were pregnant with silence, thick with secrets.

Calling the *unbecoming*, he grit his teeth through the transformation, grunting when his bones popped and snapped back to human proportions. Panting, covered in sweat and his own gore, he dropped to his knees. Black hair covered his face as he tried to remember the stories his sire had told him long ago.

His father had never talked much with Ewan, an absent father most of the time, a drunkard the rest. But once he'd overhead him while thick in his cups, swearing that his bitch whore could never screw the neighbor's runt again now that he'd marked her.

Ewan had hidden within deep shadow inside the den, trembling when his father had yanked his mother by her hair, dragging her out and laughing in her terrified face that she now bore *his* mark and she could never run off again without him knowing about it. He'd never seen his mother again after that, his father had become little more than a ghost passing in and out of his life, leaving a seven year old Ewan to care for his three younger siblings.

Ewan had marked Red.

But he didn't know how to track her, always relying on his smell, but there was none to find here. Malvena had covered all traces.

Ewan gripped his skull, tugging his hair and gnashing his teeth.

"Red," he croaked, "where are ye, lass?"

The wind stirred leaves, whispered through feathers of the dead carcasses at his feet. His body ached, screamed whenever he twitched. But he held still and tried to focus on something other than the frenetic beat of his wild heart.

"Red." He squeezed his eyes shut harder, colorful lights danced behind closed lids. "Answer me."

This time when the zephyr brushed against his nude back, a violent *bump bump* followed in its wake. His spine stiffened.

Bump. Bump.

He snapped his eyes open.

Bump. Bump.

It was like a fist knocking at the wall of his chest.

Bump. Bump. Bumpbumpbump...

He ran, following the sound of her rapidly beating heart.

Bumpbumpbumpbump. Ewanewanewan... Ewan.

"I'm coming, Red," he roared, letting the sound fill his head, his lungs, his heart, and soul. Tree limbs tore at his already ravaged flesh, but he didn't dare stop.

He couldn't smell her. But he felt her. Warmth and sunshine; her violence and mayhem. She was *HIS*, his women, all of her. Her violence, her pleasure and pain.

His vision narrowed down to a pinprick, dodging trees the best he could, covering his eyes when he couldn't avoid a slapping branch. Running faster, panting desperately for air around the fire ripping through his chest.

Rocks tore up the soles of his feet. He slipped on the blood, forced to run up the hill with both hands and feet. Nails splitting as he clawed his way up.

Ewanewanewanewanewan....

The moment he crested the hill he heard her everywhere.

Ewan. Ewan. Ewan.

He stopped, grasping onto his aching side, lungs heaving as he twirled. Everything was dark and black. Ewan wiped the stinging wetness out of his eyes, the salt left a bitter sting behind.

"Red!" he roared, brogue so thick it sounded more like riyad.

Then a flash of bright pink energy sparked like a firework's display above the enormous tree lines a hundred yards ahead.

One breath in. A deep breath out.

In and out.

Arms pumping.

Leg muscles flopping like a dying fish out of water. He tripped on a stone, rolling down the hill the rest of the way. Barely registering the fresh cuts and scrapes as he forced his battered body to stand up. He tried to run, but could barely do more than hobble. Adrenaline was the only thing he ran on now.

"Ewan! Come quickly. Come." It was Danika's voice. "She needs you, boy. Come."

He broke through the trees, following the grunts and groans and the impossible to miss stench of brimstone. That noxious, sulfurous odor that leaked from Red's pores when in a killing trance.

At first it was only shadows on a ground, but then he got closer and horror gripped his spine in an icy fist.

Malvena was bound, her body thrashing as Red kneeled on top of her. Black iridescence pulsed from Malvena's body and Red cried as the black light turned to flames around her.

***

Violet was trapped, unable to break free of the contact as Malvena's powers siphoned into her. Each vaporous inhale was a blade, ripped her up from the inside.

It was too much. Too much pain. Too much power. Her skin felt like it would rip off her body, she was bloated with darkness, on the verge of an explosion, and still her greedy soul inhaled.

She couldn't stop.

Couldn't stop.

Aunt Mir had knocked Malvena out with a direct bolt of power to her temple, then she'd told Violet to open her mouth.

She convulsed.

"Take it in, Vi, all of it," Aunt Mir's words were small, and the pain was so, so large.

Violet willed her body to stop. To close her mouth. Told her brain no more. But she was so hungry. So hungry.

Jerking, fingers digging like claws into Malvena's tiny shoulders, Violet drank and drank. That dark soul twisted in her gut, churned through her bowels.

Malvena stopped jerking. Her once lovely face now contorted into a wordless scream.

Hands shook Violet.

"Stop...ple..."

Something hot and wet seeped from her nose and ears.

"Nay, stop..." A deep burr, a desperate growl.

Ewan.

For a moment joy replaced the fear. With one final pull, Violet inhaled the last of the dark fairies soul. A mummy stared back at her, desiccated skin covered a tiny pile of bones, then erupted in a giant tower of flame. Fire licked at Violet's face, but she didn't pull back, even as she sizzled and burned.

She was going to die.

The madness, the darkness, it spread insidiously to her head, through her veins, down her legs. She screamed. Clawing at her skin to relieve the sensation of a million ants biting, before it drove her mad.

"Get it out," she cried, doubled over as the agony of a bloated belly ready to rupture, drove her to pound her fists on the ground.

Smoke began to billow from her fingers, out her nose. Her insides quaked, churned like a pot of boiling stew. Eyes burning, she racked her fingers down her face.

She pleaded, begged, not knowing what words came out of her mouth. Then large hands gripped the corners of her face and a pair of lips slammed down on hers. She screamed her agony into its mouth, shoving the alien power down, down, down.

Clutching tight to a savaged back, she sunk her nails in while the violence poured out. The agony turned to relief as the twisted soul transferred out of her body.

"Red." The voice was gentle, so soft. More a breath of sound.

Ewan. She trembled, he'd found her. Saved her. *Love you. Love you so much*, she thought over and over even as she poured more and more death into him.

She didn't notice his tight hands growing slack on her waist, letting Malvena go felt so good. She could breathe again, see again. Violet opened her eyes and stared into a sunken pair of golden ones.

Finally noticing how lax his mouth was on hers, she jerked back. The corners of his eyes were sliced open, bloody tears tracked down the sides of his nose. He was a mass of bruises and cuts. Purple skin mottled the bronze.

"Ewan," she cried when he collapsed on top of her.

She barely had enough strength to brace his heavy weight.

"He's fine, Vi," Aunt Mir's stern voice filled with compassion. "Ye did well, and so did he."

"He's dying," Violet cried, running her fingers through his matted hair, remembering the agony of being filled with that level of malevolence and power.

"Nay, girl," Aunt Mir's large blue eyes blinked solemnly back at her. "Nay. He's a wolf. His body will expel her poison."

Ewan's forehead was wet, and with more than just sweat. A strange oily residue coated her fingers. He was shaking, teeth grinding as his back arced and muscles jerked.

Violet held onto him, grateful beyond words for what he'd done, praying to the gods Aunt Mir was right and the poison would leave his body. She kissed his clammy cheek, his forehead, and nose. Uncaring that he tasted bitter, or that a hint of what'd possessed her, now leaked through him. She wanted him to know she was here, just as he'd been for her.

A strange gurgling sound rumbled from his gut, and then he moaned. Knowing what was coming, Violet turned his face.

Ewan shuddered, retching over and over and over. It seemed impossible that he could spew up so much, but it just kept coming--a steady stream of sparkling black substance.

Tears blinded her vision.

"He's okay, Violet." The one named Danika patted her arm gently. "He'll live."

She sniffed, and nodded. "I know, it's just…"

Danika's blue eyes were kind, her face motherly. So different from the cruel mask she'd worn when grappling with Malvena. "He still loves you."

A choking sob gripped her, and she shuddered through her tears as he continued to release all of the Black's power.

She'd put him through so much, tried to kill him, herself. Why would he ever care for her? How could he? She couldn't have. In fact, she'd hated him for decades, each day letting the hatred fester and boil into a wound so deep, she'd refused to listen. Almost killing any chance she'd ever had at happiness.

Violet was a bad person. Who would want to love that?

She stroked his sweaty forehead. "I'm so sorry, Ewan. I believe you. I trust you. I'm sorry I couldn't say it before. But you have to be okay. You have to… Because I… I want to know you. I want to mate you too."

Finally he stopped. Taking deep cleansing breaths before, with a loud moan, he turned to glance at her. A crooked smile curved his cracked lips. "I'd do it again, to hear ye say that."

She smiled and nuzzled the top of his head. "It's true."

"Well, alls well that ends well. Is it not, Mir?" Danika's voice was light, happy.

Violet smiled and Ewan nodded. "Thank the gods," they said in unison.

Ewan low crawled away from the glistening puddle that'd now began to froth like a witch's brew.

Miriam stood silent, a sad smile on her face. Her hair was now fully white, her skin so aged it immediately sent a chill down Violet's spine. She'd been so worried with seeing to Ewan, she hadn't noticed her Aunt.

"Aunt Mir?" She stood on shaky legs. "What's happened to you?"

Ewan's strong warm hands clamped down on Violet's shoulder. She leaned into him, comforted by his solid presence.

Danika gasped. "Miriam."

Miriam fell to her knees, her head hung low and her entire frame seemed to literally wither before their eyes. In the span of seconds she was aging rapidly, skin turning spotted and livered. Clumps of hair began to fall in patches. She turned bloodshot eyes toward Danika.

Danika fell to her knees, her wand was in her hand and she blasted a pink bolt at Miriam's head. "Return to what you once were," she said in a voice that shook.

Mir chuckled, the sound ancient and threaded through with feebleness. "It's okay, Dani. Truly, sister."

Fat tears dripped from Danika's nose. Violet's throat seized up, and a sound like an animal dying wailed from her throat. Ewan grabbed her, pulling her to his bloodied chest, crooning softly in her ears.

Danika pulled Miriam's head to her bosom, rocking back and forth.

"What have you done, Mir? What have you done? You said you were strong enough to hold her? You said--"

"Ssh. Donna fash yerself," Aunt Mir closed her eyes, "it wasn't just this, sister. I'm tired. For centuries I battled time outside our realm, keeping Malvena contained was simply the straw, Dani."

"But you said we'd hide, we'd travel--"

"No, sister," Aunt Mir's voice was reed thin, a barely there whisper, "ye did." She touched Danika's cheek. "The roses, Dani, remember the roses."

"What?" Danika was sobbing now, large waterworks fell down her face. She sniffled, wiping her nose.

Ewan's soothing up and down motion on Violet's back grounded her, kept her sane in a world that felt like it was beginning to unravel around her.

"Grab my hand tight, now," Aunt Mir said, urgency lent her weak voice strength.

Danika held on, and then she gasped when the black bolt of Malvena's power headed like a missile straight towards them.

It whistled past Violet's ears, she shivered at its passing.

The Black power was headed for Danika's wide blue eyes. The Black was one of the *Ten*, the power could never fully be killed or contained. It needed a host and would not be denied.

With trembling fingers, Aunt Miriam pulled her wand from her pocket and touched the tip of one of Danika's knuckles just as the black bolt met her face. A wash of pink energy exited the tip of Miriam's wand.

"To me," Miriam wheezed, and then the power flowed like a conduit from Danika into her. Miriam cried out, smiling as the energy filled her skin, making her glow from the inside out with differing shades of black and pearl.

Suddenly her hair began to regrow, turning a deep luscious mahogany as a rosy flush filled her cheeks. Her skin firmed up and with a happy sigh, Aunt Mir opened beautiful lavender eyes.

"Mir!" Danika cried, wrapping her up in her arms. "I thought you were dying. Oh, blessed be, sister. Blessed be."

Aunt Miriam smiled and Violet sobbed, but this time with relief.

"You're one of the *Ten* now, of course. It all makes sense. Galeta can never force you into bondage. How foolish I was... how--"

Miriam hushed Danika with a swift shake of her head. "Nay, sister. I'm here but for a short time."

"But, Aunt Mir, how can you say that?" Violet interjected, her heart returning to its normal rhythm. Safe in Ewan's arms. "You're so healthy and perfect."

Ewan's Adam's apple bobbed along the top of her head when his deep voice cut in. "Because the Black corrupts all it touches, Red." There was a tenderness to his words, like he was trying to break it to her easy.

Aunt Mir's lips quirked. "Aye."

"Wha?" Violet glanced from his face to hers and back again.

But finally she saw what her joy hadn't registered before; black had begun to bleed through Aunt Mir's eyes, overtaking the lovely lavender.

"In three or four centuries," Aunt Miriam said, "I'll be worse than Malvena. The power grows worse, never better. It doesn't matter that my heart is pure now, hers was too. Once. There's only one way to contain the Black."

"I won't kill you!" Danika shouted, her eyes were bloodshot, her lips trembled.

"I donna want ye too, sister. I knew when I choose this path all those moons ago, that this was where I'd end up." She touched the tip of her wand to her chest, the power flowing out of it was black as shadow now. "I've chosen my path."

"No, Mir. No." Danika shook her head, grasping onto her Aunt's shoulders.

"We won, Dani. We kept my girl safe. It's over now. I'm so tired, could ye deny me the rest?"

Danika bit her lip and Violet buried her nose in Ewan's chest. She couldn't look, couldn't face whatever was about to happen.

"No, Mir, I can't." Danika's soft words tickled Violet's ears.

"Aunt Mir," Violet whispered.

Eyes, nearly entirely black, glanced at her kindly. Her Aunt looked so young, so beautiful. As she'd remembered her in the beginning. Her Aunt had held her when she cried at night, read to her when storms raged beyond their home, cooked, cleaned… loved her.

"I love you." She didn't say the words so much as breathe them from the depths of her heart.

Aunt Miriam nodded, a serene smile graced plump pink lips.

Heart shattering, Violet squeezed her eyes shut, wishing she could crawl inside Ewan's skin, nestle always in the warmth of his body. Forget this night, the look of acceptance in her Aunt's eyes. Her Aunt had a stubborn streak, she might seem meek and mild, but when Miriam set her mind to something, she'd never veered off her course.

Violet hiccupped, gulping down the hot ball in her throat.

"Ssh, Red," Ewan crooned, his hand trailing fire and goose bumps along her skin. Over and over his hand ran up and down, down and up.

Violet lost herself in the hypnotic rhythm. Ignoring the bright flare of light behind her lids. She wouldn't look. Couldn't see what her Aunt had done to herself.

"Oh, Mir," Danika sniffed. "My sister, my sister."

"It is done, Red." Ewan's warm breath caressed the side of her neck.

Terrified, she took a deep breath, and like ripping off a band-aid, looked.

Danika was kneeling, murmuring softly to the earth.

"Where did she go?" Violet pleaded, glancing around, desperate to see her Aunt. But there wasn't a trace of her in the trees. She'd gone, vanished.

Ewan led her toward a softly crying Danika.

Violet frowned, glancing at him, a question on her tongue, when she noticed Danika gently cradling a black seedling. Its long stem swayed in the gentle breeze.

Danika looked at her. "The roses, now I know what she meant."

Reaching out a hand, Violet silently asked to hold the seedling. With a trembling shudder, Danika passed it--almost reverently--to her.

Violet ran her finger along the smooth stem.

"The tree is a giver of life. Though full of dark magic, its wooden heart will always remain pure," Ewan whispered.

Danika knuckled tears from her eyes. "Miriam did know how to contain the Black's soul. Her sacrifice will not be in vain. I will plant her in the roses. It's what she wanted."

Violet wasn't sure, but when she closed her eyes, it felt like her Aunt's voice filled her head with a bell like strain and the words: *I love you too*.

Chapter 18

Violet ran, bare feet kicking up stones. Her heart pounded. Snow fell in thick clusters. She couldn't escape him. He was so close.

Then she heard him.

He was running, panting.

"No," she yelped, and then he was on her, tackling her to the ground.

White light exploded off his body like flames, then Ewan was kissing her face, her nose, her chin. Growling as his hard erection drove into her thigh.

"I won," he snarled, voice more beast than man, and he nipped her chin.

She laughed, blood singing, adrenaline pumping. "No fair. I told you to give me a ten second head start."

Golden eyes glowed in the deep twilight. "I lied."

"Oh, who cares," she moaned, desire coiling down her stomach, making her toes curl.

His body was warm, like a thermal blanket, heating her even as the snow drifted lazily around them.

It'd been a year since that night, a year of laughs, sadness, and hope. Hope because Violet knew she was more than the darkness inside her. Ewan had showed her. Loved her.

"I adore ye, Red," he whispered in between trailing hot kisses along her throat.

She thrust her hips up, excited by the friction of his skin rubbing along hers. Wet and ready, she moaned.

"I love you too, Ewan. Always."

She bit him, just like he liked it. Marking the spot above his heart with her teeth. He hissed, and thrust harder.

"You're mine. All mine," she said, pressing a kiss against the bite.

He tugged on her nipple, and she arced, gently scraping her nails on his head.

Desire flooded her, made her moan and groan. Her nails pierced the sensitive skin of his skull.

He growled, white teeth bright in the liquid moonlight.

She traced the curve of his lips. "My, what big teeth you have."

Ewan snapped them at her. "The better to eat ye with, my dear."

Violet laughed, a sound of pure unadulterated joy. "Then what are you waiting for? Need you now," she mumbled, dizzy with pleasure.

"Mmm, like this," he rumbled, deep voice a hot caress against her breasts.

Then his hot hard length slipped inside and Violet rocked on him, riding the spiraling staircase that would take her beyond the here, above the clouds.

"Forever," he whispered.

And that's just how she wanted it. In his arms, making love… forever.

Epilogue

Danika touched the large oak tree. A thicket of roses surrounded its gnarled black base. Galeta had been furious that Miriam had outwitted her. But it was a victory Danika could not rejoice in.

It was a wound to know her friend was lost to her forever. All that remained was a gnarled old oak.

"Thank you, Mir. Thank you for loving like you do, for protecting that girl. Ewan is madly in love and Violet feels the same. I planted more roses last week. Not sure if you noticed." She sniffed. "They're blacks, I thought they were appropriate."

She sighed, glancing at the wild abundance of roses. Every night since planting her best friend within the small rose garden, she'd returned and planted one new rose. There were whites, reds, yellows, orange, pinks, creams… an explosion of color that she knew Mir would have wanted.

"I love you, sister. I'll never forget. But I must return to the mortal realm, Jinni's mate is in trouble. I know all will be well, but…" Danika stuttered as the fresh pain lanced through her heart. "I must go, dear. I'll be back tomorrow."

She stood, dusted off her spider silk skirt, and grabbed her pouch of fairy dust. Sprinkling the gold flecks liberally on the garden.

The roses swiveled, blinking rose colored eyes gratefully back at her. They never talked here, as if they knew that were rooted on sacred ground.

"You're welcome," she murmured to them, then patted the tree one last time.

Heat infused her palm and in her heart, she knew Miriam had thanked her too.

A word from the Author:

Marie Hall has always had a dangerous fascination for creatures that go bump in the night. And mermaids. And of course fairies. Trolls. Unicorns. Shapeshifters. Vampires. Scottish brogues. Kilts. Beefy arms. Ummm... Bad boys! Especially the sexy ones.

On top of that she's a confirmed foodie, she nearly went to culinary school and then figured out she could save a ton of money if she just watched food shows religiously! She's a self-proclaimed master chef, certified deep sea dolphin trainer, finder of leprechaun's gold at the end of the rainbow, and rumor has it she keeps the Troll King locked away in her basement. All of which is untrue (except for the food shows!), however, she does have an incredibly active imagination and loves to share her crazy thoughts with the world!

If you want to see what new creations she's got up her sleeves check out her blog:

www.MarieHallWrites.blogspot.com.

Also, if you loved this story please leave a review, reviews make her very, very happy!

Stay tuned after the recipes for a special sneak peek of Jinni's Wish: Kingdom Book 4, due December of 2012.

Cheshire's So Ono Poke:

Ingredients

- 4-ounce ahi, diced (Hawaiian tuna)
- 1/8-ounce chives, chopped
- 1/4-ounce ginger, finely chopped
- 1/8 teaspoon Hawaiian chili pepper
- 1/2 teaspoon chopped ogo (fresh seaweed, if you can find it, if not dry will do, but not too much or you'll taste nothing but seaweed)
- 1/2-ounce sesame oil, for taste
- Hawaiian alae (red sea salt)

Directions

Cut Ahi into small cubes and mix all the ingredients together. Serves 4.

Hansel and Gretel's Gingerbread Cookies:

(Tastes Best When Served by a Witch!)

The dough must be chilled for at least three hours and up to two days. The cookies can be prepared up to one week ahead, stored in an airtight container at room temperature. When the dough is rolled thin, it will bake crisp and almost cracker-like. Yet, when rolled thick, the cookies turn out plump and moist. In either case, the flavor will be complex and almost hot-spicy.

Ingredients

- 3 cups all-purpose flour
- 1 teaspoon baking soda
- 3/4 teaspoon ground cinnamon
- 3/4 teaspoon ground ginger
- 1/2 teaspoon ground allspice
- 1/2 teaspoon ground cloves
- 1/2 teaspoon salt
- 1/4 teaspoon freshly milled black pepper
- 8 tablespoons (1 stick) unsalted butter, at room temperature
- 1/4 cup vegetable shortening, at room temperature
- 1/2 cup packed light brown sugar
- 2/3 cup unsulfured molasses
- 1 large egg
- Royal Icing (recipe follows)

Directions

Position the racks in the top and bottom thirds of the oven and preheat to 350 degrees F.

Sift the flour, baking soda, cinnamon, ginger, allspice, cloves, salt and pepper through a wire sieve into a medium bowl. Set aside.

In a large bowl, using a hand-held electric mixer at high speed, beat the butter and vegetable shortening until well-combined, about 1 minute. Add the brown sugar and beat until the mixture is light in texture and color, about 2 minutes. Beat in the molasses and egg. Using a wooden spoon, gradually mix in the flour mixture to make a stiff dough. Divide the dough into two thick disks and wrap each disk in plastic wrap. Refrigerate until chilled, about 3 hours. (The dough can be prepared up to 2 days ahead.)

To roll out the cookies, work with one disk at a time, keeping the other disk refrigerated. Remove the dough from the refrigerator and let stand at room temperature until just warm enough to roll out without cracking, about 10 minutes. (If the dough has been chilled for longer than 3 hours, it may need a few more minutes.) Place the dough on a lightly floured work surface and sprinkle the top of the dough with flour. Roll out the dough 1/8 inch thick, being sure that the dough isn't sticking to the work surface (run a long meal spatula or knife under the dough occasionally just to be sure, and dust the surface with more flour, if needed). For softer cookies, roll out slightly thicker. Using cookie cutters, cut out the cookies and transfer to nonstick cookie sheets, placing the cookies 1 inch apart. Gently knead the scraps together and form into another disk. Wrap and chill for 5 minutes before rolling out again to cut out more cookies.

Bake, switching the positions of the cookies from top to bottom and back to front halfway through baking, until the edges of the cookies are set and crisp, 10 to 12 minutes. Cool on the sheets for 2 minutes, then transfer to wire cake racks to cool completely. Decorate with Royal Icing. (The cookies can be prepared up to 1 week ahead, stored in airtight containers at room temperature.)

- ROYAL ICING
-
- 1 pound (4 1/2 cups) confectioners' sugar
- 2 tablespoons dried egg-white powder
- 6 tablespoons water

Make ahead: The icing can prepared up to 2 days ahead, stored in an airtight container with a moist paper towel pressed directly on the icing surface, and refrigerated.

This icing hardens into shiny white lines, and is used for piping decorations on gingerbread people or other cookies. Traditional royal icing uses raw egg whites, but I prefer dried egg-white powder, available at most supermarkets, to avoid any concern about uncooked egg whites.

When using a pastry bag, practice your decorating skills before you ice the cookies. Just do a few trial runs to get the feel of the icing and the bag, piping the icing onto aluminum foil or wax paper. If you work quickly, you can use a metal spatula to scrape the test icing back into the batch.

Dried egg-white powder is also available by mail order from The Baker's Catalogue, 1-800-827-6836. Meringue powder, which is dehydrated egg whites with sugar already added, also makes excellent royal icing; just follow the directions on the package. However, the plain unsweetened dried egg whites are more versatile, as they can be used in savory dishes, too. Meringue powder is available from Adventures in Cooking (1-800-305-1114) and The Baker's Catalogue.

In a medium bowl, using a hand-held electric mixer at low speed, beat the confectioners' sugar, egg-white powder and water until combined. Increase the speed to high and beat, scraping down the sides of the bowl often, until very stiff, shiny and thick enough to pipe; 3 to 5 minutes. (The icing can be prepared up to 2 days ahead, stored in an airtight container with a moist paper towel pressed directly on the icing surface, and refrigerated.)

To pipe line decorations, use a <u>pastry bag</u> fitted with a tube with a small writing tip about 1/8-inch wide, such as Ateco No. 7; it may be too difficult to squeeze the icing out of smaller tips. If necessary, thin the icing with a little warm water. To fill the pastry bag, fit it with the tube. Fold the top of the bag back to form a cuff and hold it in one hand. (Or, place the bag in a tall glass and fold the top back to form a cuff.) Using a rubber <u>spatula</u>, scoop the icing into the bag. Unfold the cuff and twist the top of the bag closed. Squeeze the icing down to fill the tube. Always practice first on a sheet of wax paper or aluminum foil to check the flow and consistency of the icing.

Traditional Royal Icing: Substitute 3 large egg whites for the powder and water.

Sneak Peek: Jinni's Wish

Chapter 1

"What kind of name is that?" Paz Lopez hopped on one bare foot, while simultaneously gripping the cell phone with her chin as she attempted to slip her blood red pump on; very nearly breaking her neck in the process when she stumbled over the corner of her cream shag rug. "Dang it," she hissed.

She could already picture Richard rolling his eyes on the other end of the line. "Diabolique."

This time, she was the one to roll her eyes. Plopping down on the edge of her unmade bed, doing what her father used to always say: *work smarter, not harder*. So much easier to put shoes on when sitting, instead of hopping around like a broken jack in the box.

"I heard you the first time. But that doesn't sound like any kind of carnival I'd want to visit. Sounds creepy."

"Aww, come on, chicken. Todd and I are going and it's sorta lame that all you ever want to do on a Friday night is vegg in front of that dinosaur you call a t.v. and down 2.2 glasses of vino."

She loved her brother, she really did. But ugh… she rubbed her nose, stomach churning with nerves and irritation. Now was so not the time to be talking about carnivals, or whatever the hell this Diabolique place was. She had an art show in an hour, today was her make it or break it day. It'd taken months for the hottest gallery in town: *Moderne*, to even agree to potentially hosting an exhibit for her.

Of course they hadn't. She was too new. But she had a friend, who knew a friend, who knew a guy who had an exhibit scheduled and was in need of ten more paintings to fill the space. Fast forward several boxes of tissues, lots of chocolate, and probably two (okay three) bottles of champagne later, Paz was here. Ready to break out. Become a name. Finally.

If only her stupid nerves would settle down and stop making her feel like she was totally going to puke all over her pearl gray goose down comforter. Pinching her nose, she counted slowly to ten. But only got to three before Richard starting acting obnoxious as usual.

"I know you're there. I hear you breathing." He proceeded to pantomime harsh deep breaths. "Answer me, or I will stalk you. I know where you liiiiveee."

Giggling, she yanked her purple head pillow off the bed and shoved it against her stomach. Maybe pressure would ease the knee knocking nerves. "You're really annoying."

He snorted. "Yeah, well Todd loves it. So tell me you're coming."

Paz shoved about a week's worth of bras underneath her bed and lifted the teal shirt off the lampshade she'd tossed aside carelessly last night. Jeez, she was really a slob. Maybe when she got filthy stinking rich she could afford a maid.

"Are you coming to my show?" She plucked at her bejeweled skirt. Her first and only attempt at making clothes. Skirts were supposedly so easy to make.

Lie.

She'd had to undo the stitching four times before she felt certain she wouldn't zip it up and have a wardrobe malfunction. Namely having the stupid thing fall down around her ankles when she stepped off her elevator into the lobby of her swank Chicago digs.

Though swank was sorta stretching it. She wasn't sure the 500 square foot broom closet she currently called home could ever be considered swank, but she had a great address in the hippest part of town and with any luck, she'd be moving to that penthouse suite after tonight.

"We wouldn't miss it." His voice was warm, reassuring, and Paz couldn't help but smile. She loved her brother. "But Todd told me to ask you now, because we both know how you get when you're talking about your art."

"No I don't." She tossed the pillow away, fiddling with the large cream flower on her black cable knit sweater.

"Pfft. I didn't even have to tell you how you act and you're already defending it. So answer, sis. I'm not growing any younger."

"Fine." She stood, grabbing her purse and wallet off her green distressed thrift store night stand. "I'll go butt face. But I won't promise to like it, so there."

"You don't have to like it, but you do have to visit Madam Pandora's tent with me. Bye!"

"What?" Her brows dipped, but all she heard was the buzz of an empty line.

Rolling her eyes, she patted her flat blunt bangs and took a deep breath, ready to face her future. Her stomach nosedived. Well, unless she had to puke first.

***

The Chicago fairgrounds were magical at night. Neon lights lit up the park like a fireworks display. Crowds clamored from one red and white pinstriped tent to the next. Buttery scent of popcorn wafted in the air, tickling her nose.

"Mmm, I'm hungry," Paz groaned when her stomach growled.

Todd's expressive light brown eyes twinkled merrily as he hugged her against his broad chest. A good foot taller than her, with chestnut brown hair, and tanned good looks. Gorgeous and so her type, if it wasn't for the fact that he was totally off the market.

"On me then," he said, voice light and carefree. "A treat for my favorite artist…"

Richard gripped Todd's waist, dark brown eyes glowing merrily, rich mocha skin gleaming shades of bronze beneath the neon glow of the Ferris Wheel. Perpetual black cowlick shading the corner of his left eye. "The only artist you know," he finished, digging into Todd's chest.

Todd clamped onto Richard's hand and kissed the knuckle. A look passing between them that made Paz's knees turn to jelly. What would it feel like to have someone look at her that way? Not that she was old, only 27, but still, long enough to crave what she'd never known.

There'd been passion, maybe some toe curling moments with past boyfriends, but nothing that had ever stuck beyond month six. Maybe she was cursed.

But she'd sold all ten of her paintings. She smiled, biting her bottom lip… well on her way toward that maid she'd always dreamed of. So maybe not that cursed.

"Okay, I'm so gonna barf if you guys keep looking at each other like that."

Todd smirked, patting her head like she was a dog.

So not cool.

She gave him the evil eye. "Not a dog, Todd. Go get me my popcorn," she clapped her hands, "and make it a large. With butter. Momma's got a serious hankering from some greasy fat tonight."

Todd saluted and winked. "Anything for you, baby?"

Richard shrugged. "Trying to watch my carbs. Whatever you have I'll share." Then he sighed, a silly mopey I'm-so-incredibly-happy kind of sound and again Paz couldn't help feeling like the third wheel.

"I love him," Richard whispered, like he wasn't even really saying it to her.

She nodded, tucking his cowlick back. "I know. Aren't you sure you'd rather me, yanno, be home and stuff tonight? I mean, this is your one year anniversary. Why in the world would you want me here? Shouldn't you be bow-chica-wow…"

Richard tugged on the end of her thick black hair.

"Hey, ouch!" Paz slapped his hand away.

"You're disgusting. And no. He loves you as much as I do. Besides, Madam Pandora's awaits."

A cool rush brushed against Paz's legs. She was wearing thick stockings, and had traded in the killer pumps for a more ankle friendly pair of sparkling silver flats, but she probably should have grabbed a thicker jacket.

Even with the sweater underneath, she was still starting to shiver.

She grumped. "Why do you want me to go there so bad? What is it anyway?"

Glancing around, Paz frowned. The carnival was definitely as creepy as she'd expected it to be from the sound of the name. Diabolique, made her think of devil. Coming from a strict Catholic upbringing, anything to do with Mr. Red, Bad, and Evil still made her skin get the creepy crawlies.

Not to mention the carnival was just strange looking. Aside from the garish striped tents, and neon lights, the rides were all black. Thick, dark black. Blending into shadow if not for the lights affixed to the rides.

At first she'd had a mini heart attack when they'd bought their tickets, thinking maybe this night wouldn't suck so hard after all. The man selling them behind the booth had been hot. No scratch that, he was way hotter than hot. Which sounded really lame, but how else could she describe the panty melting smile of his straight white teeth. The artfully arranged blond surfer hair, like liquid gold the way it'd gleamed beneath the light. And his face, oh man… she couldn't paint something so pretty. High cheekbones and hard square jaw, dimples when he'd grinned.

But then she'd looked at his eyes--glowing green eyes--and something inside her had shrunk away from letting him touch her when he'd handed her the change. She'd been pretty sure those hadn't been contacts.

And what was even weirder about this carnival was that everyone one looked just like him. Well, not *just* like him. But everyone working here was hot. Uber, smokin', 'I'd sell my firstborn to have wild monkey sex with you' kind of hot. And they all had strange glowing eyes.

Which seemed to phase Todd and her brother not at all.

"Hello!" Richard snapped his fingers, making her jerk. "Did you hear a word I said?"

She grimaced. "Umm…"

He gripped his forehead. "That's a no. I said," he stressed the 'd', "that I want you to go because Brody and Luke came here last night and they said they got their fortunes told and it came true."

Paz snorted. "Oh my gosh, that's ridiculous. You do know that's stupid, right?

They're all quacks out here."

He looked hurt, and then annoyed. Richard shoved his hands into his jean pockets. "You're coming and I don't want to hear boo about it."

"Boo about what?" Todd planted a peck on Richard's cheek.

The effect was instantaneous. Richard smiled, leaning back into Todd's large chest.

"Mmm, popcorn." Paz reached with greedy fingers for the steaming brown paper sack Todd handed her. "Yummy, yummy, yummy. Love," she plopped a warm, buttery kernel in her mouth and groaned, "love, love, popcorn."

Richard grabbed one out of her bag and tossed it at her nose. She swatted at it.

"And you say I'm weird. At least I've never written an ode to my food before."

She stuck out her tongue.

"So are we going?" Todd asked, taking a bite out of his fried twinkie.

White cream oozed out the side and Richard moaned. "Fried twinkie, Todd? Cruel."

Todd laughed.

Richard rolled his eyes. "My baby sister insists Madam Pandora is a quack."

"You know what," Todd said, and then took another bite, Richard swallowed hard, brown eyes wide as he stared at that twinkie like it was his lover.

Paz knew her brother was drooling, twinkies were his kryptonite. Todd was cruel. Which was probably why she loved him so much, he made her brother suffer. As he should.

"I totally thought so too, but then when Luke told me what she said, you can't fake that."

Wrinkling her nose, Paz nibbled on a piece of popcorn. That'd gotten her attention. "What happened?"

Growling, Richard stole the last bite of twinkie from Todd's fingers and popped into his mouth with a so-there look.

Smirking, Todd licked his lips. "She told him that he'd forgotten to pay his electric bill and that when they got home the power would be off."

Snorting, feeling pieces of kernel jam in her throat, Paz coughed and then chuckled, wheezing around the bits still caught in there. So lame, she'd expected maybe Madam Quack would have said they'd be struck by lightning, or their dog would be run over. Electric bill? Get serious. She wiped tears from her eyes, ghost of a laugh still on her tongue. "Duh, she works for the power company after hours. Totally doable."

Richard rolled his eyes. "Paz, I came to your art show. Now you're coming with us."

Shoulders slumping, she licked the buttery goodness off her tongue. "Richard, seriously, that sounds so lame and I don't want to blow ten bucks on something like that."

Todd and Richard shared a glance. A wordless conversation passing between them that always made her both jealous and happy. She wanted that so bad, it was a desperate yearning in the pit of her gut, the depths of her heart. But she couldn't deny how happy it made her to know her brother now had it. He deserved it. Though she'd die before ever telling him that.

"We'll pay," they said at the same time.

One dark hand and one light hand gripped her elbows, steering her (willing or not) toward Madam Quack's tent.

"Ugh," she groaned.

Ten minutes later she was staring into the deep lavender eyes of the most gorgeous woman she'd ever seen. Midnight oil black hair, smooth alabaster skin, and the plumpest red lips that would have made even Steven Tyler green with envy.

Add to that that Madam Quack wasn't wearing a gold lamay turban, purple silk robe, or looking into a crystal ball. Paz felt totally out of her element--hard to laugh at someone when they looked as sane and gorgeous as Madam Pandora did.

The tent was low lit a dark red, casting strange undulations upon the tarp walls. Paz gripped the wooden arms of the plush, floral patterned chair she sat on.

Pandora (because Paz refused to think of her as Madam Pandora any longer) sat in front of her, long legs crossed. Sparkling black cocktail dress draping like bats wings to either side of her. Red lips pursed and staring at Paz with an intense gleam in her strange colored eyes.

"Your brothers want you to be happy."

Paz licked her lips. Didn't take a rocket scientist to figure that out, especially considering Pandora had very likely seen them drag her inside, ordering Paz to stay put or the popcorn got it.

"But you're successful, you made a lot of money tonight."

Paz narrowed her eyes.

"Paintings, was it?" Pandora cocked her head, feathers on top of her tiny hat flopped forward.

"Oh please, this is insane," Paz shook her head, "you probably heard one of them mention it. Why do you waste people's money this way?"

Pandora smiled. "Because you'll come. Though," she cocked her head, "I'm very good at what I do."

"I'm sure you are."

What a waste of her time and Todd's money. Paz stood, ready to head back out.

"Sit down," Pandora's voice brooked no argument, a shiver of heat zipped down Paz's spine. Not fear, not exactly, but wariness.

She sat.

Pandora tapped blood red fingernails on her knee. "Go to Alaska."

"What?" Paz snorted. "Alaska? Are you nuts? What's in Alaska?"

"He is."

Paz's heart skipped a beat. He, as in *he*. The one? Prince Charming? Her Todd?

"Yes. The one. You're Prince Charming. You're Todd."

Her mouth flopped open. Probably wasn't pretty, but holy freaking cow bat man, how had she done that? "I didn't say that--"

"Out loud?" Pandora lifted a pencil thin brow. "You didn't have to. I told you, I'm good at what I do."

Heart thudding almost painfully in her chest, Paz's left leg began to bounce up and down. So many different reasons why that was a cracked up idea floated through her mind.

Pandora pressed her lips into a thin line. "Stop over thinking this, Paz…"

"Wait?" She held up a hand. "How do you know my name? I didn't tell you--"

She waved her hand. "You need to go. He needs you, he's waiting. And he doesn't have much time left."

"Alaska?" Her voice sounded strained. Why was she even listening to this woman? This was so stupid. Totally dumb. And yet… "Where in Alaska?"

"Book a flight to Anchorage." Pandora leaned forward, intense eyes never swerving from Paz's face. "You have to leave tomorrow."

"Tomorrow?" she squeaked. "This is nuts. You're crazy. I'm crazy." She laughed, voice sounding totally unlike hers. So why was she suddenly sweating, suddenly desperate to believe this lie?

"He's dying, Paz, and only you can save him. If you don't leave tomorrow, it'll be over. He'll be over."

Something close to pain hammered behind her closed lids. Paz squeezed her arm rests, nails digging in so hard she felt one break.

"You're... lying?"

Pandora shook her head. "I never lie."

***

How had she wound up here? Thirty thousand feet up in the air, flying to Alaska? Alaska of all places! Paz had gone to sleep last night, desperate to forget it all. But an ache, a gnawing need for truth, had begun to bloom in her chest.

What if it was true? So she'd be out a couple hundred bucks--which would make her royally pissed, since she'd been saving for a screen press--if it wasn't true. But there'd been dreams last night. Lots of them.

A blue faced man, features distorted, but with hope shining in liquid black eyes. She'd woken up in tears and within seconds phoning the airport to confirm a roundtrip ticket to Anchorage.

Turbulence seized the plane and she yelped, biting down on her lower lip hard as her gut toppled to her knees. She hated flying.

Hated. It.

Why oh why, was she doing this? Time away from the carnival, the dream, made her think suddenly this was the stupidest idea she'd ever had. Richard and Todd had certainly been shocked, for a brief thirty minutes their wide eyes had made her feel brave, powerful. But now... the plane dipped, and she flopped in her seat, now she was just scared.

From the moment she'd stepped foot on the plane she'd gotten a strange sense of something being off kilter. Weird. But she'd ignored it, thinking she was just being the chicken Richard always accused her of being.

So she'd found her seat, not needing the compartment space, she'd packed light.

Literally she was flying to Anchorage with tickets back the very next day. Why had she done this?

She groaned when another round of turbulence tilted the plane.

She had no idea what she was looking for. Who she was looking for. She'd scanned the faces boarding her flight with an obsessive need to know if maybe one of them was Mr. Wonderful.

Then he'd sat next to her.

Heart pounding, trying to hold down the saltine crackers she'd gnoshed on earlier, she glanced at tall, dark, and decadent sitting next to her. He was gorgeous.

Bronze skin two shades darker than her own, dark unruly hair that curled against the nape of his neck, and liquid black eyes. The eyes had made her think of her dream. It hadn't been a huge stretch for her to think maybe it'd been him.

So she'd waved, and smiled.

He'd sat next to her, his delicious scent of clover and moss, teasing her senses. Paz had waited for the friendly smile in return. Nothing.

Like he'd not even seen her.

When the attendants had taken drink orders, he'd ignored her too.

He didn't read, didn't move, didn't do a single thing. Which totally creeped her out. Stepford wife, or husband in this case, total weirdo.

The plane jolted again, this time listing deep to the side.

"Ladies and gentlemen," the pilot's voice came on over the loudspeakers, *"please put your trays in the upright and locked positions, we seem to be experiencing a bit of turbulence--"*

"Oh sh--" the co-pilot cried and then there was static.

But that wasn't the worst part, because now the plane was dipping forward, faster and faster.

Suddenly Mr. Creepy latched onto her hand, squeezing tight.

"Look at me," he said, and oh man, so embarrassing that as they're crashing and getting ready to become nothing but a memory, all she could focus on was the flutter of her stomach at the sound of his whiskey deep voice.

Adrenaline spiked her veins, kids and women screamed. Oxygen masks dropped from the rough turbulence that shook her around like a rag doll.

"You'll be fine. You'll be fine," he said and she nodded.

His eyes were so beautiful. Not black like she'd first thought, but a deep inky well full of stardust. His thumb caressed her knuckles, and she knew fire seeped through her skin, deep into bone.

A strange whistling rang loud in her ears. Paz lifted up on her toes, wishing she could run away. "It's just like the movies," she whispered.

He licked his lips and man they were nice. Thick and begging to be sucked on. "What?" he said.

Tears crept into the corners of her eyes as her stomach bottomed out. A baby was crying. "The sound of death."

His touch was so nice. So real and warm.

"My Todd," she whispered as her vision blurred. He was looking at her, with an ache, a soul deep connection.

She'd finally gotten it.

Paz screamed when the plane pitched on its side. His grip tightened.

"Close your eyes, Paz," he whispered.

How did he know her name?

Glancing over her shoulder, he licked his lips, and she didn't miss the dilation of his pupils.

"We're close aren't we?" She knew they were, gravity was pinning her against the seat. The ground had to be only seconds away. Her body shuddered, tightened with goose bumps. Death breathed down her neck.

"Close your eyes, head on your knees. I'll be here when you wake up, I promise."

She dug her nails into his fist, but he didn't flinch.

"What's your name?" she breathed, back of her neck tightening.

They were close, within a second of crashing. The plane unnaturally quiet as people prayed, cried softly, or closed their eyes and waited for the inevitable.

His smile was so achingly real, alive. She sniffled, throat working back a hot tide of tears.

"Tristan Black."

Nodding, she dropped her head to her knees and squeezed her eyes shut. Her fingers still threaded through the hard strength of his.

She'd finally found him. Prince Charming.

So not fair.

There was a deafening whistle and then nothing else.

Books by Marie Hall

Kingdom Series:

Her Mad Hatter (Book 1)

Gerard's Beauty (Book 2)

Red and Her Wolf (Book 3)
Jinni's Wish (Book 4) Coming Soon
Hook's Pan (Book 5) Coming Soon

The Witching Hour: Grim Reaper Saga

Available now!

Chaos Time Series: YA Time Travel Series

The Girl in Amber Flame (Book 1) Due Jan. 2013

Ashes in Snow (Book 2) TBA

Genesis Trilogy: YA Paranormal

Forbidden (Book 1) TBA

Death Series: Adult Urban Fantasy Series

Death and the Witching Hour (Book 1) 2013

Death and the Hallowed Night (Book 2) 2013

Printed in Great Britain
by Amazon.co.uk, Ltd.,
Marston Gate.